# The Amulet of Visimar

## Eugene Weaver

# Preface

†

I remember the first time I watched Christopher Lee don the black cape for Hammer Studios in his full color and full-blooded portrayal of Bram Stoker's titular character, Dracula, written in 1897. I first saw him resurrected from the ashes by his butler, Klove, in the wonderfully atmospheric *Dracula: Prince of Darknes* (1966) in all its blood-drenched (for its time) glory.

I immediately fell in love with director Terence Fisher's take on Dracula and how truly terrifying Christopher Lee was, made even more so by his distinct silence, uttering not a single word with his red bloodshot eyes, his exposed large fangs accompanied by menacing hisses. Along with the great Sir Christopher Lee, the movie has it all: the gothic Castle Dracula, looming high in the mountains, itself a character, and the distinctly noticeable uptick in onscreen violence this sequel managed to produce.

Since then, I have watched it and every Hammer Studios' *Dracula* film countless times, enjoying each one in its own unique way. The *Dracula* series ran from 1958 to 1974 with *The Legend of the 7 Golden Vampires,* although with 1973's *The Satanic Rites of Dracula,* in my opinion the true closer in the long-running series, as this was Christopher Lee's final performance donning the cape as the count for Hammer Studios.

Along with *Dracula,* Hammer Studios produced a great number of wonderfully gothic films in their horror heyday of the 1950s, 1960s, and early 1970s. Films I came to love through the years, watching them over and over. *Twins of Evil, Vampire Circus, Countess Dracula, The Reptile, The Devil Rides Out, Plague of the Zombies,* and, of course, their own take on Universal's *Mummy* as well as *Victor Franken-stein,* usually portrayed by the late great Peter Cushing.

These films from a long-ago bygone era are the inspiration for this novel you hold in your hands. There's something utterly iconic and creepy about old, cobweb-filled castles where dark and evil things lurk around every corner and, especially, in the dreaded dungeon. Far below the castle perched on the mountain is the requisite small town with fearful villagers and a pub (its owner usually played by the always reliable actor, Michael Ripper) where the locals gossip and fight about what might be lying up in the old, creepy castle with its nefarious history of violence and depravity. The Constable and the Bürgermeister, of course, find a spot in the story, and what Hammer film wouldn't be complete without one or two lovely damsels in distress?

Well, it's all here. *The Amulet of Visimar* is my love letter to all things "gothic horror." I hope you enjoy reading it as much as I enjoyed writing it.

# Part I:

†

# The Rising

**A**Pricolici (pronounced /pri.ko¹litʃʲ/) is a werewolf/vampire fusion in the ancient Romanian folklore. Similar to a Vârcolac although the latter can also symbolize a goblin whereas the Pricolici always has wolf-like characteristics, they have the ability to transform into ordinary people or animals. The Pricolici are undead souls that have risen from the grave to harm living people.

# Chapter 1:

†

# J Curse You

*Romania, 1774*

lfred Burns looked up at the castle in front of him as the night sky slowly gave way to dawn, then fixed his steely gaze on the man tied to a large stake in front of the foreboding stone structure. An empty coffin lay open near the bound man. A vampire hunter feared throughout Europe, Burns had heard rumors throughout this region of Romania about this castle built on a mountain overlooking the small village of Burnmere roughly eight kilometers away. He was here now with his executioner, Charles Schaus, to pass sentence on the very subject of some of those rumors.

The information they were given would either free the parties in question or pass judgement on the condemned.

The sentencings usually consisted primarily of burnings at the stake, drownings, or in some rare cases, beheadings, depending on what the guilty ended up confessing. While not as quick to pass judgement as the local superstitious townsfolk, their word was final. Once sentencing was brought down, there was no more discussion. They were, indeed, judges, jurors, and executioners.

A small group of ten townspeople had been ordered to follow the vampire hunter and his executioner up the mountain. And what a trek it had been. Wolves lurked in the shadows up the rocky, treacherous path, though none had attacked due to the townsfolk keeping watch with their torches, which the wolves stayed clear of.

Several of the bolder townspeople had cautiously entered the castle and upon searching the various rooms, discovered the sleeping man in a casket and quickly taken him and the coffin outside. While still in a weakened state of slumber, the man was now bound to a large stake that had been erected earlier upon the vampire hunter's arrival.

Alfred, a thin, stern man in black attire and a wooden crucifix around his neck, looked over the small crowd that had followed him to carry out the sentencing. The bound man, Antonin Visimar, had been taken by surprise but hadn't attempted to flee, holding his head high when the townsfolk had him in their grasp, dragging him to the stake.

"He's tied securely, your honor, and we've placed the proper kindling at his feet; it appears that this wasn't the only body we found inside the castle," Charles said quietly to Alfred, who had been tasked with finding Visimar. The townsfolk set one more coffin on the ground at Burns' feet.

"Well, Charles, my friend, it appears we have what we need here. Proof," Alfred shot back sternly.

Walking up to Antonin Visimar who stared at him coldly, he saw a beautiful amulet hanging around the man's neck. A round, smooth, shiny, solid-gold encrusted faceplate housed the beautiful glowing oval shaped gemstone inside. The gemstone reflected different colors depending on which side the light hit. Holding the amulet in place around the imprisoned man's neck was an equally beautiful golden necklace. The amulet itself was roughly three inches around with the gemstone housed directly on top of it, the gold acting as a seal, keeping it locked in place against the outer housing.

Alfred took it into his hand, admiring its beauty. This would fetch a pretty penny back in England once his tour of Eastern Europe was complete. Better yet, it would make a lovely a gift for his beloved wife, Miriam.

He yanked the amulet and golden chain from the man's neck and inspected it. It was mesmerizing. Almost hypnotic. He felt the slightest hesitation, as if the necklace itself was resisting his grasp. *Nonsense,* he thought.

Antonin cried out, seeing the shining amulet now in Alfred's hand. "My amulet! Given to me by my master!"

"Silence!" Alfred shouted, and with his free hand he grasped the crucifix around his neck, raising it in front of the bound man.

Immediately, Antonin Visimar screamed, turning his face from the cross.

Alfred stared at the man with long black hair combed over his head, pale skin, and dark eyes. He was dressed exquisitely in what appeared to be expensive clothes, especially considering the meager village which the castle overlooked.

He took his eyes from the young man tied before him to the young woman lying in the second coffin several of the villagers found inside the castle upon a further, extensive search of the lower level. Alfred peered down into the opened casket. She was pale skinned with brown hair past her shoulders and dressed in a white nightgown. She appeared to be sleeping but her lack of a heartbeat said otherwise.

"How in God's name can she still look as though she just recently passed? She's dead and cold as ice!" a heavyset villager with messy hair and a large belly said as he touched her pale, white dead skin.

"Witchcraft!" an old woman toward the back of the crowd shouted.

Looking back up at Antonin Visimar, Alfred spoke loudly for them all to hear. "As all present know, I have been authorized by the holy Church of England to seek out and destroy witchcraft in its many forms, including the vampirism that has infested Europe. Antonin Visimar, for the crime of witchcraft and for what can clearly be seen as the murder of this young woman in front of us, you have been condemned to death by fire. Upon your death, your castle shall be razed to the ground. Does the condemned have any final words?"

Silence fell across the courtyard.

Alfred looked at the amulet he held in his hand and tightened his grip on it. A trophy. *His* trophy.

Charles Schaus held the torch high in the air for all to see but all eyes were on Antonin Visimar as Alfred gave the nod and the torch was tossed onto the kindling under his feet.

Flames immediately spread and quickly engulfed the man tied tightly to the post as he cried out for all to hear. "I curse your name, Alfred Burns! You invade my home and steal from me! This is merely flesh that you burn, but I will rise up from the grave to avenge myself and complete the work set about by my master, the Prince of Darkness! The legend of the Pricolici is true, as you will all soon see! In my absence, the creatures of this forest will do my bidding, and in one hundred years I shall return to complete my master's work. And the town of Burnmere will *burn*! Mark my words!"

Antonin Visimar looked toward the forest at the yellow glowing wolves' eyes peering out at him. He screamed in agony as the fire engulfed him, then quickly subsided as his body continued to burn until a shell was all that remained.

The villagers hung their heads at the grotesque display in front of them.

"It is done," Alfred said loudly, looking over the crowd.

The woman lying in the coffin in front of the charred corpse of Antonin Visimar opened her eyes. The sun had begun to set and the little light that peered through the forest had dimmed.

She opened her mouth exposing two long, pointed fangs jutting out in place of her canine teeth. Quickly leaping up out of her coffin, she shrieked at the sight of the villagers and the burnt corpse. Under the skin on her back, a pair of large bat-like wings ripped forth and opened wide. She flapped them quickly, trying to escape the sunlight.

Executioner Charles Schaus was nearest to her and reached out, grabbing the flying creature by the leg. He was a strong man with large, muscular arms and had no problem pulling the woman back to the ground. Seeing what the man was doing, the increasingly powerful woman in the sheer nightgown turned on him, wrapping her large bat-like wings around him.

Charles carried a long blade on one side of his executioner's pants and a large wooden stake to drive through the hearts of the infernal beasts known as vampires. Unfortunately, neither weapon was drawn and despite his strength, he was no match for a turned vampire once the sun set. Her superhuman strength was quick to overpower him.

Alfred immediately saw his traveling companion was in grave danger and ran over, ripping his crucifix from his neck and bringing it up in front of him.

"Get off of him, you cursed beast!" Alfred shouted but the damage was done. The vampire had bitten down into the open and vulnerable neck of Charles Schaus. Her two long, extended fangs pierced his flesh and instantly drew blood. She clung tightly to him while she drank.

The small group of onlookers began screaming, several jumping forward to help the flailing man along with Alfred, who touched his outstretched crucifix to the side of the vampire's head and caused her to shriek in pain.

Her fair skin instantly began to sizzle. Alfred pulled the crucifix away as melted flesh came with it, sticking to his cross. Pushing his revulsion for this evil beast out of his mind, he, along with the several courageous villagers that came forward to help, grabbed hold of her and attempted to pull her off the dying man.

Glassed-over, white, dead eyes turned to stare at them. She released his throat from her sharp-toothed grip and hissed at her assailants. Blood poured out of her mouth onto her white gown. With her free right hand, she swung at Alfred, nearly connecting with his face.

Charles, with two large puncture wounds on the side of his neck, bled profusely as he tried to stop the flow of blood with his left hand, his right hand drawing his stake. The men attempting to pull her off of him gave him the precious few seconds he needed.

As she turned her face back to him, ready to bite down once more, Charles slammed the stake through her soft chest, driving it right into her heart. Blood bubbled up onto her white gown. The vampire shrieked in pain while Alfred and the men lunged forward once more, trying to pry her off of Charles who had now gone limp, the entire front of his shirt drenched in warm, crimson red.

Still shrieking, the vampire woman leapt forward, attempting to grab anyone near her. All, however, had backed away once she relinquished her grip on Charles. She cried out in pain and dropped to her knees, her wings flapping slowly, trying to take her up and away from her assailants, but it was no use. She was dying, for good this time.

She saw her end nearing, her thoughts traveling back to when her master had turned her centuries before and the countless nights of hunting that had followed. She looked over at the charred body of Antonin Visimar then at Alfred Burns who still gripped the amulet. This was her master's amulet! She hissed at him then fell to the ground.

Choking on her own blood and the blood of Charles Schaus, she attempted to speak but was cut off by the blade that had been at the executioner's side and now resided in Alfred's hands. Slicing through her neck, it instantly severed her head from her body.

With his foot, Alfred kicked her head away and pulled the stake out of her chest. Silence fell across the villagers.

"Help me with the bodies," Alfred said coldly.

A few men moved forward, helping Alfred carry both bodies to the burn pile below Antonin's smoldering remains. The bodies were tossed on top of the flames and ignited.

The headless female vampire went up in flames immediately, much like Antonin Visimar had minutes earlier. It was well known and documented in and around Eastern Europe that vampires, while essentially immortal if left undealt with, burned quickly and were susceptible to death if beheaded and pierced through the heart by a sharp wooden object.

The vampire's severed head was tossed onto the rekindled flames as well, instantly exploding into a ball of fire.

"Now, burn this castle and let's make haste to leave these cursed woods," Alfred said, sounding defeated at how horribly wrong this series of events had gone, leading to the death of his executioner.

Several torches were thrown into the castle, quickly igniting it. As smoke and fire spread and began pouring out of the castle windows, Alfred looked at the burnt bodies in front of the burning castle.

Satisfied at finally completing his mission, even at the cost of losing Charles, Alfred shouted to the listening townsfolk in front of him, "It is done! Henceforth, this land is forbidden. It has been tainted by Satan and his evil minions. Do not think just because Antonin Visimar has been vanquished that evil is gone from this place. Stay clear of this place, spread the word far and wide!"

In his coat pocket, safe and sound, the glowing warmth of the amulet whispered to him again, a mere thought, barely acknowledged, embedding itself deep in his subconscious like a weed that would go unattended. *Take me, keep me safe, and in one hundred years, I shall return.*

Little did the man realize that he and his linage were now marked and under its control.

There had been ten townspeople with Alfred Burns and Charles Schaus that day, entering the forest and traveling to the castle to exact vigilante justice. Only five exited the forest back in Burnmere. The rest had been taken by the now significantly more aggressive and hostile wolves that stalked them through the miles of treacherous terrain back to the relative safety of the village. Of the remaining five, none would live longer than one year, all succumbing to the ever-present threat of wolves and the harsh elements surrounding their small village.

Safety would be a fleeting thing henceforth. The ancient evil had been disturbed and vengeance would follow, for the Burns family line and the unfortunate souls of Burnmere.

✝

Two individuals remained hidden in the nearby forest, watching the horrible events unfold, the day Burns and the townspeople had visited the castle. The young man biding his time had watched the burning of his master from deep in the woods, watched as Sophia Brassard was awakened from her slumber, staked through the heart, beheaded and burned.

He watched as the castle he had served his master in for centuries went up in flames, though he knew it could be fixed back to its former glory. But there was nothing he could do for the woman, and good riddance to the brutish man she had killed.

His master, though, needed him. Once the invading, thieving murderer and townspeople of Burnmere had departed, Marcel made his way to the charred corpses, dragging out the remains of Antonin Visimar, unrecognizable in his current state. Bundling up the body in a sheet, he carried the body back to the castle.

Looking toward the tree line, he saw Ingrid had returned from hunting at night in a distant village, no doubt enjoying the thrill of new scenery. She moved quickly, avoiding the ever-creeping sunshine.

"What has happened here?" the beautiful blond woman said, rushing toward Marcel, looking down in horror at the burnt carcasses on the ground.

He ignored her, focusing on his master, and walked into the still burning castle.

Behind him, he heard the seductive and ferociously evil Ingrid Brassard scream in fury at realizing the charred remains of her sister were spread out in front of her.

The smoke, while thick inside the main great room, was manageable as Marcel quickly made his way down a long walkway to the altar room near the rear of the castle. He took note that while much had been burned, numerous rooms were left untouched.  Furniture and drapes throughout the large castle, however, had been incinerated and were keeping the fire burning.

Once he got to his master's altar room, he heard distant screaming inside the castle as Ingrid flew through the tunnel down one of the towers to the murky depths of the dungeon floor below where she called *home*.

*Many will suffer at her hands for this grave misdeed,* Marcel thought, for once thankful the evil woman had been turned by Antonin Visimar many years prior.

His master's room was sparse but lit up by a random torch thrown inside earlier by one of the townspeople. A large stone altar sat in the middle of the room. Many had given their lives on this very altar. Some willing, most not. A pentagram smeared in blood had adorned the front but now cast a burnt ashen image from the fire that had spread. The mark of the Beast.

He placed the body of Antonin Visimar on top of the altar, uttering, "Master, a mortal took your amulet. But you will live again. And you shall have your revenge."

# Chapter 2:

†

# The Beginning
# of the End

*Burnmere, Romania 1874*

Lily-Rose Burns walked through the field near the cottage she was staying in on the outskirts of Burnmere, deep in the heartland of Romania. The beautiful golden-haired young woman, twenty-four, had been staying in the cottage rented out to her by a pleasant elderly woman named Rozalia Sitek for several weeks since arriving in Burnmere, against her sister Juliette's wishes.

Upon her arrival, Rozalia Sitek had met her merely by chance, stopping the clearly lost new arrival to Burnmere and asking if she could be of any assistance. When hearing her reason for the unannounced visit to a town no one ever visited, Rozalia took pity on the girl and offered her cottage at the edge of town as a place to stay while she did her research and history on the castle high in the mountain above.

For the next few weeks, Rozalia kept a watchful eye on Lily-Rose, who was preoccupied with a troubled look most of the time, and clearly there for reasons more elaborate than just research. Rozalia continually warned Lily-Rose about the perils of the castle. "Stay away from that place where evil still lives!" she told the girl whenever they ate meals together.

Lily-Rose knew the old woman was watching her and wanted to keep as low a profile as possible. She slipped in and out of the cottage silently, not wanting to be seen.

On most days, the fog covered the nearby castle up the mountain, but today it had broken through. Almost as if it were calling to her.

Today was the day.

The castle, of course, was the reason she was here in Burnmere in the first place. Staring up at it now, she gripped the gold encrusted amulet around her neck tightly. It was warm to the touch. Her long, pale blue dress flowed in the breeze, a gift from her sister back when Lily-Rose was still living in England.

She had traveled lightly, with numerous eyes raised at the oddity of a young woman such as herself traveling alone. She carried with her a suitcase full of clothes, a few personal belongings, and of course, the amulet that now adorned her neck, given to her on her eighteenth birthday. Her mother had passed it on to her, having received it from her own mother, passed down generations since Lily-Rose's great-grandfather took ownership of it.

Each generation told the same tale of how the amulet came into their possession, as well as its importance to this particular region. The amulet had come to their family from this part of the world one hundred years prior, in the very town of Burnmere. And now it had returned *Almost by its own will,* Lily had thought more than once since she first felt the pull toward this strange little village.

She had arrived in Burnmere by train and then horse-drawn carriage from an older man who said little other than issuing a warning about their destination and the bad omens that had haunted Burnmere for centuries.

Lily-Rose had made a few friends in the small town, one of them a man named Caspar Voit, an attractive and kind man who forged horseshoes for the population of Burnmere. The friendship might have blossomed if she had accepted Caspar's advances, but a love interest had been the furthest thing from her mind since leaving England.

She had even attended a Sunday morning Mass, something she had gotten out of the habit of doing back in her hometown of Summerhost, England. She considered going to Confession for what she was about to do, what her better judgement kept telling her not to do. Sitting through Mass had been nearly unbearable for the young woman, but she knew this could be her last time inside a church, close to the presence of God.

Since arriving in town, she had heard the rumors about the castle from the townspeople. About women, some as young as thirteen, having vanished under unknown circumstances through the years, never to be seen or heard from again. Rumors that a demonic entity still lived within the walls of Castle Visimar. Rumors that someone, or something, would come down to the village at night and steal girls for their own nefarious purposes.

No one dared to visit the castle. Even the authoritarian bürgermeister of Burnmere and his constable would not visit the castle to investigate these strange disappearances. It had been deemed off-limits permanently, with the bürgermeister claiming that wolves from the hills were responsible, which was likely true. The hills were littered with them. No matter how many were killed, more would spring up. It was as if the castle itself continually produced more of the infernal beasts.

Rumor had it that a vampire once lived in the castle, or something similar to a vampire. Lily Rose knew what had occurred one hundred years prior, when her great-grandfather had been here. Of the man put to death for witchcraft and the amulet taken from around his neck upon death. The amulet that had allowed the man to live for one thousand years if the rumors were to be believed.

Now, as she looked up at the ominous castle with its high towers and dark stone exterior, she thought back to what had caused her to take the long journey to Burnmere in the first place.

✝

She had been shopping for a dress with her sister Juliette in Summerhost, England on a sunny Wednesday afternoon. Their father had died in a construction accident when they were both little and their mother, Hannah Burns, had passed away several years prior due to a sudden illness. Dress shopping was something they had both enjoyed doing together when their mother was still alive, and was a way for Lily-Rose to remember her.

She missed her mother dearly and wore the amulet she had given her around her neck nearly every day. Juliette had made it a point to let her mother know she had no interest in an amulet that seemed somehow, evil. Even if it was a thing of true beauty.

"Excuse me, but that is a lovely amulet you have around your neck, I must say! Where did you come into contact with such a beautiful item as this?" a well-dressed man that appeared to be in his thirties said respectfully.

Catching Lily-Rose by surprise, she stumbled over her words. "Um, why, thank you, sir. It was a gift from my mother."

"Ah, a gift from your mother. What a thoughtful gift. What a thoughtful mother you must have," the man, dressed entirely in black, said softly with the slightest hint of malice.

Looking at the man's dark eyes then up to his large top hat, she suddenly felt alone. Even in this store where other women mingled around shopping for themselves. Lily-Rose continued to stare at the man. Stare into his eyes, much like he was doing to her.

"May I be so bold as to ask where your mother got the amulet?"

The noise of the shop faded. Women still mingled and talked, but no sound could be heard. The only sound was the dark man's voice. His handsome demeanor had suddenly changed. His eyes turned darker, his skin paler.

She couldn't look away from him, only answer his question. "My grandmother gave it to my mother. My grandmother received it from my great-grandmother who received it as a gift from my great-grandfather," Lily-Rose answered in an almost trance-like state.

"Ah, yes. Passed down through generations of Burns. And what, may I ask, was your great-grandfather's name, my dear Lily-Rose?" the man said icily.

"How did you know my—?" Lily-Rose began but was cut off.

"That's no concern of yours. Answer me, now," the man said in his now entirely threatening tone.

"Alfred Burns was my great-grandfather," Lily-Rose uttered, staring into the man's now black eyes, seemingly under his spell.

The man leaned forward and whispered into her ear, "You will bring the amulet to my master near a town called Burnmere in Romania, in the Carpathian Mountains. You will leave immediately. Find a way and do it. You will come up with a reason, do you understand?"

Lily-Rose was getting lightheaded staring into the evil man's eyes. She felt as though she might faint under his hypnotic, icy stare. "Yes," she began to say as she started to stumble over backwards as the amulet around her neck emanated a low heat.

Before she hit the ground, the dark man reached out a long and bony hand. His fingernails were pointed, and the skin seemed to be stretched over the bones. He caught her arm and turned her hand palm up. With his index finger, he plunged his sharp fingernail into her exposed hand, causing blood to immediately gush from the slice he had made. He was so close she could smell him. He smelled like black liquorish, a cross between anise and fennel. It was pungent to her nose and was the last thing her mind processed.

Just before Lily-Rose fell unconscious, she thought she saw the man take a vial from his black suit coat and touch it to her bleeding palm. Then, in her hypnotized state, she fell backwards, hitting her head on the floor.

Later, she woke to a group of women standing over her and Juliette on her knees gently shaking her. She was still inside the dress store, but the mysterious man was nowhere to be seen.

"Did you see him? Did you see the man in black?" she asked her sister. Her eyes darted from Juliette up to the group of women and store owner that had gotten a handkerchief to stop her cut from bleeding out onto his floor.

"Lily, what are you talking about? The only man in this store is the manager," Juliette answered softly, tenderly running her hand through her younger sister's long hair.

The women looked at her puzzled before one of them cleared her throat and said, "Ma'am, your sister is right, there was no man in here. You seemed to be talking to yourself over here. I noticed you. Looks like you dug your fingernail into your palm."

Juliette helped her sister to her feet. "Come on, my dear sister, let's get out of here. You need to rest."

Nodding in reply, Lily-Rose looked at her palm then over to her bloody finger. *No! I saw him, he was here!* She looked around the room once more then hurried out of the store with her sister's arm wrapped around her. The owner and the onlookers watched them leave with skepticism before quietly talking to each other in hushed tones about the odd incident with the confused young woman and her sister.

✝

Continuing to stare at the castle that she had watched since arriving in Burnmere almost two weeks prior, Lily-Rose knew it was time to pay it a visit. It had beckoned to her shortly after her odd incident in the dress store. Haunted her dreams. During many nights of restless sleep, she had seemingly been transported to the very castle she was staring at now, traveling up the dangerous mountain on horseback with the man from the dress shop.

*Come to Burnmere, come to me, bring me my amulet now!* Those same words echoed through her subconscious not only in her dreams but her waking hours. They haunted her, but more importantly, beckoned her and commanded her continually. Until seeing no other option but to obey its call, she had set off on her trek to Romania.

She looked down at her left hand where a small scar remained from the mysterious man's sharp fingernail that had pierced it nearly one month ago.

Right after it happened, she had begun making plans, bought her train ticket, and told her older sister where she was heading. A fight ensued as Juliette pleaded and begged her younger sister not to go to Romania on a wild goose chase. But Lily-Rose insisted that she would return safely with answers about what had happened to her great-grandfather and the true mystery of the amulet she wore around her neck.

The well-educated and more reserved Juliette tried to talk sense into her head-strong younger sister, but it fell on deaf ears. Argument after argument, day after day, as Lily-

Rose continued preparing for the long journey to Burnmere, distraught, her sister Juliette did the only thing she knew to do. She wrote to their uncle, Henry Burns, brother to their now deceased and much-loved mother and one of the most unpleasant people they knew, offering to pay him to travel part of the way with Lily-Rose. He reluctantly agreed, much to Lily's dismay, but she also begrudgingly agreed.

The large, heavyset man in his mid-fifties with a thick mustache and too-tight suitcoat for his figure wasn't much for conversation and was none too impressed with the girl's insistence on traveling, but he looked after her as best he could. Money was money, something Henry had precious little of, so being a chaperone on a train for a disobedient relative was good enough for him.

The Burns family had dwindled down to only a select few relatives after Lily and Juliette's parents both passed, something the sisters had always found strange, people never lived to a ripe old age in the Burns family. Accidents and illness seemed to plague many of them. Those who remained no longer lived in England and had moved on to the United States, setting up shops in the various boroughs of New York City.

Lily-Rose had tried to steer clear of the rather unpleasant man and once the train arrived in Bucharest, he was happy his time with her had ended. He did as Juliette had instructed, however, and found her a carriage ride to Burnmere. And that was the last Henry would have to deal with the disobedient Lily-Rose; he took the same train back to Summerhost as soon as boarding began, thankful for the money Juliette offered.

Henry Burns himself wouldn't live to see his fifty-sixth year, dying later that same year from a massive heart attack.

Lily-Rose sighed and walked to the edge of the field where wheat flowed back and forth in the breeze. She wasn't entirely sure why she hadn't gone immediately to the castle when she had arrived. Fear? Yes, but not just that. She felt as though she was being made to wait. Whatever beckoned her to Burnmere did things on its own time. Ever since the incident, she knew her destiny lay behind whatever the castle walls held. *Why? Why must I go to this ominous place?* She didn't know. She just knew she couldn't stop its draw back in England and she surely couldn't now.

Since meeting the strange dark man back in Summerhost, and even more since arriving at Burnmere, the amulet around her neck had begun feeling warm. She couldn't explain it, the supernatural aura of the amulet and the strong pull it had on her, bordering on obsession. She desperately feared the beautiful gem adorning her chest and, at the same time, she felt inexplicably drawn to it and to whatever it wanted from her.

She knew she was here to deliver this artifact back to its rightful owner, up in the castle on the mountain. It was only a matter of time before she would be required to travel up there, and though the ominous feeling of her ultimate demise loomed large, there was nothing she could do about it but wait for the call to come forth.

The kind and chatty Rozalia Sitek had continually warned her about traveling past the field and up into the mountain behind the last house in the village. Lily-Rose agreed, knowing full well what her true intentions were in this dying village in the middle of nowhere.

She clenched the amulet around her neck tightly. As though emanating its own power, its supernatural warmth on the bare skin of her chest seemed to possess her. She knew from the moment her mother had put it around her neck for the first time that it was special. Her mother had informed her upon gifting it to young Lily-Rose that she herself had never worn it, but had kept it safe until she felt beckoned to gift it to one of her daughters. Once it had passed on to the next generation of Burns descendants, Hannah died.

One hundred years later, Lily-Rose would soon be tasked with traveling back to its home. And nothing she could do would stop it. She was called forth and could only obey.

Suddenly, her eye caught a dark-suited man sitting atop a black horse at the entrance to the woods where a small path led up to the castle. How long had he been there? Why had she not heard the horse's hooves on this rocky terrain?

The man looked toward her, but his face remained shrouded in darkness. He didn't utter a word, just stared. Without thinking of any potential consequences for her actions, Lily-Rose moved toward him, glancing up again at the looming castle in the distance. The fog was back and nearly covering it in its entirety.

When she looked back at the man, he was in front of her holding out a long bony hand, sharp fingernails adorning each finger. The same hand that had grabbed her and cut into her palm some weeks earlier.

His grotesque hand waited, outstretched. She put her delicate, warm hand into his. It was cold as ice, but strong. In an instant, the man pulled her up onto the horse behind him. Glancing back, he uttered, "Hold me tightly."

She did as he commanded, and barely had time to clasp ahold of the stiff man as he kicked back on his horse and took off into the forest up the winding mist covered trail leading toward the castle.

The man felt cold, even through his black suit, and Lily-Rose was instantly shivering. But she didn't let go, she couldn't let go, this was her destiny unfolding before her. She felt instantly repulsed by the faint hint of anise or fennel on the man. She and her sister grew up teasing each other about black liquorish. They both hated it and would dare the other to eat a small piece when visiting the local candy store. It was as if the smell he cast was warning her, *you aren't going to like this one bit*. It dawned on her that this was the same smell that hit her nose as she passed out in the dress shop one month prior.

Farther up they went, the trees covering the little sunlight there was until it appeared as if night had fallen like a thick blanket over the entire mountain. Howls from wolves could be heard through the tree cover. Lily-Rose held onto her rider's waist tightly, looking into the forest as he continued galloping up the treacherous trail leading up to the castle. She saw yellow eyes peering out at the them as they passed, eventually losing count of how many she saw on their trek upwards.

Lily-Rose wasn't sure how long she was on the back of the horse with the man in black, but her cold body could barely take it any longer and his strong smell repulsed her more and more the longer she was near it. She shouted up to the man, "How much farther?"

The man didn't acknowledge her but kept moving forward, the horse breathing heavy as rocks and dirt crunched under its hooves. Numerous times she was sure he would lose control of his steed and they would both fly off, smashing into one of the nearby trees surrounding their winding path with their sharp branches. They rounded another bend where the tree cover appeared to be thinning out and the branches were barren. Thorny vines grew along the path they rode.

Over one more steep incline lay the castle in front of them. The rider charged up it and before long the front gate came into view. He rode through it, then pulled back on the reins, slowing then bringing the horse to a halt. Gravel and dirt shot forward then slowly fell back to the ground. All was quiet. It was as if the animals, if there were any nearby, were too scared to make a sound for fear they would meet the same fate as the young woman who had been brought to this infernal, hellish place.

The man climbed off the horse and once more held out his bony hand to Lily-Rose. She took it begrudgingly and was pulled off the horse quickly, landing on her feet roughly onto the ground.

He released her hand then began walking toward the castle entrance. Lily-Rose clenched the amulet tightly around her neck, glancing back, somehow knowing she wouldn't be seeing the village, or anything in her old life, again. She followed the dark man toward the large doors of the castle.

Hearing fluttering and a squeaking noise, she looked up at the dark sky to see hundreds of bats circling over the ominous castle. The closer she got to the massive doors, the louder the noise seemed to get, as if they were excited by the presence of their latest guest.

# Chapter 3:

†

# The Town of Burnmere

Below the castle where Lily had just been delivered on horseback by the dark man sat the small town of Burnmere. It lay deep within the forests of the Carpathian Mountains in the heart of Romania. Shrouded in fog, sitting near the peak of a particularly large mountain, the castle sat ominously overlooking the small village whose population was now just slightly over one hundred.

Even several miles from the village, the castle was still much too close for the villagers and was the source of much hushed gossip. The looming dread and stories the townsfolk shared kept everyone uneasy.

People didn't get along much in the village of Burnmere. It was as if the fog-enshrouded castle on the mountain that overlooked them held them in a grip of fear and paranoia. Most of the townspeople that had the means to leave did so years earlier. The rest lived a solemn and depressing existence, fearful of each other and of what had once lived inside the castle. Hours bled into days, days bled into weeks, months, and years.

The town of Burnmere was small enough that most people walked from their homes to their destinations. An occasional horse-drawn carriage made its way through the cobblestone streets, and sometimes bicycles were used as transportation, but with the road conditions continually deteriorating, walking was usually the best option.

One tiny schoolhouse was all that was required for the twenty school-age children that lived in Burnmere.

Most of the town's news was discussed and gossiped over in the village pub, aptly named "The Pale Horse," in reference to the book of Revelations. Though most everyone in and around Burnmere were farmers, there were also several small shops in town, including a general store where most groceries were purchased, a dentist office, doctor's office, post office, iron working mill, butcher shop, horse stables belonging to a grumpy old man named Maxwell Murrey and his wife Jane, and a small shoe repair shop.

St. Joseph's, a small Catholic church in the town square, had stood there since the town's creation several hundred years prior. Mass was held every day at 6:30 AM and on weekends. A vigil Mass was held every Saturday at 10:00 PM followed by two Sunday morning Masses at 8:00 AM and 10:00 AM. The village of Burnmere was a religious town. It had to be, considering the rumors that continually swirled around the castle and what evils lie within its walls. Too many unexplained deaths had made everyone painfully aware of their own mortality and the approaching afterlife.

Father Jannick Gustloff was nearing fifty. While he tried to keep in shape, he always struggled with a bit of a larger stomach, due to his "occasional" heavy beer intake at the Pale Horse. The townsfolk had come to respect the large, graying man with a well-groomed beard. He was certainly rough around the edges with a bit of a drinking problem, but very much a man of the cloth that would give his life for his meager flock if called to do so.

The frail, old bartender and owner of the Pale Horse, Armin Falck, often teased Fr. Gustloff when he brought a large beer over to his usual table. "Did ya hear about the priest that got stuck in the backwards little village?"

To which Fr. Gustloff typically replied, "Yep, he heard the beer was free."

But jokes like this were not uttered today. Today was more solemn than many others in their small town. The pub, usually a lively place in Burnmere, was solemn for those sitting around its roughly ten tables.

The priest was absent, as he was presiding over the funeral of young thirteen-year-old Aline Koltz at the local cemetery beside St. Joseph's several hundred yards from the Pale Horse. The recent death of the minor, coupled with the mysterious disappearance of the outsider, Lily-Rose Burns, had everyone on edge, more so than usual.

Marco Seiler took a long swig from his beer stein and wiped the foam off of his top lip. The thirty-five-year-old, nearly six-foot tall, broad-shouldered brutish man with chiseled features was a regular fixture at the Pale House after working his field just outside of town. Marco used to be a handsome, strong man, but the years in Burnmere hadn't been kind to him and neither had his wife. He had always expected that good things would come to him if he was a good husband and worked hard, but neither his marriage nor his work seemed to have panned out as the years ticked by. He ran his thick hand through his black, messy hair and slammed his beer down on the old, wooden table.

Several nearby patrons glanced up in surprise at the loud thud that echoed through the pub. When several noticed it was Marco, they quickly looked back at their own beer steins in silence, not wanting to engage.

"What is it, Marco?" Falck asked from behind the bar while filling up Nick Schoeler's beer stein from a large keg behind him. Once the mug was filled to the top with the golden colored ale, Falck picked up a nearby beer comb and wiped excess foam from the top of the mug, handing it to Nick then looking toward Marco's table close to the bar.

"This town, that's what, no one wants to talk about what happened. You realize each year more and more people move out of this god-forsaken place? That or they just vanish. The town is dying, in more ways than one it seems, and no one gives a flying fuck!" Marco grumbled.

Several patrons got up and left the pub quietly. Noticing this, Falck called out, "See you guys tomorrow, have a good night."

The door closed behind the customers and once more a hush fell across the solemn pub.

Marco picked up his beer, taking another large swing, then set it down and looked up to see Nick Schoeler had turned around on his bar stool and was staring at him.

"Well, what the hell are you looking at? Huh?" Marco all but shouted at the middle-aged thin, white-haired man in old, tattered clothes before adding, "Mind your business, you damn drunk!"

At this, Nick swiveled around on his bar stool to face Falck once more and mumbled, "Look who's calling who a damn drunk."

"What did you say? Speak up, you sonofabitch!" Marco shot back.

"Guys, come on. Today? Of all days to cause trouble in my bar, not today. Show some respect. A girl is about to be buried over at Gustloff's parish. Snuffed out in the prime of her life!" Falck called out, glaring at both Nick and Marco.

He knew the men had no love for each other. They were relatives, as were most people in the small village, but their great-grandparents had disliked each other, and it trickled down to the kids and then grandkids. That was how it had been ever since he could remember.

Looking away from Nick, Marco shook his head. "We never get outsiders here. And when we do, they vanish. While we continue to die off and then we bury the truth along with more bodies!"

"Now's not the time, Marco," Caspar Voit said calmly from a nearby table, glancing over at him. The strong, blue-eyed man in his early thirties forged iron in his small shop in Burnmere, primarily for horseshoes. Unlike Nick, Caspar could handle himself.

Marco looked at the blond-haired man who was pulling apart a piece of bread at his table. A half-drunk beer sat in front of him. The sound of several glasses being set down could be heard as more patrons got up and moved for the exit.

Falck shot Caspar a look that said, *Please, no trouble.*

Looking from the frail old bartender to the large, brutish man in a stained white buttoned shirt and a tattered pair of brown pants, the same thing he wore nearly every day, Caspar picked up his beer stein and took a gulp then stood to his feet and cleared his throat.

"You got something to say, lover boy? When exactly *is* a good time? When the entire village has been completely depleted of life, maybe then?" Marco shot back, taunting Caspar. Jealousy of the budding relationship between Caspar and the now missing Lily-Rose Burns boiled in his veins.

Ignoring him, Caspar looked toward the bar at Falck and nodded before turning to leave.

"Hey, I'm talking to you! You don't get to tell me to shut up! You, of all people, you hear me!" Marco shouted, standing to his feet and wavering a bit from the copious amounts of beer he had drunk.

Caspar attempted to ignore him, but Marco wouldn't desist, now making his way toward the cool-headed man.

"Marco, no!" shouted Falck as Nick and the few remaining patrons watched the scene unfold.

Stumbling forward, Marco took a large swing at Caspar, but the completely sober and significantly quicker Caspar easily ducked away from the heavy man's haphazardly flung fist.

Due to the alcohol and power Marco had put into the missed punch, he fell off balance, tripping over himself and crashing onto the table Caspar had been sitting at seconds earlier. The table's legs gave way under the two hundred and fifty-plus pounds, causing it, along with Marco, to come crashing to the ground, Caspar's half-drunk beer spilling on top of him.

Standing back and looking down at the pathetic man in front of him, Caspar offered his hand to help him up. Several chuckles punctuated the embarrassing stand-off that Marco was losing, mostly from Nick Schoeler.

Shaking his head, Falck quickly came around from the back of the bar over to the broken table and a very humiliated Marco, now rolling over onto his back. He shook away both Caspar's attempt at help as well as Falck's, then shot Nick a look of pure unadulterated hatred.

"You get the hell away from me, both of you, damnit! I'm no cripple!" Marco shouted, pulling himself up to a sitting position. His shirt was covered in beer. Angrily, he got to his feet awkwardly on his own. Falck stepped back to give the large man room while Caspar continued on to the door.

Shaking himself off, Marco fixed his angry gaze on Caspar and shouted out, "You little shit! I'm the only one that sees what's going on here! That damn thing that lives inside the castle, whatever it is, is not dead! It's getting stronger and it's going to eventually kill us all, mark my words! That's where your precious Lily-Rose is!"

The room fell silent. Caspar stopped moving toward the opened door where Bürgermeister Samuel Hartjenstein now stood, taking off his hat that resembled a kind of makeshift crown. Dressed in his official uniform, the law in Burnmere played the part well. In his early forties, the man was large and imposing with a thin beard and mustache and slightly graying hair combed back over his head. His piercing eyes darted from Caspar to the pathetic looking Marco then over to the bar's owner.

He walked through the doorway into the now silent room, a flintlock pistol at his right side and a thick wooden club attached to a belt loop on the other. He hefted up his well-ironed blue military pants and adjusted his military suitcoat adorned with several self-awarded medals as a way to command authority.

He ran a hand over his mustache before speaking. "What's going on in here?' Bürgermeister Hartjenstein asked calmly.

No one spoke. Not even Marco.

Caspar kept his eyes peeled on the proud man as Bürgermeister Hartjenstein moved toward an obviously ashamed and nervous Marco, looking him over with an air of contempt.

"What happened here?" Hartjenstein asked again, with a hint of impatience.

"That little blond-haired bastard was trying to start a fight!" Marco said, trying to control the volume of his voice.

Falck attempted to interject a comment about it not being a big deal, but Hartjenstein raised his hand for silence. A hush fell over the bar once more.

"Today we bury a young Aline Koltz, snatched before the prime of her life at the age of thirteen and here you are getting drunk at the pub and starting fights!" Hartjenstein said, raising his voice.

Marco, trying to bite his tongue, couldn't resist. "And how did she die, Bürgermeister?"

Swiftly, Hartjenstein slid out the club at his left side from its loop, raised it and brought it down against Marco's neck before he had a chance to defend himself. Marco immediately dropped to the floor once more, this time crying out in pain at the abrupt blow.

The Bürgermeister stepped back to look down at his handiwork, then across the  room at the few patrons still remaining until his eyes fell on Caspar who was now stone-faced, glaring back at Samuel Hartjenstein.

He hated the bürgermeister. The man had let the power given to him go to his head. More of an authoritarian than an actual keeper of the peace, he ruled over the town with an iron fist.

Hartjenstein seemed to delight in throwing his authority around the small village. Even overrunning the town constable, Theodor Hecht, the officer and keeper of the peace who had been elected to his position by the people of Burnmere. It was Samuel Hartjenstein that called all the shots and had final say in matters both large and small. The bürgermeister ran the show and kept tabs on everything in his own power-hungry way.

No one liked him, but he had come from the city of Crownhaven with the highest recommendation. It had been surmised by many across Burnmere that the elected Crownhaven city officials had wanted to get rid of the man, so they assigned him the position of bürgermeister for an unspecified amount of time. He had arrived five years earlier and under his rule, even more people fled.

Under Bürgermeister Hartjenstein's rule, taxes were raised significantly, and everyone knew it was to line the unmarried man's pockets. He had seen an opportunity in this dying small town and seized it, something he hadn't managed to do back in Crownhaven before getting booted out.

"I suggest you go to the funeral, pay your respects to the late Aline Koltz, if that's where you were heading. I'll talk to you later," Hartjenstein said icily to Caspar.

Caspar remained emotionless, then turned and walked out of the pub.

"Get up, Marco," Hartjenstein said coldly.

Nick, still sitting on his barstool, felt bad for the man. Even if Marco had instigated it, he knew Marco wanted what was best for their town but had a terrible time showing it in his usual drunken state.

Marco struggled to his feet looking miserable, drunk, and humiliated with a neck that would certainly be black and blue the following day from the crack of Hartjenstein's club.

"That's better. Show a little respect for yourself. You're a mess. And from the looks of it, you owe Mr. Falck a new table," Hartjenstein said firmly, staring at Marco's glazed-over eyes.

"Now, sir, that's not necessary, I am sure I can get—" Falck began but was quickly silenced by the waving of Hartjenstein's hand.

Hartjenstein continued to stare at Marco. "The way I see it, a table such as this should be roughly one day's wage from your field work. Tell you what, I'll be lenient, you can stop by my office tomorrow and pay it. No need to take care of this today. Bring in the funds tomorrow or I'll be forced to toss you in the pen for public intoxication and destruction of property. Do I make myself clear, Mr. Seiler? A simple yes will suffice, I'm growing tired of this discussion and your ugly drunken red face."

Deep down, Hartjenstein hated his job, but he needed to keep this miserable town under his thumb so he could do his *real* job with as little interference as possible. He fully intended to bleed the people of Burnmere dry before moving on to greener pastures after his disgraced and embarrassing departure from Crownhaven years earlier.

Defeated, Marco hung his head in shame, nodded and replied, "Yes sir."

Bürgermeister Hartjenstein glanced at bartender Falck, gave the slightest nod, adjusted his hat back on top of his well-groomed head, turned and walked out of the pub.

Inside the pub, Falck tried to speak to Marco, but the man pushed a chair out of the way and headed toward the washroom, no doubt to attempt cleaning himself up before going home to his sure-to-be angry wife.

Nick took a sip of his beer and said, "Another wonderful day in Burnmere. This time complete with a girl that died under, shall we say, questionable circumstances?"

Falk replied, loud enough for Marco walking toward the washroom to hear, "Best you keep that to yourself. Little good it'll do discussing such things around the bürgermeister. He'll start in with claiming we're all nothing more than superstitious drunkards and we'll end up with a night in the constable's jail and a fine tacked on each of our heads."

Pausing before entering the washroom, Marco bit his bottom lip in anger. He couldn't stand Nick and hated the "pretty boy" looks of Caspar, but at least they knew something wasn't right in Burnmere. It hadn't been right for over one hundred years,  since that castle on the mountain first appeared in the fog, no one remembering exactly when it was built. All they knew was who, or what had lived there.

Shaking his head, Marco walked quietly into the washroom to lick his wounds. Nick slapped his coins onto the bar, nodded at Falck and made his way over to the door.

Falck called out, "Where you headed?"

"Paying my respects, I suppose," Nick replied without turning around, leaving the depressing Pale Horse.

# Chapter 4:

†

# Graveyard Ruminations

Caspar made his way down the street, stopping for a passing horse-drawn carriage passing by with an elderly couple sitting atop that gave him a brief nod, Maxwell and Jane Murrey. Though Maxell was usually a bit grumpy, overall, they were good people that frequented his shop for their horseshoe needs. They had a nice assortment of horses in their own stables, though there wasn't much use for them anymore as few people came and went from the town.

Many people had relocated away from Burnmere as the years ticked by, and so many of its residents had moved permanently from this world. Those that remained had little choice, due to a number of factors: health, age, or financial constraints being the most common. Others felt it their duty and obligation to stay in the town where their ancestors grew up and planted their roots. Those with little to no remaining family saw little reason to move, as they had no ties elsewhere and Burnmere was the only home they knew. Packing up and moving to an unknown land was far too difficult for the remaining residents.

Caspar headed past a row of small shops on one side of the street. A shoe repair shop and a clothing store with a meager selection of attire for men, women and children along with fabrics for those that made their own clothes at home. On the other side of the cobblestone street were several small homes all leading toward St. Joseph's. Little gardens grew on their properties and small pots of flowers adorned their windowsills. Not all was gloom and doom in Burnmere.

Directly beside the church, a small gathering of towns-folk stood solemnly around the grave of young Aline Koltz. Her mother and father stood in front of Father Jannick Gustloff while he concluded the burial rites.

One of the bystanders in attendance was town constable Theodor Hecht, fifty-eight years old and weathered by the hard times he and his wife had endured after she had been diagnosed with late-stage cancer, as well as the mostly bleak lives of the people and town of Burnmere. He got the brunt of the official workload in town, thanks to the bürgermeister—collecting the numerous taxes, communicating with the villagers on new bylaws that Hartjenstein wanted implemented, as well as listening to all of their many complaints about the deteriorating town they lived in.

He took down their comments, assuring them he would see what could be done, knowing full well they would nearly all fall on deaf ears with the bürgermeister. He knew it and the townsfolk knew it, but such was life in Burnmere.

Making his way to the kindly older gentleman, Caspar hung his head reverently as the dirt was shoveled on top of the lowered coffin into the cold ground below by several older gentlemen. He glanced at the girl's parents who clung to each other, sobbing at the tragic loss of their daughter. She had been an only child, making this all the more difficult to endure.

In the sky, gray clouds descended fittingly over the town and seemed to settle on the cemetery. A light drizzle began to fall as many in attendance issued their words of sorrow and condolences to the grieving parents, including Nick, who had made his way from the Pale Horse. After a bit of mingling, most shuffled out of the cemetery as the funeral ended.

Remaining in the tiny cemetery were Caspar, Constable Hecht, Fr. Gustloff, Nick Schoeler, the town doctor, Joachim Heuberger, and the parents of young Aline Koltz. While Fr. Gustoff put his hands on the shoulders of the grieving parents, Nick made his way to where Caspar and Constable Hecht stood talking near the side of the small stone church. The two men spoke while shielding their heads from the dreary weather above.

Caspar said, "Lily-Rose up and skips town three days ago, only here for a few weeks. Then, two days ago, Aline Koltz doesn't come back from her early morning chores in the barn. Later, found dead right by the woods leading up to…"

Constable Hecht nodded grimly, glancing over at Caspar then at Nick who stood close enough to hear them. The forty-three-year-old Nick was one of the aimless men in town quickly approaching middle age. Drunks that whittled away their days and nights in the Pale Horse, listening to and passing on gossip while drowning their miserable lives in cheap beer. Nick was a nobody, even in a town such as Burnmere. Not married, siblings had long since moved on, a loner who worked odd jobs around town. Cleaning out horse stalls and sweeping out the church; most of the money he made went directly down his throat in the Pale Horse pub.

Constable Hecht liked Caspar. Upstanding, well kept, good businessman. But in this town, no one fully trusted another. Not with that castle and the evil that seemed to waft down, twisting its way through the village plagued with disappearances and murders blamed on the wolves of the nearby forest. An oppressive evil clung to the land and the people that lived on it.

"You took a liking to that pretty little lady that rolled into town, didn't you?" Hecht asked.

Caspar eyed the constable. He knew what the man was insinuating and understood why he was asked the question; he also knew town gossip, especially in this size village. The woman hadn't been here long so she could have moved on. However, plump old Rozalia Sitek had kept a close watch on Lily-Rose since her arrival and had been quick to let both the constable and Bürgermeister Hartjenstein know that her belongings had been cleared out of her rented cottage at the edge of town. So, for all the gossip running through the village about her disappearance, it was completely logical that Lily-Rose may have just moved on.

"Yes, I did. We talked several times when she came into town. I told you before, but it bears repeating, she wasn't planning on being here long. She was just here to do research on the legend of the castle and this entire area. Said she might have ties to this part of the country but didn't elaborate further. That's about it," Caspar said, glancing over at the parents of the young, deceased girl leaving the grave site with their heads hung low.

Constable Hecht mused, "Well, a girl's either skipped town quickly or is missing, and I know for a fact no one took her out of Burnmere by carriage, so she just up and walked out of town? Hell, no. Far too dangerous. Nearest town is, what, twenty-five kilometers from here? At least. More foul play in a town riddled with foul play. A pretty young newcomer vanishes, then a day later this mess with the murdered thirteen-year-old girl." He turned to look at Caspar. "You were the last person to be seen with Lily-Rose."

Nick took this moment to chime in, wiping the drizzling rain from his face. "I've seen a lot in my time here, Constable. You know as well as I do that Caspar here is no killer. Hell, I can't stand Marco, but one thing we agree on is what's going on in this town. Girls go missing, never to be found again, and the few that are found are ripped to shreds? Aline Koltz was left behind after her murder. And we all know it was a murder. Not some damn animal like the bürgermeister would have us believe."

"Constable, Caspar, how do you do? How is Claudie doing?" Fr. Gustloff approached the group, having escorted the grieving parents from the cemetery.

"I'm doing well enough. Claudie, however, seems to get worse each day. Poor thing is wasting away before my eyes. I love that woman. Thank you for asking, Father."

Fr. Gustloff nodded, feeling sorry for the man and his wife of thirty-five years. Theodore was a good man but didn't have much of a spine. He certainly wasn't suited for the job of constable, but the pickings were slim and he was a damn sight better than the bully Hartjenstein. The news that his dear Claudie had cancer, diagnosed by the physician of Burnmere, just about did the man in.

Doctor Heuberger now joined them in the dank, depressing cemetery after saying goodbye to his neighbors Finn and Anna Sessler who shared their growing fears for their own ten-year-old child, Patrik. *Another tired and fear-filled family, likely to move out of town, and good for them if they do,* he thought.

The fifty-year-old town physician had moved from Germany to Romania ten years earlier and found himself in Burnmere after his wife Dora wanted to find a "nice quiet home" near the Carpathian Mountains. At the time, Joachim had gone along with the move, quickly finding a job as the much-needed town physician. Once he realized the town was dying, literally, he was trapped. The dwindling population of Burnmere needed him and his wife refused to leave. After five years, she died, one of the many forgotten faces that came to Burnmere and never left. Though her death was a result of a horse-riding accident and not the dreaded "wolf attack," it wasn't without its oddities.

The morning after her burial, the doctor had discovered her gravesite hadn't been covered. The gravediggers Fr. Gustloff hired at the time were local town drunks, known for their relative incompetence. However, upon being questioned, both swore the grave had been covered shortly after the funeral the previous day after all in attendance had departed. No more was made of the issue and the dirt was covered atop Dora Heuberger's grave once more.

As the years went on, Joachim wished he had opened his beloved's casket. To make sure the body was indeed still inside. He wondered during many lonely nights alone in his small home how many other gravesites may have been violated by the evil still lurking up inside Castle Visimar.

The three townsmen looked up gravely at the priest and physician who now stood with them. Father Gustloff clasped his hands over his stomach as they all nodded a *hello*. "This is not good. Lily-Rose Burns goes missing. Then this young soul is found dead a day later. Constable, how many more girls will go missing or worse, turn up mutilated before we—"

"Before we what, Father?" Bürgermeister Hartjenstein exclaimed, striding toward the small group of men. "Well, before we what? What am I not doing that you feel you need to take care of yourself? I feel you're best served hearing confessions and presiding over Mass and little else."

"And burying young girls, so it seems," Father Gustloff added, shooting the bürgermeister a cold glance.

"We live close to forests. I've said it before, but it seems to need to be hammered home with you paranoid lot of superstitious town gossips, there are wolves in those forests. This is what happens when people aren't careful. Doctor, you said it yourself, the girl had numerous bite marks. Her throat was ripped out. Drained of her blood. How many wolves have been shot here? Countless," Bürgermeister Hartjenstein said in a half-hearted tone that revealed even he didn't completely buy what he was trying to sell. He glanced at the doctor for some sort of acknowledgment.

Clearing his throat, the heavy-set Joachim scratched his short beard and replied in a deep, German accent, "I did indeed confirm the markings on the girl's body appeared to have been from some sort of feral animal. However, I cannot confirm it was a wolf. The markings could be wolf, but from some of the claw markings, it looks as if something was sitting on top of her. Wolves don't sit atop their victims."

"Enough of this nonsense, the both of you! This whole town seems to be slipping further and further into paranoia," Hartjenstein replied angrily, then, sensing he needed to show remorse over the tragic death, added, "Listen, I am broken up about the death of that young girl as much as the rest. I know about the mysteries surrounding that damned castle up on the mountain, but we must keep law and order around here! If we need to station more men to stand guard in shifts around our perimeters, then so be it. But all this ghouls and witches nonsense I will simply not tolerate!"

The group fell silent, each man knowing full well the bürgermeister had no intention of stationing men around the perimeter of the town. No one would volunteer for that job. That *non-paying* job.

Nick chimed in, risking upsetting the already irritable bürgermeister all the more. "Paranoid or not, this isn't normal. Lily-Rose, then one day later, Aline Koltz turns up dead?"

Caspar spoke up. "Lily-Rose has a sister. She told me so herself. Apparently, her sister strongly disapproved of her trip here and sent along her uncle as a sort of unwanted chaperone. This sister, I recall her name is Juliette, knows

Lily came here, and it's only a matter of time before she's going to come looking."

Hartjenstein shot him an icy glare. "Then it will be a wasted trip. Her belongings are gone! She left this god-forsaken town, good for her. Furthermore, if there was foul play, you, Caspar, would be the first person I would question. Now, I know the stories that are whispered here in Burnmere. Constable, I am continually disappointed in your performance. I do your job for you, it would seem."

Theodor Hecht cleared his throat and stammered out, "And what might that be?"

"Putting an end to stories about vampires and witchcraft up in the castle, that's what! It's superstitious nonsense from a town filled with superstitious people with nothing better to do than come up with reasons why they can't better protect their loved ones from the local wildlife! To hear you all talk, one would think we're dropping like flies. When was the last disappearance before this recent unfortunate accident with the thirteen-year-old?" Bürgermeister Hartjenstein all but shouted.

Caspar hadn't taken his eyes off the nasty man since he arrived. He hated the bürgermeister. Every time he had to interact with him, he felt a growing need to punch him in his smug face. He wasn't scared of this tiny man in a large man's body. He remained silent as Hartjenstein continued flaunting his authority.

Fr. Gustloff, however, tried not to look at the mean-spirited, hateful man in front of him but couldn't help glaring out of the corner of his eye. *Unfortunate accident, my ass. The work of the devil is never an unfortunate accident.*

Constable Hecht answered, "Usually, these disappearances are spread out. Sometimes several years go by. Hell, I don't know."

Hartjenstein wiped his moustache with his fingers. "That's right, constable, you don't know. So, keep your damn mouth shut," he hissed at the man he had no use for.

Theodore Hecht hung his head and kept his mouth closed. He was good at that after years of being berated by the despicable bürgermeister.

Hartjenstein glared at the four men who had fallen silent once more. "One last reminder: the forest is off-limits. The castle is off-limits. I already have to deal with animal attacks around town, we're not going up into those hills on a wild goose chase. No doubt, the woman you were hoping to bed down decided it takes more than a witty pick-up line from a miserable small-town ironsmith to get her into bed. Since she likely heard I don't allow anyone to visit that damned infernal castle, she moved on. And I should reiterate once more, if I were to suspect foul play, you, Caspar Voit would be the first person I would be looking into as a possible suspect."

Caspar glared at the egotistical man that had all but proclaimed a tiny and pathetic dictatorship over Burnmere. His fists clenched tightly as he restrained himself from smashing Hartjenstein's nose in through his skull.

"Gentlemen," the bürgermeister said, giving a slight nod before turning around and leaving the cemetery without uttering another word.

Nick looked around quickly at his companions. "Well, best be getting home. It's getting close to dinner; my buzz is wearing off. Have a good evening. As good an evening as you can have in a place like this."

Nodding, Joachim said, "I'll come with you. I need to get home and clear my mind of this incident with the young girl. Gentlemen, I know this sounds strange, but I feel it in the air. Something evil. I can't explain it …"

Father Gustloff, Constable Hecht, and Caspar nodded their farewells as Nick and Joachim turned and left the cemetery.

Sighing heavily, Constable Hecht said, "Victor Reis gave the official cause of death as, you guessed it, animal attack. You know Hartjenstein though, the quicker she's in the ground, the quicker we all move on. If Lily-Rose has indeed disappeared, this will have been the quickest double unsolved crime the town has ever seen. Usually, these disappearances are spread out. Sometimes several years go by. But as the bürgermeister himself so eloquently put it, I don't know."

"I'm going back inside the church. I've got a bottle of whiskey. Think I could go for a glass. Anyone want to join me? I wanted to wait until Nick left. He'd take me up on my offer and likely drink us all under the table," Fr. Gustloff said with a chuckle, trying to avoid any more discussion about the bürgermeister and his continued ill treatment of the kind old constable, Theodore Hecht.

Smiling, Hecht shook his head, "I wish I could but duty calls. If I go in smelling like booze Hartjenstein will have my ass. Plus, I've got paperwork to fill out."

He fell silent. They all knew the paperwork he was referring to. Aline Koltz.

"Anyway, have a good night, gentleman," Hecht said, nodded, then turned and left.

Looking over at Caspar grimly, Fr. Gustloff said, "Join me for a drink. I want to share something with you now that we're alone."

Caspar looked into the priest's eyes. More bad news. He could sense it.

"One drink. Then I've got to get home." He followed the father who was already heading toward a small side door leading to his parish.

The church had candles lit throughout the sanctuary. A small confessional occupied the far corner of the room with roughly thirty pews lining the church, fifteen on each side. The altar was minimal, a large cross propped behind it against the wall. The priest's chalice sat on the altar atop a white cloth while the eucharist resided in the ciborium off to the side locked away in the tabernacle. Resting in the center of the altar was the monstrance, a beautiful cross considering how dreary and oppressive Burnmere was.

Fr. Gustloff walked past the altar, bowed, then made his way toward the sacristy in the rear of the church. Caspar followed suit, dipping his finger in the holy water font by the side door and making a sign of the cross, bowing briefly in front of the altar. He tried to make it to Mass but he couldn't help but feel as though God had abandoned them all. He headed back to Fr. Gustloff's small sacristy and walked in.

Jannick pulled out two glasses, dropped them with a thud onto his desk then pulled out a bottle of Justerini & Brooks' Irish Whisky. "Sorry, no ice," the weary priest said, pouring a double for each of them. He kept the cap off and slid the bottle to one side.

Handing the glass of J&B over to Caspar, Fr. Gustloff raised his own. "To little Aline Koltz."

"And to the missing Lily-Rose Burns," Caspar added, clinking his glass against Father Gustloff's.

"Here, here," Jannick said, taking his glass of Irish whisky down in one large gulp before sitting down in his old wooden chair. He grabbed the bottle and poured another shot, then looked up at Caspar.

Caspar saw the middle-aged, tired priest had something he wanted to get off of his chest, and the warm amber liquid would loosen his lips. He raised his own glass and also took down the burning liquid, grimaced, and set the empty glass down onto the table next to Jannick's.

A second shot was poured but Caspar didn't pick it up, not yet He wanted to hear what Jannick had to say first. "What is it, Father?"

Fr. Gustloff ran his thick hand through his dark, graying hair and sighed heavily. "Lily-Rose Burns. That name struck me. It has history here in Burnmere. I pulled some of the records from town hall. One Alfred Burns once passed through here. He was, how should I say this? Commissioned by the Church to hunt down and destroy vampires throughout Eastern Europe. A vampire hunter. The little information I have of him from official church archives reveals the man oversaw the execution and destruction of several dozen condemned individuals. Were they actual vampires? Who knows."

He paused, watching Caspar's expression turn from curiosity to disgust.

Fr. Gustloff raised his glass and took shot number two down, setting the glass back onto the table. "He mainly stuck to parts of Eastern Germany but made his way as far as Romania, right through Burnmere, one hundred years ago. I should say, I do not and have never approved of the Church's stance on these supposed witch and vampire hunts. Burning people at the stake. Drowning people. Beheading people. Hogwash, I say! It flies in the face of the Good Lord's teachings in the holy gospel. But what do I know? I'm an old drunken priest with a bad heart leading Mass in the ass end of Eastern Europe to people that once were deeply religious and now seem to have given up all hope. Still, they need a shepherd. I haven't given up hope completely, it's why I'm still here."

Caspar picked up his second glass of J&B, now wanting it more than ever after this bit of information. He quickly slammed it down and set the glass back on the table. Fr. Gustloff raised the bottle to offer him one more, but he declined with a wave of the hand. Jannick, however, poured himself another, this time capping the whisky after filling his glass a bit fuller than the previous two.

Caspar said, "Well, we now know why Lily-Rose was visiting. Her research was accurate, I suppose. I am assuming this Alfred Burns had something to do with the count that once lived there?"

Fr. Gustloff responded, "Count Visimar: the owner of the castle, now long deceased. Executed by one Alfred Burns. Look, I understand why Hartjenstein doesn't want people going into that forest leading up to the castle. He's not wrong in saying wolves have killed people in these parts. But you and I both know there's more to it. Lily-Rose was here sniffing around for a reason and it's certainly not just research. She vanishes then the following day a girl is brutally murdered in the wee morning hours. Joachim said it best, evil. There is an evil presence that seems to be growing stronger. I've felt it even before these latest two incidents. Come to think of it, since Lily-Rose arrived I've felt a growing sense of dread that the worst is yet to come. I can't shake it, Caspar. Hell, even the fog that covers that damned castle on the mountain seems to have gotten thicker and closer to this town. It's all leading to something sinister, I fear."

"Father, I need to get home. What are you getting at, exactly?" Caspar said, sighing and running a hand through his wavy blond head of hair.

"I'm not sure yet. But can you think of anything about Lily-Rose that stood out to you? Anything at all?" Father Gustloff asked, hoping for even a small nugget of information that could piece together her having gone missing and the young girl's death the following day.

Shaking his head, Caspar was about to say no then stopped and thought for a second. "An amulet. She wore it around her neck. Some type of gemstone housed inside a golden locket. She seemed obsessed with it, saying it was a gift from her mother who had passed away earlier, that it had been in the family for years and she tried to always wear it as a keepsake. The odd things is, she said she felt as though she had been bewitched by it, but never elaborated further. She was obviously troubled, Father. I mean, who would come here of their own free will?" He frowned and pondered his empty glass on the table.

"Anything else?" Fr. Gustloff asked leaning forward.

"Come to think of it, yes. I didn't give it much thought until, well…until now with all that has happened over the last three days. She had a scar on the palm of her hand. Looked like a healed cut, pretty deep. I asked her about it, but she shrugged it off and didn't want to talk about it. Just mumbled the word, *bewitched*. For such a pretty young woman, she sure seemed troubled."

Fr. Gustoff thought back to Lily-Rose sitting by herself the previous Sunday at the morning Mass. He had made eye contact with her and noted her expression: *Troubled*. Nodding at this bit of information, the priest cleared his throat and stood to his feet, extending his hand to Caspar who also stood up, taking his hand.

"Thank you for the drinks, Father," Caspar said making his way to the door.

"Be careful out there, I fear this is only the beginning. Too many coincidences on the one-hundred-year anniversary of one Antonin Visimar. I wonder if this amulet you speak of may play a part in this as well?" Father Gustloff replied curiously.

Caspar shrugged to indicate he was just as baffled by it all as the father, then quickly turned and left the church without a word.

Outside, the drizzle had turned to a steady rain. It was now dark outside. His conversation with the priest had raised questions. Who was this Alfred Burns vampire-hunting character? How did his visit here one hundred years prior tie in with his great-granddaughter, Lily-Rose? And the amulet? Was that of any significance in her disappearance, or the cut on the palm of her hand? Did this mysterious and long deceased Count Visimar's estate up on the mountain have something to do with Lily-Rose or young Aline Kotze or the numerous others throughout Burnmere's checkered history?

Tugging his thick brown coat up over his head, he pondered these thoughts as he made his way back to his ironworks shop and small cottage he called home beside it. He was ready for the day to come to an end and blissful sleep to take him away from the misery that was Burnmere.

The streets of the small village were empty as usual once night fell. The only noise to be heard was up the street at the Pale Horse pub where Armin Falck was locking up and calling it a day. Even in the rain, the man had to go for his nightly cigarette stroll.

Once Falck was out of sight, Caspar looked at the streetlamps flickering dimly against the soft rain, suddenly feeling very much alone and vulnerable. He walked faster to his home, quickly making his way to his front door. Reaching into his coat pocket, he pulled out his key and nearly dropped it, he was so nervous. Something about the night felt even more evil and ominous than ever.

He quickly inserted the key into the lock and twisted. The bolt retracted, and the door swung open. Entering, he heard something echo in the distance, possibly from the outskirts of town but he couldn't be sure with the rain muffling the sound.

Squinting into the darkness, Caspar wondered, *could it be coming from the direction of that damned cursed castle?*

It lasted only a split-second, but he knew what it sounded like. A man screaming for his life.

# Chapter 5:

✝

# The Death of Aline Koltz

*Three days earlier...*

The sky had turned black above the hazy fog surrounding the mountain as Lily-Rose entered Castle Visimar. She felt an overwhelming desire to turn and run for her life, but she knew that was no longer possible. It hadn't been possible since the man in black had visited her a month prior in the dress shop in Summerhost. Oppressive thoughts flooded her mind. *I have been bewitched and now this is my fate.*

She reached up and clasped the amulet that adorned her neck, warming to the point of being nearly unbearable against her bare skin. So far from home now, this small relic was her only tie to her sister and her family. The door behind her closed with a loud thud, making her visit feel more like a permanent residency.

The tall man in a black tuxedo and top hat that he now took off stood in front of her, looking her over. His hair was black and tightly combed over his skull. Dark eyes peered at her, through her, it seemed. Lily's first thought at seeing him now inside the dark, ominous castle was that he looked like a funeral parlor director.

Lily-Rose felt vulnerable under his gaze, her low-slung blue dress revealing just enough of her chest to make her feel self-conscious. Her wavy blond hair hung past her shoulders, her blue eyes complimenting her dress stared back at the sinister-looking man. His eyes went to the amulet around her neck.

"Allow me to formally introduce myself. My name is Marcel Metzinger, I'm the caretaker and overseer of my master's estate, Castle Visimar. Do make yourself at home. The master will see you shortly. I shall prepare a hot toddy to warm you," he said flatly, putting his hands behind his back and staring down at her.

Without waiting for a response, he turned and left the large great room, off to a door on the side, closing it behind him and leaving her completely alone. But she didn't feel alone. She felt as though eyes were watching her, unseen eyes.

Scanning the room, she made her way to the large fireplace that, lucky for her, had a fire roaring. The stone walls in the large great room were at least thirty feet high leading up to a ceiling that vaulted to a point in the middle. Certainly one of the peaks she had seeing all the way down at her cottage.

Several hallways led to other areas of the castle, with numerous doors lining the walls. One stairwell near the wall by the fireplace led to the upper floor.

Above the fireplace hung what appeared to be the house crest. A shield with two spears making an X and a dragon wrapping itself around the shield. Chiseled into stone under the crest were the words *Castrum Visimar: domus aeterna tua*. She had taken a Latin course in school many years ago and could read this well enough: "Castle Visimar: Your Eternal Home."

She couldn't take her eyes off of the words etched into the stone. She could almost hear them spoken directly to her. Sentencing her. *Replace home with damnation* she thought. She desperately wanted to flee but knew her bewitched body and spirit could not. She was too weak. She longed for her dear sister, now so very far away.

Ever since that day in the dress shop, her dreams had been haunted by a figure shrouded in shadow. Tall, ominous, evil. She dreamed about the very village she had traveled to. The castle. The forest leading up to it. Everything about Burnmere had plagued her dreams leading up to her arrival. Something was beckoning and controlling her. She truly felt as though something otherworldly, something purely evil, had indeed bewitched her and was now toying with her.

*The amulet. Bring it to me.* Those words had echoed through her head countless times over the past several weeks, and now she had obeyed the voice. She was here.

The walls in the great room felt as though they were closing in on her even if the room itself was enormous. She stood by the fire but couldn't get warm, her blue eyes darting back and forth, wishing the creepy Marcel Metzinger would come back, much as she already despised him.

The large double doors were closed, their steel-hooped handles and long, thick metal lock sealing her inside. Surely, it wasn't locked from the outside. *What if I fight this curse on me and make a run for it now? But where? The wolves in the forest will rip me to pieces.*

Lily-Rose approached the double doors but was stopped by Marcel who had somehow appeared behind her, creeping in so quietly she hadn't heard him enter. On a small saucer in his hands rested a glass filled with an amber colored liquid. *Hot toddy.*

"Going somewhere? Here's your hot toddy," Marcel said coldly, pushing the cup toward her.

Instinctively, she reached out and took it, raising the cup to her lips. Before drinking, she smelled it. Whisky, honey, lemon. It was indeed a hot toddy. She drank it down. The best and only good thing that she had experienced since leaving the relative safety of her rented cottage.

She wished Caspar Voit would come rescue her. She could tell the friendly, handsome man had a kind heart to go along with his good looks and muscular physique. But she knew whatever was calling to her was stronger than Caspar. Stronger than all in Burnmere or Romania, for that matter.

Someone, or more likely, some *thing* resided in Castle Visimar, and she was about to meet it. Her amulet burned warmer still. She considered taking it off but thought better of it.

Taking the empty cup and saucer from her hands, Marcel motioned for her to follow him.

Reluctantly, she moved forward, staying close behind him while he made his way deeper into the castle. At the end of a long, dimly lit, cobweb-strewn hallway adorned with torches on either side, they came to a closed door. Marcel reached his thin, bony hand forward and took hold of the handle. She looked at his pointed fingernails and thought back to it piercing the flesh of her palm. She shuddered at the horror of being in the same room with a man who had willfully caused her such harm and set in motion her journey to Burnmere.

She understood now more than ever that she had been unable to resist, no matter how much she had struggled against it. Even her sister's pleas had fallen on deaf ears. She knew full well that the amulet and its owner had found her and taken possession of her. Her fate had been sealed with the piercing of her hand and the drawing of her blood back in England.

The door opened and Marcel motioned for her to enter. She looked at him nervously, but his dark eyes showed no pity, no feeling. Dead. Cold.

She entered the dark room, its only light a single torch against a back wall that spanned at least twenty feet in height. Once inside, the door behind her closed and she felt Marcel's hand against her back, pushing her forward.

Wrapping her arms around her chest protectively, feeling the radiating heat from the amulet, she moved in further, looking around while her eyes adjusted to the new darkness. The room smelled moldy and old. But the smell wasn't what truly chilled her. It was the unholy presence of whatever had bewitched and beckoned her all the way from England. She turned to Marcel, looking up at him pleadingly, but the eyes staring back at her were merciless.

She turned back to the room to see the outline of a figure shrouded in darkness standing below the single torch. Beside him, two sets of glowing yellow eyes peered out. She heard a low growl. A hand raised and the animals quieted at once. *Wolves*, she thought.

"Your blood, taken from my assistant. It is the blood of a descendent of Alfred Burns, am I correct?" a low, deep and sinister voice spoke.

Lily-Rose stared ahead at her host.

"You will answer me, now."

Stuttering her response, she replied meekly, "Y-yes. I am his great—"

Marcel shoved her from behind with his cold, dead hand. "You will address our master as Count," he said coldly, his breath on her neck reeking of rotten meat and the black liquorish scent she hated so much.

Her mouth, dry and parched from the utter fear and dread coursing through her body, struggled to form words. Her bottom lip trembled, and though she wanted to burst into tears and run from the room, run from the castle all the way back to her sister in England, but she couldn't, and she knew it.

Clearing her dry throat and trying to compose herself, she said quietly, "Yes, Count. I am his great-granddaughter, Lily-Rose Burns."

"Your name means nothing to me, you mean nothing to me. What you wear around your neck, however, is of great importance and the reason you are not only here, but still alive. You will do as you're told, exactly as you're told. Then, when I have used you up, you will die. That is a certainty, do you understand?"

The amulet grew hotter around her neck as cold tears spilled down her cheeks. She knew this to be true, this was why she had been summoned here, why her thoughts had been haunted by this place every waking and sleeping moment since the dress shop. Her fate was sealed in this evil, god-forsaken place and all she could do was utter, "Yes, Count. I understand."

"Come closer, I want to see the amulet around your neck. The one your great-grandfather stole from me one hundred years ago. I can feel its heat now," Visimar hissed.

Her eyes grew wide with terror as she moved toward the figure shrouded in darkness. The amulet felt as though it might burn her flesh. This man, if it was a man, possessed a vial of her blood. She felt more and more violated with every second she was trapped inside this room.

Her feet moved forward but she hadn't moved them. She now stood in front of the shadowed figure; next to her sat two of the largest wolves she had ever seen. One black, one gray. She saw fangs bared and heard low growls, then closed her eyes tightly.

"You will look at me," Count Visimar said coolly, his words burrowing into her brain like a snake. The voice was the same one that had haunted her thoughts, the invader of her very mind and soul.

She opened her eyes. A pair of red eyes stared back at her. "Offer me your throat," he said, more a hiss than a human sound.

Lily-Rose tilted her head back, her bare neck open to him. Wrapped around it was the glowing, hot amulet, in all of its shining white and multi-colored splendor.

The Count looked at his prized jewel, returned to him one hundred years later. He leaned forward and inspected it, then ripped it from her neck.

Lily-Rose gasped but continued to keep her throat exposed, not daring to look down. The man, or creature, was now directly in front of her. Inches from her throat.

Count Visimar held the amulet in his long, pale hand. His red eyes roaming from it to Lily-Rose. "The golden chain it was connected to. This is not the same chain. Where is my chain?"

Swallowing hard, Lily-Rose whispered, "I gave it to my sister Juliette. She refused to take the amulet, so I gave her the chain instead as a birthday present. I don't think she ever realized it had been connected to the amulet…which was a gift passed down from my mother. I wanted her to have a part—"

"Silence!" the count hissed, at which both wolves stood to their feet and snarled at her. She could feel their breath on her hands.

Lily-Rose fell silent at his command, trying not to move a muscle for fear the wolves would tear her to shreds.

Count Visimar's glowing red eyes fell on Marcel who stood away from them, close to the entrance into the dimly lit room. "You, *fool*!" Visimar shrieked.

Instantly, Marcel hung his head in shame and tried to explain. "Master, I knew nothing of a chain, or a sister, only the amulet that—"

"Enough!" shouted Visimar, once more alerting both wolves to prepare to pounce, as if waiting for their command to attack.

The room fell silent for a moment before Visimar spoke again. "For one hundred years I have waited for my amulet and revenge on the descendants of Albert Burns. I tasked you to find it. All of it, not a mere piece of it! And you failed me. The complete amulet must be restored to me for our master's return! You will bring me the chain and the sister of this girl. Or mark my words, your suffering will be eternal!"

"Yes, my master," Marcel said quietly, keeping his head bowed. *This is not my fault* he thought bitterly but remained quiet.

Count Visimar turned his attention back to young Lily-Rose. "As for you, my dear descendent of one Alfred Burns. You will be my nourishment as well as my master's eternal slave upon his awakening. A small price to pay for your great-grandfather's thieving, murderous misdeeds. And soon, your sister will join you."

Lily-Rose felt hot tears stream down her cheeks. She closed her eyes tightly, feeling her blood pumping through the veins in her neck.

Two rows of sharp fangs sunk into her waiting neck, instantly piercing her carotid artery as the sharper, longer two sunk deeper than the rest. The grip of the creature's lips was tight against her flesh as it began sucking, sealing the unbreakable, evil bond this evil presence had over her. She couldn't resist. This was her destiny.

Her life drained swiftly from her neck into the creature's waiting mouth and down its throat. Her limbs went limp. Fog crept into her mind as she slowly lost consciousness, the life and breath slipping from her. Her blood spilled forth onto the floor beneath her where both wolves quickly lapped up the crimson red, hungry while their master drank.

The room spun around her as blood was pulled from her body faster than it could pump through her veins. The creature continued to drink, greedily, until Lily-Rose could no longer keep her head up. She dropped her head forward, eyes nearly closed.

As darkness overtook her, she noticed the skin of the thing drinking her dry. Pale, almost blue, the thin veins with purple running through them. Was it her blood now coursing through its veins?

The last thing she saw were the wolves at her feet, lapping up every spilled drop of her blood. And then, empty blackness took her.

†

Lily-Rose opened her eyes and looked around, quickly realizing she was no longer in the room with Count Visimar but a large dungeon or possibly a basement. She lay on cold dirt, staring up at several torches adorning the walls, giving minimal light to her surroundings. Sitting up, she immediately reached for her neck and felt the bite marks from some time earlier.

She felt no pain pulsing through the wounds on her neck. However, she was terribly cold and starving and she needed to eat. The pain in her stomach hit her hard and caused her to double over in agony. *How long have I been here?* Her amulet was gone and her clothes were covered in dried blood. Disgust at the violation she had endured soon overtook her need to sate her stomach's hunger pangs.

She stood to her feet, looking around the enormous space at several coffins haphazardly strewn about on the ground. She assumed she was deep inside the castle, bottom level, most likely. *I'm so hungry!* Doubling over in pain, she held her stomach again. She had never felt this kind of ravenous need to eat.

The bite on her neck from Count Visimar had surely been fatal. She had felt the life drain out of her, hadn't she? Yet, here she was, in some sort of limbo state. *Or worse.* She shuddered at the thought of what she may have turned into after her ordeal in that darkened room.

She wished she had something to change into from the blood-drenched blue dress she wore. She hurried over to the nearest coffin and instinctively grabbed hold of the lid, easily opening it. Inside lay another woman, this one younger than her, with blood smeared around her mouth.

Reaching into the coffin, Lily-Rose touched the beautiful woman's face and, as if suddenly experiencing the actions of the sleeping woman, she was instantly taken out of the gloomy dungeon and into the sky. Leaving the dark castle and flying just above the treetops that lined the path leading down into the village of Burnmere.

Lily, or the body she was transported to, leapt forward with superhuman speed and power. She glanced back and saw two large bat-like, bony wings draped tightly in human flesh making large flapping motions while she lunged forward. She felt as though she were looking through someone, or some*thing* else's eyes. Numerous black and gray wolves running through the forest stopped to stare up at her. Huge bats zigzagged alongside her in the sky.

The village came into view quickly, and Lily-Rose landed softly onto grass on bare feet, right behind a small patch of trees near the forest on the outskirts of town. It was still dark outside.

A young girl with a long, braided ponytail was carrying pails into the barn to feed the few cows inside. She watched the girl enter the open stall doors then dump the grain into a trough where the cows started to eat. When she had finished, the girl walked back out, closing the barn doors behind her— no doubt a task she performed every morning.

The girl looked up, but it was too late. Lily was on her before she had time to scream. Outstretched inhuman clawed hands grabbed her by the shoulders, throwing the stunned girl to the muddy ground. Lily, now on top of her, sunk her fangs into the girl's neck and bit, pulling on the flesh, ripping it off of the stunned girl's neck.

In an instant, half of the girl's throat had been ripped out. Her eyes wide in horror, she gasped for breath that would not come, choking on the blood filling her lungs and spilling out onto the muddy cold ground.

While she struggled to breathe, Lily used her claw-like appendages to rip through the girl's dress, tearing it to pieces while ripping into the girl's stomach. Feeding. Rabid in her blood lust, feasting on the girl until she was drained of nearly all of her blood.

In less than a minute, it was all over.

She raised her head, wiping her blood soaked mouth then looking down at the murdered girl whose eyes were open in a frozen stare of terror. Looking around, she felt a presence beckoning her. She was required to return to the castle. And not obeying her master would mean dire consequences. Mainly, no feeding for an even longer period of time. Which was utter and nearly insufferable agony.

Satisfied with her meal, she leapt up and in one fluid motion, took to the sky once more, flapping her wings in the wind that carried her upward toward the looming fog-covered castle in the mountains above.

The morning sun was just starting to creep up behind distant hills, yet another sign she needed to get back to the castle immediately.

In the distance, a scream was heard followed by someone shouting, "Aline! Oh my lord, no! Please, no!" The parents of the young girl had likely discovered her mutilated body. This had little to no effect on the winged creature that sailed up the mountain, nearly brushing the tops of the trees to avoid being spotted in the fog that draped the mountain forest like a thick blanket.

She didn't enter the castle through the front double doors but flew up to one of its open towers that loomed high above the rest of the structure. She dove into the opening and immediately shot downwards until reaching the very bottom of the castle floor.

Landing on the cold dirt, her wings collapsed back into her body as she morphed back to her human form. She bent over the open casket laying haphazardly in the earth and climbed inside. Her work was done. The coffin lid closed, shrouding her once more in sweet darkness.

Lily-Rose opened her eyes, tears streaming, horrified at what she had not only witnessed but experienced. She looked down at the woman inside the coffin whose memories she had just lived and who now stared up at her with dead, glazed eyes that cast a yellowish glow.

# Chapter 6:

✝

# Screams in the Night

Armin Falck lived above the Pale Horse in a tiny room with a small washroom and a kitchen that served as a living room as well. He was thankful for even this humble place of residence. He had no wife, little money, and no true friends—unless the drunk townies at the pub counted as *friends*.

Because of this, at times, he needed to get away from the humdrum of his boring daily existence of pouring beer and shots of whisky for the depressed patrons of Burnmere. He did this by taking evening strolls around the several blocks of uneven cobblestone road that ran through the small village. Long enough to suck down one hand-rolled cigarette after the Pale Horse closed at night, the one bright spot in his day.

This day, especially, his craving for nicotine was amplified after the tussle between Marco and Caspar and the visit from the cold-hearted bürgermeister himself, Samuel Hartjenstein. One busted table later and the bar had nearly cleared out.

After Hartjenstein's tough guy speech, he was certain the fine Marco owed would never touch his hands, nor would the broken table get fixed until Armin himself replaced it or just got rid of it altogether. Based on the continually diminishing number of patrons at the Pale Horse, he guessed the latter would probably be the case. No need to waste funds he barely had for a table no one would use anyway. Such was life in Burnmere.

The drizzle continued, but his hat worked well enough to shield his face and, more importantly, his rolled cigarette from getting wet and extinguishing. Strolling down the silent street, he looked at the darkened houses that were mostly businesses or long-abandoned homes. Slowly, the town of Burnmere was indeed dying. More and more people fled, and those who stayed stuck to themselves.

He passed Marco's house, one of the few still occupied in this area of town. A dim light shone through his window with the drapes closed. He felt sorry for the man whose life had dealt him a bad hand. A dead-end marriage in a dead-end town working dead-end jobs. Drinking what was left of his life away. He had one kid, a son, but he had left home at a young age to go find work and a better life. *Good for him,* Armin thought. He might actually make something of himself now that he didn't have the oppressive weight of Burnmere and his sad parents resting on his shoulders.

Another long drag on the cigarette. He sucked in the nicotine, burning the back of his throat, then blew out the cloud of smoke. It was a nasty habit, but in this town, it brought him much-needed, sweet relief.

Something caught his eye just past the Seiler residence. A shadow moving where all should have been still. He wasn't able to make out what it was, but he had the feeling he was no longer alone.

Shifting his eyes back and forth, Falck took one more drag on his cigarette then tossed it and picked up the pace. In his many walks on this same stretch of road, he had only one near run-in with something he thought was a wolf several years ago. Whatever it was, it had run off quickly. This felt different, it was as though he were being watched, possibly even stalked. The drizzle continued but the wind and seemingly all other outside noise ceased. Falck found it to be simply too quiet.

"Sonofabitch," he muttered nervously to himself, his eyes shifting back and forth. He jammed his hands into his coat pockets and kept moving, glancing back quickly to see if anything was there. A pair of glowing yellow eyes stared out at him through two trees roughly thirty feet behind him. That's when he heard a growl somewhere up ahead.

He turned his head slowly. On the cobblestone street directly in front of him stood the largest black wolf he had ever seen, its own pair of yellow eyes staring through him.

Taking two small steps back, he glanced back to see another wolf, this one gray, come out from the tree cover it had been stalking him from and moving onto the cobblestone road.

He was pinned in. The wolf in front of him only had to leap several feet forward to grab him and the wolf behind him was steadily approaching. Looking back at the black wolf in front of him, he saw it now bared its fangs, large and pointy with saliva dripping from them.

He immediately bolted toward the nearest house as fast as his old legs could go, but his right shoe caught the end of a broken cobblestone, sending him face forward onto the wet earth, nearly knocking him unconscious. He rolled over onto his back, sure he had broken his nose. He felt warm liquid dripping down his face along with the light, cold drizzle of rain.

Groaning at the pain pounding through his skull, he searched frantically for the wolves. They were no longer on the road. They were now on either side of him, baring the largest fangs he had ever seen.

Falck did the only thing he knew to do at this point, he screamed as loud as he could. He was cut off in mid-scream by one set of jaws biting down onto his face while another bit into the side of his neck. Both pressed into his flesh while shaking their powerful heads.

He raised his arms in a vain attempt to fend them off, but the wolves bit down harder, ripping his face and neck from his body, killing him. They quickly bit into the man once more, this time pulling him toward the woods, fighting each other greedily over the freshly killed man.

†

Marco opened his front door and peered out with a small lantern, searching for the source of the scream that was far too close to his house for comfort. Joining him was his wife of nearly eighteen years, Everly. The two stood shoulder-to-shoulder in the doorway, but it was obvious there was no love between them.

They had married when she was just seventeen after getting pregnant with what she hoped was merely a drunken one-night stand among many other drunken one-night stands, none of which had led to a baby. The biggest mistake of her life had been marrying this worthless bastard and not taking the opportunity when it presented itself to smother her newborn with a pillow while he lay crying in her bed.

She had turned even meaner in recent years. Angry at the world. Angry at the lousy upbringing her parents had given her: a drunk for a father and a mother who ran around on him before he caught her in bed, murdering both her and her lover. She never saw her father after that and was left in the care of an older brother who sexually and sometimes physically abused her from age eleven until she moved out at the young age of fifteen. When her brother lay on top of her, sticking his *thing* into her when she was barely a teenager, the one thought continually etched into her brain was, *There is no God, for what God would let this happen to her?*

From there it was a downward spiral of interchangeable men, all spilling their seed into her, until one actually succeeded in impregnating her. She remained angry that she had a son with this worthless drunk that couldn't keep a job even in a shit-hole town like Burnmere. Angry that her son escaped this miserable life while she suffered on.

She wanted to leave Marco many years ago, but the boy kept them together, even though they loathed each other. Once he left, the mold was set, she had nowhere to go, no means, and no one to go with. She was stuck in Burnmere and came to accept that cold hard fact. *Just eek out the rest of your life and die. Then this miserable existence will finally be over.*

Now thirty-seven and feeling more like sixty in a shit-hole town saddled with a no-good drunk, Everly went from being mean-spirited to downright evil, constantly looking for ways to antagonize her husband, making the citizens of Burnmere turn the other way when they saw her coming.

A skinny woman with a tangled mess of hair, Everly had long since quit caring about her looks. Something she blamed exclusively on her husband's inability to bring home enough money to buy her nice things. Instead wasting his time and money in the Pale Horse, drinking with people he didn't like, spending money he didn't have.

Tonight had been an especially bad night in the Seiler household. Marco had come home reeking of beer and displaying a nasty bruise on his neck, explaining the incident back at the Pale Horse to her, and she in turn, screaming at him for the loser he was.

Marco had left the house earlier in the day, already angry after Everly told him she would have been better off in a life of prostitution instead of the hell he had drug her through the past nearly twenty years. Now no decent man would have her due to her haggard looks, all of which she claimed was, of course, his fault.

He hated her. Hated the smell of mothballs on her clothes that she wore all week. Her sagging breasts he hadn't touched in years. Her unkept and unwashed hair. Once more, his fault she would say. *Not enough money for soap to properly wash myself!* While there had been much talk in Burnmere of vampires and witches in the region, as far as Marco was concerned, the real witch resided in his home.

Still, in a town like this, divorce or even separation would only make matters worse. Primarily, he would have no place to go, nor would she, so, they continued their awful existence together.

The death of the young girl had shaken up Marco. Under the rough exterior and typically grumpy disposition, a kind heart still beat inside his chest. He felt terrible for the grieving parents. This followed by the disappearance of the beautiful young Lily-Rose, someone even in his long-past best years he would never have been able to approach, was deeply upsetting.

Of course, the handsome and well-spoken Caspar had to come along and started courting her. He hated that deep down he admired the young man—not that he would ever tell him that. But Caspar did the best he could with his business in Burnmere, even hiring on Marco several years ago for a larger job.

But the meaner Marco's wife got, the meaner and more off-putting Marco got to those around him until he truly had no friends. Yet another example of Everly collecting another win in their silent battle of wills.

"What was that? Sounded almost like Armin Falck. I recognize that old geezer's raspy voice," Everly said beside Marco in the doorway. Her breath, reeking of old food and rotting teeth hit his nose and he recoiled in disgust, stepping away from her slightly.

She noticed this and snorted in disgust. "Go see what that's all about. He's your friend and it sounded bad. Too close to my house for comfort," she said, deliberately getting closer to his face.

Closing his eyes in disgust and anger, he replied, "You mean, our house."

"Just go out there and see what the hell that was about. Or should your frail wife do it for you?"

Shaking his head, Marco, who minutes earlier was looking forward to blissful sleep, the best part of his day, pulled on his coat and grabbed an old rusted-out shotgun near the front door.

"That piece of shit won't even fire. Good luck," Everly sneered as he moved out into the darkness.

Now standing outside, Marco shook his head, pushing hateful thoughts of his wife out of his mind. The drizzle was letting up, but the cobblestone street was still wet. At this time of night, under these conditions, he needed to be careful. He had fallen before in the wintertime on these continually worsening roads and it had cost him several weeks lying on his back. A truly miserable period of nagging and grumbling from his significant other.

He hadn't told Everly that the crash he had taken to the floor of the Pale Horse earlier had done a number on his hip, knowing the limp would have caught even more hell from her along with the fresh black-and-blue mark across his neck. Possibly even a slap across the face. While he hated her, he never raised his fist to the woman, or any woman for that matter. He knew better.

He walked in the direction the scream had come from. A scream, now that he thought about it, that had been abrupt and cut short. His corner was the worst off, near the outskirts and closest to the forest. The businesses here were shuttered for good and the few residents that lived anywhere near him never spoke to the Seiler's.

"It's so damn dark!" he mumbled to himself, now out of sight of Everly. He instantly started to favor his bruised hip from the tumble he took earlier.

He crept forward slowly in the darkness, holding the small lantern and hoping it had enough kerosine to keep from snuffing out. He moved closer to the trees where earlier, glowing yellow eyes had peered out at the old bartender, Falck.

Up ahead, he heard movement on the cobblestone road, footsteps. Quickly swiveling where he stood, he held out the lantern and with his other hand lifted up his old shotgun and pulled back on one of its two hammers, not sure if either worked any more.

"Who's there?" he called out.

The pain in his hip was a distant memory as fear, ice-cold fear, replaced it. Something was out here in the dark with him. He could feel it.

# Chapter 7:

†

# Stalking Prey

Lily-Rose had lain in the dungeon of the castle for several days, unconscious from what should have been a fatal wound from the vampire creature that lived upstairs within the castle walls. How she still lived and felt no pain, other than the unrelenting hunger, was a mystery to her. She suspected it had something to do with what Count Visimar's bite had done to her. She wasn't dead, but she wasn't fully alive either.

She had read about vampirism years ago in school and always found the subject a little silly. *Flying bat-creatures that drink blood and only come out at night, sure!* Now, however, she wondered if the legends had more truth in them than fiction. She was living proof that something incomprehensible to the logical mind was at work here—as were the hideous beings living within the walls of the castle.

No sunlight shone through the dungeon walls. She was still haunted by her vision of flying through the sky to murder young Aline Koltz. She stared at the woman, alive but very much dead, inside the coffin on the cold dirt of the cellar floor.

When the woman opened her eyes, Lily-Rose jumped back in surprise. The woman slowly climbed out of the coffin and stood to her feet.

She was elegant in appearance, even if ghostly white. Her long, straight blond hair fell down her back. A white, sheer gown draped over her naked body, the blood around her mouth and bright red, pouty lips so bright it seemed unnatural against her pale face.

Standing on the cold dirt in her bare feet, she locked eyes with the blood covered Lily-Rose. A slight breeze rolled through the large, open, earth-covered basement they stood in. Lily-Rose didn't say a word, too frightened by the images running through her mind of the cold-blooded murder and cannibalism she had witnessed. She was sure the blood on this woman's mouth was the child's.

"You must be Lily. Lily-Rose Burns. A descendent of Alfred Burns. My, my, how very pretty you are."

She walked over to where Lily-Rose stood, causing Lily to quickly back up defensively, but there was nowhere to go. She had no idea where the exit was in this infernal place.

"My name is Ingrid Brassard. You didn't ask, how very rude of you. A true descendent of the man who murdered my master one hundred years ago. Who stole from him and burned him at the stake along with the lovely Sophia Brassard."

Lily-Rose looked with wide-eyed terror at the incredibly alluring and beautiful woman that seemed to get closer and closer to her with each word until she was standing directly in front of her. Lily grabbed her stomach and doubled over in pain.

Ingrid raised her pale hand and touched Lily's neck where the bite marks had been, now nearly healed. "Oh, my. Poor girl, those are hunger pangs. My master Antonin has given you a gift, but you must feed. And I am to help you with that. You see, my dear Lily-Rose, you have been bitten by a vampire and are one of us now. Or, I should say, once you've made your first kill, you are one of us. A creature of the night that can live eternally. Until my master decides to end the new arrangement, that is."

"Get away from me!" Lily-Rose shouted, backing away once more.

Laughing menacingly, Ingrid continued to speak, her eyes almost glowing, no longer looking dead. "My beloved Antonin has his amulet once more, most of it anyway. He shall have the rest of it soon enough. Then, once he recites the sacred incantations from his scrolls, our one true master,

The Pricolici, sent from Lucifer himself, will be reborn and arise to begin his reign on earth."

She paused, staring at Lily-Rose with a broad smile spreading across her full lips. "The town below will be swallowed into eternal fire. Fire from our master! Your dear great-grandfather temporarily stopped him one hundred years ago. Unwittingly, mind you, by his theft of the amulet and its powerful gemstone. Now, there will be nothing to stop us. Nothing! Your sister comes here now, traveling with a man. She is to be your first, just as my sister, Sofia, was my first two hundred years ago. After I bit into her sweet flesh and she was turned, we were tasked with hunting for fresh blood and meat for our dear Antonin until your great-grandfather arrived, murdering my beloved sister and Antonin himself. Your sister, however, will be a fitting end to Alfred Burn's legacy. And revenge for not just Antonin's murder but the murder of my sister, Sofia."

Ingrid thought back to one hundred years prior when, from a safe distance in the forest, she watched her sister Sofia arise from her coffin to be staked and burned in front of their home, along with their dear Antonin Visimar, the man who had turned Ingrid into a creature of the night.

"No, please, stop!" Lily-Rose pleaded. She couldn't bear to hear her sister may be in danger. She had been bitten. She felt it in her veins, an evil virus now pumping through her. She was doomed. But her sister...

Ingrid had her backed against the far wall of thick stone covered in dried mud. Lily-Rose had nowhere to turn. The ghostly woman pressed her nearly naked body against Lily who was trembling, her dress covered in her own blood. She felt the woman's icy breath on her face. It smelled like blood. She felt cold hands running up her bloody dress, over her body, until they held her face in place.

"I kept a bit of the young girl's blood on my mouth just for you. A taste of what you can expect from your sister," Ingrid said in an almost whisper. Leaning forward and holding her head tightly, she kissed Lily-Rose on the mouth.

Lily tried to keep her mouth shut as the beautiful vampire creature smeared her lips and open mouth across her own, pushing her tongue against the frightened girl's tightly-closed lips. The blood of Aline Koltz was on now on Lily-Rose's lips and, to her horror and surprise, it tasted delicious.

Unable to fight back any longer, Lily's lips parted and she opened her mouth, taking the vampire woman's tongue into it. Utterly revolted and instantly aroused, she stood in the corner of the dungeon room at the mercy of her assailant, desperately licking the blood from inside Ingrid's open mouth, then around her full lips, in an attempt to clean every bit of the child's blood from her murderer's mouth.

The tiny portion she was able to ingest immediately eased the sharp pains she felt moments ago. Sweet and life-giving.

The vampire woman pulled back from Lily-Rose, satisfied the girl had gotten the taste of another human's blood.

"You will feed or the feeling of being burned alive from the inside out will be with you every waking second. I know this because I was once like you." Ingrid wiped the girl's saliva off of her now nearly cleaned face, watching as Lily-Rose shamefully wiped her own mouth off, licking her fingers greedily.

"Don't worry. You won't feed often, it doesn't take much to sustain us. But you will feed. Until your sister arrives, I will help you, my dear," the woman said with a smirk. And at that, she moved away from Lily-Rose, backing up a short distance until she stood in the center of the room. She jumped up and with superhuman strength leapt into the air, landing on the ceiling of the dank cellar room roughly fifteen feet up. Her hands and feet clung to the ceiling, somehow sticking to it while she hung upside down.

From her vantage point, she looked down at Lily-Rose, still in the corner looking up at her. Her thin white gown draped away from her body, exposing her nakedness. A pair of large wings pushed their way out of the woman's open back, long and flesh covered.

*If angels have wings, so do demons. Something this creature certainly is,* Lily-Rose thought.

Lily-Rose saw the woman sail through the air, with wings that now flapped just as they had in the vision. No longer beautiful, the woman was thin, deathly thin, with leathery skin stretched across her bones and eyes that now sunk inward and glowed yellow. Her thin, white, see-through gown fluttered to the dirt below as any semblance of gender disappeared. Long, bony fingers with claws scratched at the air. Fangs protruded from a wide mouth. Long, pointed ears adorned the sides of the creature's head, her once blond hair now a sickly gray that clung to its host body haphazardly.

The mutated creature, barely human and more feral-winged beast, flapped its wings and quickly shot through a large opening with bars in the side of the wall, vanishing into the night sky.

"Her body contorted to fit through those bars!" Lily-Rose said to herself, astounded and appalled by what she had just witnessed.

Alone for the first time since awakening in the room, Lily-Rose tried to push the nightmarish images she had been made to take part in since arriving at the castle earlier out of her head. She glanced up at the torches that brought a small amount of light into the dungeon and began looking for a way to escape the hell she found herself in.

✝

"Don't shoot!" a voice called out in the darkness.

Marco knew that voice. "Caspar?"

From beyond the shadows, Caspar Voit stepped out, holding his own rifle, a bolt action breech loading rifle relatively new to these parts of Romania. He looked at Marco then past him toward the dark forest.

"What the hell are you doing in this part of town!" Marco said, immediately confrontational.

Caspar chose his words carefully. "Marco," he paused, hoping his greeting was enough to keep things amicable. "I heard a shout from over at my place. It was in this direction and I felt it best to come take a look. I assume you're doing the same?"

Marco stared at him, contemplating telling him to fuck off back to his cozy little home in the middle of town. Grunting, he replied, "Heard the same thing. Wife thought it sounded like Falck, which would make sense, I suppose. He goes on his evening strolls smoking his cigarettes often enough."

They both fell silent, continuing to stare at each other. Caspar proceeded cautiously. "About earlier, everyone's nerves are on edge."

"Just stop right there. I've got to come up with money I don't have to pay that sonofabitch Hartjenstein for a table I broke because of you getting in my *fucking* business!" Marco hissed as loudly as he dared in the dark on this ominous night.

Raising his hand in peace, Caspar replied, "Look, Marco, I didn't know it would go like that. I know you've had a bit of a rough go of it lately."

"I do not need your sympathy, you hear me? So, if you don't mind, you can leave. Fuck right off back home with you!" Marco said even louder this time.

Another noise that sounded like a growl came from over by the tree line.

Marco quickly spun around, holding out his lantern as Caspar moved forward, raising his rifle toward the noise. In the darkness, a pair of unblinking yellow eyes appeared.

"Holy shit," Marco said.

"Holy shit is right. That thing takes one step out of that tree line I'm blowing its head off," Caspar whispered.

Marco nodded, raising his shotgun as well. Several more yellow eyes appeared. They counted ten total. Five wolves against two men.

"Marco, we are officially outnumbered," Caspar said, his voice shaking with fright.

"That we are," Marco muttered, staring at the glowing eyes, suddenly feeling his mortality in front of him. If the creatures those eyes belonged to leapt out, they were most likely dead.

Caspar kept his rifle aimed, now beside Marco. "These wolves are getting more and more aggressive. And, for the record, I don't think one of these killed that young girl."

Surprised at his admission, Marco raised his eyebrows, glancing at the man standing next to him. *Are we working together? What the hell is happening?*

Marco took a step forward, stretching out the lantern as far as he could, trying to get a look at what was in the trees. What he saw was a pair of legs, covered in blood, quickly being pulled back into the darkness. The pants and shoes appeared to be the same worn-out ones Armin Falk wore every day.

"Oh shit!" Marco said, lowering his lantern enough to shine down onto the grass near the cobblestone road where he presumed Falck had been attacked. It was covered in blood.

Caspar's eyes opened wide with terror. "We have got to get the hell out of here. Now, Marco."

"Agreed. Let's go," Marco replied equally rattled.

They started to step back when one of the glowing pairs of eyes locked onto them. "Your time will come soon enough," a woman's voice hissed from inside the dark tree cover.

Caspar and Marco looked at one another, confirming they had both heard the voice, when immediately a figure shot straight up into the air. The men looked up to see a human shape with large, flapping wings holding the body they had just seen dragged into the tree cover. As quickly as they had seen it, it was gone under cover of the night sky and blanket of fog that hung over the forest. Whatever it was, it was heading toward the castle.

With their heads turned toward the sky, they hadn't noticed several wolves had crept out of the woods and were slowly walking toward them.

"Caspar! Look!" Marco shouted, spotting them: a huge black one, an equally large gray one, and a smaller, dirty-white furred wolf.

Marco didn't wait for Caspar and pulled the trigger on his shotgun. A slug exploded, sending a powerful spray of pellets from its barrel, connecting with the white wolf's hind quarters. It ran back toward the woods with what looked to be a mortal wound.

Caspar didn't have enough time to raise his own weapon, he turned and ran with Marco, neither saying a word nor turning to see if the wolves were in pursuit. But they were. Growls sounded from behind them, growing closer.

The men quicky reached the Seiler home where Marco tried the door handle but immediately found it was locked. He pounded on it, screaming, "Open up, Everly! Now!"

The gray wolf reached the fleeing men first. Caspar still didn't have time to raise his gun, so instead he swung it with all his might, connecting with the wolf's head, knocking it off balance right as the door unlocked and opened.

Both men spilled inside as Marco pushed the visible shaken Evelyn out of the way and slammed the door shut, locking it behind him.

Marco and Caspar panted and leaned against the closed door, looking at each other. Marco opened up his break-action shotgun and expelled the used shell. One slug remained in the barrel next to it. He quickly went to get more slugs for his shotgun.

"What in the hell is going on and why is Caspar Voit in our house! And which one of you just fired your gun out there in the middle of the night?" Everly shouted angrily, trying to mask her fright at the bizarre turn of events.

Marco remained quiet as he rummaged through a nearby drawer in the kitchen which was barely a kitchen at all but an icebox and a stove with some barren shelves where food should have been.

Realizing her husband wasn't answering, she turned to face the handsome Caspar. "Well? Someone going to tell me just what in the hell is going on here?"

"Wolves, Mrs. Seiler. There're wolves out there, killed one person. We think it was Armin Falck but we're not entirely sure," Caspar said grimly.

"What?" was all that Everly could muster, not comprehending what was happening.

Caspar peeked out the front window. The street in front of the house was empty, no sign of the wolves anywhere. "Looks like the coast is clear. Not sure for how long."

Having found several more slugs, Marco walked cautiously toward the window, joining Caspar and peering out.

"I don't believe any of this horseshit! Get out of my house!" Everly yelled at a shaken Caspar, pointing a bony finger in his face.

"Shut up, woman!" Marco yelled, glaring at his haggard, angry wife.

Silence fell across the room, Everly stunned at the ferocity of her husband's tone. In recent years, the man had shut down. They bickered but since their son Christoph had left, he became even more of an empty shell. But not so right now. Whatever happened to them outside must have been big. Her mind went to the scream she heard earlier.

Everly backed up as Marco went back to the window with Caspar, who asked him, "What you do think?"

Marco replied, "If you don't mind staying in this dump, I strongly suggest you remain here for the night. Tomorrow, we'll tell Constable Hecht what we saw. Something is happening, something evil. Don't ask me how I know, but I can feel it."

Caspar nodded. "Thanks for the offer. I should try to make it back home though."

"Oh, cut the shit, Caspar," Marco responded coldly. "You know as well as I do that going out there right now is the very last thing you should do. I'm going to say it again, you and I both saw something take off into the sky after *speaking* to us! Sleep on the couch. Thank the good Lord neither of us were bit. Tomorrow after talking to Hecht, we head to St. Joseph's and ask Fr. Gustloff about organizing a town hall meeting. We've got to warn people."

"Did you say Armin Falck was taken into the air?" Everly asked, visibly upset, her eyes darting from Marco the Caspar.

Ignoring her, Caspar kept his eyes on Marco. "I spoke with Fr. Gustloff this afternoon. I don't know about you, but I'm not going to be able to sleep for a while. I might as well tell you what he told me."

Marco nodded and walked to the kitchen where he opened the ice box and produced two bottles of beer, cracking them both open and flipping the caps onto the kitchen table. He sat down at the table, putting the beer on the table with a thud while holding the other out to Caspar.

Caspar took the beer from Marco's outstretched hand and had a seat opposite him.

Everly walked to the window and peered out. Something caught her eye; a pair of glowing yellow eyes. They stared at her intently and, while a part of her wanted to turn and shout to the men what she was seeing, she remained quiet. It was as if she were in a trance, unable to look away from the glowing yellow eyes, inexplicably drawn to whatever it was. Then, just as suddenly as the eyes had appeared, they vanished.

Glancing at Everly staring out the window, Caspar found it odd, the seemingly dream-like state the woman appeared to be in. He was about to say something when she seemed to snap out of it.

Shaking her head, puzzled, Everly made sure to close the blinds completely. *What just happened?* She felt oddly warm and uncomfortably aroused, something she hadn't felt in a lifetime. Whatever had been out there had completely taken over her mind while their eyes were locked, searching her thoughts, seeing what she yearned for.

She turned to the two men, enemies, now sitting across from each other in her pathetic kitchen. Caspar, who had continued watching her out of the corner of his eye, quickly looked back to Marco when she glanced at him. She felt as though she had been caught doing something suspect and devious. Her husband listened as Caspar told him about his conversation with Fr. Gustloff earlier. Neither was the wiser for the odd interaction she had just had, or so she hoped.

Outside, the rain picked up again with significantly more strength, washing away the blood from the cobblestone street and the trail of crimson leading into the forest. As if the horrors of the night had never happened.

The largest black wolf on the mountain slowly turned and headed back into the forest after its brief connection with Everly. Clenched between its jaws were the remains of the mortally wounded wolf Marco had shot earlier.

# Chapter 8:

†

# Prayers and Ruminations

After the winged demon jettisoned out of the large, cavernous room, Lily-Rose quickly decided to investigate nearly every square inch of the dungeon she was trapped inside. She had reluctantly opened the other two coffins resting in the dirt, and thankfully, they were empty. She wouldn't have to attempt to fend off another two creatures.

She assumed one of the coffins was meant for her, and the other for her sister Juliette, once her sister was taken and bitten as she had been. *A final bit of revenge for her great-grandfather's apparent misdeeds.* The monster Count

Visimar and his henchman Marcel lurking somewhere above her would first have to get the necklace from her admittedly quite resilient sister. If Count Visimar followed through with his threats, the Burns lineage would likely end with her and her sister walking the earth as part of the living dead like her captors. Soulless creatures of the night.

Upon further investigation, she surmised there were potentially two ways of escape. The first was a large square opening on the ceiling. But with the walls so high, there was no way of getting to it. She assumed this was how she had gotten here, and likely how Ingrid traveled through the castle.

The second was the window the evil woman had flown out into the night sky. Approaching it, she took a deep breath and began to climb the stones that jutted out of the wall to the ledge with the barred opening. It was larger than she first thought, roughly five feet in diameter. She found this task relatively easy despite the sharp pains in her stomach which she now knew were from her...hunger. Otherwise, she felt stronger than she had in years. Leaping from one stone to another until reaching the opening roughly ten feet high up the wall, she peered through.

Freedom was just outside the window, through the large rectangular opening lined with thick bars. The winged demon that called itself Ingrid Brassard had contorted its body to squeeze through the bars and easily navigate its way out of the basement dungeon. *Is that what will become of me?* She thought back to the monster that had forced itself onto her in this pit, its blood-covered tongue in her mouth that she took and drank from.

Lily-Rose shuddered then nearly wretched in terror and disgust at her dire situation. Thoughts tormented her, of not being able to resist the tempting allure of warm blood pumping through veins to quench the fiery thirst she now felt. What if it was her sister? She felt she wouldn't be strong enough to resist. She had to escape this prison.

"How do I get out of here and if I do, where do I go? Oh Juliette, please don't be coming to this hell on earth!" Lily-Rose cried out, staring out through the bars of her prison. It was still nighttime outside, but she saw that soon it would be dawn. In the distance, she could clearly see something flying toward the castle. It was carrying what appeared to be a limp, lifeless body.

As quickly as she could, she made her way down to the dirt floor beneath. When she was nearing it, she leapt and easily landed on her feet. Lily-Rose began moving backwards until her foot unwittingly hit one of the empty coffins laying on the ground, causing her to fall backwards on top of coffin.

The creature that had once been the beautiful Ingrid Brassard flew through the bars, still in gaunt demon form, bringing a gift which she rammed through the bars and threw down onto the dirt, landing haphazardly and spayed out.

The carcass of a man lay at Lily-Rose's feet. Most of his clothes were ripped off, as was most of his face along with his neck. Deep scratches gutted the man's chest, his organs ripped from his body.

Lily-Rose fell to her knees and wretched onto the ground beside the corpse, but nothing came up. She was starving. In this instant, she truly wished for death, something she felt she had likely already experienced at the hands of Count Visimar. But this time, she wanted permanent sleep. It had to be better than this horrific existence. How far she had come over the last three days. Haggard, covered in blood and starving.

"Eat," Ingrid said, standing over her, transformed back to a completely naked woman, blood covering her. Blood that Lily-Rose instantly craved.

Turning her head away from Ingrid, Lily-Rose heard her laugh which infuriated her. She hated this woman.

"The choice is yours. Eat what I've brought for you, or maybe the rats are more to your liking? You'll find them if you look hard enough. Or, you can clean me," Ingrid lifted a dirt-covered bare foot, streaks of blood smeared on it, out in front of Lily's face.

Lily looked up; she could smell the blood on the dirty foot in front of her, instantly craving it. The retching had caused her more pain in her stomach and she was quickly learning that his would sustain her.

"Go on, clean my foot, descendent of Alfred Burns, that pain you feel will go away. For a bit," Ingrid said, smirking at her, moving her dirty, muddy, blood-drenched foot right under Lily's nose.

Fighting the desire with all her might, she slapped the foot away from her face. Ingrid quit laughing, her face suddenly turning angry. "You don't deny me, ever!" she hissed before her foot came back up, this time not to offer it. She kicked Lily, her foot landing across her right cheek, sending her to the dirt.

Instantly grabbing her face, Lily looked up at Ingrid, eyes filled with hate. Ingrid grinned. She enjoyed seeing the newest addition to the Visimar family lying on the ground in front of her.

Suddenly Ingrid looked up toward the ceiling, distracted. "Yes, my master," she uttered, then looked back down at Lily-Rose who was attempting to get to her feet. Ingrid quickly shoved her back down with the same bloody foot.

"Down, doggie. Now, eat," Ingrid said with an evil grin, looking from Lily-Rose to the mutilated corpse of Armin Falck. Then, she shot up once more onto the ceiling, crawling to the square opening like an insect before vanishing up through the exit. Still naked, covered in blood.

Lily looked around the empty room once more, her eyes falling to the bloody corpse. Her heightened sense of smell picking up the scent of the fresh kill laying before her. Instantly her mouth began salivating. In her desperate state, she thought back to Mass the previous Sunday and instantly dropped to her knees, put her hands together, and bowed her head. In desperation, she began to recite the Lord's Prayer.

†

Inside Antonin Visimar's chamber room where several days earlier he had regained his amulet, minus the golden chain, he stood behind his stone altar. One of his wolves, the black one, sat beside him waiting for a command.

Marcel had left immediately at Antonin's demand to bring Lily-Rose's sister Juliette to the castle. Visimar knew the necklace itself wouldn't be powerful enough to lure the sister to him, as the amulet had done after Lily had been bewitched, but she would come to the castle. Of that, he was sure. Marcel would do what was required of him. Or else. Then, the necklace would be reclaimed by its rightful owner and once it had…

Antonin's mind drifted while he rested his hand on top of the black wolf. Not even Ingrid, his always faithful vampire bride, lover, and murderess could touch either of his wolves without having her flesh torn into.

As he stewed about Marcel's incompetence at failing in his task to retrieve the entire contents of the amulet, he thought back to when he first arrived at the castle. Built under mysterious circumstances that were now the thing of legend, many throughout the land whispered that the devil himself erected the mighty castle with the help of demons, a rumor he never bothered to dispute.

Long before Count Visimar took up residency in the castle, a wealthy man from the Middle East, well versed in alchemy and witchcraft and known only as "The Traveler," enlisted slave labor to build the castle, possibly in the early second century. Built to house a sacred gemstone of great beauty found shortly after the crucifixion of Jesus Christ, its sole purpose was to bring about Satan's long reign on earth until Christ himself returned to vanquish him and his legion of demons.

The Traveler had acquired the gemstone and amulet it was housed in while traveling through the land now known as Syria. Along with the amulet, he was given a scroll of otherworldly incantations that would need to be rehearsed and recited in order to restore an ancient evil housed inside the amulet itself and bring back to life an evil creature that would come to be known throughout the land as the Pricolici.

Years passed, and The Traveler grew closer to perfecting the incantations needed to raise the Pricolici from the fiery depths, but he wasn't powerful enough by himself to complete his master's resurrection. He was vanquished by invading Hunn armies around the mid-third century. The gemstone, however, survived theft, hidden deep within the castle walls by its owner.

From that point on, many tried to take up residency in the castle but never stayed long. Large amounts of money changed hands with various individuals coming far and wide seeking the sacred amulet that had been rumored to be hidden within its walls. Quarrels as to who actually owned the castle would rage on for centuries until, finally, Antonin Visimar himself arrived almost by accident.

Unbeknownst to him, the castle and what lie hidden deep within its walls had called to him when he was a young man traveling through Romania in the Carpathian Mountain region. Soft whispers had echoed through his head, beckoning him up the mountain toward the castle, an urge he couldn't explain or run from. He had the sense he had been chosen for something specific. His old life—parents, loved ones, family, place of birth—all would become a mystery to him. He was to be born again when he reached his destination in the Carpathian Mountains.

His travels soon led him to the fog-covered mountain where the castle stood. He knew, in an instant, his destiny lay inside the castle walls. It was beckoning him, the whispers in his head becoming louder and more insistent. *Come to me, find me and bring me back. I will make you immortal and you will rule with me eternally.*

Though many before him had unsuccessfully attempted the climb through the thick fog cover, the wolves and bats claiming their lives, he made it to the top. He sensed that he had been *permitted* to the top.

Standing at the entrance to the huge stone structure, he waited until a large black wolf approached him from the side of the castle and stopped in front of him, staring into his eyes. At first, the man was frozen in fear. Then, as if he could read the wolf's mind, he stripped his clothes off, throwing them to the ground, knowing, in his trance-like state, he had to obey his master.

The wolf changed before his eyes into something much larger and far more ferocious. It stood on its hind legs, significantly longer and thicker than that of a human. Its broad, fur-covered chest rippled with new muscles as the wolf's head mutated, becoming larger and more menacing. Its snout protruded from its face while its large sharp fangs grew even larger. Yellow piercing eyes stared at him, *through him.*

Antonin lay upon the dirty, muddy ground, waiting for the beast to have its way with him, for he knew instinctively that is what it wanted.

Moments later, he awoke as though he'd been asleep for hours. Recalling what had just transpired, he found he was without clothes. In his nakedness, Antonin stood to his feet, noticing scratches covering his body. He ached from head to toe but he put this filth-covered clothes back on and headed toward the castle.

The doors opened, as if the key to his admission was lying with the wolf. He entered and found his destiny set into motion. Quickly, his youthful good looks changed. His dark hair became darker, eyes became black. His new and now eternal master, who had appeared to him in the shape of the Pricolici beast moments before, again whispered deep inside his mind, telling him where to find the gem encased in a mysterious golden mineral, leading him to the altar room.

He instinctively made his way through the dimly lit and musty castle to the alter room, once inside, he peered down at the altar, he saw it crack open, the gemstone locked inside the amulet revealing itself at long last. He picked it up and observed its magnificent beauty. The beautiful gemstone shone brightly in the darkened altar room. He continued to stare at it, mesmerized. It belonged to him now, and he would do what had been asked of him, what the voice deep inside his head told him.

*Learn the ancient scrolls, then recite them and bring me back to my former glory. This is your calling. Do this for me!*

Years passed, and he grew accustomed to his new life inside the castle. He began learning a long set of resurrection rites written in blood on scrolls left behind by the Traveler, tasked with reciting them in their entirety once he had perfected them which would likely take centuries.

More years passed. He took a particular liking to two sisters he had slept with in a nameless, now long forgotten town, and the one called Ingrid he decided to use. Sex meant little to Antonin; power and death were what fueled his existence. That and the allure of bringing to this world the creature that had tainted his body forever. A body now devoid of its very soul.

Ingrid had been bitten, almost willingly, in the early hours of the morning several days after they met, hundreds of years ago, and taken back to the castle where she stayed until her appetite could no longer be sated with the rats in the cavernous dungeon. She took her sister as her first kill, sealing her and her sister's fate to the eternal life of the night-prowling vampire.

Marcel had come to him when Antonin visited Aix-en-Provence, France shortly after the sisters became part of his family. He took the young man easily, swiping him up into the night sky after leaving a local tavern. Marcel was bitten, dead, and then reborn Antonin's servant. He needed someone to tend to his affairs, run his many errands while he was gone, and collect curious travelers that managed to avoid the hungry, prowling wolves of the mountain. All who dared enter the forest of the mountain soon became food for the new family living inside castle Visimar. No one was spared.

Marcel, however, wasn't permitted to feast on humans, not at first. That was reserved for Antonin and the sisters Sophia and Ingrid, something Marcel was envious of whenever he was in their presence. Marcel was one of the living dead, made to feast on dead animals of the forest and inside castle walls, barely above mere humans on the food chain, and he knew it.

Many more years passed as Antonin continued learning the incantations scribbled in the scrolls. He studied the antiquated passages about resurrecting the ancient being with wolf-like attributes, created by the fallen angel Satan himself, that would rule the earth in his absence until the final days. This Pricolici had been vanquished by several priests around 457 AD, sent back to the hell it was created in by mysterious means.

The old texts offered detailed information about what the shining gemstone housed inside the amulet was used for. The writings indicated that it had supernatural healing properties and had once belonged to a Maji whose name was Melchior. The gemstone had been gifted to the blessed Christ child of Nazareth. How the gemstone came to have healing properties and immense power wasn't explained, but whatever the case, it was a means to bring back Antonin's master.

*The true master!* he thought. *Not some Shepherd boy that willingly hangs on a cross, pathetic!*

The time came when the incantation rites were getting close to perfection. Antonin knew this, and he was also told so deep in his subconscious mind. A whisper that soon, he would be ready. Correct pronunciations, proper dialect, even the tone in which the incantation was to be performed had to be perfect for the resurrection rites to work properly. And he was growing closer to mastering it all. Even the watchful Marcel was impressed at his master's growing knowledge of the ancient text, listening to him recite particular passages over and over. Year after year.

And then Alfred Burns came, taking what was rightfully his.

Now, looking down at the shining amulet, Antonin smiled grimly as Ingrid walked into his chamber, still naked and covered in the blood of Armin Falck. The wolf at Antonin's feet growled as she glided over to where he stood, nearly shrouded in darkness.

"Another one taken; I gave his body to the girl. We shall see if she can withstand the hunger pangs. I don't think she can," Ingrid said menacingly, looking down at the wolf who bared its teeth at her. She looked away, back up to her master.

Nodding, Antonin replied, "If Marcel fails in bringing the sister to me, it will be your job to see it through. You must not kill her. She is to be Lily's first, as I have stated. Do you understand? It will be a final sacrilege to the name of Burns."

"Yes, my master."

"Soon, we will begin the full cleansing of the town below us. We've been biding our time, not drawing too much attention apart from the local superstitious peasants. I am confident the gold necklace will come back into my possession. Then I will finalize the rite of resurrection of our lord from his ancient slumber, opening the doorway to hell and completing what I had nearly achieved one hundred years ago.

"Yes. And I will be there at your side, master," Ingrid hissed.

He looked at her, suddenly aroused. "Once the lord of this world returns to power, I will be at his right hand, and you shall be at my side. Then, I will give the sisters whose great-grandfather attempted to thwart my task permission to destroy themselves."

A thin smile crept across Ingrid's lips as she sensed his arousal at her beautiful, blood-covered naked body. She moved closer to him and kissed his cold lips. The blood of the dead bartender from Burnmere crossed from her lips to his.

Tasting its sweetness, he hungrily began licking her face, much like Lily-Rose had done earlier. Antonin's features contorted from his hundreds-of-years-old self to a much younger and handsome man. He allowed Ingrid to strip his clothes from him then lifted her onto the altar and had his way with her.

His wolf looked on as their bodies further transformed, melded, and contorted, now taking on the appearance of bat-like mutations, similar to the bats that flew above the castle that Antonin himself controlled. Once transformed, they wrapped around each other in their own grotesque form of intercourse.

Ingrid moaned and bit down onto her master's skin, his blood flowed onto her as she greedily lapped it up. In their own unholy and unnatural way, they both climaxed as rabid animals atop the altar. The wolf watched on with yellow piercing eyes, snarling at their unholy union.

"Now, go. It is dawn. See to it that the girl sleeps. This is my command," Antonin whispered to his mistress.

Nodding in reply, she glid silently out of the room, her feet barely touching the cold stone floor as she slipped a sheer white gown over her head once more.

Opening the trap door on the floor near the great room, Ingrid leapt down, falling several stories into blackness through her own passageway before landing in the dungeon that doubled as her slumber room. There were several ways in and out of the dungeon below through the large hole in its ceiling; this was the most immediate from her master's altar room.

Seeing Lily-Rose on her knees, her hands clenched together, head bowed, Ingrid screamed, "How *dare* you!" and rushed over to where she knelt.

Lily-Rose didn't look up but continued saying the Lord's Prayer followed by a "Hail Mary" and a "Glory Be," praying the rosary she had learned as a young girl at her local parish back in England.

Ingrid hissed in fury, "There are no prayers in this castle!" She noticed the corpse of Armin Falck lay untouched.

"Our father, who art in heaven, hallowed be thy name…" Lily-Rose continued.

Sunlight began to stream through the steel barred opening on the side wall. It was time for Ingrid's slumber and Lily-Rose to begin her new cycle of sleeping through the daylight hours. Ingrid began to weaken as daylight continued to creep in, lighting up the dirt.

"You will sleep, damn you!" Ingrid shouted.

"Thy kingdom come; thy will be done…on Earth as it is in Heaven. Give us this day our daily bread…" Lily continued mumbling to herself, keeping her eyes closed.

Rushing over, Ingrid stood in front of Lily-Rose and grabbed her. But the girl fought back, shoving her away. Ingrid had to get to her coffin, Lily realized. Even in the upper floors of the castle, during sunlit hours, she was vulnerable. Her consecrated coffin in the dirt was her reprieve. Otherwise, she was mere mortal, weakened of her hideous powers.

Lily-Rose stood up with renewed confidence, staring her adversary directly in the eyes. "And forgive us our trespasses, as we forgive those who trespass against us. Lead us not into temptation but deliver us from evil."

Ingrid glared at Lily-Rose as she backed toward her casket. "Have it your way. If you don't sleep, you'll become even weaker. Especially since it appears you aren't eating. Remember, that's your meal. You can eat now or in a week when it's good and rotten. The choice is yours." She slid into her coffin and the lid closed.

Lily-Rose, alone in the silence of the dungeon, was relieved to be rid of the heinous, evil woman. But she knew she needed to sleep and to eat if she was to get out of the dirt-filled pit in this hellish castle.

"Sleep on it, Lily," she said quietly and walked over to the coffin farthest from her captor. She opened it and climbed in, hardly believing she was actually doing it. However, once inside its confines she fell asleep almost instantly. As her eyes closed, she uttered, "'For thine is the kingdom, the power, and the glory, forever and forever. Amen."

The lid closed, sealing her in darkness followed by what she hoped would be dreamless sleep.

# Chapter 9:

✝

# Something is Coming for Us

**D**awn arrived in Burnmere. The rain had ceased and as was typical, the layer of fog continued to blanket the mountain, shrouding the castle almost completely.

The previous night, Caspar had told Marco what he and Father Gustloff discussed earlier over several shots of J&B scotch whisky. About Alfred Burns, vampire hunter, who one hundred years prior had vanquished one Antonin Visimar. About the beautiful amulet Lily-Rose wore everywhere she went while in Burnmere, and the scar on her palm that she didn't want to discuss.

While they talked, Marco's wife Everly had watched them with contempt. However, she kept her mouth shut, thinking of her interaction with what was out in the darkness. Everly couldn't shake the image from her mind, for it had lodged itself deep into the recesses of her subconscious, now biding its time.

She decided Bürgermeister Hartjenstein would hear about all of this. The bartender of Burnmere being lifted up into the sky, wolves openly attacking these grown men with guns. She would, however, leave out her own odd experience.

Caspar sat up on the rather unpleasant smelling and thoroughly uncomfortable couch he had gotten several hours of sleep on the night before. Rubbing his eyes, he looked around the room. It was quiet in the Seiler household, if this could be called a household. Dirty dishes piled up in the pitiful kitchen and everything smelled of old food, old furnishings, and uncleanliness.

In an instant, he felt truly sorry for Marco, married to easily the most unpleasant woman in Burnmere, possibly even all of Romania. A son that had abandoned him, no job, no life. Just existing until an early death that was all but certain with his drinking.

The door leading outside opened quietly and Marco walked in, holding his shotgun. They locked eyes, Marco breaking the uncomfortable silence.

"Morning. I'd ask how your night's sleep was but from the looks of it, I can guess."

Caspar chuckled, which drew a grin from Marco as well. "I appreciate you letting me sleep on your couch, for what it's worth. It wasn't safe out there last night."

Walking into the living room, Marco set his shotgun down beside him on the single chair that he typically claimed in the evenings, brown and worn down to a state of disrepair. He groaned as he sat.

Noticing this, Caspar asked, "Are you unwell?"

Marco looked at him, debating whether to tell him about his hip. "Just tired. Hip's acting up."

Caspar immediately thought back to the tussle the previous day at the Pale Horse, assuming the hip issue was from the tumble he took. His eyes then fell onto Marco's black-and-blue neck from the clubbing he had taken from Bürgermeister Hartjenstein. Once more, he felt sorry for Marco, but they had more pressing matters at hand. A new day could bring new problems. Namely, that Falck had possibly been taken up into the air by God-knows-what.

After their discussion had ended the previous night, Marco had gone back to his bed to find Everly asleep. Snoring loudly, as she usually did, taking up more space than she needed, another typical move to assert her dominance over him.

He had crawled onto his side and slept uncomfortably for several hours before waking up to find her gone. *Thank God* he thought upon opening his eyes at the crack of dawn finding his bed empty. She typically got up before him so she could berate him for this too. "Sleeping in again, instead of going to work like a real man, you lazy bastard!"

However, she wasn't in the house at all. Caspar had been fast asleep on the couch, so he took it upon himself to investigate the surrounding area around his house where the incident last night had occurred.

"I took a stroll around the block earlier this morning. Traced our footsteps, including the run to the house, and found nothing, not a thing. It rained pretty hard last night so I figure the blood we saw was washed away. I was hoping to find something that confirmed what we saw. We did see that, right? A man was lifted up into the air and then vanished? I mean, I keep telling myself it happened but now I'm starting to wonder, did it?"

"It happened. Sure as I'm sitting here on your couch, Marco. Whatever that was in the shadows spoke to us before flying off with a corpse. We need to warn people. This town has had heaps of misfortune, but this is different. I truly feel this is leading up to something, and whatever it is, it's bad." Caspar stood to his feet and stretched from his uncomfortable night.

"Well, that's just it. Hell, I was spouting this same stuff yesterday in the Pale Horse when you..." Marco stopped, shooting Caspar an unsure look.

Caspar responded quickly, "You and I may have our differences. A whole hell of a lot of them. But on this, I am sure we are seeing eye to eye. And there's a few more in town that will hear us out on what happened."

Nodding at the attempt at comradery, Marco continued Caspar's thought. "Fr. Gustloff, Constable Hecht, I assume that German physician fella, Doctor Heuberger and Nick Schoeler…that sonofabitch."

"The enemy of my enemy is my friend," Caspar replied, wanting to avoid the tangled web of long-ago injustices and hurt feelings that had created bitter rivalries in Burnmere.

"I suppose you're right, if everything you told me last night is accurate. Hell, if even part of it's accurate, we have bigger problems than our own bullshit," Marco said quietly, looking out his window.

Nodding, Caspar held his tongue. He was glad things were friendlier now between himself and the man just twelve hours ago he would have happily gone fist-to-fist with in a street brawl.

Marco spoke again, trying to formulate a plan in his brain. He ran his hand through unwashed, messy black hair. "Maybe a town hall, a meeting of the minds. At the very least, we've got to make sure people are staying off the streets as soon as the sun sets. Particularly the kids. Aline Koltz was taken just before dawn. This town doesn't have many kids but those that are, aren't safe. Hell, none of us are."

"Agreed. Best place to do that would be St. Joseph's. Fr. Gustloff would welcome everyone willing to hear us out. A few rings of the church bell and we could get the better part of the town gathered there."

"I haven't been to Mass in ages. I haven't made confession in I don't know how long, hell, I don't know if I even believe in a higher power other than the evil that lurks in the woods and castle up in them hills," Marco ruminated. "God decided long ago he'd rather stay clear of my house. And rightly so, I suppose. Not a damn good thing has come out of it, other than my boy, and he did the right thing and skipped out of this hellhole, away from *her*."

They both fell silent; Caspar didn't know how to respond. He wasn't a well-practiced Catholic either. In a town like this, it was hard to be. He went to Mass, but his faith was probably not much stronger than the disgruntled, sour man that sat across from him.

Breaking the silence, Marco continued, "Still, I would tend to agree, the church is likely the best place to try to rally everyone together. I suppose, however, doing so does come with its own unique set of risks."

Marco and Caspar looked at each other, knowing full well what the other was thinking.

Caspar was the first to say it. "Hartjenstein. No way he'll let us have a town meeting. Even if Constable Hecht is all for it and implements some sort of a curfew until we figure out what the next steps would be."

"First, we need to get to the Pale Horse. I'm fairly certain that was Falck last night, but we need to be sure. Then we talk to the priest and Hecht. In the meantime, I need to figure out where the hell Everly got to," Marco replied, picking up his shotgun.

Hopping up, Caspar grabbed his rifle as well, time for talking was over. "I'm going to make a pit stop at my place. I'd like to get more ammo and some food."

Marco grew quiet. He hadn't offered his guest any food and knew better. His parents had taught him at a young age to show kindness to those you invite into your home. But that was a long time ago, and another Marco before Everly came into the picture.

Seeing Marco fall silent, Caspar gave him a friendly slap on the arm. "Come on, we've got work to do."

Marco's hardened facial features softened at someone in this godforsaken town showing him a hint of kindness. He nodded at Caspar and they walked out of the house, closing the door behind them, no longer full-blown enemies.

The two began making their way to the center of town, to Caspar's house, then the Pale Horse, and finally, St. Joseph's.

As they walked, Caspar breached the topic of Marco's missing wife. "Is it normal for Everly to be gone like this in the morning? Should we be concerned? Last night when she was staring out the window while we were talking, I meant to say something, but I assumed she was making sure whatever we saw out there was gone. I wonder if she saw something herself? She seemed almost as if she were in a trance."

Thinking it over, Marco answered, "That woman has a mind of her own. Is it odd? Yes. Did she see something outside last night? If she did, she certainly won't tell me. She won't give me the satisfaction of being right. About her not being there, well, we aren't used to guests at our place so she may have taken off early to run errands. I expect to see her milling around the square more than likely. She has a few acquaintances in town she might be yapping to."

"Think she bought what we were talking about last night?" Caspar asked cautiously, not wanting to upset a comradery forming. A man's wife was typically off-limits as a topic, but the situation was worsening so discussions like this seemed necessary.

Marco shook his head. "I doubt it. Although she heard the scream. She knew damn well *something* happened out there. I have a strong hunch so did some townsfolk after I fired my shotgun."

"We're going to find out here soon," Caspar added as they neared his home.

It was still early morning but much like any other day, the few people that were already out and about kept their heads down. This being a weekday, the roughly twenty kids in town were arriving at the tiny building off the main street leading out of town. The schoolhouse was basically a one-room cottage that had been transformed into a makeshift classroom at the insistence of the bürgermeister that nothing larger was needed.

The school's previous location had been significantly larger with better amenities, but Hartjenstein had immediately set up his home base there after kicking the school out. Much to the old schoolteacher, Miss Shalner's dismay, which she had voiced quite loudly in the last town hall meeting three years earlier. Ada had been reduced to tears, with the townspeople furious and shouting insults and profanities at Bürgermeister Hartjenstein.

After that, he squelched any more meetings that involved the entire town. Small meetings were still permitted but the final say always fell to him. Caspar thought about this seeing the schoolkids shuffle slowly into the small building. Miss Shalner was standing by the door and saw Caspar and Marco heading toward Caspar's house. The thin, gray-haired woman gave Caspar an odd look which he returned with a brief wave. Then, she disappeared into the cottage, closing the door behind her as the last child filed inside.

Marco knew how odd this must look. A rather well-respected man such as Caspar, from the "good" part of town, if there was such a thing in Burnmere, letting a man such as himself into his house.

Inside Caspar's cottage, the space was clean and well kept, although not much bigger than Marco's. Still, from the looks of it, he made a decent enough living as the ironsmith even with the hefty taxes the bürgermeister collected.

Caspar grabbed some extra ammunition and several extra slugs from a shotgun he previously owned. Grabbing the six slugs, he handed them to Marco. "In case you run out of your own. And in case we need them, which I feel we will."

Marco warily nodded his thanks, taking the ammunition from Caspar.

After offering some food to Marco, who gratefully took it, they ate a bit of dried fruit and some other odds and ends from the kitchen then headed over to the Pale Horse.

One block away, the Pale Horse was unsurprisingly dark. Old Armin Falck never opened his doors this early. As they approached, a stray dog rounded the corner and ran past them as if chasing something, but there was nothing in front of it. It was whimpering, as if had been frightened by something unseen. They watched the dog run off, past the schoolhouse.

"That mutt stays around the Pale Horse, Armin feeds it leftovers. Where the hell do you think he was heading in that much of a hurry?" Marco said, puzzled.

Caspar continued to stare in the direction the dog had run—the exit out of town. He shuddered as an icy feeling of dread crept through his entire body. "I don't know Marco, but I don't like it."

He knocked on the Pale Horse's front door. Armin Falk lived up the stairs in a tiny apartment and would ordinarily be up there or in the bar prepping for the day. After a brief wait, they knocked again, peering in through the window on the door. It was dark.

"Well, he's not here. But I have a good idea where he is. Up in that damned infernal castle," Marco said grimly.

Glancing over at him, Caspar nodded, thinking the same thing. "Come on, time to go talk with Fr. Gustloff."

It was eerily cold outside, and the sky was filled with gray clouds. A breeze continually ran through the town, typical due to its proximity to the mountain, whipping downward through the village. The previous night's rain made everything damp and dreary. Most mornings, Burnmere was a sad and depressing place, even in the early spring month of May.

The church doors were closed as Caspar and Marco walked up the cobblestone pathway leading into the humble house of God. The outside of St. Joseph's Parish was white with a cross mounted on the top peak of the church. While far from elegant, the church was easily the most appealing-looking building in town, aside from Bürgermeister Hartjenstein's renovated schoolhouse living quarters.

Caspar and Marco entered the church, both blessing themselves with the holy water in a small stoup just inside the double doors. They set their guns down by the doorway and saw that Fr. Gustloff was cleaning up after the 6:30 AM Mass that had just ended. This being a weekday, very few people showed up for it, most sticking to the Day of Obligation Sundays or Saturday evening vigils.

Caspar cleared his throat.

Without looking up, Fr. Gustloff said quietly, "I was wondering when you would show up. Surprised to see you with Marco."

Marco and Caspar glanced at each other then approached the father.

"Last night, did you hear—" Caspar started but was cut off.

"Yes, I heard the gunshot, if that's what you were going to ask. Which one of you shot in town? Bürgermeister is none too pleased. Already paid me a visit before Mass, said he would find out what that was all about. I knew it came from your end of town, Marco, but with things being how they are between you and the illustrious Samuel Hartjenstein, I thought it best not to stoke the fire by giving him what he wanted. Confirmation that someone fired a gun last night in the wee hours."

"That would have been me, Father," Marco said, suddenly ashamed.

Looking up at the large, unkept man then at Caspar, Fr. Gustloff said half-jokingly, "I never in my wildest dreams thought I would see the two of you together."

Marco immediately spoke up. "Wait, now, we aren't friends. We're just, I don't know how to say this, dealing with the same thing." He paused and looked at Caspar who had been nicer to him over the last eight hours than most anyone in town ever was, give or take. He cleared his throat then hung his head.

Moving forward, Caspar said urgently, "Father, we need to talk to you about what happened last night. It's Armin Falck, we have reason to believe he was taken up to the castle."

"Something is coming for us, I can feel it," Marco added.

"Is that so?" a voice from behind them said sarcastically.

Fr. Gustloff was the first to see the man standing in the doorway of his parish and he sighed heavily.

Bürgermeister Hartjenstein stood inside St. Joseph's, and he had company. On one side of the well-dressed man stood Constable Hecht, and on the other stood Everly Seiler, scowling.

# Chapter 10:

†

# The Hounds of Hell

One hundred years earlier, Marcel had lain the charred, burnt corpse of his master on the sacrificial altar inside Castle Visimar the day he had been burned at the stake by Alfred Burns. Marcel had been beside himself.

After that fateful day, Ingrid had murdered several young girls in distant villages, bringing their bodies to her master, slicing their throats open and letting their warm blood fall on top of Antonin's remains. Incantations were spoken to go along with the butchery, but he had continued to lie still and devoid of life.

Ingrid and Marcel both knew the reason the seemingly immortal Antonin Visimar remained dead was that the amulet with its shining gemstone had been taken. The gemstone that could give the gift of healing as well grant great power, along with the golden chain and locket, now resided with the Burns family where it would be passed down to several generations before coming *home*.

May turned to June on the mountain, and on the sixth day of the sixth week since the horrible injustice had been done to their master, something changed. It wasn't the blood of a young virgin girl that stirred life again from the charred remains of the Count, but wolves. One black and one gray wolf appeared on the doorstep of the castle, their cold eyes staring through Marcel.

Marcel understood immediately that they had come to be sacrificed, given to Castle Visimar by an ancient, dark evil. The amulet was gone but Antonin needed to live once more, for only he knew the incantations, only he had been tasked with his master's resurrection. So, a gift had been brought forth—by Lucifer himself or one of his demons—to restore Antonin's lifeblood, so he could find and return the amulet and bring about the great and powerful Pricolici's return with the proper incantations.

Marcel followed the wolves back to the altar room. They knew where to go. Once there, they both gently hopped up on top of the altar and stood over the remains of Antonin and waited.

Ingrid entered the room, beckoned by Marcel. "Are we to sacrifice these beasts to our master?" she asked coolly, watching the beautiful wolves staring at her.

"This is what must be done," Marcel answered grimly, not looking at his begrudging partner in crime.

Slowly, Marcel moved forward with a large knife in hand, feeling fear course in his veins as the wolves snarled at him, their yellow eyes glowing in the nearly black room. Even Ingrid, who stood behind him watching, retreated slightly.

These two wolves were different from the rest that roamed the forest, they had an otherworldly aura about them. In the shadows of the altar room, the wolves grew larger, their bodies contorting as bones and ligaments snapped and shifted under their skin. Their teeth grew longer and more pointed.

Marcel and Ingrid both instinctively bowed their heads slightly in reverence while the two beasts morphed further, now rising up to stand on their back two legs. Their chests expanded with new muscles forming, their front legs now more like arms from which claws grew. A significantly extended snout protruded from their still mutating heads.

Once the transformation was complete, the two werewolves, sent by the lord of all evil beasts, stood above Antonin, looking down at what barely resembled anything living. Suddenly, the creatures of the night tore into each other, ripping at each other's throats with wide, open jaws. Claws slashed across furry torsos, spilling blood onto the altar and splashing onto the cold floor, but more importantly, covering Antonin's corpse in crimson.

Marcel and Ingrid had seen much since they had been chosen to serve their master, but nothing like this. Wolves coming to their doorstep of their own free will, changing into massive beasts that quite literally ripped each other to pieces. Ingrid shed tears. Not tears of happiness or fear or sadness, tears of overwhelming dread.

Dropping to his knees and placing his forehead to the bloody stone floor, Marcel could no longer watch the horror unfold in the altar room as both creatures continued to destroy each other. Blood splattered the walls, the floors, and the two servants who dared not move.

"The beast has sent its own creations, possessing these woodland creatures, to revive our master," Marcel whispered in awe, only glancing up briefly when he heard both werewolves falling to the ground near him, dead.

The blood on the altar of Antonin, resting on top of the remains, began to smoke, turning a sickly black, like tar.

All in the room heard a voice like a serpent's hiss rising from the altar: "Live for me and fulfill your destiny, bringing me to this world. The gemstone and gold that surrounds it. You have one more chance, if you fail, you will drown in a fire of your own making."

Marcel and Ingrid lay prostrate on the cold floor at the sound of the ancient voice that echoed through the altar room.

The smoldering black blood seeped into the crusted-over remains, twisting and turning inside the corpse, pumping through veins that now sprang back to life. Internal organs formed while a newly revived heart pumped black sludge throughout the revived system. New skin began grafting itself under the burnt skin as the shriveled body grew once again, filling out until Antonin's normal height was restored.

Time itself seemed to stand still inside the altar room. Two dead beasts lay on the stone floor. Ingrid and Marcel lifted their heads, looking on at the unfolding horrors in front of them.

The charred remains of Antonin moved, first the arms, then legs. Slowly, the dead outer skin crumbled as the now moving body underneath gave way to new flesh. It stood up as more dead skin fell from its torso. Raising its arms to its face, it tore the remaining blacken, burnt flesh from its head, revealing a born-again Antonin Visimar.

He slowly wiped his freshly grown black hair back over his head and opened his eyes. They gleamed yellow and black before turning back to their original human color.

Standing before his two servants, the perfect specimen looked down at them in his unashamed nakedness.

Ingrid rose to her knees, bowing before him as Marcel had also done. He looked at the two dead beasts at the foot of the altar, sacrificed for him. A gift to him from the fallen angel himself. He breathed in the dank air of his chamber room and raised his hands.

"Rise," he said calmly.

With heads bowed, Marcel and Ingrid stood up, not daring to look at his face until he commanded them to do so. All was silent once more for a minute.

The reborn Antonin spoke calmly but with the utmost authority. "I would thank you for my return if you hadn't failed at your tasks earlier. Because of your failure, your sister Sophia is destroyed. She waits for you in the afterlife, Ingrid. And you will be reunited when I give the command. Until then, we have much work to do to bring about the great Pricolici's return to this world. You will not fail me again. All three of us must not fail again."

"Yes, master," both Marcel and Ingrid mumbled.

Antonin continued with a whispered hiss, "In the abyss, I saw the master. The great and mighty Beast. He showed me what must be done. The amulet will be found and brought back here if we have to search the whole earth. Marcel, you will be tasked with searching for it. The line of Alfred Burns will be forever destroyed for what he has done here on this scared ground! But the golden amulet and the stone encrusted within *will* bring forth the triumphant return of our master, and he will rule this world once the resurrection rites have been, at long last, properly recited. Until then, I must continue learning the scrolls."

"Yes, master," both Marcel and Ingrid once more replied.

"Do not fail me, do not fail my master," he uttered coldly.

The room fell silent once more. Antonin climbed down from the altar, staring at the two dead beasts at his bare feet. He bent down and stroked the blood-covered fur. "A gift from our master, to watch over us and see to it that we do not fail Him again. They gave me the gift of new life, and now they will stay with me. Arise, my friends."

Both of the werewolf carcasses instantly moved. The stomachs of each expanded and stretched.

"Stand back," Antonin muttered, standing aside as he bit into his wrist and tore it open, spilling his own blood onto the dead creatures.

The large werewolf carcasses began twitching and contorting. Smoke rose from the remains. Bones cracked and shrunk. The blood each had spilled earlier for Antonin now mixed with his resurrected blood, seeped back into their open wounds, sealing themselves up while flesh pressed in on healed bones.

Marcel and Ingrid quickly moved back so the rest of the transformation could occur.

New snouts protruded from newly formed skulls, followed by torsos and legs. Soon, the creatures had been fully mutated back to their original wolf-life selves, no longer resembling large wolf-men but massive four-legged beasts of the forest.

The new creatures stood to their feet, shaking off the blood from their previous selves. The gray wolf and the black wolf had been reborn, the black blood of their master Satan and the new blood of Antonin pumping through their veins. They looked around the room, yellow eyes peering at the three beings that stood before them.

Both approached Antonin, standing beside him as he stroked their heads. The beasts looked at Marcel and Ingrid, growling.

Nodding his approval, Antonin spoke with authority. "Until I have the amulet back in my possession, I will continue perfecting the incantations set forth for the mighty Pricolici's return. We shall feed on the fresh blood of the villagers near and far. Burnmere is damned. Those that remain will slowly be killed, by our hands or by the fangs of my pets and the wolves of the forest. They will know the true meaning of fear even as they deny that I have returned, and with me, my master, once the amulet is back where it belongs."

Once more, the servants uttered, "Yes, my master."

The wolves beside Antonin howled.

The fog surrounding the mountain and castle was thick, nearly shrouding it from view in Burnmere, while newly resurrected Antonin and his vampire lover Ingrid slept in his chamber room with his pet wolves. There was much to do in the hundred years that would follow.

☦

Marcel left the castle immediately upon his master's orders to find the amulet. He had failed Antonin once before by letting him burn at the stake, and he vowed to never do it again. But in neglecting to get the entire amulet back, he had unknowingly failed yet again. This was his final chance, failure again would lead to his damnation, sooner than expected.

He had, however, always been a faithful servant to his master, even when Antonin and Ingrid continually mistreated him. Ruminating on that fateful morning when Alfred Burns arrived with his executioner and the townsfolk, he knew deep in his tainted, black heart, there was nothing he could have done differently. In fact, doing anything but staying hidden as he had done would have resulted in his own demise at the stake, which in turn might have meant Visimar would never have been reborn. The same could be said for the heinous Ingrid Brassard. How the count had found such a detestable woman to serve him was beyond Marcel's comprehension.

He recalled a time far back in his past when he wasn't like this. He was a young man in France. *Was I happy? Happier than this miserable life, I suppose.* Glimpses of a mother and father in his youth, now long since gone from the world, and maybe a sibling, he could no longer recall. Before Visimar, he at least had fleeting moments of freedom and maybe even happiness.

Once he was turned by the vampire's bite, his life consisted of luring men, women, and children alike to the forest and castle above to meet their grizzly demise.

An eternity of serving his master. And when his master had gotten his full use out of Marcel, he would be destroyed for good. And then, hell, or whatever darkness was after this sad life, awaited. *Which might be for the best.* Marcel knew if he had the willpower, he would have ended his miserable existence himself at Visimar's resurrection one hundred years earlier.

*But how do you kill someone who is already dead, or, in limbo between two worlds?* It was something he had contemplated many times over the vast number of years he remained on earth. His connection to Antonin Visimar was permanent until Antonin himself broke it or someone else took it upon themselves to destroy the creature that Marcel had become.

He should have been given the great gift Antonin bestowed on Ingrid and her sister. Instead, he was living but dead. He had no fangs, no wings, no real substantial god-like powers. His existence would always be that of lowly servant to his master Antonin Visimar. The minor powers he was given, hypnosis and being able to slip by undetected with relative ease, were just that, minor. He killed with a knife or his bare hands, but never for sustenance. Only self-preservation or at the command of the count.

For now, he continued his trek across Romania, thinking how sweet it would be if he were the true, rightful heir to the amulet and gemstone. He had certainly earned that right for all he had done in service to his master. His true master was not Antonin, anyway; his true master awaited its resurrection inside the castle once he fulfilled his task. Until then, he was forced to remain as Antonin's slave for countless centuries, awaiting the day he would be tossed aside like the insignificant being that he was.

His plan was to intercept Juliette, convinced the sister of Lily-Rose would indeed be coming for her and would likely know she was in Burnmere. He hoped his intuition was right. He would then use his powers of persuasion to bring her to the castle with him, thus making his task easier.

Marcel rode hard through the day on the black horse and carriage he had taken from the castle's stables, his mind repeating one persistent thought. *She is to be Lily-Rose's first after the amulet's chain is back to its proper owner. I must not fail, or it will truly be the end of me.*

# Chapter 11:

†

# Meeting of
# the Minds

**B**ürgermeister Hartjenstein stood with his arms at his sides, inspecting the three gentlemen inside the church looking sheepish at having been *caught in the act.*

"I seem to have a knack for walking in on conversations at the most inopportune time, don't I? Twice yesterday, in fact, at the Pale Horse watching you once again make a total buffoon out of yourself, Marco. And later in the cemetery, talking to my constable about werewolves, witches, ghouls and all of that nonsense with that drunk Nick Schoeler and

Joachim Heuberger, the most levelheaded one of your sorry lot."

Unable to hold his tongue, Caspar lashed out, "We wouldn't have to sneak around and talk in hushed tones if you'd do your job."

Marco was taken aback. This was something that would normally come from him, not upstanding Caspar Voit. He glanced over at Father Gustloff who held his head high. This man of God wasn't going to be intimidated by the bully that stood in front of them.

Hartjenstein wore a thin smile on his lips. "Is that so? Interesting story I heard from Mrs. Everly, here. Marco, this poor woman didn't get a wink of sleep last night. Seems as though the two of you were out firing guns in the middle of the night, inside town limits, I might add."

This immediately got Marco's attention. "What did you say to him, woman? You know we were being chased by something out there!"

Everly piped up, "Your imaginations. That's what was chasing you two last night. Then sitting in my kitchen telling scary stories that include this priest here! Sad state of affairs it is if this is the best shepherd we have leading his flock, I must say!"

Father Gustloff, Caspar, and Marco all knew the woman never went to Mass. She was as far from religious as humanly possible. But here she stood, adding self-righteousness to her long list of unpleasant attributes. All three men held their tongues.

"Well, then," Bürgermeister Hartjenstein said, clearing his throat, "the two of you will need to pay restitution for the illegal use of firearms inside city limits for no apparent good reason."

"No good reason!" Marco exclaimed. "Our town bartender was very likely murdered then lifted up into the sky and taken to the castle! How is that not a good enough reason?"

"I just came from your neck of the woods, Marco, and there was, as I suspected, nothing. No signs of foul play, only scared townsfolk because of that discharged gun of yours in the wee hours of the night. As for old Armin Falck, if he doesn't turn up later today then I shall personally be questioning you further, Marco Seiler! About what you *were* firing your weapon at last night!"

Marco took a step forward, furious at the man's sudden insinuation that he may have been the cause of the bartender's disappearance.

Hartjenstein quickly took his club out of its sheath and took several steps forward. Behind him, Everly crossed her arms, grinning.

Constable Hecht tried to stop the bürgermeister but knew it was best to keep quiet.

"Not in this house of God!" Father Gustloff shouted right as Caspar stepped between Marco and the bürgermeister before the club was to be brought down on his head.

"How *dare* you interfere with the law!" Samuel Hartjenstein shouted in Caspar's face, their eyes locking in a silent battle of wills.

Caspar didn't blink, nor did he turn away from the bully.

The room instantly fell silent.

"Go on, bring that club down on *my* head and see what happens," Caspar said with quiet determination, continuing to stare down the bürgermeister.

"Now, look, everyone," Constable Hecht exclaimed, attempting to diffuse the situation. "Father Gustloff is right. This is a house of God, and this type of thing shouldn't be dealt with inside its doors. Maybe we can talk like civilized people outside?"

Marco stepped forward. "I can take care of myself. I was the one that fired my shotgun. Caspar didn't discharge his rifle at all."

Not taking his eyes off Caspar, Hartjenstein replied to Marco, "Is that so? Does he speak the truth, Caspar?"

A long pause followed; Caspar wanted to make the man wait for his answer. "I suppose so."

The bürgermeister spoke, "Well, then, I shall be confiscating your weapon, Marco. I assume yours is the one that looks as if it could fall apart when the trigger is pulled?" He looked at the shabby old shotgun, picking it up and inspecting it, then continued, "You leave me with no choice. And, in addition to the table you broke yesterday, I will have my constable here issue you another fine, both to be paid today, in full. Be glad I'm not having you arrested. My leniency and patience only go so far. You continue causing trouble in a town where it seems as though everyone is already on edge."

"Maybe that's because some truly vile things are happening. I buried a thirteen-year-old yesterday afternoon, if you've forgotten," Father Gustloff said in a controlled tone.

"I haven't forgotten," Hartjenstein said smugly. And with that, he turned and walked out of the church with his head high, slinging Marco's old shotgun over his shoulder nonchalantly.

Left behind with Constable Hecht, Everly contemplated turning and leaving with Hartjenstein but figured it best to stay put, enjoying being the instigator of this latest setback for her husband.

Once the bürgermeister had left, Constable Hecht was the first to speak. "I'm sorry, Marco. From what the bürgermeister told me earlier, that table you busted yesterday is going to set you back one hundred leu, and then there's the discharging of the weapon that I'll need to confiscate."

"Ha! Like he has that kind of money! Fat chance!" Everly exclaimed.

"You've done enough damage, Everly, why don't you kindly get the hell out of here?" Marco replied bitterly, then added, "Pardon my language, Father."

"No need to apologize," Father Gustloff shot back.

Caspar grinned at this dig at Everly.

Scowling, Everly did the only thing her feeble mind knew to do when she felt she had been slighted, she lashed out. "You bunch of wimps. I would expect as much. A chicken shit constable, a priest that averages—what, thirty people in here a week? A pretty boy that can't seem to find the little harlot that rolled into town a few weeks ago and you, you miserable piece of dung, why I put up with you is beyond me." She stared daggers into Marco.

"Constable, would you kindly please escort Mrs. Everly out of my church?" Father Gustloff said, calmly but firmly.

"Mrs. Seiler, why don't we just," Constable Hecht attempted while raising his hand toward her arm.

Instantly, she swatted it away angrily. "Don't you touch me! You keep your hands off me!" she screamed, backing toward the door.

They all watched the woman, except Marco whose head was turned away in embarrassment, as the fury on her face turned to a slight grin. She had the final word, much like the bürgermeister.

She exited the church, leaving the four men standing alone in silence.

After a brief pause, Caspar attempted to say something to ease the tension, clearing his throat.

Marco raised his hand, stopping him. "Don't say anything. We have bigger problems than the likes of them. Constable, I can pay for that table, the expelled gunshot within town limits, I don't think I have the funds."

Clearing his throat, the constable looked over at the three men standing before him. "I'll take care of it. Marco is right, Armin Falck is missing. I heard the scream last night and checked around town early this morning, but I still can't locate him."

The group pondered their next steps for a moment, then Father Gustloff spoke. "I'm continually puzzled as to the bürgermeister's insistence on looking the other way. What will it take? Why must the man constantly deny what is right in front of all of our faces?"

"Money," said the constable. "I shouldn't speak on this but with things getting worse around here, it must be said—he is quite wealthy. Much of the town's taxes line his pockets and are spent on lavish items to adorn his cottage. I did a bit of digging and Crownhaven certainly didn't want him. He was pulling the same stunt over there until he was supposedly, *relocated*. And now, we're stuck with him, for better or worse."

Everyone fell silent, angry at their predicament and the man who seemed to foolishly turn a blind eye to the evil that surrounded them in order to slowly siphon the town dry of the meager money it had.

"What exactly did you two see last night?" Father Gustloff asked Caspar and Marco.

At that moment, Nick Schoeler peeked his head into the church. "There you are constable! I was going to ask you where in the hell—oh, sorry, Father," he paused, seeing who was standing in front of him. "What is God's name is Marco Seiler doing at St. Joseph's?"

Immediately, Marco's calm demeaner shattered and he fired back, "Listen here, you little bastard, I have every bit as much right to be in this church as you, you miserable old drunk!"

"Ha! Looks like the pot calling the kettle black from where I stand! Speaking of black, your neck looks like hell!" Nick fired back.

Constable Hecht was about to intervene, but Father Gustloff stopped the argument dead in its tracks. "Both of you, enough! This is a house of God, and all things considered, we have to quit fighting amongst ourselves. If you plan on continuing this nonsense, do it outside. I can almost certainly assure you the bürgermeister will happily take his club over both of your heads and fine you for something you didn't do, making you pay with money you don't have! Do I make myself clear?"

Silence fell through the church as Marco rubbed the black-and-blue mark across the side of his neck, looking at an equally sheepish Nick. They both shifted their eyes guiltily over to Father Gustloff. The man was typically jovial and friendly, but these were serious times.

Nick glanced over at the holy water font then dipped his bony finger into it, blessing himself.

"Go on, Nick, what were you saying?" Constable Hecht prodded.

"Ahem, well, I was going to ask you where the he…er, where in the world our bartender is? I sometimes swing by before he's officially open to grab a nip of whiskey to start the day. Not always." He paused and inadvertently looked over at Marco, as though in competition with the man to see which was the biggest loser. Marco returned the glance, almost as if knowing what he was thinking.

Nick continued, "Back door was unlocked so I went inside. He's *always* there, so I figured maybe his ticker finally gave out and he keeled over dead upstairs in his room. I wasn't breaking and entering, constable. Just so we're clear."

Constable Hecht nodded and motioned for him to continue.

Nick realized he had everyone's attention, a rare thing for him. "So, I walked around the bar, no sign of foul play, then I went upstairs and it was not only empty, but his bed was made. And his supper was sitting there, uneaten. What happened?"

Caspar spoke up, his frustration and anger growing. "I'll tell you what's happening. There's something evil going on up in that castle and the surrounding mountainside and it's continually invading our town. Has been for years. And no one has done a damn thing about it!"

An uncomfortable silence fell across the men as they all nodded their silent agreement at Caspar's words.

"Falck is the latest mystery. I believe Marco and Caspar here can shed a bit more light on it," Constable Hecht responded, looking at the two men as if awaiting their response.

Caspar then told the tale of the previous evening's events, starting with the scream he heard upon arriving home from Aline Koltz's funeral, and ending with holing up for the night in Marco's house.

Father Gustloff, Constable Hecht, and Nick all listened with rapt attention to all of it, including the surprising detail of Caspar Voit spending the night in the house of Marco and Everly Seiler.

Marco added, "One other thing, and it might be nothing, but Caspar and I, when we were looking in at the darkened bar on the way here, saw the stray dog Armin feeds from time to time run past us. And I mean, that thing *ran* all the way out of town."

This extra bit of information reminded Nick of something. "Yeah, I saw that mangy mutt run out of town on my own way to the Pale Horse. Thought it was odd but figured someone gave it a swift kick in the ass for being the nuisance that it is."

Constable Hecht said, "So, what's next? I'm of the mindset that regardless of how absurd something may seem, if the information lines up, it's worth looking into. And this here is certainly that."

Caspar added, "We can't call a town hall meeting. There is no way Bürgermeister Hartjenstein will allow that. Going house to house is too cumbersome and time consuming. I fear whatever is up in that castle on the mountain is going to continue upping its menacing visits."

"The amulet," Fr. Gustloff began, getting everyone's attention. "Caspar spoke of an amulet that young Lily-Rose wore. Is there anything to that?"

Marco nodded. "I saw it too. Around her neck. Though I didn't get a close look, it appeared quite valuable."

"She said she felt as though she were bewitched by it," Caspar said grimly. "I'm more and more of the mindset that the amulet may have something to do with her visit to this town. That, along with her family's history with the castle."

The word *bewitched* caught everyone's attention. Most of all, Father Gustloff. "Yes, you mentioned this yesterday, Caspar, and it is indeed an interesting theory and one we should consider. What is the connection to the castle? No one visits the castle, ever. The wolves will tear anyone who tries apart. But everything bad in Burnmere seems to originate from that damned forest and, more to the point, that castle up there."

"So, what do we do? Sit by while people continue getting picked off?" Nick said coldly, his mind thinking of Bürgermeister Hartjenstein throwing sand into the gears of any real plan they could concoct.

Caspar spoke up. "We all saw the remains of thirteen-year-old Aline Koltz. Then Marco and I saw what we believe to be Armin Falck being taken in the direction of the castle. I have to believe that Lil-Rose is trapped up in that castle. She's a direct descendant of the man who killed Count Antonin Visimar a hundred years ago, and I think that amulet has something to do with it."

"Again, it comes back to what the hell can we do?" Constable Hecht asked, quickly adding, "Sorry, Father."

Father Gustloff didn't acknowledge the slight infraction as the room fell silent, all of them deep in thought.

Marco finally put into words what was on everyone's mind: "We go up to the castle and kill whatever is living inside it."

All eyes fell on him. Then, one by one, they all nodded in agreement.

# Chapter 12:

†

# A Choice
# for Juliette

All was quiet inside Castle Visimar. Ingrid was in her slumber, and Lily-Rose had also succumbed to the daylight hours and slept in the coffin provided for her. Marcel was off somewhere far west of Burnmere preparing to collect Juliette Burns and the gold around her neck. Antonin Visimar, however, was wide awake.

Since his rebirth after Alfred Burns invaded his home and burned him at the stake one hundred years earlier, Antonin had become something more than just a vampire. More than a creature of the night. He found that he could do a great number of things now that he was unable to do before, staying awake in the daylight hours being one of them.

He wasn't as powerful, he was aware of that. His powers weakened when the sun arose, but this hadn't made him less dangerous. If anything, he was more animalistic in the daytime. The sunlight angered him, it was extra hot to his skin even in cool temperatures. Thus, he would hunt from time to time during the sunlit hours of the day, just for sport or out of boredom. The blood, while still delicious to his lips, wasn't as important for his survival as it had once been.

More important, however, was his mastery of the incantations of the sacred scrolls. He was ready, all he needed now was the final piece, the golden necklace that adorned the Burns sister's neck. The powerful gem that the amulet housed called to him, beckoned his presence. It was incomplete, for now, but that would change soon.

When it was complete, the Pricolici would come forth and together they would burn bright. He at his master's right hand, below him Ingrid, while Lily-Rose and her sister would watch on helplessly as entire towns and villages fell at the feet of his master.

Burns and his lineage had temporarily stopped his dark master from its triumphant return, but all was about to be made right. They would pay for the misdeeds of their great-grandfather, suffering eternal agony. Lily-Rose was halfway there already, soon her sister would complete the transformation.

The stone cast a glow inside the housing it was encased in, now that it was back in its rightful place. Antonin stared, mesmerized, at the stone that dated back to the birth of the Christ child. Its power was unmatched in the right hands. *His* hands. He would succeed where the one before him had failed. He was now fully confident in his abilities to recite the incantations that would complete the ritual bringing forth the Evil One.

*It will happen here in my altar room, when the amulet is complete. And it will be glorious.* Antonin thought, staring at his prize. He held it tightly in his hands as his two wolves sat on either side, watching him, waiting for his command.

He could sense the gold chain getting closer. He could feel it in his ancient bones, where there was an aching for everything to be completed. He had nearly achieved it one hundred years earlier and soon, it would finally come to fruition.

*Don't you fail me, Marcel.*

His mind drifted to Lily-Rose and how sweet her blood had tasted. He considered pulling her from her slumber to have his way with her, but she was to be his master's upon his return. The amulet had shown him this when he had retrieved it from her earlier. *She will fully turn after killing her sister, then she will be his. But before that, she must eat. She must feast or her pain will be boundless.*

He could sense the rotting corpse of a man Ingrid had brought lying in the dungeon; his body would soon turn putrid. The choice was hers. Feast now on fresh meat, or feast later on rancid flesh. Ingrid would see to it that she followed orders.

*The sister comes now, it is all falling into place, very soon, the town of Burnmere in its entirety, will perish* Visimar heard the voice deep in his subconscious. "The rising of the mighty Pricolici comes soon," he muttered aloud.

Once more, he looked at the amulet and the small, jagged crystal-like stone in its center. He felt its power making him feel *alive*. Tilting his head back, he opened his eyes wide, now turned a dark sickly red, his mouth stretched open beyond its limits, pulling, then tearing flesh. Sharp teeth shone in the dimly lit room, the two larger fangs jutting out even further, his skin pulled back tightly over his face.

Antonin Visimar released a mighty, inhuman shriek in his excitement for his master's soon return. It was the shriek of the damned, echoing through the castle hallways, reverberating up through the castle towers and shooting out through their openings far above, then drifting through the fog-covered sky.

The wolves beside Antonin howled in unison with their master. Together, all three created an otherworldly call to arms. Wolves in the forest perked their ears and stood to attention, immediately baring hungry fangs and snarling. They too began howling, their sounds carrying up into the blowing wind and fog.

The birds of the forest quickly took flight, away from the howls of the damned and toward Burnmere.

Antonin Visimar then lay on his altar, clenching the amulet and closing his eyes. There was much to be done when night fell, but for now, rest.

†

Juliette Burns had traveled much the same trek that her sister had, by train from Summerhost, England to Bucharest, Romania. Now, in the early morning hours upon their arrival at the train station, she had lost track of how long her trek across Europe had been. Several days had passed, and after the first, time seemed to blur in a continuous string of rural sights as it chugged along.

Though she had made light chit-chat to pass the time, her mind was on her missing sister. The two, while they had their fair share of differences, were inseparable, until now. Juliette would not be at ease until young Lily-Rose was found safe and sound and they were heading back home.

Finally at her destination, she stretched and stood to her feet, filing out of the train with the rest of the patrons in Bucharest, Romania. She hopped off the steps of the train cabin, her auburn hair blowing in a breeze that felt refreshing after being cooped up.

She had given her sister some time after departing with their Uncle Henry, much longer than she should have, but Lily-Rose was an adult and could make decisions on her own, even dangerous ones such as this. The sisters had not fought much growing up together, but this had been different. For the first time in their lives, they got into shouting matches over Lily-Rose's insistence on traveling to Romania. Letting her go, even with a chaperone, was something Juliette had regretted from the moment the girl left home.

Now, sensing she might be in danger, Juliette's worry overtook her and she decided to make travel arrangements of her own. She feared something nefarious was at work under the surface of Lily-Rose's insistence on coming to the tiny Romanian town of Burnmere and was compelled to seek her sister out immediately.

Juliette was beautiful in her own, unique way. Her younger sister Lily-Rose, while more outwardly attractive, lacked the sweet innocence that had followed Juliette since she was a child. Slight freckles dotted her cheeks, and her delicate frame made her appear even younger than her twenty-nine years, something she was cognizant of and made sure she wasn't taken advantage of—particularly by members of the opposite sex. Yet another thing that differentiated her from her sister.

Her soft brown eyes inspected the carriages in front of her. All with men hungry with the hopes of finding someone looking for a ride.

One man with black hair and almost mesmerizing eyes called out to her, "You, ma'am! Can I help you get somewhere? You look like you need a ride!" His large black horse scraped its hooves against the cobblestone street as if hungry to get moving.

Juliette pulled her hair out of her face, her pretty gray dress flowing with the breeze.

She didn't answer, looking around at her other options. However, the rest of the riders appeared busy suddenly, avoiding eye-contact and running to other potential customers. A portly older gentleman puffing on a pipe, who had raised his hand to ask if she needed his assistance, now looked away. It was as if she were no longer seen by any of them except the dark-haired man with the top hat perched atop his head staring at her directly.

After one more sweep of her options and realizing there was only one, she walked over to the man and introduced herself. "Hello, sir. My name is Juliette Burns, I have traveled from Summerhost, England and I am in need of—"

She was cut off by the pleasant but mysterious man in front of her, now holding out his gloved hand to her. "A pleasure to make your acquaintance, my lady. Odd that you say your name is Juliette Burns. You remind me of another customer I helped get to where she needed to go in the Carpathian Mountain region. Her last name was Burns as well, if memory serves."

Instantly widening her eyes, Juliette cried out, "My sister! Lily-Rose! You saw my sister?"

"Yes, indeed. Lily-Rose, she said her name was. Pretty young woman that one, and very pleasant, I might add!"

Marcel said politely, trying to hide the excitement he felt standing in front of the last piece of the puzzle for his master to complete the ritual. Around her neck was a beautiful gold necklace that complimented the rest of her attire.

"Seems as though I came to the right carriage rider after all," Juliette said, once more glancing at the other riders, several of whom had been looking at her and the mysterious man but averted their eyes quickly when they saw her look their way. "Strange," she said to herself.

The tall man watched her intently, saying nothing for a short time.

Juliette suddenly felt her necklace turn slightly warm against her skin. This jogged her memory about something Lily-Rose had said before she left, about the amulet beginning to feel…warm. She had dismissed it at the time.

Marcel glanced up at the men nearest his carriage, his eyes turning dark. *Stay in character, she needs to go with you willingly.* He shook his head slightly, focusing his attention back to his prey. "Don't worry about them. Most of them are old drunks. You would be best served by using my horse and carriage to get you where you need to go. I can get you there quickly and inexpensively!"

"Well, sir," Juliette started.

"Please, call me Marcel Metzinger."

"Mr. Metzinger, I would very much like to go to my sister. I fear she is in some trouble. She left one month ago and I am here to bring her home," Juliette replied, looking over the carriage she was contemplating hiring.

"Burnmere, very good! You wish to go to Burnmere!" Marcel replied, trying to hide his excitement.

"Yes, that is the town. So, she is there! Well, Mr. Metzinger, what is your rate?" Juliette questioned, more to buy herself time than to bargain with the man. He seemed well kept and pleasant enough, but something under his good-natured demeanor felt off. Juliette was a perceptive woman, even a bit suspicious, much more so than her younger sister. Maybe it was the way his eyes darted nervously, or the urgency of his wanting her to hire his services. Still, the man had been Lily-Rose's driver and knew the route.

"Ma'am," Marcel began.

"Oh, please, call me Juliette."

"Miss Juliette, I will charge you upon arrival to your destination," Marcel exclaimed, adding, "Furthermore, I live near Burnmere so it's on my way; therefore, the rate will be much less."

Something deep in Juliette's subconscious told her to walk away. The man wasn't accepting pay up front, this was too much of a lucky coincidence. Too much of a good thing was usually not a good thing at all, in Juliette's estimation. And his smell. She got whiffs of black liquorish, her least favorite candy by far.

*Get into the carriage, so we can make haste to the castle and the deed is done!* Marcel thought as he stared into her eyes. She seemed to be a tougher nut to crack. The spell he put on her younger sister back in Summerhost had been easy.

Juliette looked back at the man nearest them who had been glancing up periodically during their conversation. He averted his eyes once more when he saw her looking at him. Glancing back at Marcel, whose eyes had suddenly taken on a more sinister look, she made her decision.

"Mr. Metzinger, if you'll pardon me," Juliette said calmly and, picking up her suitcase, walked over to the man nearest them.

Fury clouded Marcel's mind. *That bitch! That dirty bitch!*

"Sir, can you get me to Burnmere in a day's time? I can pay handsomely."

The man, a portly older gentleman with a balding head and a pipe hanging from his mouth, looked at the woman then over to Marcel who was staring daggers through them both, going so far as to move forward several steps before stopping and reconsidering it. The train station was bustling with people, including several police officers on duty patrolling the platform.

The older gentleman leaned in close to Juliette. "Ma'am, Burnmere isn't a place you should be going. A young lady such as yourself and all." Then he leaned in further, adding, "Especially with an unsavory gentleman such as that."

"Will you take me or not? I must be going. My sister awaits my arrival," Juliette replied urgently.

"Yes, ma'am, I will take you. Not that I want to go that direction, but better me than him. Name is Daniel Kolb. Pleased to make your acquaintance. Step aboard and watch your footing, I'll help you with your luggage."

"Juliette, pleased to meet you, and thank you. I feel as though that man may be up to no good," Juliette answered in a near whisper.

"Aye, young lady, you would be correct. Sometimes intuition and a strong sense of self-preservation can be a good thing, yes?" Kolb responded quietly.

Smiling thinly and giving the portly old man a slight nod, Juliette climbed into the open carriage and Daniel closed the door behind her. He picked up her suitcase and stored it in the rear, securing it in place, then headed toward his horse, an older Hucul breed that had seen better days.

Daniel prepared to climb up onto the carriage when he inadvertently glanced in the direction where Marcel had been minutes earlier. But the man and his horse drawn carriage were gone.

Nodding to himself, Daniel spit onto the ground, lit his pipe once more and snapped the reins, "Come on, Baba, let's go, old girl."

The horse slowly began clip-clopping down the cobblestone street, out of the train station.

Glancing behind him, Daniel noticed the woman was wearing a shiny gold necklace. "If you don't mind me asking ma'am, that necklace is quite something. You may want to put it away once we reach Burnmere, it's a poor little village with some unsavory people and an unsavory past, if you catch my drift."

"It was a gift from my sister. I fear for her safety, and I fear for my own if I must be honest. Especially after that man back in the train station," Juliette trailed off.

"Keep that intuitive head on you, young lady. Where we're going, I fear you shall most certainly need it," Daniel said grimly.

The gold necklace grew closer to Burnmere and castle Visimar. Behind it, a man shroud in black with a large top hat followed on his black steed and carriage.

# Chapter 13:

†

# Everly's Opportunity

Everly stood outside the church, trying to decide what to do next. She had betrayed her husband, something she relished. However, if Marco were to go home it would certainly be an all-out fight, something even she wasn't in the mood for. Not after Caspar and Marco had stayed up most of the night talking about ghouls and werewolves. While she didn't believe it, she knew what her eyes saw. Two glowing wolf eyes in the darkness, calling to her, beckoning her. She remembered how the beast's gaze had made her feel warm all over. Deep in the recesses of her mind, she felt a connection that she couldn't quite explain.

Noticing Bürgermeister Hartjenstein walking back toward his large home she wondered aloud, "When was the last time I bathed?" She smelled herself and she stunk. Dirty clothes, unbathed skin, unbrushed teeth, and unkept hair. She had once, many years ago, been an attractive woman. Firm breasts, trim, lust-filled eyes and a knack for getting most of the young men to swoon over her. Until Marco Seiler knocked her up, the single worst moment of her life.

Bürgermeister himself was handsome enough, in a town where handsome didn't apply to ninety-nine percent of the population that was now down to roughly one hundred. Watching the well-dressed man enter his home near the church, she suddenly felt aroused, a feeling she hadn't felt in countless years. Sex with Marco had ceased a long time ago, and thank the good Lord. She hated that smelly large oaf grinding on top of her for mere minutes before spilling his disgusting seed into her. She *hated* the man. What a sweet release it would be if she could bed another man.

"But I look and smell hideous," Everly mumbled to herself as she contemplated her next steps. "I'm only thirty-seven, that's not that old," she reasoned. Her best years were now far behind her and likely her worst years still ahead if she continued on the path she was on. The meager number of women in town had dwindled considerably through the years. Some from the woodland creature attacks, others married off by Father Gustloff, and the luckiest escaping the dead end that was Burnmere, never to return.

Everly wondered where the few children in town would ever find love once of age. Those that could still produce offspring tended not to. The town was quite literally on its last dying breath, she was convinced this was its last generation. And rightly so, the town needed to die. But first...

Impulsively, she made her way to Bürgermeister Hartjenstein's home. *Time to be brave and maybe if I'm lucky...* Her thoughts went to the beast's eyes staring at her as she peered out her window the night before. The warm feeling in her stomach returned. She felt courage she hadn't felt before. At the very least, she might get some food for bringing to Bürgermeister Hartjenstein's attention the little mob that had formed inside St. Joseph's parish.

Raising her hand to his door, she glanced back and forth, making sure no one saw her at his doorstep. Small towns mean big gossip. She could always blame the visit on her husband for any number of infractions. The entire town knew of the couple's outright hatred toward each other.

Everly delivered several raps on the door with a few shifty-eyed glances up and down the currently empty street. The kids were in school and most everyone else was either working their jobs or at home.

Bürgermeister Hartjenstein's door opened slightly. "Yes, what is it? I thought that business over at the church was taken care of!" he exclaimed upon seeing the shifty-eyed woman standing at his doorstep.

Choosing her words carefully, Everly replied, "Well, it's like this. My husband, he's a harsh man, we both know this. On top of that, he doesn't farm so we have nothing to eat. And I was hoping to inquire about a possible job. You know, something that would benefit you, good sir."

Taken aback by the suggestion, Bürgermeister Hartjenstein's curiosity got the better of him. "Dear woman, I don't have any jobs for you, or anyone else, for that matter. Between that frightfully incompetent Constable Hecht and I, we can manage the town of Burnmere just fine I suppose. What exactly are you suggesting? What service could you provide? We are a very poor town, Mrs. Seiler."

He was clearly lying and Everly knew it. The man was wealthy, made so by a town he continued to steal from, her included. It was certainly one of the reasons he continually turned a blind eye as the string of mysterious incidents occurred in and around Burnmere. He would likely move on when the reserve was dried up completely.

Everly peered just past the bürgermeister's opened door into his living quarters, easily nicer than anyone else's in town, most of whom were farmers in some fashion. As little actual money changed hands in town, food was the primary source of bartering and trading of goods. She assumed his luxury came at the expense of the hard-working townsfolk who were continually taxed far too high given the condition of the town that saw no improvements. She envied his niceties befitting a significantly more upscale town than Burnmere.

"If you would just let me in, sir, I can convince you that what I have to offer will make your job easier and possibly help you bring in more money for the town. You know, improvements and the like," Everly said sheepishly, hoping the allure of money would gain her access into his house.

"I just got done with my breakfast and haven't had time to tidy up what will all the commotion earlier this morning." He paused, looking the haggard woman over. He could smell her body odor, but underneath the grime, he sensed at one time she had been an attractive woman.

"Please, just hear me out!" Everly pleaded, putting her hands together as if praying to him.

"Fine, come in, but make it quick. I have things to do and a married woman inside my home won't look good. Especially one married to Marco Seiler," the bürgermeister exclaimed in disgust.

Everly stepped through the door into his well-appointed living room. She moved over to the couch, wanting to sit down then looking for permission at Hartjenstein who had closed the door behind him.

"Yes, yes, go on, take a seat," Bürgermeister Hartjenstein answered in a slightly annoyed tone, resigned to the fact that this persistent woman was going to share what was on her mind, one way or another.

"Would you be so kind as to get me a glass of water?" Everly asked in what she hoped was a sensual, soft tone.

Bürgermeister Hartjenstein was quite taken aback and surprised that someone, anyone, from Burnmere was being amicable toward him. "Of course," he said quickly, and went to fetch her a glass of water.

She looked around the room at the elegant furniture, fancy lampshades, nice…everything. She hadn't seen such niceties in more years than she could count, if ever. He came back and handed her the glass of water which she happily took, making sure her fingers touch his slightly when taking the glass from his hand.

"Tell me, Mrs. Seiler, what do you have in mind that would benefit both me and this town? Well? Out with it," Samuel exclaimed hastily.

Everly took several gulps of water, gathering her courage, then set the glass beside her on the solid oak end table and stood to her feet. "I think you would best serve the town of Burnmere if you would allow me to clean myself up, make myself look presentable and all, and then put me in charge of all the bookkeeping, maybe even assist Constable Hecht. He's quite old, you know."

Trying not to laugh, Hartjenstein shot back, "And why on earth would I need a bookkeeper and why would Constable Hecht need your help?"

Everly continued, "Because a detailed record of your finances will better help you to not just save more but collect more from the townspeople. I see how you live, quite nicely, I must say. But wouldn't you like to live even better? You need a good secretary that can handle all paperwork. Furthermore, Hecht isn't very, how shall we say, aggressive in carrying out your law and order through the town. I can help with that too."

Now intrigued at the possibility of syphoning more funds from the dim-witted, superstitious townspeople, he indulged her. "Yes, I suppose that would be nice to have more detailed records here. But your husband would certainly never let you do anything of the sort, you must know that."

"Samuel, can I call you that?" Everly began but didn't wait for a reply, continuing, "You don't need to worry about him. He won't do anything. In fact, if you want to beat him down more than he already is, this would be ideal. Hire me on as the official secretary of Burnmere."

A smirk came across Samuel's face. "What's in it for you? I don't have funds to just throw at a new employee," his eyes shifted guiltily as he uttered this lie. He knew full well much of the town's taxes fell back into his pockets instead of the increasingly needed upkeep for the dilapidating town.

Everly had slowly been taking steps toward the bürgermeister, now standing directly in front of him in the middle of his living room.

"That's just it, Samuel, I don't need much. A place to clean up and look presentable. Food, because Lord knows I barely eat at home now as it is. That's really it. Oh, and one other thing."

She leaned forward and put her lips against his, roughly attempting to shove her tongue into his closed mouth.

The bürgermeister's eyes widened, not just at the surprise kiss being laid upon him but her smell. Immediately, he pulled back, holding her away. "What on earth are you doing, woman?"

"What do you think I'm doing? I'm showing you what I can do *for* you," Everly responded. She knew she smelled bad, but this was her opportunity. This was it, she had to press forward, regardless of her appearance.

"You, ma'am, are a married woman! You come into my home and proposition me! *Get out!*" he all but yelled.

Everly shook her head, "No, I'm not leaving. Not until I show you what I am capable of."

She dropped to her knees in front of the stunned man and grabbed hold of his trousers, pulling him in toward her. He began to resist but Everly quickly put her hand against his clothed crotch and began rubbing.

"Everly Seiler! You stand to your feet this instant!" the bürgermeister shouted, but Everly continued.

She undid his trousers and pulled them down. *This is your chance, Everly.* She grabbed hold of his bare buttocks and, moving him forward, took his now semi-erect penis into her mouth. His resistance quickly faded, and any attempts to pull himself away from the aggressive woman ceased. His erection quickly hardened and in little less than a minute's time the man was moaning in pleasure, even placing his hands on the back of Everly's head, swaying with her movements.

With her free hands, she pulled the top of her dress down, revealing dirty and sagging breasts, rubbing them against Samuel's bare legs. She continued sucking and rubbing until he orgasmed into her mouth.

Satisfied at what had taken place and what was now all but a sure thing with their arrangement, she wiped her lips of his remaining semen and stood to her feet, her exposed breasts hanging from her opened dress that barely clung to her hips in her standing position.

Bürgermeister Hartjenstein immediately pulled up his trousers, buttoning them back up. He was stunned, disoriented, just as she had hoped, caught off guard and unable to resist. *You're now in charge, Everly.*

As Samuel struggled with the last button on his trousers, Everly took the opportunity to tell him the new business proposal. "I believe we have an agreement? I am your personal secretary, for now. But I would greatly like to assist our constable as well. I can leave your house with these still hanging out and scream, or I can put my dress back on and none will be the wiser," Everly stated, glancing down at her exposed breasts before adding, "I will require new clothes and food. I can start as early as tomorrow. That should give you plenty of time to inform Constable Hecht of our business arrangement, should it not?"

Looking at the woman's dirty breasts, Samuel nodded briefly and replied, "I certainly like the idea of better kept tabs on the finances of Burnmere. And you do not require compensation other than food, clothes and ahem, possibly bathing and hygienic needs, correct?" Bürgermeister Hartjenstein stated, as though trying to justify this.

Contemplating this, Everly decided to press further. Nodding, she replied calmly, "That is correct. Though spreading some of your good fortune around a bit will certainly help to keep my mouth shut about what was just inside of it minutes ago. So, you may want to consider that when paying Constable Hecht his monthly salary. I will certainly make it worth your time, as you've seen."

Hartjenstein began shaking his head in protest, but Everly was already turning away from him to walk toward the door. "You will see that I have a great number of skills that have been untapped for many years. I would very much like to start my new position tomorrow. With a nice new dress, I might add. I will arrive at, shall we say, nine o'clock AM? We can start with paperwork. There aren't many people in town so getting them all documented should be a relatively easy task, don't you think?"

Not waiting for a reply, Everly began pulling up her dirty dress. On her way to the door, she grabbed an apple from his coffee table in the center of the living room. She didn't glance back, walking out his front door and into a new beginning for herself.

She passed the Pale Horse pub, the eerie silence surprisingly frightening as last night's events played in her head while she continued on her way home. The scream, the gunshot, Marco and Caspar bolting into the house, terrified. Both of them talking about all types of witchcraft into the wee hours of the night. The yellow eyes peering at her from the edge of the forest.

Everly shook it off. *Don't think about that nonsense, your new life begins now.*

She glanced up into the sky. The fog seemed even heavier, blanketing much of the mountain. Only the vaguest outline of the castle could be seen from her vantage point.

The creeping sense of dread returned. She heard wolves howling in the distance but could see nothing in the fog-draped forest past her small home.

Smirking to herself while keeping a keen eye on the nearby forest, she uttered with a hint of uncertainty, "Werewolves and witchcraft. All nonsense from paranoid and superstitious people."

Walking into her house and gently closing the door behind her, she peered out the window, hoping she would catch a glimpse of whatever she had seen the night before.

She turned from the window to find, sitting in the far corner near the bedroom, the largest black wolf she had ever seen staring at her intently with glowing yellow eyes. It was the same wolf she had seen the night before. She immediately felt the connection they had made the previous night.

Backing up, she contemplated making her way to the door and running, but as her hand grabbed the door handle, she froze. "What do you want?"

The wolf continued to stare, then Everly heard a soft voice deep in her mind, as if the beast were speaking its thoughts into hers, *My master requires your assistance.*

The wolf walked into the bedroom, and as it did, it began transforming from its wolf shape, growing larger until it stood on its back legs, until it was something between a wolf and man.

Everly, mouth agape, in a trance-like state, moved forward into the bedroom and closed the door behind her.

# Chapter 14:

†

# Plans and Confrontations

"So, how exactly shall we attempt a climb up that mountain?" Nick asked Marco as calmly as he could, scared out of his wits at what was currently being proposed. Marco looked at Caspar who nodded, knowing what Marco was thinking.

"The Murreys have a stable full of horses. We'll go there, and each take one and ride fast and ride hard up that mountain," Caspar said confidently.

Nodding, Marco added, "My hip hurts like a sonofabitch but that's the safest bet, if such a thing exists in this plan."

"Do you think old man Maxwell will just let us up and take some horses?" Nick asked, knowing full well he was a stern and gruff old fellow.

Before Marco or Caspar had a chance to answer, Constable Hecht chimed in, "We certainly don't have many weapons. I mean, a few rifles, I suppose, but against those wolves we're as good as dead, with or without horses."

"I think Jane will help us out with regards to acquiring horses," Caspar said, looking over at Fr. Gustloff. "Furthermore, we have a holy man among us. We need to think outside the realm of what we've believed our whole lives as being real. Marco, you and I both saw a body being lifted into the sky and flown off. That cannot happen, it simply cannot. But it did. And if what we saw is real, then there must be a higher power that can intercede on our behalf."

He paused, looking over every man's solemn expression. He continued, "The bites on Aline Koltz weren't made by a wolf. They were made by something…other."

"What do you mean by 'other'"? Constable Hecht asked.

Caspar shook his head, trying to rationalize what he was about to say. "I don't know, demon, vampire, creature of the night, something supernatural that can fly. Joachim said it himself; those bite marks were not made by a wolf. There's no bears in these parts, so what then? The point I'm making here is that we go up there with not just rifles but with crosses, with cannisters of holy water. We go up there with stakes to ram through the heart of whatever lives up there."

Nick, staring out the window, interrupted to say, "Sorry to interrupt, but, Marco, you might want to see this."

Curiosity crossed Marco's already troubled face as he moved toward the window. Outside, up the hill and past the church, Everly was leaving Bürgermeister Hartjenstein's house, holding her head high, not hiding the fact that she was leaving another man's house. One well known for hating her husband.

Fr. Gustloff, Constable Hecht, and Caspar joined Marco and Nick as they watched Everly spit onto the cobblestone street, take a bite of an apple, and make her way past the path leading to the front of St. Joseph's. They all saw her glance at the church then continue on.

"What is Everly doing leaving the bürgermeister's house?" Constable Hecht said out loud before falling silent. Whatever had taken place inside that house, it wasn't good. He inadvertently glanced over at Marco as did all of the men, uneasy and unsure as to how he would react to this latest unpleasant development.

Fr. Gustloff stood beside Marco and rested his hand on the man's shoulder. "Marco, if you would rather hold off on this and go home..." he started to say.

Quickly brushing Fr. Gustloff's hand away, Marco turned to face the men. He was sure whatever his wife had been up to inside his arch-enemy's house was far from good. He shuddered at the implications but a small part of him wasn't surprised. His life was shit and this was the culmination of it.

The men in the room waited for his response.

His eyes went from the floor up to the faces of the men in the room. "I think…that we don't have time to spare. It's still morning, so I say we pack what we need, meet back here, get the horses and head up that mountain."

Silence followed as each man ruminated over Marco's proposition. Leaving today, barely time to plan. But the alternative was another night of likely another victim. Things had escalated dramatically since Lily-Rose had arrived, all of it seemingly leading to something bigger than any of them could put their fingers on.

Caspar was the first to respond. "I'm in. But we don't have much time."

Nick suddenly felt a slight tinge of empathy for his fellow town drunk, Marco. Just slightly. "I'll help out. It's a pretty shaky plan, but what the hell else am I going to do? The bar appears to be shut down until further—."

He was cut off by Fr. Gustloff. "There is an evil in that castle. It's been up there for longer than this town has been in existence. And now that evil is growing stronger. I cannot go with you. My heart cannot take it. I'm forty-nine but I feel seventy. Furthmore, I am a man of the cloth and attempting something like this without proper approval from the Church would cause significant damage if it is discovered, I would likely be ex-communicated and removed from this parish. My place is here. I must stay behind."

"Gentlemen, I would like to help, really, I would. But Bürgermeister Hartjenstein will have my ass, and my wife Claudie, well, you all know she's not in the best health," Constable Hecht said glumly. Years in Burnmere certainly hadn't boosted his already low confidence. Especially after Hartjenstein begrudgingly took him on as constable, taking every opportunity to beat the man down verbally, making sure to keep the aging man humble and meek, always looking to him for guidance. And that was how it had been since they had each filled their respective roles.

"Suit yourself, constable, we understand. I would hope you keep this to yourself. At least for as long as possible?" Caspar said quickly, fully understanding the constable's need to stay behind. He was the law in Burnmere, if in name only. He thought for a moment then added, "Keep your eyes peeled, and your ears to the ground. Bürgermeister Hartjenstein will be on the war path, I fear."

"Of course. I'll keep the peace as best I can, it's my job, I suppose, and I'll do what I can with regards to the bürgermeister," Hecht replied, suddenly feeling quite cowardly. Which, if he had to admit it, he was. He knew the town was run by a greedy madman; he knew his say meant nothing, but his options were painfully limited.

"Pack up, then meet back here at noon. Constable, I suggest you let the doctor know what's going on, I think it's safe to say he's one that we can trust. He's got his ears to the ground, so to speak, and we need more people like him able to speak truth in this town. All agreed?" Fr. Gustloff stated.

Everyone nodded in agreement, including Constable Hecht who opened the church doors to leave. Hearing something above, he looked up. "Gentlemen, come here, you need to see this."

All four men exited and stood right outside the church. Caspar noticed the schoolteacher Miss Shalner and her class also standing outside, several blocks away, staring up into the sky. Other townsfolk scattered throughout the main street of Burnmere slowly made their way outdoors, all of them looking up.

"What in God's name is going on here!" Nick said in a stunned voice.

Flapping noises and buzzing sounds emanated from above them where large flocks of birds all flew away from the mountain and from Burnmere in a long string, as if flying toward Noah's Ark in the Old Testament. Fleeing certain doom.

"They know something we don't," Marco said gravely, watching the birds of all sizes and colors flee Burnmere.

"I believe we are all here in agreement," Fr. Gustloff uttered. "Time is of the essence, gentlemen, you need to gather some personal belongings for your trip up that mountain." He turned and quietly walked back into the church, making the sign of the cross as he entered, closing the doors behind him.

Marco glanced over toward the bürgermeister's house where Hartjenstein stood outside watching the fleeing birds and noticed even some flying insects traveling with them. He glanced down at Marco and their eyes locked. Marco didn't look away, it was Hartjenstein who did, in what could only be construed as shame and embarrassment. His eyes trailed back up to the sky, then, in a huff, he returned to his house, slamming the door behind him.

It was a small victory for Marco against a truly despicable man, but a victory nonetheless. Whatever had happened inside that house earlier with Everly was nothing good. Everyone around him knew it and, more importantly, Bürgermeister Hartjenstein knew it, he could tell from the look on the guilty man's face. Marco sensed that this could be the beginning of the end for the town's bürgermeister. Everly had likely wrapped her talons around him and gotten him to agree to something he would very quickly come to regret.

The birds and flying insects vanished out of sight once they passed the small village. Once gone, an eerie silence fell over Burnmere. No one spoke, and even the school children stood in silence, taking in the paranormal activity that had just occurred.

"This tracks with the old dog that took off earlier up by the Pale Horse," Caspar said grimly.

"I was thinking the exact same thing," Marco replied, nodding in agreement.

"Be careful up there. I'll do what I can to keep Hartjenstein at bay and in the dark as to your whereabouts. And Marco, that table, don't worry about it," Constable Hecht said quietly.

"Thank you, Theodor. I appreciate that," Marco mumbled, still stunned at the sight he had just witnessed and the stare-down with Bürgermeister Hartjenstein.

Constable Hecht left the church grounds, making his way to his office up past the butcher shop and small grocery store.

At the schoolhouse, Miss Shalner glanced over at the church and the three men standing in the doorway. Her typically stern face had been replaced with a look of genuine worry and concern for not just herself but the children whose wellbeing she was entrusted with.

She put her head down and motioned for the kids to go back inside. They had finally started making noise after the strange occurrence above, while the rest of the town seemed to quietly go back to what they were doing.

As Nick began walking away from the church, Caspar called out to him, "You still planning on taking a hike with us later after that display we just saw?"

He stopped and turned his head slightly, giving a quick nod. Then, with his hands shoved in his pockets, he turned and left for his own place.

Caspar saw his gun still propped up against the outside of the church. Picking it up, he tossed the loaded bolt action breech loading rifle over to Marco who caught it in midair.

"What the hell are you doing, Caspar? You need this gun!" Marco exclaimed.

"Go to your house and get packed up and I'll see you back here soon," Caspar said, turning his attention toward Bürgermeister Hartjenstein's house.

Marco nodded, unsure what Caspar was planning. He turned and headed home. Back to a waiting Everly.

The morning was hazy and the fog that enshrouded the mountain completely had lifted just slightly, enough for the peaks of Castle Visimar to cut through. As Caspar made his way to Hartjenstein's house, he glanced up at the dim outline of the castle.

He knocked on the bürgermeister's door and waited. After a few seconds the door opened with Hartjenstein muttering, "Just what the hell do you_"

Caspar pushed his way into the house, shoving the man aside. Looking around he asked, "Where is it?"

"How dare you push your way into my home!" the bürgermeister shouted.

"Where is Marco's shotgun? I need it," Caspar replied coolly, glancing at him while still scanning the well-appointed living room.

"You will get the hell out of my house this instant! Rest assured; charges will be brought against you!" Hartjenstein continued.

At this, Caspar turned and got within an inch of the bürgermeister's face, unblinking and in an icy calm voice, replying, "I'm going to ask you once more, where's the shotgun that you stole from Marco?"

Changing his tune immediately, the bürgermeister tried backing away but was unable to as he was against a wall. "And why do you need it?" Hartjenstein asked quietly, his bluff now being called.

"Where...is...it?"

Pausing, Hartjenstein's eyes shifted to the right.

Caspar looked over and, sure enough, in the corner of his kitchen lay the shotgun taken from the church. Without batting an eye, Caspar pulled away from the man, walked over and picked up the shotgun, then returned to the visibly shaken bürgermeister.

Once again directly in his face, Caspar stared him in the eyes.

Instantly, Hartjenstein felt guilt cross his face and looked away. Meekly, completely deflated by the sudden aggression, he once more stated his case. "You simply cannot barge into a man's house and take what doesn't belong..."

He stopped, realizing what he was saying. Silence fell in the house.

Caspar could tell the man was eating his words, so he let them stew just a bit longer.

"This town and the people in it are dying. Literally. And you're up here in your lavish house furnished with people's hard-earned money, fucking around with another man's wife," Caspar said in a cold, calculated voice. He was officially done taking this man's shit.

Hartjenstein could see in the man's eyes that he meant to strike him, hard. And in a fight like this, Bürgermeister Hartjenstein would be pummeled. His *all bark no bite* demeanor had officially been called out, and he was backing down like the coward he truly was. They both knew it.

Averting his eyes from Caspar's fury, he felt again his tight grip on the town of Burnmere slipping. First, with the aggressive Everly and the forced blowjob, followed by her blackmailing him into giving her an actual job. Then the stare-down he lost with the woman's husband, and now this unpleasantness with Caspar Voit.

Utterly defeated, Hartjenstein went limp and refused to look up at Caspar.

After an awkward silence, Caspar moved away from him, toward his door.

As he reached for the handle, Hartjenstein uttered, "What are you going to do? I mean, I admit the birds were a bit strange. And I suppose it is odd that the bartender Falck's lights aren't on..."

Caspar didn't reply. He exited the house of the defeated bürgermeister and closed the door behind him, his eyes instantly going up to the mountain. Shrouded in the fog, the outline of the castle loomed large. Even on this overcast day, the fog seemed alive as it circled the castle and the mountain he would soon be traveling up.

He quickly left the Hartjenstein residence, hoping he would never have to set foot inside it again as long as that man was in power, if what he had could even be considered power. He headed back to his own humble home to get provisions for the long and dangerous journey ahead.

# Chapter 15:

†

# The Trek
# to Burnmere

Daniel Kolb pushed his horse Baba hard through the Romanian countryside. He knew these parts and the sooner he could get his young passenger there, the sooner he could make his way back home, away from Burnmere. He knew the rumors and what came out of that dreadful, fog-shrouded mountain at night and wanted no part of it.

At the same time, he felt compassion for this kind-hearted young woman that chose him over the downright creepy man with the icy stare back at the train station. He puzzled at the quiet departure of the mysterious man that had seemingly hypnotized Juliette before she was able to come to her senses and pull away from his gaze.

Sure, Daniel was nothing to look at and the other strange figure could be considered alluring to a young, beautiful woman, but one thing that man was not was *safe*. He would see to it that she arrived safe and sound, he had given her his word on that.

Mountains covered with thick forests passed by them along with large fields of various crops, the sky was pleasantly blue, and the air felt good on Daniel's face. However, these pleasantries were far from his mind. His mind was focused on the mysterious man that vanished. *Where is he?*

Earlier, when Daniel had stopped briefly for old Baba to drink a bit of water and rest her weary hooves, he had asked Juliette if she cared to join him up front for a bit. She happily obliged and had been sitting beside the friendly old man for roughly one hour making light chit-chat.

Daniel, turned slightly to look behind him. Nothing but the dusty road they were traveling on.

Juliette asked, "What is it? I've noticed you looking back. Are you seeing something?"

Daniel thought for a second before replying, "It's nothing. I just want to get you to your destination as quickly as I can."

She sensed he wasn't being entirely honest with her but didn't pursue it further. However, from that point on, Juliette glanced back periodically, instinctively clutching the gold necklace around her neck.

She thought back to when her sister told her she was coming here to investigate their great-grandfather's history, and Juliette's resistance to this plan. She hated how things had been left between them. Looking back on their tense conversations, Juliette couldn't help but feel her sister was under someone or some thing's spell. Her sister, while spunky and at times, flirty with the opposite sex, was still logical. Not so when it came to her traveling alone to Burnmere deep in the Carpathian Mountains of Romania.

All they had at this point, was each other. *Damnit, Juliette, why weren't you more forceful?* She shook her head angrily over her last interaction with her dear sister Lily-Rose before she left in a huff with their Uncle Henry for the train station.

She had a sinking feeling the closer they got to Burnmere that her sister was indeed in seriously grave danger. Dread was slowly creeping up on Juliette, though she couldn't point her finger to what it was exactly. The countryside was truly beautiful and, other than the strange carriage driver that accosted her at the train station, it had been an uneventful journey thus far. *The eyes on that man, though, so black. He almost seemed dead.* She shuddered at the thought. Where did he go?

Numerous patches of trees lined either side of the road as they passed, all filled with birds. Even the skies seemed crowded with birds of various shapes, sizes and species hovering high above.

"Why are there so many birds in this area? It seems as though there are hundreds upon hundreds. Don't you find that odd?" Juliette said puzzled, staring up into the sky above.

Nodding, he replied, "Aye, it is indeed odd. There are no lakes or rivers in this region, they seem to be lost, or fleeing."

"Fleeing? From what? What could cause hundreds of birds to do this? Weather?" Juliette suddenly felt a shiver course through her.

"There's much to flee from in this area of the Carpathian Mountains, ma'am. This, however, is quite an anomaly. Even for someone such as me that has seen a lot in my day," Daniel said as his mind drifted.

"What do you mean?" Juliette replied, now curious.

"Well, in another life, I used to be a priest, but it seems as though it wasn't for me. Years ago, I lost a part of my faith and haven't seemed to gain it back. Without it, I could no longer lead my flock. The Lord, however, works in mysterious ways. I feel like He isn't done with me yet, I'm just waiting for a sign, I suppose you could say," Daniel said contemplatively, his mind going to the mountain that he was certain the birds had traveled from. Most everyone knew of the legends that swirled around this area. Vampirism, devil worship, witchcraft, and murder. Sacrifices to an unseen, evil entity. His priestly prayers returned to him as he thought of the darkness surrounding the Carpathian Mountain region.

"If I may be so bold, what happened, Daniel? What could happen to make a man of the cloth lose his faith, even part of it?" Juliette asked, looking over at the elderly carriage driver, now deep in thought.

He shrugged. "Missy, I've seen more hate, anger, gossip, infidelity, jealousy and bitterness to last several lifetimes. All from people that happily took communion, week in and week out. They'd go to confession, do their bit, and I'd do mine. Rinse and repeat. I blamed myself, I was their shepherd and I wasn't leading properly, I suppose."

"Doesn't everyone deserve second chances, though? Juliette answered.

Glancing over, Daniel replied, "That they do, but after about the fiftieth time, or maybe it was the five-hundredth time, I simply became discouraged to the point of checking out. I know God gives us all free will but to take advantage of His love over and over? I couldn't take it any longer. Hanging it up and doing something a bit easier has been good for my soul. So, it's been me and old Baba here ever since," the old man paused, contemplating a bit then added, "But I'd be lying if I told you I don't have some regrets and feel as though I abandoned my parish when it needed me the most."

"Fair enough. Everyone has to follow their own path, and if yours is to take me to Burnmere to find my sister, then you're right where you belong," Juliette said evenly.

They both fell silent. Staring out at the landscape, Daniel thought on his faith, the people he had left years ago, regret and sorrow for a flock he felt he simply could no longer lead as they needed him to.

The country had changed dramatically since their departure from the train station much earlier in the day. City life had turned to rural country, the small towns they passed through giving way to quiet and serene landscapes of grassy hills and forests. This part of Romania was poor countryside, made up primarily of farmland, and relocating was difficult if one had nowhere to go and had lived here most of or all of their lives. Those living in the small villages that littered this region continued to eke out their existence as the towns themselves slowly died off. Such was the case in the town they were heading toward.

Juliette and her driver both remained lost in thought, both feeling the presence of true isolation surrounding them. She thought of the flocks of birds, all in unison, traveling away. To her, it felt as if it were a bad omen of what lay ahead for her. She kept her mind on her sister. *I'm coming, Lily-Rose, I'm coming.*

The morning had turned to near noon. Stopping to give Baba a rest and to stretch their feet, Juliette climbed back into the carriage and was thankful to get some much-needed sleep on the next leg of the journey. She was exhausted from all the travel and wished it to be over. Knowing full well that this same trek would have to be repeated to get back home, but at least Lily-Rose would be safe and sound with her once again.

"Miss Juliette, up ahead, see that mountain?" Daniel exclaimed, pointing up ahead and glancing back at her as she was waking up from her nap.

Sitting up and leaning forward uncomfortably in a seat whose cushion should have been replaced years ago, Juliette looked in the direction her elderly driver had pointed. Several miles in the distance, straight ahead on their current path, stood a low mountain with clouds surrounding it.

Juliette's brow furrowed; she instantly didn't like the imposing look of the mountain. It wasn't just the thick tree cover that gave her pause, it was the dreary sky above what she could now make out as a small town below the looming, oppressive mountain. Most of their trip was bathed in beautiful sunlight, but this town had a swirling gray cloud of despair hanging over it. Maybe it was the fog rolling off the mountain that blanketed the sky. Whatever it was, it was an ominous sight.

"Daniel, what's the story with the fog on the mountain up there?" Juliette, now fully awake, said over the clip-clop of Baba's hooves.

Glancing back at her, Daniel replied, "That, young lady, is the mountain where Castle Visimar resides. Many a superstition surrounds that place, one of which is that the very devil himself lives inside that mountain, awaiting his return to earth. But that's just what us religious folk talk about."

"And do you believe that?" Juliette replied, continuing to lean forward, staring out at the village and mountain above.

She was met with silence. That uneasy feeling in the pit of her stomach grew the closer they got. They would likely arrive in Burnmere in a matter of minutes at the rate they were traveling. She felt both excitement at being reunited with her sister and dread at what loomed high upon the mountain.

"Daniel, I should have asked you earlier, but once I find my sister, can you tell me how easy it will be to find a way back to Bucharest to the train station?" Juliette said, then added, "I fear that finding her then getting her to come home with me might be challenging. That town doesn't look welcoming."

Daniel pulled back on the reins to slow Baba down a bit to better converse with the young woman. "I can certainly return for you. Old Baba here is getting up there in age as is her owner. But I fear for your safety, missy, and I want to see you and your sister make it safely back to England." Daniel pondered, thinking to himself a bit then adding, "So, if you require my services, I can meet you in two days' time, right at Burnmere's entrance to pick you up. If it's all the same to you, I would rather stay out of town. Is this agreeable to you, missy?"

Juliette replied, "That's very kind of you, good sir. I truly appreciate it, and indeed, two days' time should suffice."

"I hope you find your sister and stay safe," Daniel said with genuine concern. Nodding to himself, he added, "There are indeed some other covered wagons that come through here to replenish the town general store and the pub. However, I've never been inside Burnmere."

She sensed he would rather not make the trek back to this part of the country anytime soon if he didn't have to. "I could probably get a ride from one of the delivery wagons, don't you think?"

Daniel contemplated this, wishing he could just agree that was the best and most convenient plan for her, but he couldn't. "I wouldn't rely on a transport to get you and your sister back to Bucharest, Miss Juliette. I shall be here, that is a promise."

The dirt road turned to cobblestone and Baba slowed as Daniel pulled back on the reins of the old horse, coming to a stop at the entrance to Burnmere. An old crooked wooden sign hung on the side of a small stone building where the dirt path turned into a crooked cobblestone street. It read, "Welcome to Burnmere: Population..." The number had been scratched off and what remained looked ominously like a solid circle. Or a zero.

Juliette noticed most of the town consisted of identical stone buildings or wooden structures. All were small, old, and all in need of updating and renovations. Smoke wafted up from chimneys, and signs adorned the fronts of buildings with businesses' names. The first stone structure upon entering town, Juliette learned immediately, was the town schoolhouse.

"End of the line for you. I will help you with your luggage and be on my way," Daniel said, stopping just short of the school building and climbing down from his driver's seat. He opened the small carriage door and offered his hand to Juliette, which she graciously accepted.

She stepped off the carriage onto the cobblestone street, peering into the town in front of her, trying to avert her eyes from the fog-shrouded mountain that seemed to lord over every square inch of Burnmere.

Daniel fetched a pail of water and some feed for his weary horse then retrieved Juliette's suitcase.

Juliette commented, "You won't take your horse into town to feed and rest?"

"No, not here. I will give old Baba here a bit of rest then we shall be on our way. I will be back in the agreed upon two days' time. Right here, in this very spot, to pick you and your dear sister up, unless old Baba or I meet our Maker before then," he joked, pulling out his pipe and lighting it.

Juliette didn't share in the old man's humor. This place was devoid of that, and she relied on him and old Baba to get them back to the train station, back to safety.

Noticing her grim expression, his demeanor sobered. He picked up the water can and empty feed bucket from Baba who was swallowing her last bit of grain and stored it back inside the rear of the carriage. He walked back to Juliette who gave a thin smile, knowing it was time for goodbyes as well as payment.

Juliette retrieved the funds owed to her kind driver from her suitcase and attempted to hand him the money.

Looking down at her outstretched hand, Daniel took several more puffs from his pipe and glanced around the town where several people were meandering through the old streets, none of whom were in a hurry, why would they be? Where was there to go in a town that had seemingly died many years prior?

His grim facial expression told Juliette all she needed to know. She pushed the money toward him further. "Here, Daniel, take it."

Breaking his attention from Burnmere, he took it, wrapping his own hands around hers. "Juliette, listen to me carefully. This town, it is a cursed place. Please, take care of yourself, I fear for your safety. I hope you find what you're looking for, truly I do."

"I hope so too, Daniel, and thank you for taking care of me back at the train station. I should hope I never see that menacing face again. I will be here in two days' time awaiting your arrival to take my sister and I back home."

He nodded, replying, "I will say a prayer for you on my trip back." He didn't wait for a reply but turned and climbed back up to his seat on the carriage. A quick flick of the reins was all it took for Baba to begin trotting away from the eerie village. Daniel didn't once look back as the horse turned his carriage in the opposite direction of Burnmere. He was thankful to be leaving and was already dreading the return trip in a short two days' time. But the sisters would need him.

It was shortly after noon, but the skies looked as though dusk were about to fall. Gray clouds hung over the fog-covered mountain, shrouding everything in shadow.

As Daniel and Baba left the immediate area, something caught his eye to his far left. He could have sworn he saw movement but when he looked in its direction, he saw only trees and hills leading up to the mountain past them.

Inadvertently, his eyes traveled up to the mountain. Looming high atop it was the outline of Castle Visimar, several of its high towers peeking through the fog. He shuddered and quickly turned in his seat, making a sign of the cross, then gave the reins a good shaking to coax Baba to move a bit faster. The old horse happily obliged, as if sensing her master's discomfort with their current surroundings.

Juliette watched Daniel, Baba and the carriage pull away, going from a trot to a near run. Considering where she was and the odd journey they had taken since leaving the train station, this didn't surprise her; it only frightened her more.

She turned and walked into the town of Burnmere, noticing a group of roughly twenty children outside the schoolhouse. The kids weren't so much playing as milling around the tiny grassy area, periodically looking up at the sky then over to the mountain, all seeming to either be deep in thought or talking quietly to each other. They looked dour and sacred, as did the old, gaunt woman that stood at the doorway glaring at the newest arrival to Burnmere.

Juliette attempted to give a wave, but the skinny old woman immediately shouted, "Children! Come in! Recess is over! Now!" The kids quickly filed silently back into the building, several of them looking at the new arrival in town and giving her a half-hearted wave. Instantly, her heart broke for the children who appeared trapped in this depressing, sad town. Once they were inside, Juliette noticed the old woman giving her one last quick and untrusting glance before shutting the door behind her.

"And that is how I shall be greeted throughout this village, I fear," Juliette said with a shudder. Bucharest wasn't anything like the beautiful town of Summerhost, but it was a beacon of joy and bustling life compared to this place.

Shaking off her initial jitters from this new, alien place, she made her way further into town. It was time to get some answers.

†

Daniel's eye had indeed caught something. Marcel and his black horse had been silently following them through the countryside, just far enough away to keep out of sight. Juliette was to come to the castle willingly, not by force. Attacking the old man and taking her by force was against his master's wishes. It would have been quite an easy task, but he resisted.

Instead, he and his horse were protected from their eyesight. Protected by the darkness and evil that had the land in its tight grip. The necklace had arrived in Burnmere, and now it was that much closer to its rightful master. Marcel decided to bide his time. The woman would come to him; she couldn't resist. Not with the allure of the necklace this close to the castle. He would call on the woman and she would come to him. Then he would whisk her off to Castle Visimar much like he had done with her sister several days earlier.

Marcel quietly circled the town from a distance, wanting to get the woman up the mountain during the daylight hours, if possible. He knew what was at stake. *Do not fail me again.* Visimar's words echoed through his rotting brain.

The large black horse pushed forward, toward the edge of the forest, close to Rozalia Sitek's cottage where Lily-Rose had once been a resident. There, he waited for his prey.

# Part II:

†

# The Falling

"And the great dragon was thrown down, the serpent of old who is called the devil and Satan, who deceives the whole world; he was thrown down to the earth, and his angels were thrown down with him." (Revelation 12:9)

# Chapter 16:

### †

# Lily Awakens

In the cavernous dungeon within Castle Visimar, Lily-Rose slept. But the sleep was restless, her thoughts and dreams plagued by her captors. Marcel, the slave, Ingrid, the bride, and Antonin, the master all seemed to be in a continuous state of pursuit of the young woman whose blue dress was no longer drenched in her own blood but was now vibrant, as was the one wearing it.

She dreamed of running through the forest, away from the castle, but no matter how fast she ran, her pursuers were always gaining ground. As if they were simply toying with her. *Playing with their food.* On and on the running continued down the tiny winding trail Marcel had traveled earlier when taking her to the castle.

On either side were wolves of various sizes and colors. They kept pace but never attacked. Leading the charge were the black wolf and the gray wolf, both of which had stood by their master in the altar room as he sunk his fangs into her neck then lapped up leftovers.

*What do they want? Why are they pursuing me?* She kept running, tripping over a fallen branch and landing hard on her face. She felt the dirt and rough surface of the mountainous region scrape her body. A large, outstretched branch scraped against her chest, ripping her skin open. Instinctively, she put her hand against her fresh wound.

Marcel, Ingrid, and Antonin appeared to be floating slightly off of the ground. They came to a stop, as did the wolves that now encircled her. Feeling completely vulnerable and helpless, she shouted out at the creature in front of her, reciting the Lord's prayer while a swell of large vampire bats circled above, as if they too were waiting for a quick meal of her warm blood.

Ignoring her prayers, Antonin hissed at her angrily. Marcel, however, was gone. Ingrid was no longer there either. She glanced over on either side of the surrounding forest. No wolves.

A transformed, mutated Antonin, now resembling a man-bat, hovered slightly off the ground and raised both arms as if in a mock crucified state. He looked at her with hate-filled eyes that glowed yellow, then red, then black, a continuous stream of mutating pupils, all trained on her. His body was contorting, fangs protruding from his wide mouth, skin pulled back tightly across his skull, ears pointed and black hair falling out before her very eyes. His neck appeared to be extending while his arms grew longer and bonier.

He was naked now, and as she glanced down, she saw he was devoid of any manhood. Skin continued to pull tighter around his frame as Antonin, or the thing that called itself Antonin, looked past her into the forest. Something was coming, she could hear it. Footsteps? Was someone coming to help her?

She didn't have time to turn around to look, the monstrous beast in front of her let out an unholy scream, its mouth widening further and further across an already inhuman face.

Lily-Rose woke up to complete blackness. For a few seconds, she thought everything that had happened to her in the last month was all a bad dream, and she had just awakened in her nice, warm cozy bed back in Summerhost. It was still the middle of the night, hence the dark room.

Except she wasn't back home. Raising her hands, she hit the top of the coffin she lay inside. No soft cushion beneath her, just cold, hard wood. She was surrounded by it. She immediately felt herself grow cold but that wasn't the worst part. The hunger gnawing at her stomach was nearly unbearable, as though she hadn't eaten in weeks and her stomach had resorted to eating away at her insides to quench the hunger pangs.

*Keep it together, stay calm, Lily.*

She pushed against her coffin and the lid popped open. Dim light hit her eyes, causing her to squint at the pain. It hurt to see daylight, she realized, which made her temporarily forget about her stomach that seemed to have a small fire smoldering inside of it.

Climbing out of the coffin, she surveyed her surroundings. Same dungeon, just a bit brighter inside, revealing only two options for escape. The ceiling hole that Ingrid had crawled up through and the barred window in the side of the wall where Ingrid had flown through with the corpse that still lay on the ground.

She eyed the carcass, and instantly her stomach gurgled and rumbled. *Just a bite to take away this searing pain!* She tried to avoid it, but the slashings and bites had exposed meat and coagulated blood. The sight of the blood instantly made Lily-Rose think of the forced kiss from Ingrid, and her licking every bit of the young girl's blood from Ingrid's smirking face.

"I hate her," Lily-Rose said aloud, looking toward the coffin where the demon creature now slept, waiting for the daylight hours to pass so she could once more do what seemingly came natural for her, torment her and kill people.

The corpse she recognized now as the bartender of the Pale Horse in Burnmere. Her mind went to the charming Caspar Voit, a man who, in the short time she became acquainted with him, she imagined being in a relationship with.

Something Lily-Rose hadn't planned on, as romance had been the furthest thing from her mind since her encounter with the dark man in the dress store.

Caspar and she had shared a bit of their past with each other; he asked about the beautiful amulet around her neck and she asked why in the world he would want to live in a place such as Burnmere.

Lily thought back to his response. "My ironworks business is quite lucrative, and people here rely on my services, so…here I stay, for now." Then he had smiled warmly at her and she had reluctantly returned the smile finding it hard to resist the kind man's likable personality.

The man stirred up a warm feeling in her stomach, the feeling one gets when the possibility of sex suddenly becomes a strong reality. She felt it and she sensed he did as well. But she knew she was in Burnmere for another matter, not romance. Called forth by the owner of the amulet, and now this was her new reality. Bitten by a vampire and told that she would feed on her sister, completing her transformation into a living dead creature of the night. Damned for eternity to this hellish existence. Killing to sate an appetite that would likely never be satisfied. All because of a great-grandfather she never knew. *Is this what is to become of me? Is there no hope? No God?*

"I should be asleep right now, but I willed myself awake. Now I just need to will myself out of here," she said quietly.

The blood on her blue dress had hardened. She pulled the garment off; thankful she wore a thin slip underneath. Freed of the uncomfortable confines of its snug, form-fitting cut, she could now move about more easily. She certainly had her strength back, even with the hunger pangs and constant pressure on her eyeballs. She was certain this newfound strength came from the bite that Antonin had *blessed* her with. She thought of the awful experience and rubbed her neck. *I died. He killed me and through that evil creature's blood, I came back as some sort of purgatory being.*

Lily-Rose stood in front of the murdered bartender that was now little more than raw meat for the taking. As she stared at it longingly, she felt her dry, parched mouth become wet with saliva. She breathed in heavily, smelling the corpse on the ground. *It's right there! Make this pain in your stomach cease. Even just a little bit, one small bite!*

She dropped to her knees, then got onto all fours, taking in the smell, saliva dripping from her mouth onto the dirt below. The cold of the dungeon and the thin slip that hugged her naked body were no match for the heat she felt suddenly coursing through her body. It was as if every inch of her could sense the best orgasm of her life mere seconds away, all she had to do was *eat.*

Lily's heart slammed hard in her chest, beads of sweat forming on her forehead. She opened her mouth and ran her tongue across her top row of teeth, two of which seemed suddenly more pointed that before, as if preparing for the meal before her, pushing up against the smaller human teeth that surrounded them.

Bending down slightly so the meat would fill her nose all the more, she breathed in the succulent smell of blood and flesh. The saliva could not be stopped, it was now a constant string forming then dripping from her mouth onto the ground as well as the dead body laying right in front of her. The smell was making her delirious as she realized she couldn't resist, until,

*Our Father, who art in heaven…hallowed be thy name…*

Lily-Rose wretched and dry heaved then quickly fell backwards, away from the corpse. Instantly, the heat she felt in her body subsided. The two fangs that had protruded out of the top row of teeth painfully pulled themselves back in and the saliva quickly dried up. Along with this, the burning stomach pain came back with a vengeance. She doubled over and writhed around in the dirt, clenching her stomach, her chest, her head. All seemed to have gone from an almost lustful heat to burning, angry pain.

"Thy kingdom come, thy will be done, on earth as it is in heaven. Give us this day, our daily bread and forgive us our trespasses as we forgive those who trespass against us." After speaking the words aloud, she glared over at the coffin in which she was certain Ingrid still lay sleeping.

"I don't think that applies to you, honey," Lily-Rose said coldly, then with all her strength, she pulled herself back to her feet and did her best to ignore the corpse. She walked around the dungeon again, over to the opening with the bars. Inspecting them above, she thought aloud. "I tried before so I don't think I can squeeze through there… That bartender's body was forced through by the demon witch, but me? I've got to try again."

She walked toward the wall and felt around. Recalling that it had been relatively easy to traverse up to the opening earlier, she ignored the pain in her stomach and began climbing up the ten-foot ascent once more. This time was even easier, as she remembered which stones to grab hold of to ensure a proper foothold.

Once she reached the large opening, she grabbed hold of the bars and pulled with all of her might. They wouldn't budge, which didn't surprise her. What the bars did offer however, was stabilization. With her feet dug into the creases of the rounded stones that made up the dungeon walls, and her hands gripping two of the bars tightly, she hoisted herself upwards until her feet now rested on the ledge of the opening. Once more, she did this with relative ease, surprised by her newfound strength post-bite.

She thought of Ingrid flying through the air, turning into a winged demon. Was that what awaited her? *Only if I kill and feast. I must not! No matter how intense the pain!*

Looking down to the ground below, easily ten feet down, Lily-Rose knew there was no way she could have attempted this without the newfound strength and determination that came from the bite Antonin had inflicted on her the previous night. The thought of his blood coursing through her veins repulsed her, but that very supernatural blood could be the source of her escape.

Shaking the bars once more, Lily knew there was no chance of them breaking free from the stone bonds they were encased in. She wasn't strong enough to pull the bars out or stretch the steel they were constructed of. *But can I squeeze through?*

She glanced back at the coffin she had climbed out of, then to the food provided for her by the generous Ingrid, then over to the demon woman's coffin. "I should have found a way to stake you through the heart," Lily-Rose muttered, then turned back to the bars once more.

Focused, Lily-Rose looked past the bars at what would await her if she did indeed escape—trees as far as the eye could see. The ground consisted of dirt and weeds, and along with the typical wooded landscape hung the dense fog. *How can I possibly make it out of here through that?* Her mind briefly went to the wolves that had chased after her and Marcel as they road on the back of his horse through the mountainous region. She would deal with that later. Priority one: escape this literal hell hole.

She placed her forehead against the bars and with all her might, pushed against them. *Please let this work.*

Her head pushed through the bars, although it shouldn't have. It wasn't humanly possible, but she wasn't entirely human anymore. Her eyes widened at this small victory. Now that her head was through the bars, she pushed her arms through and then her torso followed. She felt her body contort, her ribcage sinking in almost as if her ribs had turned into putty, then as she moved forward, they extended back to their normal state.

"Here goes nothing," she said, gripping the bars with her free hands and pushing the rest of her body through, spilling out onto the cold earth and landing with a thud. She couldn't believe it, could have sworn it was impossible. But that was before she became a guest of Castle Visimar. Before she had met all of its inhabitants.

"Didn't count on a silly girl like me being this resilient, did you?" she uttered on all fours, glancing back through the bars at the coffin where her captor lay sleeping.

She stood to her feet, her bare feet. While it wasn't deathly cold, it certainly wasn't *warm*, with the sunlight permeating the cloud cover and fog. Night, however, would be a different story, she had to get moving immediately. Realizing she felt the cool air around her gave her hope that not all was lost. "I'm not completely changed yet, and I'm not going to be, either," she muttered.

Looking around, she was thankful to see no wolves in her general vicinity. She knew she had to move; with each passing minute, the daylight would soon turn to dusk which would turn to nightfall. And then the demon creature would surely awaken, and her retribution would be swift.

Now that Antonin had his amulet, maybe he wasn't aware of her escape attempt? Maybe he was focusing more on what he intended to do with it once he got the necklace around her sister's neck? She thought of Juliette, sweet Juliette, who had urged her not to go on this trek, literally begged and pleaded before outright yelling at her. But it had fallen on deaf ears. She had been marked and had to go, she couldn't resist the draw of the count as well as what she assumed was a hypnotic spell the dark man in the store back home had bewitched her with. Now she felt just as urgently the need to get out of here.

No longer hesitating, she began her trek around the castle to its front entrance, where she would start a quick descent down the mountain, back to Burnmere. Perhaps she could find Caspar, and the town doctor whose name escaped her at the moment. What she really wished for was her dear sister Juliette. Just to see her again, to say how sorry she was at their last conversation before abruptly leaving Summerhost. She knew she hadn't been able to stop herself, but she hated how things had been left, regardless of whatever awful curse had been put on her.

The castle was huge; however, it was relatively easy at ground level to walk around its perimeter. She didn't want to stare at it for longer than she had to, but her eyes inadvertently kept glancing up. The castle oozed a sinister, evil aura. Its thick stone walls blackened by what looked to be a fire that must have taken place many years prior. Thick cobwebs draped over large portions of the unkept exterior along with heavy plant growth now visible in the daylight hours. High up were several peaks, the same peaks she had seen when looking at it from a distance, back in the relative safety of Rozalia Sitek's cottage at the edge of town.

Reaching the front, she found the path that led down to her hopeful freedom. Glancing back one last time at the sprawling and foreboding castle that had been her home for the last several days, she thought of the amulet that the evil being inside was now in possession of. Shaking her head, she turned and began the journey down the mountain.

It wasn't long before glowing yellow eyes peered at her through the foggy tree cover. Growling hungrily.

# Chapter 17:

†

# A New Traveling Companion

**M**arco tried the front door of his home; it was locked. He didn't want to deal with Everly, so he dug through his pocket and produced the key, unlocking and opening the door. At first glance, it appeared that Everly wasn't inside.

"Thank the good Lord for small fav...." he began but his hopes were dashed.

"Well, there you are. All done with your little vampire hunting club with the rest of the rejects?" Everly stood in the doorway of their washroom, her hair wet, combed and no longer ratty. Her dirty face had been cleaned, and though she had a towel wrapped around her, he could tell she had washed with the meager soap they had on hand. He also noticed deep scratches on her chest and thought of her leaving Bürgermeister Hartjenstein's house, shuddering at the thought.

He remained silent, looking at her. He knew why she had attempted to clean herself and he figured where the scratches came from, repulsing him all the more. The woman had no shame. *Wash all you want, you're still a dirty wretch inside and that can't be scrubbed away, no matter how hard you try.* She repulsed him. The only good thing that had come from her was named Christoph and he had thankfully fled far from his mother and from this shameful existence.

"What, you like what you see all of a sudden? You couldn't get it up if you tried," she said sarcastically, her newfound confidence in her new career wavering just a bit. *Where did the last hour of my life go?* She had no recollection of what had taken place in her bedroom less than an hour ago. All she knew was she felt awakened, renewed in a way she couldn't explain.

Marco walked past her, grabbing an old sack cloth, and began putting items into it. He couldn't offer much for his soon-to-be traveling companions. His shotgun was gone, and he essentially had no food. Still, a few items could be of use. A canister of kerosine, a knife, an old table leg that had fallen off their now three-legged table that had never been repaired. Everly watched him look around the small house.

"What the hell are you doing?" she said with a hint of genuine interest.

He needed to get rid of her. She would run directly back to Bürgermeister Hartjenstein's if she got a whiff of him heading to the mountain. Time to get this over with.

"None of your fucking business, woman," he hissed. *That felt good.*

"Oh, really? None of my business, you say? Well, let me tell you something. Starting tomorrow, I'm in charge of bookkeeping and finances of Burnmere. Me! The good bürgermeister himself hired me on. I will begin assisting the constable as well in the keeping of law and order around here. Something this town is in dire need of." She paused when she saw him stop what he was doing and look at her. *He knows what I did.*

"Get out of my sight. You disgust me. You're the reason our son left. You, Everly are a *bad* person. Do whatever makes you happy, Lord knows I never could," Marco said coldly, staring daggers into her.

Everly and Marco had many drop-down, drag-out fights in their time but this felt different. This somehow, felt final. People in Burnmere never split, no matter how rotten the marriage was, together in misery was better than alone in a dead town. Those that sensed the end was near typically just packed up and moved, only to separate when finally free and clear of the godforsaken town.

"Why you…" she paused, she wasn't sure how to respond. "I hate you! I *hate* you! What you represent, everything about you! I hate our son because he came from you. And now I plan on bettering my situation. Improving my—up to this point—wasted life, stuck with the likes of you. Well, no more! A new Everly is here and you can't take it!"

Marco turned his back to her, hoping this outward defiance would chase her back to the washroom. He was right, he heard the door slam as hard as she could muster, causing something in the washroom to fall off the shelf and shatter. Turning back around, he found himself once more alone. *Thank Christ,* he thought then put the few items he thought may be of use into the potato sack and quietly left his own house of horrors. If he made it back alive, he hoped she would be gone. *If only I were that lucky.*

As quickly as he could considering his hip still hurt, he made his way back to St. Joseph's parish with the potato sack slung over his shoulder.

At Caspar's house, who was also just leaving with a few belongings, one of which was Marco's shotgun, Caspar called out, "Catch," and tossed the shotgun over to him. Marco caught it in midair, wanting to ask how in the bloody hell he managed to pry it from Hartjenstein's slimy, greedy paws.

"A gift," was all Caspar said.

To which Marco replied, "Thank you, Caspar." The thanks wasn't just for retrieving his old shotgun but for somehow standing by him over the past night and morning. Something he hadn't been accustomed to and something that was beginning to give him a much-needed boost of confidence.

Caspar nodded. The man wasn't all bad, he had just been dealt a shit hand all his life. The pinnacle of which was one Everly Seiler.

They walked in silence to the church. Once there, they saw Nick had already arrived and had brought along his old trusty rifle and little else. A knife rested in an old leather sheath on his belt but its size wasn't intimidating.

The three greeted each other with a nod then turned to face the church doors.

"Excuse me, could one of you gentlemen help me?" Juliette said, hurrying up the street to their location, watching where she stepped as she approached.

They stopped and turned to see who had called out to them. A stunned look crossed all three of their faces when they saw a woman that could only be the sister of Lily-Rose Burns, the resemblance was uncanny. She wore a flattering gray dress and had long, flowing brown hair. While not as obviously attractive as her younger sister, she was still absolutely beautiful.

With her suitcase in hand, the young woman hurried over toward the three men who, until about a minute ago, were of the same mind to get to the mountain as quickly as possible. Now, a new wrinkle in the plan stood before them.

Coming to a stop in front of them, Juliette set her suitcase on the ground and offered her hand to each of the three in turn, speaking quickly. "Hello, my name is Juliette Burns, and I am here to claim my sister. Can any of you gentlemen help me? I've come a great distance, I'm tired and I would very much like to see her and know that she's alright." She stopped to take a breath, hoping these men were not like the man she had met at the train station.

Marco instinctively looked at Caspar, figuring he would be the one to answer her question. But Caspar seemed at a loss for words. The resemblance to Lily-Rose was astonishing. Same facial features, same eyes and lips. Even their voices seemed to have a similar ring to them.

Seeing Caspar collect his thoughts, Marco brushed aside how lovely this woman looked in such a dismal town and took the lead. "Miss Burns, I think it would be best if we step into the church to discuss your sister."

She looked warily at him. He was unkept, large, and appeared to have led a hard life. Plus, stepping into a building, even if it was a church, with three strange men was the opposite of what she felt comfortable doing. Her eyes shifted from man to man, they all seemed normal if slightly dirty, two of them at least. The other one was quite handsome and well-groomed, she observed.

"He is right," a voice behind the men exclaimed. A priest stood in the opened doorway, peering out at the scene in front of his parish. "I urge you all, come inside. There are prying eyes around here."

He glanced up at the house where the bürgermeister lived. Even looking out his window, Hartjenstein had a clear shot of St. Joseph's parish, likely why he had quickly come down the previous day after Aline Koltz's funeral to see what the men were discussing. He was sure that would be the case soon if they didn't continue the conversation inside.

Juliette looked past the three people in front of her to the opened door of the church with Fr. Gustloff standing beside it, his hand motioning for them all to join him inside.

"Father Jannick Gustloff speaks the truth, we can't talk out here. Not about Lily-Rose." Caspar finally spoke, not waiting to see if the woman who claimed to be her sister would follow or not.

Nick and Marco followed Caspar inside, leaving Juliette standing by herself on the path that led to into the small parish.

"Ma'am, time is of the essence," Fr. Gustloff said, once more glancing up toward the bürgermeister's house.

Juliette turned to see where he was looking and saw a curtain closing. She looked back at the priest, suddenly feeling paranoid and vulnerable.

Fr. Gustloff said, "Come in, please. And we will tell you what we know and what we intend to do about it."

Nodding, Juliette quickly entered the church doors, continuing to glance behind her toward the curtained window that now remained closed.

"So, as you have heard, my name is Father Jannick Gustloff. Pleased to make your acquaintance." He offered his hand which she took. While he shook her hand, he gave the slightest tug, leading her into his church and quickly closed the doors behind him, going so far as to lock them. He released her hand once she was inside.

*A priest that locks his church doors in the early afternoon hours. What have I gotten myself into?* Juliette cautiously made her way into the tiny church. She instinctively dipped her finger in the small font by the entrance and blessed herself. With all of the weird occurrences since her sister had suddenly taken off for this mysterious part of the world, she could use a bit of holy water to protect herself.

She quickly inspected the chapel. It was as basic and poorly constructed as she had imagined from the exterior's appearance. But that didn't concern her, what concerned her was something much more important.

"Where's my sister? You four know something or you wouldn't be so mysterious right now," Juliette exclaimed, immediately putting her defenses up. Her driver Daniel hadn't necessarily boosted her confidence for a pleasant stay in the town of Burnmere, and the quiet and likely dangerous Marcel back at the train station still lingered in the back of her mind. He was somewhere out there, and she feared it might be close to her current location.

Fr. Gustloff responded, "Juliette, we don't have much time. But allow me to introduce you to the men that intend to find out where exactly your sister Lily-Rose is." He pointed to each man. "Nick Schoeler, Marco Seiler, and Caspar Voit."

They all nodded. She returned the gesture and immediately returned to her initial question. "So, none of you know where Lily-Rose is? Anyone here want to tell me what is going on?" Juliette said in a feeble attempt to mask her rising emotions.

Caspar looked at her gold necklace, its color identical to her sister's amulet. He made a note to ask her about it later. Now over his initial shock of seeing Lily-Rose's sister standing in front of them, he spoke up.

"Your sister was taken several days ago. We're convinced something from that castle up on the mountain came to take her. We aren't entirely sure why, but we are guessing it's a direct result of what your great-grandfather Alfred Burns did to the man that lived there one hundred years ago." He paused, letting her digest this information.

"Vampire hunting, if one believes in that sort of thing, that was my great-grandfather's supposed profession. He gave the infernal thing he had taken from the man he burned to his wife, my great-grandmother. It was passed down to my grandmother, then to my mother, and finally to Lily-Rose when she turned eighteen. So, the story goes from what my mother told us," Juliette paused.

"Then to your sister, Lily-Rose," Caspar repeated, realizing that the amulet likely did play a part in what was escalating in Burnmere.

"I hadn't thought of it much, but this necklace she gave me as a gift is part of that damned thing. I refused to wear that amulet that comes with such a horrible backstory, if one if to believe in such things, but Lily-Rose so wanted us to share in our family's history. As if she were drawn to it. So, I accepted this necklace as a gift and have worn it ever since. It appeases her, I suppose. I don't believe in vampires, but regardless, its checkered history has always troubled me with regards to it staying in our family."

"May I?" Fr. Gustoff asked, extending his hand.

"Of course." Juliette took the gold necklace off and handed it to the old priest. He looked it over, inspecting it up close.

"Interesting, this gold casts a shade I have never seen before. As a priest, I have seen my fair share of expensive artifacts in my time, many of which were solid gold or gold plated. This, however, casts a much different hue, quite beautiful, I must say. I understand why you wear it," Gustloff exclaimed, handing the necklace back to Juliette.

Marco cleared his throat and said, "Ma'am, we have decided, after the most recent death of our local bartender here in Burnmere, that we are going up that mountain to the castle. That is where we were about to head when you showed up. Time is of the essence. The hills are filled with wolves and whatever is up there comes out at night to feed."

Clasping the necklace around her neck once more, Juliette looked at the large man. He was indeed a brute, but his eyes appeared kind. She could tell this man had likely been quite handsome at one time.

She glanced at Nick, who had remained silent. "You haven't chimed in yet, Nick, was it?"

"Me? I'm just an old drunk with nothing to lose. Tired of seeing young girls torn to shreds. My life ain't worth a damn, but most others in this town are, even if they wouldn't admit it. I intend to do what I can, I suppose," Nick said, as though resigned to the fact that he probably wouldn't be coming back home.

Marco looked over at him and for the first time offered him the slightest smile. This man was weak, likely had no liver left to speak of and no hope, yet he was willing to give of himself for the good of those he lived beside. Even if they all but hated each other, the man had earned a bit of his respect.

Caspar said with some urgency, "Juliette, the birds in the sky have quite literally left this area en mass. The fog cover has become even heavier, and your sister is still missing. Time is not on our side, so we must go but once we return, you will be the first to know. Feel free to stay—"

"You said all the birds left your skies?" Juliette interrupted. "Odd you say that, because on my way to Burnmere, we passed a large area that seemed to be overrun by birds. Both my driver and I found it strange, to say the least. And ominous." She took a deep breath, as if steeling herself. "I'm coming with you, I've made it this far, and I am guessing together we can figure out what is happening up there. Plus,

I'm an excellent horseback rider, have been since I was a little girl. Both Lily-Rose and I, actually."

"Absolutely not! Where we're going, there is a good chance none will return," Caspar argued, looking to Marco and Nick for backup.

"He's right," Marco added. "The bartender I spoke of, we watched his body picked up off the ground and flown away last night. Then heard something whispered about us being next. I don't believe in vampires, but I believe what my own two eyes show me, and whatever is up there is pure evil. We intend to do what we can to stop this killing and, in the process, save your sister, if she's still alive."

Juliette winced at the insinuation that her sister might not be alive, but said nothing.

"A thirteen-year-old-girl was laid to rest yesterday, Juliette. This is serious and seems to be getting more dangerous by the hour. Your arrival in our town could make matters even worse, I'm sorry to say," Fr. Gustloff stated, looking at the woman and her golden necklace that had just dropped into their lives, throwing their plan for a loop.

"Regardless, if my sister is up there, I intend to find her. Now, you four can accommodate me, or I will find a horse and ride there myself. If I can't find a horse, I'll walk. The choice is yours. But I am going up that mountain and I'm leaving now." Juliette bent down and picked up her suitcase and headed toward the doors.

"Stop, wait," Fr. Gustloff said. "You cannot stay in this town. Not with the bürgermeister on the war path."

"My wife got a *job* working for him. She's now in charge of finances among other things so it seems," Marco added, glancing at the men as if to confirm what they suspected earlier.

"Constable Hecht already has his hands full. Another new face, one whose sister has gone missing, will cause all sorts of hell around these parts," Caspar added.

"You've put us in a pretty awkward predicament, young lady," Fr. Gustloff said sighing.

Shrugging, Juliette asked, "About how far up that mountain in the castle?"

"A few miles. If we keep moving, assuming that crusty old Maxwell lets us have a few horses, we'll be there in good enough time," Caspar answered.

They all nodded. Marco rubbed his hip; it was already giving him issues and it was only slightly past noon.

Sighing, the men looked at each other and nodded. Fr. Gustloff gave the final approving nod in her direction.

Juliette smiled thinly. She was certainly not excited about this, but she knew in her heart she had to make the climb with these people, to find out where her sister was and hopefully bring her back safely.

"Then let's go!" Juliette exclaimed, wanting to get moving.

"First, let's take inventory," Fr. Gustloff stated.

Everyone laid out what they had on the nearest pew. Caspar had brought his rifle, extra shells, a canteen of water and a bit of food. Nick had only brought his knife and a rifle, and Marco had brought kerosine, his gun, a knife and the leg of his kitchen table.

Inspecting the items, Fr. Gustloff looked at Marco, "Interesting choice of weapon," he looked at the wooden table leg.

"If the legends are true of vampire lore, I intend to push it through anything not human up there," he replied with a nod.

"I have taken the liberty to pack you holy water," Father Gustloff said, holding up a bottle. "If you are going to face what I think we are going to face, you will certainly need crucifixes as well." He paused then added, "We haven't much time, but you should let the doc know where you're heading then make haste to the Murrey's place just outside of town."

There was a jangle at the doors. Everyone froze in place, looking at each other. Everyone but Juliette, who hadn't had the displeasure of meeting the town's bürgermeister, immediately thought of Hartjenstein. Always at the wrong place at the wrong time.

"Shush, keep quiet." Fr. Gustloff motioned with his finger to his lip. He glided quietly over to the side window to peek out and see who was knocking. It continued, with more force as he peered out.

Hanging his head, he sighed heavily, "Marco, it's your wife."

# Chapter 18:

✝

# Standoff at St. Joseph's

Lily-Rose continued making her way down the narrow trail, away from the castle. Her bare feet were freezing and the thin slip she wore was certainly not enough to keep her warm. She was thankful there was a trail at all, even if it was mostly grown over. Her captors had no need for it, they could fly through the sky. It was the man that had pierced the palm of her hand, taking some of her blood, that still had need of it, traveling to and from the castle to the village and beyond. She wondered how the townsfolk below had never noticed him but attributed it to all the supernatural goings-on inside the castle and whatever gifts Antonin had *blessed* him with.

Yellow eyes watched warily but never attacked. She sensed many were keeping pace with her. She had started her trek down the mountain in a run then slowed, needing to conserve her energy. She knew Antonin's blood had given her newfound strength but her need to feed was so severe she simply couldn't continue at the faster pace.

As she slowed, so did the wolves. No other creature was stirring in the hazy forest. She squinted her eyes to see but all that surrounded her were trees, dirt, and yellow glowing eyes piercing the other-worldly fog that swirled around her. *I'm in a nightmare fairy tale and the big bad wolf is continually at my side, not letting me out of its sight* she thought bitterly.

Her eyes ached from the daylight, and for once she was thankful for the fog and gloom, certain that direct sunlight would be nearly impossible to bear. Still, she knew she hadn't fully changed into one of them, not yet at least. Much worse than the pain she felt in her eyes was the gnawing and burning sensation in her stomach. At times it was so intense she stopped, bent over, and dry heaved.

Lily-Rose could only imagine the strength she would have now if she had only torn into the flesh of the dead bartender back in the castle's dungeon. Whenever her mind went to the carcass that Ingrid had supplied her with, saliva began to formulate in her mouth and slip through her lips, dripping onto the dirt below as well as her silk slip. It was then that she would feel slight bursts of heat run through her body, as if it knew exactly what she needed and was sending her brain signals to supply it with the sustenance to quelch the hunger pangs. But no relief came.

She wondered if she could make it the entire way back down the mountain in the state she was in—intense burning in her stomach coupled with cold outer flesh. This was hell, or close to it.

†

While Lily-Rose made her way down the winding trail of the mountain, inside the castle, Antonin Visimar slumbered. He never slept in his undead state, he merely entered a deep calm, a rejuvenation period for his immortal flesh, reborn from the wolves his master sent forth. This deep calm was usually, not surprisingly, during the daylight hours as that was when he was his weakest and least formidable.

If he would have been fully alert and awake, as he had been several hours earlier, he would have sensed the girl with her own set of new superhuman powers, *gifted* to her by Antonin himself, pushing through the bars of the dungeon opening.

Antonin rested on the altar in his private chamber atop the stone slab that had laid claim to many human sacrifices, young and old alike, primarily women but sometimes men. Resting atop his bare chest was the amulet, safe and sound back to its rightful owner, almost all of it. The gem inside the locket glowed dimly in the half-darkened room lit only by the single torch on the wall above.

The gray wolf was restless, awaiting its orders to retrieve the girl it had sensed fleeing by foot who was to be a prize that belonged to their true master, not the man lying on this altar. They were, at least temporarily, beholden to this man they had granted new life to.

It sat upright, its glowing yellow eyes staring straight ahead at the entrance, ready to spring to action at the slightest of commands. It made no sound; it knew better and knew the current chain of command, at least until its true master returned. The girl must live to feast on the sister once the remaining piece of the amulet was returned, sweet revenge for the transgressions of one Alfred Burns, vampire hunter.

Antonin rocked his head slowly back and forth.

†

The rapping on the door to St. Joseph's continued, now with the added voice of Everly behind it. "Open this damned door, Gustloff! I know you're in there and I know that good-for-nothing husband of mine is hiding in there as well!" she hissed.

Sighing, Marco walked toward the door, but Caspar held his hand out stopping him and whispered, "Wait, Fr. Gustloff might be able to get rid of her."

"Who is this woman? She sounds angry," Juliette said, noticing the grim looks that had fallen over everyone's faces.

"That would be my wife, Everly," Marco answered with a sigh.

Fr. Gustloff cracked the door slightly and looked out at the angry woman standing in the doorway, now attempting to push her way inside.

"What can I do for you, Mrs. Seiler?" Fr. Gustloff asked in as calm a voice as he could muster.

"I want my husband out here, that's what. I know he's in there, come on!" she screamed, quickly slipping through the doors until she stood inside the church, looking over the small group.

"Mrs. Seiler, now is not the time," Fr. Gustloff stated.

"Oh, now's a great time. From the looks of it, there couldn't be a better time than right *now*. You all look like you're planning on going somewhere," Everly stated.

Ignoring her, Marco said to the group, "Let's go, time's a wasting."

"Don't you ignore me, damnit!"

Instantly, Juliette didn't like her. Her eyes were cold, her demeanor was unbecoming, and thus far, she appeared to be downright nasty both inside and out. She tried her best to ignore the ugly woman and grab the items they were taking with them.

"And who do you think you are?" Everly said, walking over to the new face in town. "You must be that Lily-Rose whore's sister. I can see the resemblance."

Without missing a beat, Juliette looked up and slapped the woman hard across the face. The hand connecting with skin reverberated through the small church, nearly knocking a stunned Everly backwards off her feet.

Instantly, a flabbergasted Everly grabbed her burning cheek with both hands and looked appalled at this woman that had the audacity to touch her. "Why you little," she began as she felt hot tears forming in her eyes.

"If you come one step closer, you'll get that again, only worse. Do you understand? Nod if you understand," Juliette said in a calm, controlled voice.

Everly stood in stunned silence, staring into the woman's eyes trained on hers with an unblinking, determined look on her face.

Juliette's hand twitched slightly, as if she were preparing to deliver a nose-breaking punch. Everly gave the briefest of flinches then turned to face the men. Not uttering another word, still clenching her stinging cheek, she put her head down and hurried out of the church. She didn't want any of them to see her tears of surprise, pain, and most importantly, embarrassment. Immediately, she headed up the path and onto the cobblestone street toward the bürgermeister's house on the hill.

Stunned silence filled the room as the wide-eyed men looked at each other then to Juliette, who remained stone-faced but breathing heavily.

Nick cleared his throat, breaking the silence. "Pardon my language, ma'am but, holy shit."

Caspar added, "No offense to Marco, but that *was* impressive."

"I suppose I should apologize to you, Marco, but no one calls my sister a whore, I don't care who you are," Juliette said, turning to face the large man who himself was taken aback by the powerful slap to Everly, who had it coming for the past twenty-plus years.

"You're alright in my book," Marco replied, then turned and said his goodbye to Fr. Gustloff, receiving a blessing. He made a sign of the cross, taking a crucifix from the priest, and walked out of the church. Nick and Juliette followed behind.

Caspar was the last to leave. "Father, I know you can't come along. And I'm sure it's for the best, but having a man of the cloth with us for what we are likely to encounter up there…" he trailed off.

Fr. Gustloff put his hand of Caspar's shoulder, looking him in the eye. "Son, I need to be here. The people of this town need me, plus, I wouldn't make it halfway up there with my heart, we both know that. You have what it takes to vanquish the evil that lies up there more than I do."

He handed Caspar his own personal crucifix, blessing the man and offering his hand to shake. "The Lord be with you, my son."

By the time they were outside and up the path, the bürgermeister's door was open and Everly was flailing her arms, shouting in his face and pointing down to the church.

Marco said quietly to Caspar walking beside him, "She's in charge. Mark my words, she is now in charge."

Fr. Gustloff stood in his doorway, watching the four of them walk up the cobblestone street until they were out of sight. "I fear for us all. Lord, be with them. Be with us all, amen."

They hurried toward the Murreys', passing Dr. Heuberger's office, where he met them outside after Constable Hecht had visited him earlier to inform him of their plan.

"Doc, I don't mean to sound grim, but I'm not sure if we're all coming back down that mountain. Everly Seiler is on the warpath, and I would assume Bürgermeister Hartjenstein, Constable Hecht, and Fr. Gustloff are going to have their hands full. Help them out by keeping the peace, if at all possible," Caspar informed him.

"You have my word on that. I wish you weren't doing this, but I imagine it will fall on deaf ears," the doctor said grimly.

"Joachim, you know as well as we do, there is an evil up there and it needs to be stopped. This is Lily-Rose's sister, and she has something we believe belonged to it, possibly a key to stopping the evil up there," Caspar replied back.

The doctor nodded, shaking Juliette's hand. "Nice to meet you, ma'am. I would tell you to steer clear of that mountain and what lies within, but I feel as though that has already been discussed with you."

"Nice to meet you, Joachim, and yes. I have been warned. My sister is up there and I'm not leaving until I rescue her or figure out what is happening here."

"I understand, truly I do. Be careful, all of you. I will keep a close eye on the town along with Constable Hecht." Joachim began stepping back into his small clinic.

"Watch out for my wife, Joachim," Marco said quietly.

Upon hearing this, the doctor stopped short of closing the door to his office, seeing how serious the man was. He nodded in reply and closed the door behind him.

Once at the Murreys', old man Maxwell greeted them on his front porch with a curious expression. "What brings you all out here? I don't think we've met before, have we, missy?" He extended his old, wrinkled hand toward Juliette who took it graciously.

"My name is Juliette Burns. We are heading up that mountain to find my missing sister," she said matter-of-factly.

Nick added, "And stop whatever is killing off the towns-folk."

"Is that so? You know this is against the bürgermeister's rules, right?" Maxwell replied, wrinkling his nose. The old man was the human equivalent to a raisin. All wrinkles. His wife was similar in shape and size. The had lived in Burnmere their whole lives, as had their parents. The children they had a lifetime ago had long since moved far away. The Murreys, however, couldn't part with their home and their horses.

"The bürgermeister doesn't care about any of us. Every single person in this town knows full well his rules are all about keeping us put while he robs us blind. So, it's up to us to stop whatever the hell is going on up in that castle," Marco said with cold determination.

"Is that so?" Maxwell said, slightly taken aback by the authority Marco suddenly seemed to carry himself with, something he hadn't seen out of the man before today. He looked over, seeing his wife Jane come out to the porch to join them.

She looked at the guests on her front porch nervously, stopping on Juliette, the stranger in the group. "You must be Lily-Rose's sister, you look like her. We're truly sorry that she is missing," Jane Murrey said kindly.

Nodding, Juliette answered, "I am indeed, she's up there. I just know she is."

"And you need some horses to get you where you're going, that so?" Jane continued, putting her hands on her frail hips.

Maxwell looked at his old wife, "Dear, I'm taking care of—"

"Take what you need. Stop the evil up there, everyone in town knows this place is cursed, even Bürgermeister Hartjenstein himself, though he'll deny it till his dying day.

God speed to you all," Jane cut him off, looking at all of the guests on their porch.

"Now, wait just one ever loving minute!" Maxwell began, perturbed at the sudden possibility he was about to lose four of his horses, but realizing his wife, and Marco Seiler of all people, spoke the truth. Everyone in town knew it and he had to admit, so did he.

"Maxwell, you and I have seen things no human has any right seeing in our lives," Jane replied curtly, adding, "it all comes from that castle. I'm not a superstitious person but one thing I am sure of, Castle Visimar is an evil place and if horses will get them up there faster, then go. What use are they to us here?" She paused, looking from her angry husband over to the travelers in front of her on her porch, primarily, Juliette. "But you should know, once night falls, whatever is up there feeds. And the daylight hours are ticking away. It's already nearly four in the afternoon, but from the cloud cover, you'd think it's dusk."

"Ma'am, thank you kindly. Maxwell, we will not take any horses unless you give us the go ahead. This is serious, but we won't come between you and your wife," Caspar added cautiously, knowing he needed both of them to sign off on this.

Maxwell studied the three men and the new arrival in town, Juliette, standing in front of him and shook his head. "I would say that I fear I will never see the horses again but more importantly, I will likely never see all of you again either. That includes you, missy. I hope I'm wrong, but you shouldn't be here, this place is not a place for newcomers as I suspect you have figured out by now."

"I'm getting my sister. I've traveled far and I'm not stopping. Horses or no horses," Juliette responded grimly.

Sighing, Maxwell pointed to his stables. "Then go. Saddles are in the barn, they're fed."

"You'll be compensated," Marco began but stopped. He had no way of paying the generous couple.

"Damn right, I'll be compensated," Maxwell stated gruffly before rethinking his words. He shrugged his shoulders, adding, "I suppose compensation will be succeeding in whatever you set out to accomplish. Come on, follow me." Maxwell hung his head and made his way off his porch, over to the stables. His wife Jane smiling at his stubborn agreeance to help these people out. People that were actually trying to do something, anything really…to stop what had destroyed all hope in Burnmere.

They thanked Jane then quickly moved to the stables with Maxwell who selected a horse for each of them to match up their weight and height

As they were about to mount, Caspar said to the group, "I can't promise what we're going to find up there or if we'll make it back, but damnit, we're going to try. Juliette, last chance, you sure about this?"

She nodded.

Once saddled up, they all climbed onto their new rides up the mountain, thanking Maxwell who gave them a nod, and rode off toward the edge of town where a small, nearly hidden path lay beyond the trees—the starting point for their journey up the mountain.

✝

Watching from a distance, Marcel sat silently atop his black horse, furious at the four travelers heading toward his master's castle. To the woman he uttered, "Good, you will never leave, mark my words," then began his own trek up the mountain, intent on intercepting them and thinning the herd along the way. Likely with the assistance of the creatures of the forest and, as night fell, Ingrid.

# Chapter 19:

✝

# Rude Awakening

ntonin Visimar's thoughts drifted while in his meditative state. He enjoyed this time typically, his mind wandering through countless years of existence before his untimely demise and rebirth. After the incident with Alfred Burns, he had grown more animalistic, likely from the blood of the feral animals that lay at his feet, sent to him by his master.

His body felt less human than it ever had before. The blood of the villagers rarely quenched his hunger and thirst any longer and were reserved now for Ingrid, a task she specialized in. His desires had changed but one remained, to obtain the complete amulet containing the gem dating back to Christ's birth. Once the necklace was retrieved and placed alongside the amulet the incantation ceremony would begin.

His mind drifted as he pictured the beautiful amulet. *I must revive my master, that is my mission, that is why I am here, that is why I exist.*

He knew Marcel continued on his mission to bring the remaining necklace back to him. The gold from the necklace and amulet was a mystery to him; originally black as the night, once the gem was encased inside, it had turned to the appearance of gold. The combination of the gold-colored mineral and the gem created a powerful supernatural object.

Soon, the amulet and necklace would be together again inside the castle, and the incantations recited in their entirety from the ancient, sacred scrolls the Traveler left behind so many years earlier. He was eager to find out how it would all come together in resurrecting his master. *Hopefully he will be proud of me and all of my many accomplishments!*

Thoughts and images continued swirling through his mind in his resting state, increasing in intensity. He felt the end approaching, his master's return imminent. From there on, a new world would begin. One that was to have started one hundred years ago, before Alfred Burns' arrival. Now, his lineage would pay the ultimate price. He would have preferred to do away with both of the Burns sisters instantly, but his master, the Pricolici demon, had other plans.

*Awaken,* a voice whispered in his head. Antonin opened his eyes; he was no longer alone in his altar room. Or was it the altar room in his mind? Was he still in his slumbering state? He couldn't be sure. He wasn't lying down any longer, he was kneeling at the altar. A presence was in front of him. On either side the wolves were on all fours, growling at him.

"Master? What do you ask of me?" Antonin said.

The voice whispered back, "While you slumber, plans are underway to undo all that we have worked for. You failed me once before; I am troubled by these new developments and have created a plan."

Antonin searched his mind; his master spoke the truth.

"This will be your fate if you fail me, Antonin Visimar," the voice hissed.

He then saw in his mind the wolves on either side of him lunging forward, tearing into his flesh. Their huge jaws sinking deep then ripping out large chunks. He was helpless to resist their attacks. The black wolf ripped his throat out, much like its brethren had done to the innocents of Burnmere and surrounding villages. After the wolves finished their mauling, he felt his body lifted high in the air inside the altar room. The flame from the single torch lunged upward, instantly igniting him. The fire did its job, much like it had one hundred years prior, burning him until he was little more than a charred shell.

Opening his eyes, Antonin looked around his dimly lit altar room, shaken by the vision his master had shown him. He sat up, looking down at the foot of the altar where both of the wolves sat, awaiting his command. The black wolf was now back inside the altar room after its journey to Everly's house.

*Why are they alert at this time of the day?*

"The girl!" he shouted, gripping the amulet tightly and bounding out of the room. The wolves ran after him as he raced toward the entrance leading to the dungeon.

Effortlessly, he swooped down, landing easily on his feet onto the damp, cold dirt below as the wolves remained up top, awaiting further commands.

Antonin scanned the dungeon, all was quiet. The mutilated remains of another faceless, worthless human lay in a heap on the ground. He walked past it to what had caught his eye instantly, the opened coffin.

He peered into the opened coffin, the young woman he had drunk from upon his retrieval of the amulet was not there. *Not where she should be.*

In a single jump, he leapt from the open and empty coffin to where Ingrid lay in her slumber. He ripped the lid open and inside lay Ingrid with her eyes closed, beautiful as ever in this relatively peaceful state.

Antonin grabbed hold of her, yanking her up and out of the coffin with such force it nearly cracked her spine. She barely had time to open her eyes when he threw her as hard as he could through the air, smashing her into the stone wall.

Instinctively, Ingrid's fangs protruded, her bat-like wings pushing through her pale skin and sprouting from her back, spreading wide. She contorted her body back to a standing position, ready to attack whatever had made the grave error of assaulting her in her sleep. Springing forward with wings flapping, she lunged through the air at her assailant then stopped short of latching onto him, dropping to the dirt.

Angrily, she hissed as she looked into Antonin's rage-filled eyes. He was her master and could do with her as he pleased. But she had never been awakened from her slumber and pummeled against a wall by him.

"What have I done to incur this, master!?" Ingrid said in a barely controlled tone, fighting back her rage. She was no match for this man, and she knew it.

He said nothing, pointing a bony finger toward the opened casket.

Her eyes traveled with his finger and at once scanned the room, they were indeed alone. Both coffins were empty.

"You let her escape. She was to feast, then sleep! How did this happen?" Antonin said in a barely contained rage.

"I saw her go to sleep! I watched her! My lord, I don't understand how," she began.

"Silence!" he bellowed.

She instantly fell silent. They both looked toward the bars.

"Master, the bars," Ingrid said, her eyes glaring in their direction.

"Her body is changing. She's a feisty one, figuring out how to contort her body to squeeze through. Other than your dear sister, we have never seen a scenario such as this," Antonin said, regaining his composure.

"I will retrieve her, my lord," Ingrid said bitterly.

"No! *I will retrieve her*," Antonin cut her off with teeth gritted, fuming at the Burns woman's escape. "Leave her to me. As dusk arrives, you will go to the town below, kill everything in sight. They have existed far too long, and the time of our master is nearing. We have no more use for the meat below, he will provide for us upon his return." Antonin said coldly.

Ingrid, silently raging at Lily-Rose and embarrassed at failing Antonin, asked, "So I have your permission to openly and freely kill at will all in the town of Burnmere?"

"Yes, If anyone is traversing the mountains, take care of them first. Everyone but the Burns sister, I feel the presence of the necklace nearing," he spat back, still filled with rage at this new setback.

"Yes, it shall be done," Ingrid replied. She glanced out through the bars and saw dim light still shining through. Soon dusk would arrive, and she would do what she did best, hunt.

Antonin didn't say another word. Instead, he floated up off the dirt, then shot up through the hole in the ceiling, through the castle and out its highest peak.

*You may run, little Lily-Rose Burns, but from me, there is no escape.*

Below, the two wolves exited through the front door, taking off into the forest, hunting their own prey.

The fog that hung in the air and clung to the trees seemed to travel with Antonin, swirling around him and clearing the way in front of him. Far below, the town of Burnmere lay quietly awaiting its demise. As he glided slowly through the foggy, gray sky, he said aloud, "Tonight, you all will perish, starting with the Burns sister, mark my words."

✝

Standing outside the bürgermeister's house, Everly explained to Hartjenstein what she suspected was going on. Marco and his new band of merry men were traveling up the forbidden mountain. She pointed as the men, along with Lily-Rose's sister, left the church.

Still reeling from Caspar's shaming and the forced sexual encounter with Everly, Hartjenstein had certainly had better days. He was becoming more and more intimidated by the woman standing in front of him, taking several steps back as she took several small ones toward him. Her rotten breath hitting his nose hard, he shuddered to think his member had been inside that disgusting mouth of hers, no matter how good it felt for the brief time they had indulged.

"Well, aren't you going to do something?" she shouted with newfound aggression.

"What would you have me do? When they come back down, *if* they come back down, they will immediately be arrested. But you don't expect me to go looking for them! If they're that hell-bent on getting eaten by the wolves, I say, let them!"

"If any of them come back down, I want to be there for the arrests. In the meantime, what about the priest? He has been conspiring with them! Undermining your authority at every single turn!" Everly shouted, spittle ejecting from her rotten mouth, some of which hit Hartjenstein in the face. She knew this and it brought her great pleasure knowing he was repulsed, seeing him recoil. She felt powerful, alive once more, using her ugliness both inside and out as a means of control.

"Very well, I will go speak with the priest. Go to Constable Hecht, tell him I'm coming in with Gustloff. I have a sneaking suspicion he may be in on this. Inform him that I sent you to retrieve him. I'm tired of all this insubordination!" the bürgermeister replied, buying into Everly's lies.

He quickly pushed past her. Anything to get away from her.

Everly smiled slyly, *I'm to fetch the constable. Me!*

While she hurried toward the police station, Bürgermeister Hartjenstein went to the church, sighing at the day's downward turning of events. While walking down the hill toward the small parish, he looked toward the mountain where the fog continued getting heavier and appeared to be moving, flowing down. He shuddered with a sinking feeling that the day was going to get nothing but worse, not just for him but the entire town of Burnmere as well.

On his way to the church, several townsfolk passed him, looking the other way. He knew he was hated in this town and, frankly, didn't care. A job was a job, and this was the one given to him. One that he had made himself quite wealthy over. Why should he live in misery with the rest of these hopeless cases? He had simply made the best out of a bad situation.

Eventually, he would move on and relocate once the town was truly dead and, with roughly one hundred people left, the writing was on the wall. With more elderly people dying off and the wolves continually whittling away at the rest, this town would mercifully be little more than a bad memory to all who had the good fortune of fleeing it while they had the chance. Until then, however, Bürgermeister Hartjenstein would continue to profit off of their misery. Now, unfortunately, it seemed with the added unwanted and unneeded help from Everly Seiler.

Without bothering to knock on the door, Hartjenstein pushed it open and walked through, unhappy that he had to visit St. Joseph's again in the same day. Looking around, he found the old overweight priest kneeing at the altar praying. He was saying Mass for a party of exactly one, himself.

*What the hell is he doing?* Hartjenstein wondered, moving forward and not bothering to bless himself. He had no use for organized religion or any religion, for that matter. His religion was one of *take what you need, take what you want and live luxuriously while you can, regardless of those you trample over.* Something he excelled in through his years as bürgermeister.

"What are you doing, Gustloff?" He was no father to him or anyone in this shithole town.

"Amen," Father Gustloff stated, then looked up after consecrating the bread and the wine. With his eyes closed, he ate the wafer then drank the small amount of water and wine in his old chalice.

"Peace be with you, Samuel Hartjenstein," Father Gustloff stated, opening his eyes and looking him in the eye.

"Pfft, what am I supposed to say, *and with your spirit* or some such drivel?" the bürgermeister replied coldly.

Father Gustloff nodded yes, then cleared the altar of the sacramental items and bowed deeply before turning to address Hartjenstein, knowing full well why the man was there. She had sent for him.

"So, a group of people left for the forest mountain and more importantly, the castle above. Is that correct? Or is Mrs. Seiler mistaken?" Hartjenstein said impatiently, starting to regain his authoritative posturing now that Everly was no longer in his presence and Caspar was likely in the forest now as they spoke.

"Bürgermeister, you know as well as I do, a great evil plagues this land. We are now finally doing something about it. If not the brave individuals that travel there now, then who? You? I feel your primary concern in the town of Burnmere is self-preservation and more importantly, self-gratification," Fr. Gustloff said with not just a hint of condemnation and contempt.

"How dare you make such accusations! You! A supposed man of God, what insolence! I have been tasked with protecting this village and my orders are absolute, no one is permitted to travel up that mountain! Even scum like Marco! Yet you, priest, sent them on their merry way. I watched out my window as they arrived and left. You are to blame for this superstitious mumbo-jumbo!"

"I will take full responsibility, what would you have me do?" Father Gustloff replied calmly.

Bürgermeister Hartjenstein shouted back, "I'm taking you in, that's what. I was hired to uphold the law, something our constable seems to be unable to do. Maybe I should install the Seiler woman to replace him. She stinks, but rest assured, things would get done. This lack of respect toward those in authority over this town will come to an abrupt halt."

"Things would get done, you say. Oh yes, indeed, things get done with her," Father Gustloff answered, still calm and controlled, unlike the increasingly agitated bürgermeister.

Ignoring the comment, Hartjenstein fired back, "I'm done arguing with a self-righteous man like you, let's go."

"Gladly, I have nothing to hide," Fr. Gustloff answered and turned to walk out of his parish. He blessed himself on the way out then felt a slight shove from the bürgermeister to move, his calm demeanor continuing to anger the agitated man more with each passing moment.

They made their way through the cobblestone streets in silence, townsfolk watching them as they passed. School was letting out for the day, the school children all filed out quietly one by one from Hartjenstein's old house with their teacher Miss Shalner watching the scene unfold. She glared at the bürgermeister as he gave a nod to her, knowing it would upset her. She turned around, slamming the door behind her as the last child exited the building.

Another individual watching them leave the parish was Doctor Heuberger. He nodded to the priest who nodded back, neither smiling and both knowing full what was currently at stake.

"What are you looking at? Don't you have sick people to attend to, Joachim?" Hartjenstein muttered, pushing Fr. Gustloff's back to keep him moving, nearly causing him to trip and fall on the uneven cobblestone street.

Heuberger glared at the bully then continued on his way. He knew something like this was bound to happen, which was why he was here visiting this part of town, to keep a watchful eye out. To see just how bad it may get now that a group of townsfolk had actually defied the bürgermeister's long standing orders to *never* go into those woods.

He wasn't a strong man, quite the opposite, but he knew that the only way to let evil win was for good men to do nothing. And that had been slowly happening year after year in Burnmere.

He looked toward the mountain, knowing his friends were traversing it now. Fog swirled around the castle and through the treetops in an eerie display, the likes of which he had never seen, even in this godforsaken town. The fog seemed to have a mind of its own, slowly rolling down toward Burnmere.

"Whatever is in that fog comes for us and comes for those that dared enter its domain. I fear the evil is already amongst us now," Heuberger said to himself quietly, continuing to watch the fog roll in.

# Chapter 20:

†

# Traversing
# the Mountain

ily-Rose continued on her downward trek to the town below. Covered in dirt, she was tired and hungry, constantly hungry. A hunger that got worse with every passing hour. She tried to find ways of alleviating the hunger pangs by thinking of life back in England. Thoughts of her sister and her mother when she had been alive, the sun shining down on the cottage they called home. Now so very far away, in another life.

The daylight was turning to dusk. Soon, Ingrid and Antonin would be in pursuit, if they weren't already, but the sharp daggers in the pit of her stomach were so severe she couldn't move any faster.

She pushed on, sticking to the trail and setting landmarks in front of her in an attempt to stay focused and determined to get to the next tree, large rock, or bend in the trail. The little game she made for herself alleviated the pain for a moment, but it always returned, in full force.

The wolves of the forest continued to keep pace with her. Just out of range, stalking past tree cover, watching and waiting with uncaring and emotionless yellow eyes. However, they weren't the only ones now in pursuit of the escaped Lily-Rose.

✝

Much farther down on the trail, several more pairs of yellow eyes peered through trees deep in the forest at the mountain's newest arrivals. Caspar led the way up the winding path. It was narrow but wide enough that they could ride two by two. Juliette had made her way up to Caspar while Marco and Nick rode behind them.

"Can we make it up there before nightfall?" Juliette asked, lightly gripping the reins of Ginger, her gray and white speckled horse, looking out into the trees that surrounded them on either side. They were still relatively low on the mountain where periodic flatter areas presented a nice break for the horses.

Caspar looked up to the sky. "Well, the sun appears to be on the move through the cloud cover so soon it will be dusk. We have a long way to go, but I'm confident we can make it."

She nodded then instinctively reached up and clenched the gold necklace around her neck. "What has my sister gone and got herself into?" Juliette said sadly, glancing over at Caspar.

Sighing, Caspar thought for a bit then replied, "The way I see it, and trust me, I'm no expert on the occult or any of this superstitious witchcraft really, but it all started with your great-grandfather. Then it worked its way down to the both of you. And now you're hopefully finishing what he started all those years ago. One hundred years ago, if what Fr. Gustloff said was accurate from his findings in the meager town hall records."

"I've never believed in vampires or witches or any of that stuff either. Even knowing what my great-grandfather was called, I didn't believe it. I always thought he must have been a superstitious witch hunter and part of the inquisition, murdering innocent women throughout the countryside. Yet another reason I wanted to stay far away from that amulet, I feared it had innocent blood on it. But I might be wrong about several things, it seems," Juliette replied.

"Me too, Juliette. I saw something and heard something—a woman's voice that took our town bartender. She almost hissed the words mockingly at Marco and me. I'll never forget that voice," Caspar said with a shudder.

Juliette looked ahead toward the castle shrouded in fog. "What's the story with the fog around here?

"It's always been like this in Burnmere. I attribute it to the castle. Scientifically, there might be a logical reason but I sure as hell can't find any. It's almost as if the fog hides this town from the rest of humanity, even the world."

"I was able to find it alright, with the help of a kind-hearted carriage driver named Daniel. I almost made the mistake of taking a ride from a gentleman that claimed to know my sister. He was a scary fellow; I believe he said his name was Marcel," Juliette said, shivering at the thought of the dark man.

Caspar looked at her nervously. "He said he met your sister? I've never heard that name before. Whoever he is, he doesn't live in Burnmere. Everyone knows everyone in town."

"He was up to no good and, if I'm honest, I fear we may cross paths again," Juliette said as she shifted her eyes on either side of the trail, expecting him to jump out in front of them.

Caspar grinned and glanced over at her.

"Is that funny to you?" Juliette said slightly taken aback at his chuckle.

"Oh, I believe you, I do. You seem to be able to handle yourself well, is all. You did what every living soul in Burnmere, her husband included, would like to do back at St.

Joseph's. You slapped Everly Seiler across the face," Caspar said quiet enough so that Marco couldn't hear him, although he suspected Marco could have hugged Juliette for delivering the powerful blow to a woman that truly and wholeheartedly deserved it.

Juliette looked over at him as their horse each began another steep incline around a windy bend. "No one talks about my sister that way. She has proven, especially since our mother's passing, to be quite headstrong and stubborn, but she's my only sister and I love her dearly, and she knows it."

"I'm sure she does, and I plan on doing my best to find her and help bring those that took her to justice. I was looking forward to getting to know her more," Caspar said, then thought better of saying more.

"Well now, that certainly doesn't surprise me," Juliette said with a grin.

"What do you mean?"

"I mean…you're a handsome man, she's attractive and at times rather forward, so that would make sense."

Caspar looked over at Juliette, "Oh, she wasn't forward with me, not at all. In fact, she was quite the opposite. She seemed distant and quite troubled. I mean, she was friendly, but it felt as though it was a one-sided courting." He paused, feeling slightly awkward at the direction this conversation had taken.

"That is indeed interesting. That's not the Lily I know," Juliette said. "The Lily I know would have certainly played hard to get but in her own mischievous and fun way. Not, as you say, distant. Which is exactly how she acted before leaving home. Distant and troubled,"

They both fell silent, deep in thought. Juliette glanced back at the two men trailing them who remained silent and just out of earshot.

"I'm not sure those two have spoken a word to each other since we left. If this journey is as dangerous as I suspect it will be, they should probably get along, right?" Juliette asked genuinely curious, especially about the large man named Marco.

Caspar was quick to reply. "There is certainly no love lost between those two. Hell, Marco doesn't much care for me either. In a town of one hundred, Marco and Nick are considered the two biggest, how shall I say this nicely?"

From behind, Marco shouted up, "Losers, drunks, dead-enders?"

Silence fell among the four of them.

Marco rode a few trots closer to Caspar and Juliette, then continued. "It's true, we are losers and drunks. I can't speak for Nick but the only good thing in my life, my son, Christoph, moved far away years ago. I have a wife that makes my life a living hell, and as far as friends go, what you see here is it. So, Miss Juliette, I want to do something good before I die, something that might leave the smallest mark on this stain of a town that's a positive. Not be another lost soul whose life was wasted in a bar drinking himself to death. There are innocent people being killed and I aim to put a long overdue stop to it, with the help of everyone here."

Looking back at Marco, Juliette caught his eye and smiled. Not a smile of pity, but of understanding. Something else in the smile Marco couldn't pinpoint, surely not attraction? No way. For one, he was married, even if to a completely wretched and horrible person. For another, he was *Marco*. No woman had ever truly admired him, ever. And, they had just met mere hours ago.

Marco fell silent and looked away from Juliette after their eyes had locked for a brief time. He couldn't believe he had just called Nick and Caspar his friends. Countless nights he sat at the bar arguing with old Nick, who argued back. They hated each other, or so they thought at the time. But they were, whether he liked it or not, all he had left in the town of Burnmere.

Caspar looked back at the large man, "I believe you just called us your friends, Marco. I'll be damned!" He chuckled.

Nick was grinning as well, adding, "He ain't lying, we are a pair of drunks, but right now I can't think of anyone else on this crazy trek up this mountain that I would rather be riding with. What's the saying? The enemy of my enemy is my friend?"

Caspar heard the words and shot Marco a look behind him, words he had spoken earlier to Marco. Hearing this, Marco gave each a nod in agreement.

Once more, they fell silent as their horses continued to climb higher up the trail and the yellow eyes continued to move about in between the trees. Silently keeping pace with the intruders while staying well hidden.

Nick mumbled quietly, so only Marco could hear, "You're still a sonofabitch, don't forget that."

Marco, who thought he saw something flash by from the corner of his eye in the tree cover a second ago, glanced at Nick beside him and glared, then slowly his face softened, his frown turning to a slight grin. Seeing Nick grinning back, both men began laughing.

Juliette and Caspar glanced back. "Seems as though they don't hate each other as much as they thought they did," Juliette said with a grin.

"When and if things get hairy, I know we'll all have each other's back. That's what's most important, trusting each other," Caspar said smiling.

"What happened to Marco? The side of his neck is black and blue. I felt it best to not pry, bar fight I presume?" Juliette asked quiet enough that Marco and Nick wouldn't overhear.

"That was compliments of our own Bürgermeister Hartjenstein. He truly is one nasty piece of shit, pardon my French. Having said that, he and I did had an argument yesterday and so I suppose I must take the blame for some of it. Marco was actually speaking truth, and no one wanted to listen," Caspar said, ashamed of what had taken place inside the Pale Horse the previous day.

She nodded, glancing back at Marco. Something about the large, broad-shouldered, black-haired man endeared her to him. She wasn't sure if it was the eyes that might have been soft and full of kindness at one time, and maybe, just maybe, that kindness still lived deep inside this obviously hurt and hardened man.

As they continued on their way up the mountain, Juliette told the men more about the necklace she wore, how it seemed to give off a warmth on her neck once she reached the town of Burnmere, intensifying as they continued traversing up the mountain.

"Now that is interesting, indeed," Nick said at this strange detail. "My mama, God rest her soul, used to tell me a story when I was a little boy about how, somewhere here in Europe, magic came from deep in the earth. It was black and it glowed warm, and the boogeyman came from it. Pricolici is what momma used to call it."

"Pricolici? I've heard of that. A huge beast, part werewolf, part vampire. I wasn't aware the story went that it came from deep in the earth. Do you suppose it's referring to hell?" Marco looked warily over at Nick.

"That's what my mama would say." Nick paused, recalling the story. "Legend goes that some magic stone from Bible times would one day bring the demon to life from the fiery depths below. That and a list of some kind of religious incantations read aloud. When that happened, the Pricolici would take its true form to rule the land for its master, Satan.

Free to roam the countryside hunting for naughty boys and girls, as my mama would say… " he trailed off, knowing it sounded far-fetched.

Juliette chimed in, "We had a jeweler look at the amulet a while back who claimed he had never seen such gold and surmised it may not have even been gold at all. The old man didn't want to have anything to do with it, however. I always found that to be quite strange. When Lily became obsessed with coming here, she kept touching the amulet that never left her neck. I would remind her of what she was doing and ask her why she continually touched it."

Caspar prodded Juliette gently, "And? Did you ever find out why she was touching the amulet?"

Snapping out of her memories, Juliette replied, "She said sometimes it felt warm and was making her skin itch."

Nick continued remembering more of the tale his mother would tell him. "She used to say, 'You will know the evil is awakening when the stone heats to your touch!'" He shuddered to himself, recalling how the thought had terrified him as a child, and now, as they made their way up the creepy mountain, still did.

Juliette shuddered at this connection. "I wonder how much of this is legend and how much could be truth?" She unconsciously touched her own warming necklace.

Chuckling, Nick replied, "How the hell should I know? It's a folk tale. Werewolves, vampires, magic stones, and villainous beings out to bring the dreaded Pricolici back to rule the land for its own father, Lucifer."

Caspar and Marco exchanged a long look, then Marco said what he assumed they were both thinking. "Could the legend of Pricolici actually be real? Maybe Antonin Visimar, one time holder of the amulet that Lily-Rose wore, is a follower of this Pricolici. I've heard different variations of the story myself. That this small 'magic' stone became encrusted in the vile, shapeshifting creature's black crystal from below. Then was painted and molded to resemble a priceless piece of jewelry. A priceless and evil item that a certain great-grandfather of the sisters now in Burnmere took after murdering Visimar."

"And if any of this is to be believed, your sister has possibly delivered that very amulet back into the hands of whatever is up there," Caspar said to Juliette.

"I can't believe I'm hearing this; this all seems quite far-fetched. However, something *had* taken control over my sister and pulled her to this place. So, whatever it is, we need to stop it," Juliette replied glancing at the men around her.

"Hell, I wouldn't be surprised if—" Nick started to say when his horse reared back, knocking him off its back. A large wolf jumped out from behind the tree cover, lunging at Nick, who had been trailing behind the rest of them by several feet.

Lightning-quick, Marco pulled the shotgun slung over his shoulder, cocked both hammers and aimed before firing at the wolf as it leapt through the air, about to pounce on the fallen Nick, whose rifle had slipped off the holster attached to his horse when it reared back.

The blast was deafening, two slugs blasting into the thick white fur of the wolf. Its neck exploded and it dropped right in front of Nick, killed instantly.

Nick slid away from the dead beast that lay at his feet, quickly scurrying toward the fallen rifle just out of reach in the grassy overgrowth beside him, when he saw a pair of glowing yellow eyes between two trees mere feet away.

"There's more of them!" he shouted, pulling the rifle up to his shoulder. Caspar pulled back on the reins of his horse, bringing it to a full stop, and drew his own rifle, but he didn't have a clear shot without hitting either Juliette or Marco.

Marco, meanwhile, opened the breach of his shotgun, expelling the spent shells and quickly slamming another two into the empty chambers. He closed it and pulled back on the hammers once more.

Juliette found herself in the same predicament as Caspar. As Marco blocked the path where Nick lay, she saw a second wolf leap out from tree cover where it had been stalking them.

Another loud crack echoed through the forest as Nick shot the attacking wolf in its chest. This one also fell at his feet, slightly larger than the first and coated in dark gray fur. Its teeth were frozen in a snarl with a pool of blood already trickling out of its half open mouth.

Nick jumped to his feet, but his horse Sawbuck had taken off in fright, heading back down the path at full speed. Sawbuck didn't get far; two wolves leapt out and attacked the unsuspecting animal that made the mistake of encroaching on their turf.

Looking on in horror, Nick watched as the wolves tore into the helpless horse that attempted to kick them away to no avail. One wolf bit into the horse's long neck while the other leapt onto its side at full force, bringing the horse down to the ground. With a ferocity none of the men had seen yet from any wolf in the Burnmere area, the wolves ripped the horse's leathery flesh with their teeth and long, sharp claws.

"You sonsabitches!" Nick yelled, raising his rifle to his shoulder.

"Nick, no! Save your ammo!" Caspar yelled but Nick fired once more, hitting the wolf that had its horse's neck in its clenched fangs. The brown-furred wolf thrashed violently at the blast that connected with its shoulder.

Seconds later, the wolf relinquished its grip, dropping to the ground. The horse, however, was mortally wounded and no longer struggled against the ripping, biting and tearing of the second gray wolf.

Knowing Caspar was right, Nick frowned at the dying horse, raised his gun and shot it through the head, instantly ending its misery.

The rest of the horses were spooked but a tight grip on their reins from the three remaining riders kept them still.

Caspar offered his hand to Nick, quickly hoisting him up and onto the back of his saddle.

"Let's get the hell out of here!" Marco shouted ahead, quickly motioning with his hand for the rest to follow.

"Agreed!" Juliette chimed in.

Before they turned to make haste, they saw the last wolf cease from its mauling of the horse. It stood with blood dripping from its mouth and fangs, breathing heavily. Its glowing yellow eyes staring at them, through them. Fog slowly wrapped around the carnage, swallowing it up until all that could be seen were the two yellow eyes still peering out at the survivors hungrily.

Taking off once more, they continued up the winding hill, the spooked horses breathing heavily, moving as fast as they could without considering the steep inclines and loose dirt of the trail.

Several minutes after the attack, Caspar, now in the lead, raised his hand for them to slow. Juliette pulled back on her reins as did Marco behind her.

"What is it?" Marco said from the rear.

Nick saw the reason for Caspar's sudden halt on the path. Up ahead, the fog, now heavier, appeared to be forming a thick wall of swirling white clouds they could not see past.

"How are we going to get through that?" Juliette asked bleakly, gripping her necklace that continued feeling warmer and warmer against her flesh the further up the mountain they traversed.

"I'm working on it," Caspar replied, staring ahead as the fog continued to swirl as if it were actively attempting to stop them from going farther up the mountain.

☦

From a much narrower, barely passable path off to the side of those he stalked, Marcel had been traveling silently on his own steed. This was his master's land, and he knew it well. Just as he knew the necklace that belonged to his master was close.

"Come here, little lamb, just a little further. Master was right, the sister of Lily-Rose will come to us," Marcel whispered, watching the riders get closer.

# Chapter 21:

†

# The New Law

Lily-Rose knew she was being pursued; she could sense it. Though she was unsure whether it was the bite she had received the evening before from Count Visimar or simply the eerie otherworldly atmosphere that surrounded her, she knew she was being hunted. It was only a matter of time before her whereabouts were discovered.

She looked up through the fog, above which were more gray clouds covering what was likely dusk. Forest wolves had likely picked up her scent upon her escape and been stalking her, though she couldn't see them. The fog was so thick she felt as though she were in a fairy tale, the kind her mother used to tell her when she was a little girl. Fairy tales that involved Big Bad Wolves hunting little girls. Only this was her own fairy tale, populated by very real werewolves and vampires.

She wondered how long it would take for Count Visimar and Ingrid to take flight and attempt to retrieve her. She sensed, as she had earlier, that he was likely somewhere behind her already in pursuit.

Soon darkness would blanket the forest. She had no torch, very little clothing on, and was barefoot. She no longer set markers for herself; instead, for the past hour she had been running until the pain was too much to bear then she slowed to a walk, repeating the pattern over and over.

*How will I survive the night? Keep moving, Lily-Rose you aren't dead yet,* she told herself, not yet giving up on her brief freedom from the horrors of the dungeon in Castle Visimar.

Her stomach pain came in waves. Right now, it was at its worst, the intense burning so painful she stopped and bent forward. It felt as though someone was ramming a knife that had been held over an open fire into her stomach and there was no reprieve. Just one long, constant flaming hot knife to her guts.

Lily-Rose dry heaved at the immense pain, nearly passing out. Down on all fours, the palms of her hands sunk into the dirt, her knees scratched and covered in filth. She stared at the ground, waiting for the wave of intense agony to subside even slightly so she could stand to her feet and continue on the fog-enshrouded path leading down the mountain.

While she caught her breath in the dirt, she heard a voice in her head. *I will find you, my sweet, tasty Lily-Rose. Then I will find your sister, you will drink from her, then he will take you.* Lily gritted her teeth in pain and anger. It was Antonin, speaking to her.

"You will not take my sister, you monster! I'll die before I let what happened to me happen to her!"

She pulled herself up to a standing position once more and noticed the two wolves that had been stalking her, one on either side of the path, their glowing yellow eyes peering out through the fog.

While Fr. Gustloff was being led to the small-town jail by a completely overwhelmed and flustered Bürgermeister Hartjenstein, Everly Seiler was busy berating Constable Hecht who refused to hand over any town files.

"You've been in cahoots with those men for a while now. You realize how odd it is that you, an upholder of the law in Burnmere, are friendly with the locals? That's not your job, your job is to uphold the law! Something you've exceedingly failed at. So, I'm going to ask you once more, give me the files on all of the town taxes and the citizens payment records!" Everly shouted, pointing her bony finger at the tired and old constable who sighed and hung his head.

"Ma'am, I haven't heard any confirmation from Bürgermeister Hartjenstein that you've been hired by him to go over the paperwork, and until I do, I'm not handing over any town documents. You're shouting at me to uphold the law and that's what I'm doing," Constable Hecht said defiantly. He wished he was off duty and back home with Claudie, his ailing wife. She was at home rotting away with cancer and he was being berated by a truly awful woman in the most thankless job in all of Burnmere.

Everly, loving the feeling of power this was giving her, continued with her aggressive rant. "So, what are you afraid of? Afraid I'm coming for your job, is that it? Well, listen and listen well, I'm done being pushed around! This town needs a bit more law and order. Bürgermeister Hartjenstein is being overworked because his right hand isn't doing its job!"

*She called me an "it", what a wretched bitch.* "Look ma'am, you simply cannot come in here and—" Constable Hecht began.

The front door opened to the jail and Bürgermeister Hartjenstein entered, leading Father Gustloff in. Both Everly and Constable Hecht stopped their arguing and looked at the two men standing in the doorway.

"Constable, lock him up on charges of organizing a criminal group. Forest is unsafe and off-limits, and this man helped orchestrate a posse putting them all in danger," Hartjenstein said, pushing the priest into the small room.

Instantly, a large, evil smile crossed Everly's face.

Father Gustloff made it a point to not even look at the woman, instead, focusing on Constable Hecht. "Constable," he said quietly.

"Hello, Father," Constable Hecht replied with a quick nod.

"Oh, looky here, they act like they haven't been talking. You bunch of lying bastards. You're lying! Some godly man of the cloth you are!" Everly shouted.

"Relax, I've got this under control, Everly," Bürgermeister Hartjenstein said, furious with himself for ever allowing this woman into his house earlier in the day.

Surprisingly, Everly fell silent at the bürgermeister's command. He noted that the woman only backed down at the firmest show of authority. Everything else, she just pushed forward with her crazy talk.

Constable Hecht opened the lone jail cell which typically remained empty other than the occasional night sleep for Nick or Marco if things got too rowdy down at the Pale Horse.

Fr. Gustloff stood by, awaiting his incarceration for the crime of existing in opposition to Hartjenstein. Constable Hecht flopped the keys down onto the table angrily, which Bürgermeister Hartjenstein picked up on.

"So, you disagree with me, is that it?" the bürgermeister said bitingly.

"I didn't say that," the constable retorted.

Everly stood by quietly, watching the two men begin the argument, enjoying every minute of it and hoping for it to escalate. She had, of course, been the instigator in this whole confrontation and she relished it.

"Well? Is there something else?" Hartjenstein said a bit louder.

"It's just, I'm the law here and arresting this man without talking to me first isn't protocol. Furthermore, this woman is asking for private financial information on the townsfolk here in Burnmere. Says you hired her, but that type of job comes from me as well, the elected officer of the law." Constable Hecht stopped, knowing that wouldn't go over well with either of the opposing forces in the small room that was feeling smaller and smaller.

"Why you useless little *shit*. Who in the bloody hell do you think you are that you can talk to me like that? I run this town, me! Not you, and don't you *ever* forget it!" Bürgermeister Hartjenstein shouted angrily at the constable who wanted to flinch at the hostile words but forced himself to hold his ground.

Sighing, Constable Hecht replied, "Samuel, why are you so completely in denial about what is happening on that mountain and in this very town? You've made it clear no one is to go into the forest, yet people are dropping like flies here. And they are following your rules! They aren't going into the forest, the forest is coming into our town and killing us off! The thirteen-year-old girl, Armin Falck and the still missing

Burns woman. And that's just in the past several days! I'm an old man with a wife that's dying of cancer, not that you would know or care in the slightest. I just want to put my hours in and go home to her. If there are people headed up into the mountain to confront whatever is up there, and there is indeed *something* in that castle hunting us, then I support them. I wish I could have gone along but my old bones can't take it, so God speed to those with enough courage to do what most here would never in their wildest dreams be man enough to try!" He was obviously referring to the bürgermeister himself.

A silence fell over the jail. Father Gustloff stood quietly watching it all unfold as did Everly, her smile turning to a scowl at this man's insubordination.

"First off, you will refer to me as Bürgermeister Hartjenstein. Secondly, you seem to want to go galivanting around the mountain, so have at it! You won't be missed, old man. I could do your job blindfolded! A lot more would get done here, that's for damn sure. And if I get the slightest whiff that you are referring to me not being man enough, I will skin you alive, you weak, pathetic little man! Probably weaker than your own wife. Maybe I should hire her on as constable, what do you say about that?" Hartjenstein spat back, furiously doing his best to antagonize the old man. He'd been itching for a fight ever since the woman forced herself on him earlier and Caspar had called his bluff later inside his house.

Constable Hecht calmly looked over at Father Gustloff. "Mr. Jannick Gustloff, you are free to go."

Everyone in the small room fell silent again. Hartjenstein was stunned at this seeming lack of respect and going against his wishes. Everly was eating it all up, sensing a promotion in her near future and she hadn't even put a single hour of work in on the job yet.

Looking at the constable, Father Gustloff nodded and headed toward the door.

"Stop this instant!" the bürgermeister shouted, but Fr. Gustloff continued moving.

Everly continued to watch, her newfound animal instinct guiding her. *Wait for it.*

"This man has not committed a crime; he is free to go. I am the elected official of Burnmere. Elected by the people that I serve here, and last I checked, I still make the arrests. I didn't arrest this man, let him go," Constable Hecht announced, suddenly overcome with a spell of confidence, tired of being pushed around by this weak bully with a god complex. Especially after the completely inappropriate comment about his dear, sweet wife. He wanted to kill this man for his many transgressions day in and day out. He had been allowed to get away with too much for far too long.

Fr. Gustloff made it to the door and was about to open it when Hartjenstein drew his pistol from its holster, aiming it at the priest and said shakily, "You will not take a step out that door, or I swear, Jannick, I will shoot you dead. Don't think for a second I won't."

Another click rang through the jail along with a gasp from Everly. Hartjenstein turned away from the door to face Constable Hecht, who had his law enforcement rifle cocked and aimed at the bürgermeister's head.

Everly stood slightly behind Constable Hecht and, sensing he might actually blow the bürgermeister's head off, saw her moment and leapt onto Constable Hecht's back, attempting to disarm him. This inadvertently caused him to pull the trigger on his rifle. The blast hit Bürgermeister Hartjenstein in the middle of his throat, exiting out the other side. At the same time, the bürgermeister, also surprised by the violent crack of the bullet against his neck, instantly destroying his Adam's apple, discharged his own pistol aimed at the constable's chest. This bullet pierced the air, landing squarely in Constable Hecht's heart.

Both men fell to the ground.

Fr. Gustloff ran forward toward the fallen bürgermeister. Blood poured out of the rifle's bullet hole that appeared to have connected with the carotid artery. Bürgermeister Hartjenstein coughed up blood that splashed onto the growing pool of blood from the hole in his neck.

"Samuel," Fr. Gustloff began but saw the man's eyes glazing over. He was dead. Instantly, he looked up toward his fallen friend, Theodor Hecht. A pool of blood was beginning to form around the man on the floor as well. Standing to his feet, and looking down at the man, he saw the bullet appeared to have entered into his upper chest. His heart.

"Stop right there," a cold voice said.

He looked up at Everly where she stood near the body of the constable holding his rifle. Their eyes locked as she pulled back on the bolt, discharging the spent shell from the Romanian Mannlicher Rifle, then quickly slamming the bolt action back into place, locking another shell into the chamber. She raised the rifle to her shoulder.

Fr. Gustloff slowly raised his hands, not taking his eyes off of her or her newfound weapon. He wondered if anyone heard both blasts go off, surely someone had, right? The jail wasn't near any homes and the only business nearby was the butcher shop that old Abe Radner ran. He had closed up for the day already. *If anyone heard it, they may not even know where it came from. This is bad.*

"Everly, listen. We need to get Doctor Heuberger in here, now. Two people are dead."

"Oh, we don't need to do anything. You've done enough for the both of us. You hiding my husband from me, you letting that harlot into your church. She struck me! That bitch hit me, and you stood by!" Everly shouted, trying to come up with anything her rotten brain could think of to justify this madness. Her body felt warm, this power and violence was arousing her.

"Everly, please, you've got to lower that," Fr. Gustloff began.

"Stop saying my name, I know what you're trying to do. I'm not stupid, you all think I'm some stupid old hag because of the piece of shit I shacked up with. Well, let me tell you something. Bürgermeister Hartjenstein hired me to do a job, and from the looks of it, him and his deputy are *dead*." She paused for added effect. "And that leaves me in charge." An evil smile once more crossed the deranged woman's face.

Fr. Gustloff knew he needed to choose his words carefully, she was right. Both men were quite obviously dead, and she had his gun. He looked down at Bürgermeister Hartjenstein's fallen pistol. It was a six-shooter so five remaining shells were likely still in the other five chambers. Fr. Gustloff was no killer. He was a man of God.

"What are we going to do now, Everly?" Fr. Gustloff asked calmly with his hands still raised in the air.

Everly looked around the jail, contemplating her options. *This is your time, now seize it!*

She thought of her son, Christoph, who hated her, her husband, who hated her, the man that lay at the priest's feet whose member she had in her mouth hours earlier, dead. He was repulsed by her; this priest was repulsed by her. The town of Burnmere shunned her. Her life had seemed over a mere day ago but now, she had the power, she was in control, and it excited her. *Take it! It's yours now!*

She pulled the trigger of Constable Hecht's rifle and the bullet blasted out and shattered into Fr. Gustloff's forehead, throwing him against the door leading out into the empty street beyond the jail. Everly, breathing heavy, kept the rifle pointed at her target.

Fr. Gustloff's expression was that of complete surprise. In the few seconds his shattered brain had to process what happened, he thought of Caspar, Marco, Nick, and the Burns woman, on their way to attempt to vanquish the great evil of this land.

"Peace be with you," he whispered quietly, not to Everly, but to his friends and their perilous quest against the powers of evil.

With the words spoken, he fell backwards onto the wooden floorboards, dead. Blood began pouring out of the hole in his forehead, streaming out onto the floorboards of the small jail.

Everly lowered the rifle, discharging the spent shell and slamming the bolt back once more. Loaded and ready for more. "I'm in charge," she uttered, gathering more ammunition from Constable Hecht's drawer. He would no longer be needing it.

Her body trembled as her mind filled with twisted images of having lustful sex with a stranger. Ripping and tearing at each other. Biting each other. It wasn't a man; it was a beast. She felt hot, not just from the senseless murder she had committed, but with the burning desire for this beast man to be inside her once again.

*I put my trust in you, I need you, my sweet Everly.*

She shook her head, blinking hard. Whatever had polluted it seconds ago was gone. She scanned the carnage on the jail floor, satisfied with her work, then smiled smugly and walked out defiantly into the streets of Burnmere.

# Chapter 22:

†

# Hide and Go Seek

Deep in the dungeon of Castle Visimar, Ingrid's coffin shot open. Dusk had fallen, the hunter was ready. She wasted no time in leaping out of her resting place and, while in midair, her bat-like wings shot out of her back and extended.

She took flight and shot upwards through the hole on the ceiling, up through the steep tower and out its open top into the sky.

Her master was hunting Lily-Rose. *I will take care of everyone else,* she thought arrogantly. The fog was thick today, as if it had a mind of its own. She had great vision when nighttime fell but it wasn't quite that time yet. Dusk still hung in the air; she would have to fly above it if she were to reach the village.

She took off, gliding through the sky, down to her soon-to-be hunting ground. On her way, she saw forms through the fog that appeared to be people on horseback. "Good, my first prey of the night, foolish little humans daring to enter *my* forest," she uttered as she swooped down toward fresh blood.

She landed beyond the wall of swirling fog, remaining hidden and out of view from her prey. Her bat-like wings retracted into the opened flesh on her exposed back. She wore the thin, see-through slip she had previously worn and nothing else. Peering around at her surroundings, she spotted Marcel.

"You," she said quietly as he watched the horses approach.

"Ah, you've decided to grace us with your presence, I see," Marcel said snidely, not looking over at the new arrival.

She walked over to him and before he could cover his face, she leaned in and licked it, running her tongue from his chin, across his lips and up over his right eye.

Quickly, he shoved her back as she laughed maniacally.

Wiping the foul spit from his face, he glared at her. "What are you doing here? I will take care of them. Our master's necklace is within reach. He told us she will come to him and she shall!" Marcel exclaimed.

Without missing a beat, Ingrid hissed back, "You know as well as I that the master has chosen me as his right hand in seeing the Pricolici return to this world. *Not you!* You would be wise to remember that, little errand boy!"

Marcel knew she was right, infuriating him further. Ingrid had always been Antonin's favorite while he had remained exactly as she had called him, the errand boy, blessed with eternal life, but only useful for his labor. He was about to continue the argument when a flame ignited past the fog. They both stopped arguing and looked on.

†

Juliette had offered her horse to Nick but he refused. "She needs it more than me," he said. So, he remained with Caspar as Marco brought his horse beside them.

"What do you make of it?" Marco asked, staring ahead at the wall of swirling fog.

"Nothing makes sense, at this point. All bets are off, if that legend or story or whatever it is, is to be believed. We have to push through; there appears to be no other way and just waiting here is liable to get us killed. I'm sure there are more wolves waiting for a chance at us out there," Caspar replied.

"Thanks for saving my ass back there, Marco," Nick said almost sheepishly, glancing over at the man that had been a sworn enemy for so many years.

Marco didn't reply, he simply nodded his head in thanks and mutual respect.

"We've got to move, night is going to drop on us sooner than later," Juliette said, giving the reins in her hands a quick flip. Her horse Ginger pushed forward and at this, Caspar and Marco moved their horses forward as well.

They were about to enter the thickest part of the fog bank as loose sediment underfoot caused the horses to slip on their continued climb.

Gripping the reins of his horse tightly, Caspar said, "I don't think it's wise to go into that on horseback. The terrain is much too unstable, and we can barely see in front of our faces as it is. I would rather be on solid ground to best defend ourselves against whatever is out there instead of on horses that get spooked. We've made it a good distance on these horses, but I think it may be time to part ways."

"Good idea," Juliette and Marco both said at the same time. Nick nodded in agreement and they all dismounted.

"What do we do with these horses?" Juliette asked Marco, as mere seconds later, the horses neighed loudly and all three, now free of their riders, took off running in opposite directions. Marco's steed ran into the woods. Juliette's took off back down the path and Caspar's barreled ahead into the fog.

"Wow!" was all Nick could muster at the bizarre sight. Within seconds, wolf snarls echoed through the deep tree cover, followed by the pained screech of frightened horses, then muffled snarls and grunts of wolves feasting on fresh, warm meat. An eerie silence fell over the forest for a brief period before howls began reverberating throughout, lifting up past the fog enshrouded treetops into the night sky.

Marco opened his potato sack and produced a small jar of kerosine. Next, he pulled out the wooden leg of his kitchen table, tore a piece of his shirt sleeve from around his large arm, then wrapped it around the wooden leg and doused it with the flammable liquid. Reaching into his pocket, he pulled out a small tin with several matches inside. With his thumb, he flicked the top of the match, igniting it then holding it to the cloth. Flames burst forth, lighting the dim path.

"Marco, I am glad you're with us!" Caspar exclaimed.

"There's enough kerosine and a few more matches to light up more stakes. Nick, you brought one from the church. Caspar—"

Marco was cut off by the bloody, severed head of Caspar's horse, Dutch, rolling out of the fog along the path, stopping at their feet.

"What…the…hell," Nick said quietly, staring down at the horse head then up toward the direction it had come from.

All four put their guns against their shoulders.

"We have to go through this fog. No turning back, everyone ready?" Caspar said authoritatively.

Juliette scowled and moved forward, frightened but undeterred. Marco watched her go, liking the woman more with each minute he was in her presence. She was, in every way, the opposite of Everly. Courageous, well-groomed, and deeply loyal to her kin, traveling all the way from England to find her. Everly laughed when she heard Christoph had left without so much as a good-bye to her.

*Light the way for her,* he thought to himself, pushing forward past her with his torch outstretched, lighting the way for them all.

They could barely see in front of their faces, but Marco's torch helped. Pushing forward and upwards, they continued on.

"Here's the rest of the horse," Marco said, holding his flame down to the ground. "This wasn't done by an animal, the cut is clean." He pointed at the slice at the top of its neck. Blood was oozing out of the stump onto the dirt trail underfoot.

"Clean, wasn't it?" a woman's voice hissed in the fog.

Everyone tensed as Marco extended his torch outward.

Nick, beside Marco, had his rifle extended and was shaking.

"Show yourself!" Caspar exclaimed, recognizing the female voice instantly from the previous night outside Marco's house.

Juliette, instantly filled with dread, held firm and tried to remain calm. They had formed a semi-circle with Marco now in the lead.

Out of the fog, a woman moved forward, beautiful even through the thick mist. Her sheer slip clung to her body, accentuating her curvy breasts and slender form. Two large fangs overlapped her upper lip. Her eyes flashed yellow as she stared at her prey then stopped when they reached Juliette. The gold necklace wrapped around the woman's exposed neck was her master's. The sister of Lily-Rose stood before her, the second descendent of the murderous Alfred Burns.

"Stay back, you vile woman," Marco said firmly.

"Vile? Me? Vile? Oh, you silly man, I'm so much more than vile. I'm a murderer, a seductress and a servant to the master of this world. And all of you will soon realize the true meaning of pain. My master comes, soon he will have the one that escaped, and I will bring him that pretty necklace as well as you, Miss, Juliette, is it?" Ingrid's yellow eyes fell on the woman in between Caspar and Marco.

"The one that escaped. My sister! Where is my sister!" Juliette shouted.

Caspar raised his hand instinctively to silence her. This woman in front of them was no woman, at least not anymore.

"Ah, it is you indeed. Your sister will soon be one of us, after she has drunk you dry. And then our great master will claim her as his own once he is finally reborn. You will soon bow before our great master while the rest of the town below will all be dead.

"We'll just see about that you *bitch*. It sounds like my sister escaped," Juliette hissed.

This made Ingrid laugh, it was time to show these simple mortals her true self. She had felt invincible since Antonin turned her. Even when her sister was staked and burned alive one hundred years prior, she felt that would never happen to her, the stronger and smarter of the two.

She was sneaky, always pouncing on those who were vulnerable and not expecting it, enjoying the terror in their eyes when they realized what was happening to them. Especially the young ones, taken before the prime of life, feeling their lives being sucked out of them until their eyes went blank. She was a taker, swiping children forever from their loved ones. Families torn apart, destroyed forever in mere seconds to sate her appetite as well as the boredom of having been granted eternal life. Some of the youngest simply killed for sport. Relishing in the horror the child's parents felt once they found their little one with its throat bitten completely out and, at times, stomachs sliced open like pigs.

Thinking on these horrific images she had perpetrated for centuries, she smiled, feeling a deep desire to show these mortals here her true self before she killed them all, all except the woman with the necklace.

Ingrid taunted her further. "You should have seen your whore sister when I had my way with her in the castle. You should have seen her lick the blood of an innocent child off my face. You should have seen her in ecstasy while my master, Count Antonin Visimar drank from her throat after reclaiming his property, stolen by your wretched great-grandfather!"

Ingrid opened her mouth wide and hissed as her face began to contort, skin pulling back against her bones. Her fingers extended and her body grew thinner causing her slip to drop off, revealing a hideous sexless mutation underneath. The bat-like flesh covered wings on her back shot out and began flapping.

Juliette muttered, "My sister is no whore," and was about to pull the trigger on her rifle but Marco beat her to it.

"I've had enough of this vile creature's filth," he said quietly.

At the slightest nod from Caspar, and beginning with Marco, all four guns erupted into the fog directly into Ingrid who shot backwards onto the ground with four new holes in her body.

She had been shot before but this was different. This was four against one, even if she was an immortal creature of the night, the four blasts had wounded her and would take a while to heal. *I should have gone to the village like my master ordered,* she thought.

She leapt back up on her bat-like feet, screaming in both anger and pain from the four blasts, all of which had connected with her stomach and chest area. It was a mess of red blood and tainted bat-like flesh. Resembling little of a human anymore, her true animal self was now on display, her large wings flapping, attempting to lift her up, off the ground.

Juliette moved forward, a crucifix in hand. She shoved it into the Ingrid mutation's face and shouted, "You're not leaving here, you *bitch*!"

Ingrid hissed, baring her fangs. She hated crosses and what they represented. But right in front of her was the necklace around Juliette's neck, and she instinctively reached out to take it when Nick ran up on the other side of her, splashing his blessed holy water onto her face.

The water burned the thin skin off her contorted face. This was the first time she had ever experienced something of this nature. She had never been quite sure how religious items worked in opposition to what she had become other than her outright hatred of crosses. Now she found out as the water worked like acid, searing through her skin and working its way through her jawbone. Thick brown clumps of flesh, bone and muscle tissue melded together then dripped from her melting face onto the ground.

Screaming and raising her clawed hands to her face, she tried to wipe the holy water away, but instead she tore the bottom of her rapidly melting jaw completely off. She continued shouting and screaming as she looked down at the jaw that seconds ago had been attached to her face, dissolving into the dirt below. The water made its way to her right eyeball. The yellow glow was extinguished as was the entire eyeball itself, melting off of her face and landing atop the growing pile of brown and red melting parts at her feet.

Nick jumped back as she flailed violently, not wanting to get any of whatever was melting off of her onto himself. This gave Caspar the window of opportunity he needed.

Lunging forward, he slammed the makeshift stake he had gotten from Fr. Gustloff inside St. Joseph's earlier in the day directly through her still beating, undead heart. The stake was nothing more than a broken, splintered wooden end of one of the old pews inside the chapel, but its point was deadly sharp and it easily pushed through the screaming ghoulish figure.

But Caspar didn't stop once it penetrated her flesh, he pushed her back against the nearest tree until the tip of the stake jabbed against the bark of the large oak.

Most of Ingrid's face was gone, the holy water having worked its way almost back to the gray brain matter inside her skull. The bullet wounds in her chest were no longer able to heal from the continuous onslaught of new wounds. Pinned to the tree, she couldn't even scream out as her mouth had ceased to exist.

"Step aside, Caspar," a voice behind him said grimly.

Caspar did as he was ordered. Marco moved forward, touching his kerosine lit torch against the flailing vampire vermin in front of them. It instantly ignited into flames, causing the four humans watching it in its death throes to flinch and stand back.

The fire was intense and quick to burn her into ash, as though her body was prepared to go out in such a gruesome fashion. All that was left was a smoldering pile of burning bones and ashes at the foot of the tree.

They all stood around glowing embers and smoking ashes on the ground, taking everything that had happened in and trying to process the madness.

"Night will soon fall, and I fear this thing's master is out there. Likely looking for your sister, if what this one said is to be believed," Caspar said grimly, breaking their silence.

Juliette nodded, adding, "Which means she's still alive and she needs our help."

Each found a branch heavy enough to retain a flame, and followed Marco's example, tearing a bit of their clothes and wrapping the ends. Marco spritzed more kerosine on each makeshift torch. Pulling out the small tin of matches once more, he lit the rest of the torches.

After a quick check of their inventory, they moved forward through the heavy fog with Marco once more in the lead. Now more prepared for what likely awaited them in the coming darkness. Pairs of yellow eyes periodically blinked through the trees. Growls and angry snarls echoed in the fog, both near and far.

Two sets of yellow eyes, larger than the rest, hung back farther. One set belonged to a huge gray wolf and the other belonged to the largest black wolf the mountains of Carpathia had and would ever see.

# Chapter 23:

†

# Bad to Worse in Burnmere

Marcel watched the chaos unfolding nearby. He was good at staying silent if that was required of him. Ingrid could have certainly used his assistance, but it brought him joy to see that wretched bitch suffer then have what she had considered her *immortal* life snuffed out from right under her. She had always been too confident in her own powers and the gift her master had bestowed on her.

He hated this existence. Never having sex, never knowing love or even the pain of the loss of a loved one. Even simple things like enjoying a fine meal, something he used to do in his native country France, was now reduced to eating little more than gruel or the rodents of the castle and surrounds forest to sustain his optimal weight to continue performing for his master.

He would be used until he was no longer needed, and right now, his own existence was beginning to hang in the balance. Ingrid was gone forever; it was Antonin and Marcel left. Antonin had countless years to create an army of the undead, instead choosing to keep the gift he had been bestowed and gifted with to himself and his select chosen few for reasons only Antonin himself knew. Maybe it was at his own master's command? Maybe it was out of a deep fear of the amulet falling into the wrong hands? *Look how well that went,* he thought to himself.

Regardless, he felt as though he would at long last be tossed aside once the Pricolici's return was complete after the incantations had been properly recited. *I could do that!* Marcel thought coldly, continuing to watch the four mortals make their way farther up the mountain.

He had sensed cracks in his master's armor already, starting with him being burned at the stake and robbed of the very jewel he sought so hard to protect. And now the amulet was back with Antonin, thanks to him. Yet, even with all but that damned necklace in his possession, his master couldn't do anything to save Ingrid from suffering a similar fate as her sister on this same mountain one hundred years prior.

Marcel continued watching the travelers work their way up through the fog, the wolves of the mountain staying out of sight, following them as well. With the fire they now wielded, many of the wolves remained close but not attacking. The two large ones, however, were another story. Hardly wolves at all, they were considered lycanthropes in this part of Romania, every bit as dangerous as vampires but much more brutal in their attacks.

He had always kept his distance from the two wolves Antonin considered his pets. He knew well that these beasts were no pets. They were likely extensions of the fallen angel, Lucifer himself. Mutations sent to not just revive and restore Antonin to full health but also to watch over him and make sure that everything fell into place, which it had, to a point. It was Marcel who had retrieved the missing necklace, having fulfilled his mission to go to England, take a sample of Lily-Rose's blood and bewitch her into making the trek all the way to the Carpathian Mountains.

And now she'd escaped his master's seemingly impenetrable dungeon, if what Ingrid and the Juliette woman said was true. Another mistake by Count Visimar. Marcel considered this. For centuries he had been loyal and faithful, but what would happen if Antonin failed in this task of bringing the Pricolici back to this world? What would become of him, the ever-faithful servant? Should he not think of his own interests?

He thought on these things as he continued following his prey, confident he could easily dispatch at least one of the four, but the rest would likely overtake him, and his fate would be similar to that of one very recently burned alive Ingrid. A fate he would rather not endure, if possible.

Silently slipping through the forest, Marcel tracked their movements. The fog was thick, but Marcel's eyesight was excellent. Another small benefit of having been turned, his eyes never glowed yellow like the wolves' or Ingrid's. But after he had turned countless years ago, he found that seeing clearly in the dark as well as through smoke and fog came easily for him. He had tracked many a prey for Ingrid's sister Sophia, a woman he had enjoyed being around, unlike her sister.

Now, once again focused on reclaiming the amulet and necklace, Marcel was glad to see through the fog and nightfall that was quickly descending over the mountain.

As he watched them traverse up a steep incline, he noticed the large man limping, as though favoring his hip. "If I'm to take anyone out, that one would do nicely," he mused aloud. "Although, taking out the woman ensures me the prize my master seeks. No, she is to go to the castle willingly. Maybe the skinny old man? He's way past his prime and appears diseased with alcohol from the looks of his pale, wrinkled skin. Maybe the strapping young muscle-bound man? I would have enjoyed a night with that man years ago."

Or, perhaps he would just let Antonin's wolves take care of them.

The two wolves hung back from the rest of the pack, close to their prey.

†

Everly had left the jail. Three corpses lay bleeding out of the floor inside, and she would keep them there, for now.

"So, what shall my first order of business be?" her delusional, warped mind wondered. She felt nearly invincible. The law of man and the law of God were no more, thanks to her. All that remained was the law of Everly Seiler, a last name she intended to never use again.

She could barely recall being married. In fact, she couldn't remember much of her past life. All she knew was that great things awaited her. New life had sprung up inside her and now she intended to seize the moment. Her body was beginning to feel younger, her confidence growing, and for the first time since her youth, she felt truly *alive*.

Heading up the darkening street as night fell, she bumped into the schoolteacher, Ada Shalner, heading home after wrapping up her cleaning duties and eating her supper in the schoolhouse, which was larger than the one-room closet she called home.

Everly knew the woman had always had it in for Bürgermeister Hartjenstein over being kicked out of her far-too-large schoolhouse. Why should she have such a big building for the few kids the school housed? She intended to reinforce that decision now that she was in charge. Doing what needed to be done for the town of Everly.

Immediately, Ada Shalner saw the rifle Everly was carrying in her right hand, along with Bürgermeister Hartjenstein's pistol and holster now strapped around her waist. She had pulled off Constable Hecht's jacket and put it on as well, to signify she was now the law. And while Everly wished she had a badge, the jacket would have to do, for now.

Ada Shalner's eyes went from Everly's grinning face down to the blood-spattered jacket. "Everly, what on earth happened to you? Why are you wearing the constable's jacket? Where is—" She stopped talking, a look of realization falling across her face, her eyes slowly moving up to meet Everly's.

It was too late, Everly had the rifle trained on the old schoolteacher's chin and pulled the trigger. The bullet entered under Ada Shalner's chin, shot up through her brain, and exited out the top of her skull. She only had a split second to realize her end arriving before dropping to the cobblestone street, dead, a steady stream of blood pumping from the top of her head.

"You poisoned the town against the bürgermeister, and this is what it got you. Such a shame," Everly said glibly, smirking at her handiwork and moving on. Next stop, the doctor's office.

Several elderly townsfolk, hearing the gun blast, stepped outside to see what had happened. One look at Everly was all it took to head back inside their homes, closing the doors behind them and quickly locking up.

Doctor Heuberger himself heard the gun blast and peered out his small window, watching as the crazy woman in the distance approached, carrying two guns.

Everly looked up to the sky where night had fallen across Burnmere and the mountain above. A voice deep in the recesses of her damaged mind continued to tell her, *You're in charge. I need you to do my will and cleanse this town.*

†

Antonin Visimar continued scouring the fog-enshrouded mountain for Lily-Rose. Thus far, she had remained elusive to him. Which came as somewhat of a surprise to a being that considered itself nearly god-like. His master was certainly a god. But in order for him to meet his master, he must get to the girl and her sister. He continued his search, hovering just slightly above the treetops, scanning the path below.

Lily Rose knew she was being stalked by the thing that went by the name of Antonin Visimar. She could feel his presence all around her, yet she pushed on as night fell across the mountain. She had decided to hop off the small path for better tree cover, assuming correctly that he would come for her in the sky.

Her hunger was overwhelming, but she needed her strength. She couldn't go on any longer with the pain that wracked her stomach and decided on the best course of action. She stopped in her tracks and peered around her, quickly seeing several pairs of yellow eyes blinking in the fog. Night had nearly arrived across the mountain and her sight had greatly increased. Another one of Antonin's *gifts* bestowed upon her, she suspected.

She chose her prey; the hunted was about to become the hunter. Ignoring her hunger pangs, and already beginning to salivate at the prospect of food in her stomach, she leapt forward toward the blinking yellow eyes where a small-sized wolf had been stalking her, its brown fur blending with its surroundings well enough to keep it hidden. But with night falling, Lily-Rose's eyesight was better than its own.

She jumped at the wolf, landing on top of it as it instantly lashed out, baring its fangs and sinking them into her exposed shoulder. Her hunger, however, outweighed the pain and fear she felt, trying to overtake her.

With both hands, she grabbed hold of the sides of the wolf's head and, as hard as she could, jerked it to the right. She heard the snapping of its spine from the sudden and powerful jolt. Instantly, the wolf released its death grip on her shoulder and slumped over onto the dirt, dead.

Lily-Rose sat up and looked at her wound, already bleeding heavily. She smelled the iron in the blood and it made her drool. She thought back to how she had resisted the temptation to devour the corpse in the dungeon earlier. That was a man and this was an animal, she rationalized. *I've eaten plenty of animal, what's one more?*

Lily-Rose sank her teeth into the exposed, furry neck of the wolf, tearing past the fur and thick skin until something warm and wet hit her mouth. It was the same substance she had lapped up around and inside Ingrid's mouth. She sucked the blood out of the dead animal as fast as she could, the sharp pains instantly subsiding.

Once she had drunk her fill, she considered eating some of the meat but held off. She had to keep moving, especially now that she had newfound strength. She felt great, even the bite on her shoulder felt as if it was already attempting to heal itself. She looked at the open wound and noticed the blood had slowed to a trickle.

Standing, she scanned her immediate area. No more blinking yellow eyes to be found. "Don't like it when something fights back, do you?" she said glibly to the forest. Next, she scanned the area, feeling it best to keep on heading downward, through the tree cover.

Then, in the far distance, she saw something with her improved eyesight. Four glowing lights through the trees that appeared to be moving in unison, one after the other. She squinted, hoping to make out what exactly they were.

"Lights! Those are torches!" she exclaimed, overjoyed at the prospect of something on this mountain that could potentially help her efforts to escape.

Quickly, she began making her way through the trees toward the lights. The sharp rocks, sticks, and rough terrain tore up her bare feet, but she kept moving.

In her haste, her bloody foot slipped on a particularly smooth rock, and she fell forward, landing hard on the rough ground. This being a particularly steep incline, she began to roll forward, her body smashing into shrubs and rocks on her way downward, closer to the four traveling light sources.

"Did you hear something?" Juliette said quietly, looking in the direction of the noise.

They all stopped and listened. More branches cracked, followed by a thumping sound which produced a loud groan of agony. Then all was silent once more.

"That sounded like a woman, up there!" Marco said, pointing in the direction where the sound had come from.

"It's off the path," Nick quickly pointed out, and he was right. The castle was close, if they stayed on the path.

Juliette didn't hesitate. "That's my sister, I know it is!" She left the path and entered the darkness of the woods with Caspar, Marco, and Nick following close behind.

# Chapter 24:

†

# Reunited

Marcel watched the four travelers come to a full stop when they heard the same noise he had. This wasn't a wolf; this was a person stumbling and falling. It had to be Lily-Rose! If he could secure not just the necklace but Lily-Rose as well, his master would reward him plentifully. Especially now that Ingrid was no longer in the picture.

He continued following the four travelers closely, but in his excitement, he inadvertently made his own noise. Nick, only a few yards from him, bringing up the rear of his group, called out in a loud whisper, "I think I heard something!"

Marcel froze, hoping they would keep going. Nick, however, had his rifle raised and was pointing it toward him.

Hidden by a tree, Marcel saw the four travelers wanted to continue moving forward but had stopped.

Behind him a set of yellow eyes flashed in the night. One of Antonin's wolves. A beast that had no love for Marcel.

"Come out! We can hear you!" Caspar said into the darkness.

Juliette, meanwhile, took off toward the woman's voice.

"Juliette! Wait!" Marco shouted out, seeing her run forward.

Marco saw a second pair of eyes; it was the black wolf standing alongside its gray wolf partner.

Just as Caspar took off in pursuit of Juliette, Marcel stepped out from the tree cover to reveal himself to Marco and Nick, each holding their torches out in front of them. Still little more than a shadow, his stealth-like abilities worked even better at night.

"Who are you?" Marco said defiantly, squinting to get a better look at the mysterious man in front of them.

"I'm the sisters' transportation, silly man, and I intend to take them both back to my master," Marcel said calmly.

Beside him, the two large wolves stepped forward and stood between Marcel and his new opponents.

✝

Antonin flew nearby in the sky, just above the trees in the pitch black of night, his full supernatural powers restored by the darkness. Looking down, he saw his wolves and Marcel moving in toward two men with torches, neither of whom had what he was after. He was confident his wolves would make short work of the two trespassers. He needed to get to the sisters and, more importantly, the necklace.

Looking farther up the mountain, he saw a man and a woman fleeing. *And where are you two going?* He glided silently past the men toward the remaining two travelers. *Could they have found my Lily-Rose?*

"Juliette, wait!" Caspar shouted, but it was no use. He glanced back and saw that his two traveling companions weren't behind him. "Damn it all!" he exclaimed as he kept pushing forward, hoping Marco and Nick could take care of themselves while he collected Juliette and investigated the noise they had all heard minutes earlier.

Several yards up ahead of him, Juliette came to a full stop. When he reached her, out of breath and still carrying his rifle, Caspar put his hand on her shoulder. "What are you thinking? We have to stick together, Juliette!"

She quickly bent down to the ground and cried out, "Oh no! Oh God, no, please be alright!"

Caspar looked down and saw Lily-Rose lying unconscious in the dirt. She was covered in bruises and blood and wearing only a thin slip, her feet cut up as well.

Quickly, Caspar took his thick outer shirt off and draped it over the nearly naked unconscious woman. Bending over her, he saw the bite wound on her shoulder and grimaced. *What hell has this girl been through?*

"Lily-Rose, I'm here! I knew I would find you! Oh Lily, please be alive!" Juliette cried, inspecting the badly injured body of her younger sister.

Caspar stood to his feet, flashing his torch back and forth. They weren't alone; he sensed something was watching them and it wasn't a wolf. No yellow eyes peered through the darkness, no breathing, no footsteps. But *something* was in the darkness near him. His right hand shook holding his gun. *Keep it together, Caspar.*

Juliette was beside herself with joy at finding her sister and terrified at the state she was in. How was she going to get back down the mountain in the middle of the night with no horses, and with wolves and vampires hunting them?

"You came for me," a low voice mumbled under Caspar's thick shirt.

"Oh Lily-Rose! Of course, I did! I'm here but it's imperative that we get you up. Can you move?" Juliette said kindly to her now conscious sister.

"I'm healing, give me time and I can stand," Lily-Rose responded, looking at her sister who was still crouched down beside her. She could hear the blood pumping through her sister's veins and could almost smell the fresh, healthy and very much *human* blood working its way inside her sister's body to her vital organs. Lily's bloody mouth began salivating, this woman was meant to be hers, Visimar had told her so. She would drink of her sister, that would heal her fully.

"What do you mean, you're healing?" Juliette responded, assuming her sister was simply delirious from the fall she had taken.

Already Lily-Rose was attempting to sit up, which alerted Caspar that something was amiss. The woman was on death's door just moments ago. He bent down to inspect further.

✝

Marco and Nick were left to fend for themselves. The cloud covered night sky parted momentarily, revealing a full moon that peaked through the thick forest slightly, penetrating the fog. Along with Marco's torch, it illuminated one man and two of the biggest wolves they had ever seen stood before them. What they could make out of the man wasn't much to look at, tall and thin, they could likely take him easily judging by his size. It was the wolves that were a problem.

"I've been watching you both for a while," Marcel began, speaking in a low voice. "Well done on those wolves back there. I think it's safe to say, however, you are ill-equipped to handle these two. My master will be so pleased with me. Catching two of the four that murdered his dear Ingrid. Oh, I watched that happen as well, and I should also say good work, there. I shall not miss that vile woman. However, you both must die now. But the sisters, oh, he has so much in store for them! I'm anxious to see their full transformation, especially the one that traveled from England of her own free will to attempt a rescue of her damned sister. She's a pretty one, isn't she?"

He was giggling with glee at how things had progressed. Ingrid was gone and the sisters were now within his master's grasp near the castle, which is where Marcel would take them. Juliette had been a tough one, but regardless, she was still right where she belonged. With her necklace, willingly having traveled up the mountain.

"I don't find this funny," Marco muttered coldly, staring at this new adversary he now intended to kill. He instantly felt a deep need to protect and defend Juliette Burns and would do so to his death, if necessary.

This made Marcel quit his laughing and fall serious. He looked at the wolves beside him as if to coax them along to begin the attack, at which point, they both moved forward, teeth bared at their intended prey.

"Come on, you wretched beasts!" Marco shouted, filled with rage.

Nick, standing close beside Marco, glanced over at him and muttered, "This appears to be it, our last stand. Never thought I would die beside you, of all people."

Marco nodded, not taking his eyes off the approaching beasts.

"Glad to be with ya. We appear to make a good team, I suppose," Nick added.

"Yes, indeed, now let's kill these fucking things!" Marco shouted and pulled the trigger on his shotgun.

The blast echoed through the foggy woods, connecting with the gray creature and sending it backwards. Immediately, Marcel snuck behind the nearest tree, watching again from a safe distance.

The second and bigger wolf lunged forward as Nick pulled the trigger on his rifle but, in his haste, fired too high. The bullet imbedded into a tree, close to a stunned Marcel's head, flinching at the near miss.

The gray wolf was hit in the chest, but this didn't slow it down much, though it did anger it further. Baring its fangs and breathing heavily, it ran forward again toward Marco while the black wolf bolted toward Nick. Both connected with their intended targets, knocking the men off their feet.

Marco's shotgun spilled out of his hands but he still grasped his lit torch tightly. The blow nearly took the wind out of him as pain instantly shot through his body from his sore hip hitting an exposed tree root. With the wolf breathing down on him, as hard as he could, Marco jammed his torch into the gaping, bloody hole his shotgun blast had made in the creature's chest.

The monstrous wolf howled in pain, making Marco shove the makeshift stake-torch combination farther into the animal.

Nick wasn't so lucky; the black wolf knocked him unconscious, his head connecting with the hard, rocky ground. His lit torch fell beside his body and his rifle spun free, rolling down the hill and out of sight.

The wolf opened its jaws wide and sunk its bared teeth into Nick's exposed throat, biting down and through as easily as if it were biting into a roll of bread. It was over within seconds, Nick didn't feel a thing. One second, he breathed, the next, his life was ripped from his throat in an instant.

The black wolf continued ravaging its fresh kill, now ripping into Nick's stomach with its fangs and sharp claws.

Meanwhile, the wooden stake had pierced the gray wolf's heart, flames and all. With the beast on top of him, the large, imposing Marco continued pushing the stake further and further into the creature's broad, muscular chest.

Shoving the wolf off of him and scrambling to his feet, he looked over to see the black wolf feasting on the organs of his traveling companion and newfound friend. He quickly scanned the immediate area for his shotgun but without his torch it was difficult to see.

The black wolf looked up at Marco and stopped feasting on Nick's organs. Blood dripped from its open snarling mouth, its yellow eyes supernaturally bright in the darkness. It began slowly moving toward the large man, not bothering to look down at its fallen brother that lay gyrating and twitching in the dirt.

Lit on fire, the twitching beast's fur sizzled and ignited simultaneously. Even engulfed in flames, Marco could see it was turning from beast into a beast-man. Legs expanding, paws contorting and growing long finger-like claws. Its head expanded and its snout grew. Now nearly three times its original size, it no longer moved, fire engulfing it completely. The transformation to its true form was now complete in death.

"Oh, you're in for a surprise now," a voice said from behind a tree nearby.

Ignoring the man, Marco quickly thought through what items he still had on him. Somehow, the potato sack hadn't fallen off when he was pushed to the ground and remained still crossed over his back, inside it, the kerosine and the holy water Father Gustloff gave him. And a crucifix he had tossed in as well, also from Father Gustoff. The few matches left in the tin remained in his pocket.

Never taking his eyes off the approaching black wolf, he opened the potato sack and fished out the kerosine, opened it, and threw all of its contents onto the approaching wolf that merely shook its face.

"I killed your friend, now I'm going to kill you," Marco said determinedly at the kerosine-drenched approaching creature.

The black wolf, sensing what the man was conveying, began its own transformation. Its legs grew substantially, bones cracking, muscles forming. It was able to quickly stand on its hind legs that now resembled a giant man's legs. Its arms extended, muscles bulging on longer extensions. Paws turned to fingered claws, chest expanding and growing its own muscle mass.

Finally, the ears folded back against its enlarged and mutated head, its snout the last to grow, expanding and pushing out from its face. Large teeth pushed out of its gums, now significantly larger and smeared with the blood of Marco's friend. The tail of the wolf had somehow shrunk up into its body and the transformation was complete.

The huge, black-furred werewolf creature stood before Marco in all its unholy glory, furious at the death of its partner, opening its mouth and letting out a roar the likes of which Marco had never heard before, echoing through the forest.

"And now, you die," Marcel called out mockingly.

Gritting his teeth, Marco replied under his breath, "Not today, I don't."

The wolf-mutation ran toward the ready and waiting Marco, who had reached into his right-hand pocket and, with his thumbnail, ignited a match he had dug out of the tin container. He threw it at the beast's face, immediately igniting it in flames. The wolf-mutation's head exploded into flames, stopping it in its tracks, and with its large, clawed hands, it batted at the fire spreading down its fur.

Marcel peered out from behind the tree, dumbfounded that this large brute of a man was accomplishing what no one in his memory had been able to do.

While the wolf-mutation flailed about trying to extinguish the mass of flames engulfing its body, Marco saw his shotgun laying close to where he had fallen, visible in the light created by the wolves' burning flesh. He lunged for the shotgun, once more landing on his bad hip and crying out in pain. He grabbed hold of it and opened it, expelling the spent slug and popping another one from his pocket into the chamber. Slamming it shut, he pulled back on the hammer.

The wolf-mutation continued to flail angrily, turning around and trying to find the culprit of this grave misdeed. Its eyes, severely damaged by the fire engulfing its face, fell on the man that had been its intended target and began moving toward him.

*Everly was so sweet*—the unexpected thought invaded Marco's mind. As if this beast-man had spoken it directly to him.

Shaking the morbid thought off, Marco bit through the pain in his hip, brought his old shotgun up to its head, aimed, and pulled the trigger. The slug erupted from his gun, connecting perfectly with the wolf-mutation's fire-engulfed head.

The close-range shotgun blast to the beast's already weakened and damaged head caused it to vaporize. Fiery fragments of brain matter, mutated skull, and burned fur drifted to the ground as if in slow motion.

The body of the headless wolf-mutation dropped to the ground, dead, no longer able to mutate and transform like its master had granted it so long ago when it willingly gave its life to resurrect Antonin Visimar. Like the gray wolf, its entire body erupted into flames.

Both wolf-mutations continued to burn quickly until all that would soon remain was a charred, malformed and blackened skeleton.

Marco got to his feet and surveyed the clearing where they had taken on the two wolves. Death, destruction, and charred corpses of things not human lay strewn about as he once more opened his shotgun and reloaded it. He picked up Nick's dropped torch, still lit, and held it out toward the trees.

"Two down, one to go. Come on out, you bastard," hissed Marco, whose body was wracked with pain, into the darkness of the tree cover but no reply came back.

His mind raced to remember what the wolf had seemingly spoke into his mind minutes earlier: *Everly was so sweet.* He thought of finding her in her bath towel, scratches across her chest, and pushed the grisly thought away.

# Chapter 25:

†

# A Surprise for Everly

While Juliette, Lily-Rose, Caspar, Marco, and Nick battled wolf-mutations and vampires in the mountain above, Everly stayed busy in the town of Burnmere. She had officially gone mad, possessed by the evil that had entered her when laying with the wolf. The new host that had taken over her body and willpower continued to warp her mind. Filled with rage, her bloodlust had only increased since the incident at the jail and the murder of the old schoolteacher.

Night fell as she made her way to Doctor Heuberger's place of residence. He was one of the guilty parties in cahoots with her rotten, good-for-nothing husband, Caspar, Nick, and that floozy bitch that had just shown up in town unannounced.

Her corrupted mind planned on dealing with her soon-to-be deceased husband if he made it back from the mountain alive, which she highly doubted. The same applied to the rest of the insurrectionists. *Oh, what I will do to that bitch woman that slapped me across my face. I'll slap the life out of her, is what I'll do.*

Everly's eyes filled with hate and rage at the world that had dealt her a bad hand. She quietly made her way up the small walkway leading to the doctor's house directly beside his office.

Unbeknownst to her, Joachim was prepared.

Feeling invincible, she walked up to the door, quietly gripped the door handle and pushed the knob, surprised to find it was unlocked. It was late, and likely the old German man was fast asleep. She knew he lived alone after his wife had passed almost five years ago.

Everly never gave thought to who would take over the duties of town physician if she had her way and succeeded in murdering the doctor. Even Joachim was barely able to handle the job of sole doctor in a town of one hundred souls, many of which were elderly and in poor health.

These things didn't cross her deranged, possessed mind, as revenge for unknown crimes is all she could focus on. Her hatred for her husband, for the attractive Caspar, for the son that despised her, the priest who looked the other way from her. *See where that got you, priest man? A bullet in the head.* She wondered if his invisible God welcomed him with open arms. He certainly couldn't save the so-called holy man's life! At that thought, she felt almost god-like in power. Everly, the giver and taker of life.

An evil smile crept over her face as she pushed the door to the doctor's house open. Not once did she consider she was now committing yet another crime on top of murder. She was breaking and entering.

The small house was dark inside. The stupid doctor didn't even bother locking his door at night. *You get what you deserve, you traitor! This is for Bürgermeister Hartjenstein, God rest his soul.* Yet, truthfully, she couldn't have cared less that Bürgermeister Hartjenstein was dead; in fact, she relished it. She was in charge now.

Everly walked through the door into the darkened house. All the houses, other than Bürgermeister Hartjenstein's, were small and laid out similarly. She knew exactly where his bedroom was. Then it would be as simple as walking in and blowing his brains out.

She enjoyed the thrill of the hunt and the release of the kill; it turned her on and made her think of when she had mated with the finest specimen she had ever seen, not human, something...more. She yearned for more, but she had to first take charge of this lawless town.

She had found her true calling. *Once this deed is done, I shall go back to the bürgermeister's house and claim it as my own. My new life has just begun! Soon people will learn to respect me! The new, unquestionable leader of Burnmere! I am the new supreme...*

A shotgun blast echoed through the doctor's kitchen, interrupting Everly's visions of her own grandeur and blasting her out of the opened front door and onto the walkway outside.

Pushing his chair back, Doctor Heuberger stood to his feet in the darkness of his home. He knew she would be coming for him; from his window, he had watched her making her way up the uneven cobblestone street toward his house as the moon above shorn down on her.

She had always hated him, ever since he had given her a grim prognosis on her current health. "You won't live to see fifty if you don't start eating right and taking care of yourself," he had said several years ago when she went in to check about sores that had formed around her inner thighs. She hadn't bathed in so long she had developed sores close to her genitals. The sight had been ghastly to Joachim at the time, but he was the town physician, it was his job to give news to all, even if it was bad.

Her response was swift and brutal at the time. "I'll live a damn sight longer than your wife! Still thinking something is digging up graves around here? What a damn shame this is what passes for a town physician. Burnmere is going to hell, I tell ya!"

He couldn't wait to get the foul woman out of his office, and she had never returned. Until today, that is.

Doctor Heuberger walked out of his house and looked down at the squirming, writhing woman on the ground, like a rabid animal. Her stomach was covered in blood that had splashed onto his walkway. Neighbors were now coming out of their houses to look at the damage.

A young couple, Finn and Anne Sessler, and their ten-year-old-child Patrik poured out of their house. Anne quickly covered the boy's eyes upon seeing the blood-covered body on the ground.

"What happened? We heard shots earlier!" the twenty-nine-year-old farmer asked Joachim.

"I fear we will find more bodies at the jail. We must go now and see the damage this woman may have inflicted," Heuberger replied grimly.

Nodding in puzzled agreement, the young man told his wife to get inside their house and lock the doors. In the meantime, more people had filed outside and were talking amongst themselves. The word spread quickly that the town doctor had shot the Seiler woman for breaking and entering. The most hated woman in all of Burnmere had been shot and lay dying.

Heuberger and Finn bent down to inspect Everly and the damage his slug had inflicted on her. One look told him she would be dead in minutes, the wound was fatal, and she was bleeding out. She coughed up blood and stared at her executioner with mad, rabid eyes filled with hate.

Knowing her demise was imminent, she uttered, "Don't bother sending for the priest, I killed him, and you're gonna need a new schoolteacher as well." She attempted to laugh but coughed up more blood.

Finn looked at Heuberger, horrified at this admission of guilt and even looking death in the face, Everly appeared to be defiant to the end. Picking up the bürgermeister's pistol, Heuberger looked it over and hung onto it while handing Constable Hecht's rifle to Finn.

"Come on, leave her, we'll deal with her body later," the doctor muttered angrily.

Nodding, Finn stood up and walked after Heuberger to the jail, finding on their way Miss Shalner lying dead on the street, her brains splattered across the cobblestone road. Inside the jail they encountered the horrific aftermath of multiple homicides. Father Gustloff, lying dead right inside the door. Bürgermeister Hartjenstein, shot through the neck, and finally, the good Constable Hecht lying dead in a pool of his own blood.

Heuberger, Finn and several other men in town stared, at a loss for words, at the carnage on display.

Finding himself to be the man everyone looked toward for guidance, Heuberger took charge, quickly ordering the schoolteacher's body be removed from the street and moved into the jail cell room with the other corpses until further investigations could be completed. Someone would also have to be on brain clean-up duty, which would likely be him. Finn was appearing to be a reliable helper and follower of orders in the immediate aftermath of the killings, something Joachim was in dire need of.

While the doctor tried to understand the senseless murders that had occurred in the town of Burnmere, his eyes drifted up to the fog-covered mountain. He wondered what was happening up there with the four travelers and surmised that the evil so prevalent on the mountain had likely bled down and attached itself like a parasite to the worst individual in all of Burnmere, who remained bleeding out in front of his house.

"Whatever you're doing up there, God speed to you all," the doctor uttered as he and Finn carried poor Miss Shalner's lifeless body into the jail before the town coroner, Victor Reis, would arrive later. Cause of death would be the easiest answer to come of this night of horrors for the town of Burnmere and up on the dreaded mountain above.

# Chapter 26:

†

# Things Moving
# in the Darkness

Caspar and Juliette heard the howling and snarls of wolves coming from the direction where they had left the others. "We have to go back!" Caspar exclaimed, knowing their traveling companions were in grave danger.

A weary but quickly healing Lily-Rose was now on her feet, shaking her head from her hard landing against a particularly large tree and wiping dirt off her bloody slip.

Taking hold of Lily's shoulders gently to inspect the bite, Juliette, ignoring Caspar's command, asked in a near whisper, "What has happened to you?"

Lily-Rose spilled into her sister's arms, squeezing her tightly. "I'm sorry, Juliette. I'm sorry for how we left things back home. I'm sorry that I wasn't stronger and the dark man was able to bewitch me. I was weak and now I've put you in grave danger as well!" She sobbed into her sister's shoulder.

"Oh Lily, I love you so. I would travel across the world if it meant being with you. We Burns sisters stick together! I'm here now. Tell me what happened!" Juliette said, not ready to release her sister from her embrace.

"I attacked a wolf and it bit me. Then I…killed it and drank its blood to quench my hunger pangs," Lily-Rose replied, as though in a daze from all that had happened since her escape from the castle earlier.

"You drank a wolf's blood?" Juliette replied in disbelief, pulling back from her sister.

Lily-Rose touched the necklace that adorned her sister's neck. "You came for me, and you wore the necklace I gave you. Juliette, my sister, I fear he may succeed. The owner of that castle wants to bring back an ancient evil."

Caspar and Juliette looked at each other with the realization that the story was actually true.

"I should have been watching over you, Lily, I should have been paying attention," Caspar said, looking over the horrible state the young woman was in.

"There was no way I wasn't coming here. I came against my own free will and now I've put you in danger!" Lily said, tears welling up in her eyes.

"No, we are taking you off of this godforsaken mountain!" Juliette exclaimed.

Lily-Rose frowned, her face grave. "We don't have enough time to get back to Burnmere, I fear, not with the necklace this close to his precious amulet! He is coming and once he has that necklace, something is going to rise from that castle. Antonin Visimar is real and he bit me and turned me into something...*in between*. And Juliette, you are to be my first kill before I become that thing's bride!" Her panic-filled eyes darted back and forth as if she were expecting company any moment.

"The Pricolici legend is true," Caspar uttered as he heard howls echo through the woods.

Lily nodded, speaking quickly now. "He has wolves and two others with him. The man that pierced my hand and stole my blood then bewitched me into coming here and a woman, an awful woman. She tried to force me into eating a dead body she brought to the dungeon of that castle where I was held," she said.

Her mind raced with the thought of whatever was surely on its way to intercept her sister and the necklace draped around her neck, and of what Lily herself would be required to do upon Antonin's capture of them. *I must kill my sister.*

"If it's the woman I think you're referring to, she no longer exists," Caspar said as he studied the damaged woman in front of him. He could tell she had been through literal hell and yet she had survived.

Instinctively, he put his arms around her and, like Juliette before him, gave her a gentle hug. She felt cold to his touch. Lily-Rose hugged him back. Enjoying the man's warmth, physical human contact, was something she never thought she would experience again, and it felt so good right now in this desolate forest filled with evil. A small part of what she had once been, a living human being, stirred inside her infected body.

Hearing this small bit of good news, her eyes shone with a spark of life. "You killed Ingrid? Please say it was her! The things she made me do…" Lily-Rose trailed off, her thoughts falling back to her harrowing experience in the dungeon of Castle Visimar, the naked demon woman shoving her tongue into her mouth, her taunts and threats.

As Caspar nodded yes, Juliette exclaimed, "My necklace is burning hot!" She quickly looked behind and around her. If the legend was to be believed, whatever was in this forest was growing closer. "Lily, Caspar is right, we have to get back to our friends, can you walk?"

Lily-Rose nodded slightly but didn't move. "He has the amulet, and as long as he has that and we have the necklace, he will come for us, the descendants of Alfred Burns. We have to kill him, or it, I should say. I'm barely a woman anymore, thanks to the disease that thing infected me with," Lily-Rose said.

Two separate gun shots echoed through the forest, causing all three of them to flinch instinctively.

"We need to get back to Marco and Nick! They need our help!" Caspar exclaimed, looking in the direction they had come from.

Juliette handed the torch to her sister while she kept her rifle. They all took off toward the sound of the gun shots. Lily-Rose now took the lead, as even in her bare feet, she felt her strength returning, her wounds healing.

Caspar and Juliette gave each other a worried look. Lily-Rose was alive, but she was different. They both could only imagine the horrors she had endured. Now, if what she had told them was to be believed, she was to become a full-fledged vampire *after* killing her sister. Then, she would join with the demon Antonin had planned on resurrecting at long last, bringing it back from the hell where it currently resided. It was all too much to take in at once.

Up ahead they saw Marco was talking with someone, and from his tone, it wasn't Nick. Moving forward, they heard Marco saying, "Two down one to go. Come on out, you bastard."

"Who is he talking to?" Caspar said quietly, holding his rifle out in front of him.

Lily-Rose's sense of smell had been heightened since being bit. Something familiar was in the air. "I recognize that smell."

"All I can smell right now is burnt hair and it's revolting!" Juliette replied.

They entered the clearing and saw Marco holding his torch out into the darkness. Juliette was the first to see the charred, burnt remains of what appeared to be mutated, gigantic wolves strewn out on the ground. She gasped at the sight.

Marco didn't take his eyes away from the dark forest. "Nick is dead. Killed by one of those wolf beasts, both of which are also dead."

"You killed them both?" Caspar said, surprised at what Marco had thus far been capable of.

"Indeed, I did, and whatever is still out there, I plan on doing the same with. You hear that, you bastard! Come on out, I'm waiting! I saw you earlier, now show yourself!" Marco shouted angrily.

"Nick's dead?" Caspar asked sadly, surveying the area when his eyes fell on the poor soul saying on the ground with his throat tore out and his insides strewn about his body.

Marco was silent as the full realization was hitting him that Nick was, indeed, dead.

"I know that smell," Lily-Rose walked up beside Marco as Caspar quickly went to check on Nick's body and Juliette looked around in disgust at the carnage on the ground.

Marco glanced over at her. "Lily-Rose! We're here to get you out of here, I'm glad you're alive."

"Thank you for coming for me," Lily-Rose said then added, "Fennel and anise, that's what I smell."

A dark outline appeared through the tree cover in front of them. She knew the shape of it. It was the same large shape that had sunk its fangs into her open and waiting neck the night before.

Suddenly, Lily's senses were heightened. She smelled the blood pumping through Caspar, Marco, and her sister's veins, and it smelled…delightful. Her mouth watered; her stomach pains were returning. It was as if their living bodies were beckoning her to taste them. To bite into their soft, warm necks and drink her fill of life from them.

She clenched her stomach in pain, forcing the thought of food out of her mind and looked up to the sky.

"What is that? Juliette said, standing to her feet after inspecting the burnt creatures.

They all listened. Above them, squeaks and flapping noises reverberated through the dark sky, growing louder and closer.

"Vampire bats, hundreds if not thousands of them. I saw them when I was taken to the castle by the man whose scent I smell nearby. He and his master are here with us now," Lily-Rose said cryptically, not taking her eyes off the dark shadowed figure that appeared to be floating slowly toward the clearing where they all stood.

# Chapter 27:

†

# Return to

# Castle Visimar

The shadow man, Marcel, continued to watch them. He knew the forest well and could remain hidden for as long as he liked, and he had decided to continue doing so. The large man and his friends appeared to be more resilient than he expected. Both of his master's wolves were dead, Ingrid was no more, and they still had the necklace. Yes, his master had said that the sister would come of her own free will, but Lily-Rose had slipped through Antonin's fingers.

Marcel had, since being bitten, grave robbed, kidnapped, and murdered. He had essentially given his very soul to not just Antonin, but the dark being who was nearing his return if everything played out according to Antonin's plan. *Am I a coward for waiting for this to play itself out?* Antonin Visimar's mistakes had plagued him since his death at the hands of Alfred Burns and subsequent resurrection one hundred years ago. Would Marcel, ultimately, pay for his master's mistakes, or end up with nothing after giving his very life for the count after a lifetime of servitude?

†

Gliding down until his feet hovered just above the ground, the dark figure drew closer to his victims. As it did, the fog seemed to evaporate, as if itself wanting to escape the evil that resided within it.

Caspar, Juliette, and Marco stared up at the clearing black sky that appeared to be moving in front of the moon. No longer fog covered, they could see black creatures swirling above, flapping their wings and squeaking angrily at the intruders that had, thus far, eluded their master.

The only one not looking up at the unholy display above them was Lily-Rose who continued watching the man shrouded in darkness slowly moving toward them. He was taking his time, toying with them. Seeing what they would do and how they would respond to his presence.

"I can't keep this necklace on anymore, it's burning my skin!" Juliette said, finally looking down from the sky and over to her sister.

She took the necklace off and instantly dropped it on the ground as it burned not just her neck but her hand as well. She put her hand to her neck where a red ring had formed on the skin where the necklace had been.

As soon as the necklace landed on the ground, Lily-Rose cried out as the thing that had been gliding toward them swooped down into the clearing and snatched the necklace. It now had both the necklace and the amulet itself, one more thing left: time to claim the Burns women.

As the swirling vampire bats above them flew in unison with their master, Antonin Visimar, Caspar and Marco both aimed their guns to the sky. But the creature above was too fast to get a lock on. It zig-zagged around them in a blur of flapping wings.

Frustrated, Caspar exclaimed, "To hell with this, just fire!" and pulled his trigger which easily missed its mark.

Marco dropped his torch and sack with his belongings, firing his shotgun, and saw several bats drop from the sky while the creature they were protecting remained unharmed. He quickly reloaded and aimed once more. "I've only got a few more shells left!"

Juliette joined the fight, raising her gun in the air and pulling the trigger; her blast appeared to hit the creature but did little damage. It hissed angrily, still circling them.

Bending over in pain, Lily-Rose's hunger was increasing. She instantly heaved, coughing up a thin stream of wolf's blood, spitting it onto the ground. Dropping down to all fours at the sheer enormity of the sharp, burning pain that was back with a vengeance, she screamed out in agony.

While on all fours, she glanced over at Marco's torch and his dropped sack. She reached over to see if there was anything inside that could be of some help to their situation, pulling out Fr. Gustloff's holy water first, then the jar of clearly marked kerosine. She glanced down at the burning torch beside his bag and realized what she had to do.

Juliette glanced over at her sister and saw her begin pouring something over the top of her head.

Lily-Rose turned and looked at her sister and mouthed, *I love you.*

"No, wait! Lily-Rose, what are you doing?!" Juliette shouted out, suddenly realizing what she had poured over her head.

Tossing the empty canister of kerosine aside, Lily-Rose picked up the small container of holy water and popped the lid, then grabbed Marco's dropped torch from the ground, nearly extinguished, but with a small flame still emanating from its tip.

The count landed in front of her, now a fully transformed creature of the night. Instantly, the bats above slowed into a sort of holding pattern. Time seemed to stop as Caspar, Marco, and Juliette aimed their guns in Lily-Roses' direction. They didn't fire as she was between them and the creature, and any blasts would certainly hit her.

It stood nearly seven feet tall, naked and covered in leathery skin. Long, bony arms with long bony fingers and nails at their ends clawed at the night sky in front of Lily. Its neck was abnormally long, and its mouth was wide, with two full rows of sharp fangs. On its back were enormous bat-like wings, roughly ten feet wide from end to end. Its eyes continually changed colors. Red, then yellow, then black until settling entirely on red.

The creature known as Antonin Visimar looked at the young woman then past her at its foes. It spoke in a deep, foreboding voice that didn't resemble anything that could be remotely human.

"You killed my wolves, and you killed Ingrid, well done. But that won't stop the inevitable. Tonight, the mighty hell spawn, the Pricolici, shall return and together we will begin out reign on this planet, starting with the total annihilation of Burnmere, then beyond. And this woman shall be my lord's, a gift, you could call her." He stopped speaking, his red eyes peering at Lily-Rose.

No one spoke. They all continued gazing in horror at the huge vampire creature in front of them.

Antonin Visimar looked toward Juliette then down to the necklace it grasped in its claws. Its red eyes narrowed. "You will still be her first victim. I intend to take you both back to your new home where she will feast on her sweet sister's blood. That I am sure of. None of you are making it off this mountain alive, I am also quite certain of that," it hissed as its wings extended wide, about to make its move.

Lily-Rose glared defiantly at the beast. "You're sure of a lot of things, aren't you?"

Recalling her dream where all three ghoulish creatures from the castle were chasing her down until only Antonin stood before her, she realized it was up to her to finish it, and she knew how to do it. She tilted back the holy water container, draining its contents into her mouth and dropping it to the ground.

Antonin's large body twitched, preparing to once more take flight.

Juliette watched in horror as Lily-Rose raised the still lit torch and touched it to her kerosine drenched body, instantly igniting herself.

"No!" Juliette screamed and lunged forward. Marco caught her just as she was about to jump onto her sister in a vain attempt to stop Lily-Rose from burning.

Caspar held his rifle out, not knowing what to do other than watch on in horror with the rest of them.

The Antonin creature also gazed at Lily-Rose in shock, his master's bride-to-be lighting herself on fire. "No!" it began to shriek in its deep, hissing voice.

Lily-Rose, hoping her regenerative attributes the thing in front of her had *blessed* her with would last long enough for this to be a success, jumped onto the Antonin creature, wrapping her burning flesh around its neck while suppressing screams of agony at the fire engulfing her. Her insides were on fire from the hunger while her flesh was literally burning off. She never would have guessed that self-immolation was the way she would leave this world.

Spontaneously, the Antonin creature took flight, trying to flee from the flames that were now igniting it, but Lily-Rose had a death grip around its neck. The bats above the tree cover fled at the ball of fire heading upwards toward them.

Below, Juliette screamed in terror at what was happening to her sister. Marco and Caspar were left speechless, watching the spectacularly gruesome display of fire in the sky.

Antonin zig-zagged, but this time not to toy with its prey, but rather fighting for its once-thought immortal life, much like it had one hundred years earlier from this woman's great-grandfather.

Lily-Rose no longer felt the immense pain of the fire, her nerves had been seared off. In her quickly deteriorating, foggy mind, she thought of the words she had spoken in the dungeon earlier. *Our Father, who art in heaven, hallowed be thy name.* The burning hunger in her stomach was replaced with actual flames. *Thy kingdom come, thy will be done, on Earth as it is in Heaven.* There was one last thing she needed to do. *Give us this day our daily bread and forgive us our trespasses, as we forgive those who trespass against us.* The creature was hissing and shrieking at its own impending destruction. *Lead me not into temptation but deliver me from evil.*

Putting her lips against the creature's, Lily blew her mouthful of holy water into its open mouth. *For thine is the kingdom, the power and the glory, forever and ever, amen.*

Instantly, both the creature and what remained of the burnt Lily-Rose exploded. The necklace that Antonin still clasped also ignited and shattered. The vampire bats in the sky instantly scattered, flying in all directions, and within seconds, vanished altogether.

As small burnt pieces of both Lily-Rose and Antonin floated to the ground, Juliette also fell, with Marco catching her and gently placing her on the ground. She was inconsolable and, not knowing what else to do, buried her face in his large chest. He gently put his arm around the grieving woman.

Caspar lowered his gun and rested his hand on Marco's shoulder. The forest was silent, no animals made a sound. The wolves had fled, as had the bats.

"The fog, look at the fog, it's evaporating," Caspar said quietly as he watched the fog that had enshrouded the mountain for so long slowly lift up into the sky then vanish.

They all huddled together for a bit longer before Marco spoke. "Juliette, look at me."

She pulled away from him, waiting to hear what he had to say.

"I'm sorry, Juliette." He paused, uncertain as to how to proceed. "Your necklace, could it have survived the explosion?"

Stuttering, trying to compose herself, Juliette mumbled, "I-I don't know. It was burning when I took it off but I'm not sure it could survive that." She tried to wipe away tears that continued to spill from her eyes. "Why?" she said, confused.

Marco said grimly, "I suspect that amulet is still up in that castle somewhere. And if it's there, that hidden coward, Marcel, is likely heading there now. We have to get the amulet. We've made it this far and have to see this through to its conclusion. We have to retrieve it and destroy it, to rid this place forever of this evil."

Nodding, Caspar said, "I agree but we've already lost so much; shouldn't we head back to town?" his voice trailed off.

They both looked at Juliette, still beside herself, trying to come to grips with the self-inflicted destruction of her sister. Her mind processing memories of when they were young. And then, when their parents both passed away, how they had always stuck together. Lily had been her best friend, and now she was gone. Sacrificing herself for all of them. Didn't she owe it to her to follow through with this? So that Lily's death would not be in vain?

*Pull yourself together, Juliette. Do it for Lily!*

"We're this far, and my sister did not just die in vain. We go to the castle and get the amulet," Juliette replied, wiping away her tears defiantly.

Marco looked bleakly at Juliette. "You just lost your sister. Are you sure you can do this?" he asked, kind but firm, wanting to make sure she could handle what was yet to come, especially in light of the most recent tragic turn of events.

"My great-grandfather started this, and I intend to make sure it ends with me. Let's go," Juliette replied as she stood to her feet.

They looked at each other in silence for a minute then quietly collected their things and began the rest of the hike up the mountain.

†

Once more, Marcel had watched on as his master, the ruler of his existence, was vanquished along with the necklace. He quickly and quietly began searching the immediate area where his now destroyed master had fallen. Little was left and he had to make sure the rest of Antonin's killers didn't see him. He knew time was of the essence.

*It has to be here somewhere!* Something caught his eye. Crouching down, he found what he had been searching for. His keen sense of sight in the dark, a gift from his master, had led him to the fallen shards of the golden necklace. It had shattered from the explosion but wasn't destroyed. Merely broken into several pieces, which he quickly located and collected.

He had to get back to the castle. His hopes for the travelers giving up and going back to Burnmere were dashed when he heard them discuss continuing on with the journey to the castle. If they made it to the castle, the amulet would be found and taken. *Surely, it is in his altar room! I must get to it!*

He knew they suspected he was still a threat with Juliette figuring out it was indeed him from the train station. This lot wasn't going to quit and give up, so he had to move.

He easily made it back up to the castle quickly and silently through the trees, passing the three intruders from a distance. Marcel could see they were moving slowly up the path, likely due to the large man's limp. He prided himself on how sneaky and quiet he could be. Ever since the travelers had entered the forest, he had been one step ahead of them.

Juliette would come willingly to the castle, that still held true. Otherwise, everything now appeared to be falling to him. *Have all of these years of servitude been leading to this moment for me?* He felt opportunity arise, with Antonin gone, Ingrid gone, the wolves gone. Yet, he survived! He felt a surge of confidence course through him as he knew now what he had to do. If he could complete the resurrection rites for the Pricolici, would it grant him significantly more power?

He moved on quickly, until he stood before what had until recently been Castle Visimar and said coldly, with his newfound confidence, "You treated me as a slave and now you lay in tiny pieces of burnt ash on the cold ground while I live! And soon, I will have a new master! One that will make me an heir to its mighty powers. I alone will see this through!"

Marcel walked through the large double doors into the castle, holding the fragmented necklace. He headed toward the altar room. Toward his new and much brighter immortal future.

364

# Chapter 28:

†

# Reciting the Sacred Text

"How's the hip"? Caspar asked Marco.

Glancing over at Caspar as they walked up the steep incline, Marco replied, "Could be a whole hell of a lot better, but it doesn't matter, we're almost there." He pointed at the castle up and over the last bend on the narrow path they had been on for close to an hour after the death of Antonin and Lily-Rose. Soon it would be dawn and sunlight would creep up from beyond the distant hills.

Juliette said precious little the rest of the trek up the mountain. Little did she realize when she had left the comfort of her home in England that, along with being without a mother and father, she would lose her dear sister as well. Her emotions went from utter despair to rage at the evil beings her great-grandfather had stirred up. At this moment, she hated Alfred Burns. A man she had never met who had unwittingly set in motion events that would shatter her young life.

Caspar nodded then changed the subject. "Remember when I had you doing some work in my shop? It was a few years ago."

Puzzled at the sudden change of topics, Marco looked at him with surprise. "Yes, what of it?"

"I wanted to apologize," Caspar answered, shaking his head in frustration.

"Apologize? For what?" Marco responded, now with genuine curiosity.

Even Juliette, who knew these men very little, sensed they had history. Especially in such a small town as Burnmere where likely everyone knew everyone else's business, both good and bad.

"You did good work for me, better than good, actually. You're a damn fine ironsmith. Hell, I would go so far as to call you a natural," Caspar paused as they continued up the winding road, then continued. "I considered hiring you on but knew I would likely lose business with you working in my shop and taking pay. Especially with how Bürgermeister Hartjenstein has always had it in for you. I didn't pay you what I had promised, you knew it and I knew it."

Silence fell across all three of them as they pushed forward. After a pause, Marco replied, "It's over. I've always been the town loser and I have come to accept that. Only good thing I've ever done is help bring my son into this world. All that matters now is ending well. But for what it's worth, I appreciate the apology. I would have liked working with you. But you were a little shit, and if we make it out of this alive, I expect full payment plus interest."

He looked over at Caspar and both men broke into grins then started to chuckle.

"Hell, Marco, if we make it out of this alive, I'll make you co-owner of Voit's Ironworks Shop." He smiled broadly at Marco who nodded his appreciation at what now seemed to be a fully mended relationship.

They made it to the entrance of the old, dirty, cobweb-encrusted castle with no further wolf attacks or surprise visits by vampiric creatures of the night. *What lay in wait beyond the double doors?* Juliette wondered as she stared up at the large, imposing castle in front of them.

Marco moved forward and wasn't surprised to find them locked. A minor setback. He raised his shotgun and pulled the trigger, blowing a hole in the double doors, exploding the wooden plank on the other side holding the doors closed.

Expelling his second-to-last shell, Marco popped his final shotgun shell into the chamber and slammed it shut.

Caspar moved forward, pushing the double doors open, and cautiously entered into the castle.

All three stood inside the main great room examining their new surroundings, looking for potential dangers. Torches on the walls lit the interior but everything remained relatively shrouded in shadow, as if it were built so that little to no light could penetrate its thick, stone walls.

Juliette noticed the castle crest on the stone wall. A shield with two spears making an X behind it and a dragon wrapping itself around the shield with the Latin words, *Castrum Visimar: domus aeterna tua* chiseled below.

"Castle Visimar: Your Eternal Home," Juliette said ominously, glaring up at the crest and shuddering.

"You can read Latin?" Caspar asked.

"A bit," she said then paused. "My sister could speak it much more fluently than I. Anyway, let's all hope that phrase doesn't come to pass."

"Agreed. Not sure where to go from here but we sure as hell aren't splitting up," Marco said, shifting his eyes warily around the ominous castle interior with Juliette close by his side, something he noticed and quite liked. *She trusts me. Me, of all people.*

"I've always wondered what this place would look like inside, and it certainly doesn't disappoint. I cannot wait to get out of here as soon as humanly possible," Caspar replied.

"Human likely isn't a word that applies to this place. Come on, let's start down that hallway," Juliette said, pointing.

Marco looked at her questioningly. "You seem confident; why that one?"

"Because." Juliette paused, looking in its direction then down at the floor. Dirty footprints on the stone floor led down the dark hallway to the right-hand side of the main entrance.

"Ah, good call," Marco answered, giving her a slight grin. He liked this woman. She had traveled far and lost much, yet she pushed on, determined to see this through.

Side by side, they all moved forward into the darkness.

✝

Inside the altar room, Marcel set the broken pieces of the necklace that until recently had adorned Juliette's neck and retrieved the amulet Antonin had secured behind the altar. As determined as Antonin had been to procure the necklace, he hadn't done much to actually secure and protect the amulet.

"You prideful man, that was your downfall. You weren't careful, but I am," Marcel uttered, now grinning smugly to himself at the ease with which he was able to retrieve the amulet that appeared to be waiting patiently for him.

He placed it on the altar atop the broken pieces of necklace. The lone torch cast a dim light upon the altar, just enough for Marcel to see what he was doing. He knew the incantation rites perfectly. Antonin kept the scrolls in his altar room and it was here that he had recited the words etched on them over and over, with Marcel present many times.

"Thank you, Antonin, for your diligent work, I will now take over," Marcel said with a thin smile as he lifted the scrolls from their resting place and opened the first of three.

He alone would bring the mighty beast back to this world. He would reap the countless awards and accolades from a true god, far surpassing what Antonin had ever dreamed possible, even for himself. This was his time. Taken at a young age and turned against his will into a soulless walking dead slave-man, cursed to a life of servanthood without any of the benefits allotted the likes of Ingrid and her sister, but all of that was about to change.

He stood behind the altar, one hand holding the opened scroll and the other raised upward, preparing to recite the resurrection rites he had learned over the many years. He would certainly have dressed for the occasion had he more time. However, time was limited, as the three remaining humans would certainly be nearing the castle.

The text on the first scroll began:

◯̲⊑ ⍰⍀ɰ⏃Φ̄ ⫽◯̲⍀⏄ ⌇⏃Φ̄⏃ʌ, ⊑ɰ⍀ɰ ⊬◯̲⎍⍀ ⌇ɰ⍀⍚⏃ʌΦ̄ ʌ◯̲⍙. ♀ ⍰◯̲⫛ɰ Φ̄◯̲ ⊬◯̲⎍ ⊑⎍⫛⍰⫽ɰ, ♀ʌ ʌɰɰ⏄ ◯̲⎎ ⫛⊬ ⫛⏃⌇Φ̄ɰ⍀

Translated, the symbols conveyed a message of supplication. *Oh, great lord, Satan, hear your servant now. I come to you humbly, in need of my master.*

He continued on, perfectly reciting the first scroll text in its entirety. Upon completion, he rolled it up, set it on the floor, and retrieved the second scroll.

A boom echoed through the castle which he instantly recognized as the sound of a shotgun. *They're here, sooner than expected,* he thought angrily, having only completed the first full passage of the resurrection.

He continued speaking aloud, none of it intelligible to human ears. His tongue flicked inside his mouth at the strange, otherworldly dialect. Spittle flew from his mouth as he hastily recited the second passage, his keen sense of hearing picking up approaching footsteps. *How the hell did they choose the right hallway?*

He kept reciting the next set of symbols:

⟨symbols⟩

Translating, his mind formed the thoughts. *And so, for the sake of your Earthly kingdom, grant me power to fulfill this unholy unity that you have blessed this amulet with...*

He continued on until the whole second passage was recited perfectly to completion. Deep in the recesses of his mind, he felt the being arise from its depths. Where was it coming from? Why was it here, exactly? *To rule, to take, to conquer. That's all you need to know,* his mind responded.

The altar in front of him began to shake. *It* was coming soon. He had to keep reciting the incantation aloud. He set the second scroll down and picked up the third and final scroll, opening it and once more raising his free hand toward the altar.

He continued with the third and final resurrection rites in their strange, alien dialect as the shaking continued to increase. The altar in front of him appeared to be smoking, though it was made of stone. It must be from the amulet that rested atop it.

*I beseech you, oh Satan, lord of this world, bring about the all-powerful Pricolici. Grant that I may be witness to this most unholy of births...*

As he progressed through the third rite, the altar began to crack, the gold that housed the amulet changing colors from its vibrant gold to black as the outer plating melted to reveal the amulet's true, original appearance.

The black crystal-like substance ignited, as did the remaining pieces of the broken necklace. Marcel glanced down, wanting to watch what was happening but needing to focus of the incantation rites. He raised his hands high in the air; the third passage was nearly complete.

Another quick glance down assured Marcel that he was speaking the sacred text accurately. *Keep going!* He continued in the strange dialect, doing his best to not go too quicky, despite the distractions of the noise outside the altar room and the smoking amulet. He was so close, and Marcel knew it. It was nearly complete.

The black crystal was reshaping itself. No longer solid, the fire had burned off the gold plating and was melting what lay beneath the golden exterior until the stone sat in a pool of thick, black goo, bubbling, expanding and stretching across the top of the altar while still on fire. It moved in such a way that Marcel could only surmise it was a living organism, cognizant of its surroundings.

†

They all felt the sudden vibration inside the castle. It was barely noticeable at first but quickly the stone floors began to shake.

"Come on, we have to hurry!" Caspar exclaimed as Marco nodded in agreement. Juliette had taken the lead, gun in hand, running toward what she assumed was the room they needed to get to. It was the farthest one down the long hallway, its door facing them while the others lined either side of the walls.

"I have a hunch we don't have much time left!" Juliette yelled out, no longer attempting to keep quiet, her voice rising above the low hum reverberating through the whole castle.

Fighting through the pain, Marco was having difficulty keeping up due to his hip that felt like bones grinding together. It was agonizing, but he had made it this far and, like his companions, he wasn't about to give up.

They made it to the door and, as expected, it was bolted shut.

"Marco, your shotgun got us inside this place, so have at it!" Caspar exclaimed.

"I have one shell left then I'm out," Marco replied.

"We're out of your kerosine but still have a bit of Fr. Gustloff's holy water left. We're down to the bare minimum with regards to protection here," Caspar said grimly.

"I still have this," Marco pulled out the large hunting knife he brought along from his house.

The floors and walls were now visibly shaking. Tiny particles of dirt and rock fragments were beginning to shake loose from the high ceilings throughout the castle.

"Ready?" Marco asked solemnly, glancing from Juliette to Caspar.

"Ready," they both responded, nodding.

Marco's last slug exploded from the shotgun he was quite glad that Caspar had retrieved for him earlier from the bürgermeister's house. It had been invaluable numerous times on their journey.

The door, much like the entrance into the castle itself, exploded inward and instantly, the three of them pushed forward inside. Caspar first, then Marco and Juliette. Marco, out of shells for his shotgun, had turned it around to use as a club.

What they saw inside the dimly lit room was sure to haunt them the rest of their days. Juliette recognized the man behind the altar as Marcel, the one who had a hand in luring her sister to Burnmere, which ultimately became her final resting place. *But she was burned alive, she has no resting place,* Juliette thought angerly as she quickly brought her rifle up to her shoulder and aimed.

The altar itself was a mass of black goo, dripping off of the sides and onto the floor. Bubbling and popping, small flames flared up throughout its wide exterior. In the center lay the small glowing stone, now growing brighter than any stone anyone in the room had ever seen, Marcel included.

Marco and Caspar took a second to get their bearings, but not so for Juliette. Her eyes filled with rage and she didn't hesitate, pulling the trigger aimed at thc dark man's head whose mouth was making unutterably evil sounds.

"△⋔Ш⅄, amen," Marcel said, lowering the final scroll and seeing Juliette's gun trained on him. He closed his eyes just as the bullet entered his right eye socket, traveled through his brain, then blasted out the back of his head, sending blood, skull, and brain matter against the back wall of the altar room.

He was blown off his feet. Dropping the final scroll to the floor, Marcel's body slammed against the wall directly behind him. Sliding down the wall, his body came to rest in a sitting position on the floor, his mouth slightly open and a steady stream of blood now running out of it. Next to his lifeless body lay parts of his head.

"Good shot!" Caspar called out, adding, "We burn it later, first things first—what the hell is happening here?"

Juliette, satisfied that her shot ended his life, quickly joined Marco and Caspar by the black goo-covered altar.

"Good Lord in heaven, is this what's left of the amulet and necklace?" Juliette asked with eyes wide at the swirling, bubbling black substance atop the altar. In its center was the stone.

"What do you think, Caspar?" Marco said, glancing over at him grimly. "Want to draw straws to see who attempts picking that stone up? Think it's hot like that black shit around it? Whatever we do, we have to do it quick, these walls and the floor can only take so much of this continuous vibration."

Juliette added, "I think it's imperative that the stone come with us, we can't leave it here, not after all we've seen."

"Agreed, here goes nothing," Caspar replied, shaking his head as he slung his rifle over his shoulder, reached forward, and put his finger on top of the jewel. "It's not hot." With his index and thumb, he gently plucked the stone up, pulling it from the thick black, tar-like substance that stretched like rubber.

Juliette and Marco watched as Caspar pulled on the gemstone, attempting to free it from the clutches of the elastic black goo. He managed to pull it up, away from the altar, but the foreign black substance was still clinging to its bottom side.

As if sensing someone was attempting to take its gem away, the substance bubbling atop the altar moved up and over the gemstone, touching Caspar's hand and burning him instantly. He cried out in pain as the black tar acted like an open flame, igniting his hand on fire.

Caspar's rifle slipped off his shoulder, falling to the floor as he fell over backward onto the shaking stone surface below, clenching his burning hand.

Juliette and Marco moved immediately to his side. "Holy water!" Marco cried out. Juliette quickly fished for the small bottle inside her jacket pocket, pulled it out, uncorked it and poured it over Caspar's shaking hand. The flame extinguished instantly.

Caspar was delirious with agonizing pain as the shaking grew in strength all around them. The walls formed small cracks between the stones as more dust and debris from the ceiling fluttered down on top of their heads.

Marco shouted, "We need that stone, and we need to get the hell out of here! Now! This place is coming down!"

As he spoke, a large chunk of rock broke from the ceiling, landing mere inches from the three huddled on the floor of the quickly deteriorating Castle Visimar.

## Chapter 29:

†

# Fight to the Death

While Marco, Juliette, and a severely burned Caspar continued their efforts to free the gemstone from the clutches of an evil, black liquid substance and escape a rapidly deteriorating castle, the town of Burnmere below was reeling from the murders of four of its citizens. Two of which would certainly not be missed.

Doctor Heuberger worked into the early morning hours with his neighbor Finn and the town's coroner, Victor Reis.

"Cause of death, bullet wounds, that's fairly obvious. What isn't obvious is how it all happened. This is a disaster," the thin, twenty-eight-year-old man with receding hair and small wire spectacles said morosely.

Constable Hecht's widow had arrived when he hadn't shown up earlier in the evening to find the murders inside the jail. She was still inconsolable.

The three men looked at the woman who sat with several other townsfolk on the corner near the crime scene, face buried in her hands.

Joachim nodded and said quietly so only his fellow companions could hear, "Gentlemen, you should know, we have some of our townsfolk up on that mountain right now. I fear the body count may grow before the sun comes up."

Looking at the town's doctor, puzzled, Victor Reiss replied, "People are up there? What the hell for? That place is off-limits," he said sternly, which was his natural disposition.

"*Was* off-limits," Heuberger said, looking toward the jail where the bürgermeister lay dead on the floor. "Nick, Marco, Caspar and that Lily-Rose's sister, Juliette Burns, who just arrived in town, went up there to stop, well, to end this whole damn thing."

Joachim, who had essentially taken the much-needed leadership role in town, filled both Victor and Finn in on what had happened over the last several days.

They listened in rapt attention until something astonishing interrupted their private discussion. All three men, along with the townspeople that had gathered near the crime scene, turned toward the castle on the mountain. The slightest hint of sunshine had appeared on the horizon, bringing welcomed light to the valley.

"Look! The fog, it's lifting!" Finn exclaimed, peering up at the mountain and the fog that seemed to be not only lifting, but slowly evaporating as well.

"Do you feel that?" Victor asked, looking at both men.

"Yes, the ground is shaking. It's coming from up there," Doctor Heuberger said, staring wide-eyed up at the castle.

✝

Up in the castle, inside the altar room, the black substance slid down the other side of the altar, quickly moving onto the motionless body of Marcel.

Marcel, while shot, wasn't dead. He had been bit long ago by Antonin but was never gifted the full power that Ingrid and her sister were allotted. He was, however, still alive and, over time the gunshot would have slowly healed itself.

The foreign substance slid over his exposed body, then his face, and slid into his mouth and the eyeless socket the bullet had ravaged earlier. The black goo was contracting, shrinking, as it entered the body.

On top of the altar, the remaining black goo slid off, taking along with it the gemstone that clanked to the vibrating floor.

"Get the stone!" Caspar yelled while grabbing hold of his burned hand. He had opened his eyes just in time to see the stone fall. All three of them looked on in horror as the black substance slid off the altar, across the body of Marcel, and was burrowing itself inside him.

"What is God's name..." Marco said.

"God has nothing to do with this," Juliette replied, staring in wide-eyed disgust.

The last tiny bit of black slime oozed into the opening in Marcel's right eye socket. The gemstone rested in his opened hand. Slowly, the hand closed around it. His remaining eye in his left socket sprang to life, instantly aware of his surroundings.

Marco and Juliette grabbed hold of Caspar, hoisting him up to a standing position and moving back. Even Caspar's pain seemed to fade as he looked on at what was happening beside the altar.

Marcel stood to his feet, his body growing longer. His arms extending, his legs extending, his clothes extending along with the mutating body then tearing off completely, revealing a naked body whose skin had stretched to the point of tearing open and exposing muscle underneath. His chest widened and grew while the skin around his face pulled itself off. He was now a skinless being. His mouth widened as his one remaining eyeball liquified and dribbled out of its socket. New eyes began forming to replace Marcel's old ones, the new, significantly larger ones casting a sickly red color. His skull was mutating as well into an oblong oval, jutting out the back side where the bullet exited earlier, now fully healed.

"If there is or was such a thing as the legend of the Pricolici, I believe we may be seeing it now," Marco said grimly.

The whole room was shaking, causing pieces of rock to fall from the ceiling, one of them hitting Juliette on the shoulder. She cried out in pain, dropping her rifle to the ground and grabbing hold of her injured shoulder.

Caspar pulled out the crucifix Fr. Gustloff had given him and held it out in front of him. His rifle was no longer within reach, the floor's vibrations had shaken it away to the far side of the room. They had no weapons and the room had turned to unholy chaos.

The black tar swirled and twisted around exposed muscles, the creature's transformation now nearing its completion. Large claws on the end of larger fingers. Feet that now resembled something more akin to hooves. Two large horns shot out of either side of the new creation's head, each one twisting and tilting down toward its torso. Fangs similar to a vampire's pushed out of its gums inside its widening mouth, while wolf fur sprouted across its muscular, large body.

The creature looked up as if toward heaven itself and held its hand out with the gemstone. Its thoughts reverberated through the room, through the castle, and outward across the mountain. *I am eternal! I live, and I shall take a bride to spread my seed to populate this world! The gemstone of the Christ-child is mine! My reign will bring fire to all of huma...*

Its telepathic connection to the world of the living was cut off by a searing pain to its wrist. It looked down to see a burly man with a large knife. Marco had swung down with all his might onto the creature's exposed, thick, fur-covered outstretched wrist, slicing into it with brute animal strength.

The Pricolici screamed more in anger than pain, its hand nearly severed from its mutating wrist, hanging on by a thin layer of new skin that had started forming over its black tar-like muscles.

For a brief moment, it lost control of its severed hand and dropped the gemstone onto the floor. Marco, biting through the pain in his hip, lunged down, grabbing the stone then retreating back toward Juliette and Caspar.

Black tendons shot out of the Pricolici's wrist, attempting to reconnect with its severed and dangling hand, pulling it back up toward the wrist where black goo continued leaking out onto the shaking floor below. Opening its jaws wide, exposing large rows of pointed fangs and a sickly, dark red forked tongue inside, it roared in anger at this man, this *mortal*, that had snatched the prized jewel it had waited thousands of years to be reborn through. Its unhealed hand still dangled, as without the healing stone it was now vulnerable but still powerful.

Juliette and Caspar headed for the door along with Marco, who shouted out, "We need to get out of here, now!"

While the room continued crumbling around it, the creature took its first steps, slamming its hooved, ram-like feet onto the floor, every step shaking the room more. The ground under its feet gave way, as did it, falling through the newly created hole. As it began falling, it lunged forward, landing on its stomach against the barely stable remaining stone floor that continued crumbling, its body halfway out of the gaping hole. With its undamaged left hand, it reached out, grabbing hold of Caspar's fleeing leg, dropping him instantly, face first on the ground.

Marco, grasping the stone tightly in one hand and his knife in the other, glanced back to see Caspar go down hard.

Juliette cried out, still favoring her injured shoulder. "Caspar, no! Hang on!" She watched helplessly as he was pulled toward the rapidly expanding hole in the floor.

With a bloody and broken face, Caspar looked toward Marco and shouted, "Go! Get out of here!"

Instinctively, Marco tossed his knife in the air. It clattered to the floor in front of Caspar who reached for it with his burnt right-hand, white-hot pain instantly shooting across his entire body.

The Pricolici continued to use its own undamaged hand to pull Caspar further toward it and the continually expanding hole in the stone floor.

The knife slid forward far enough for Caspar to grab hold of it as the floor continued to crumble. He quickly turned and slammed it as hard as he could into the creature's heart.

The vulnerable creature, minus its healing stone, cried out in agony as the knife pierced its newly-formed, rapidly beating heart.

Then, the ground gave way completely.

Both Caspar and the Pricolici monster disappeared through the open floor as large stone chunks fell from the ceiling. The altar was obliterated, causing more destruction as it too fell forward and through the opening in the floor.

Marco and the wounded Juliette wasted no time, running back through the long cobweb strewn hallway toward the main entrance to the castle. It, too, was falling apart. Torches that had previously adorned the walls had fallen, igniting anything that burned. Parts of the ceiling caved in throughout the hallway as did the floor. Every step they took in their sprint to the front doors caused another stone underfoot to shimmy then fall downward into blackness.

Pounding pain searing through his hip, Marco fell to the floor just as they reached the crumbling main entrance leading out of the castle. He clenched the gemstone tightly but landed hard on the injured hip and cried out in pain.

Juliette stopped and tried to help him to his feet, "Come on, Marco! Get up!" she shouted.

He shook his head and held out the gemstone to her, "Take it and get the hell out of here! Go, now!"

She looked at the stone for a brief second then at her surroundings rapidly caving in around them. "No way, Marco. I'm not leaving you behind! We're leaving together damnit, *now get up!*"

Taking her hand begrudgingly, with her help, he forced himself back to his feet.

Marco's pull on her injured shoulder sent new pain coursing through her own body, but Juliette shook it off and looked toward the front doors, still busted open from the shotgun blast earlier.

Acknowledging his brief nod of thanks, she took his free hand and together they rushed forward as the house crest above the fireplace fell and smashed to the ground, the floor crumbling beneath its weight as it plummeted into darkness. Fire was rapidly spreading from the collapsing structure, knocking over lit torches as smoke filled the rooms quickly, much like it did one hundred years prior.

"Castle Visimar: Your Eternal Home," Juliette spat out angrily as she and Marco ran through the opened double doors, the entire ceiling in the great room collapsing behind them and smashing through the heavily damaged floor.

Once outside, sunlight hit their eyes as they squinted and continued to run as fast as their weary legs and damaged bodies could take them, finally collapsing onto a nearby patch of grass, unable to go any further.

Lying on the grass, they turned around and looked up at Castle Visimar, that, for a brief period in time could be renamed *Castle Pricolici*. The entire structure shook, its two peaks on either side crumbling. One falling in on itself while the other fell into the top of the castle, bringing the roof crashing down inside the structure itself. From there, the castle caved in on every side, taking the small stables behind the castle along with it.

The ground shook violently as Juliette clenched Marco tightly, watching the chaos around them.

After what felt like an eternity, the trembling stopped. The ground ceased to shake, and all was silent. All that remained was a pile of smoldering rubble.

As dust and smoke filled the sky then began to settle atop the destruction of Castle Visimar, Marco looked over at Juliette who was softly crying. They were tears filled with pain, suffering, and most of all, anger. Anger at the senseless death of her sister, Nick, and then Caspar. All had given their lives to save the town below and potentially, if the creature's legend was to be believed, the very world itself.

Marco hung his head. He had almost given up and would be dead now if it wasn't for this woman who, the day before, he hadn't even met. He looked at the gemstone in his hand.

"How close were we to seeing true chaos rule this land?" Juliette said, looking down at the shining stone in Marco's hand.

"Too close," Marco replied, then handed it to her. "Here, this belongs to you, Juliette. It's been in your family for a hundred years and should stay there."

She smiled and took it, instantly thinking of her dear sister. She clenched the stone tightly then stood to her feet. "Come on, we need to get back to town and tend to our wounds. We'll both have a lot to answer for."

Nodding, Marco glanced up, replying, "I've never seen the sky look so clear."

Juliette joined him. He was right, it was a beautiful morning on the mountain and the sun shone brightly down on the town of Burnmere below.

"Think we'll encounter any more wolves on our way back to town?" Juliette asked shakily.

"No, it's over," Marco replied firmly.

They slowly made their way back to the town of Burnmere where the residents had also had an active night, culminating in watching the fog lift after what seemed like countless years followed by the complete destruction of the castle on the mountain.

Marco was correct, the only thing dangerous about the trek back down the mountain was the steep incline they both had to navigate in their current injured states. If any wolves remained, they had retreated their own hiding spots and avoided the humans completely.

Most of the walk back down the mountain was in silence, each lost in their own thoughts and regrets, playing out the events of the last day in their heads. Nick, then Lily-Rose, and finally, Caspar had succumbed to the evil of the mountain and its inhabitants.

Juliette looked over to a silent Marco. "We never saw what happened to Caspar. He fell through the floor along with that Pricolici thing and then…" she paused and trailed off, unable to find words for her fears.

Marco grew more solemn. "I'm afraid I can't imagine how anyone could survive that."

"Marco, I'm sorry for all of this. I'm sorry that my great-grandfather took that amulet that essentially housed the very monster we defeated." She looked down at the jewel in her hand. "You'll be a hero in Burnmere. Thanks to you and Caspar and Nick, a great evil was averted."

"I assume I will be jailed rather than welcomed as a hero," Marco sighed, resigned to his fate and deeply grieved over the loss of his two traveling companions.

"Well, the future isn't written yet," Juliette said firmly, glaring at the town that was growing closer and closer.

# Chapter 30:

†

# Back in Burnmere

Doctor Heuberger stared up at the destruction high in the mountain. He, along with the rest of the town, had watched as the castle crumbled to the ground. Some even cheered but this was no time for celebrating. Cold-blooded murder had occurred in the town of Burnmere, this time not from the evil on the mountain but one of their own.

The town was in a state of shock, more so than it had ever been. The few that could manage to help did so quickly and without complaint. Finn's wife Anna agreed to handle any families with children showing up for school that hadn't found out about the death of their teacher, Ada Shalner.

It was early afternoon when the town coroner found Doctor Heuberger returning from old Rozalia's cottage, where he was filling in the old woman on the limited information they had on Lily-Rose's whereabouts, and asking if the girl had left any belongings behind that might help solve the mystery of her disappearance.

Wiping his sweat-covered face off, Reis cleared his throat and motioned for Heuberger to talk in private, away from listening ears. Taking the hint, the doctor looked around to make sure they were far enough away from Rozalia, then fixed a tired gaze on the coroner. "What is it, Victor? I'm beyond tired and don't see any rest coming in my near future."

"Look, it's the Seiler woman. You need to see her body," Victor said quietly, looking at Joachim urgently.

Shaking his head, Heuberger replied, "For the love of God, I do not want to see her. I would rather see anyone else, dead or alive in this town, more than that woman."

Reis didn't move, he just stared at Heuberger, motioning for him to follow to the coroner's office.

"Fine, but make this quick. There's so much to do and I haven't eaten in I don't know how long," the doctor said with a sigh.

"You'll be glad you didn't eat. Trust me, come on," Reis said grimly, leading the way to his shop.

Turning back to Rozalia, a well-known gossip in town who had strained to hear their hushed discussion, he said firmly, "Rozalia, I have to go. I promise you'll know what happened to Lily-Rose as soon as I do."

"Oh, thank heavens. Thank you for keeping me informed. Such a nice girl, that one," Rozalia replied then turned and walked toward another group of women who were likely gossiping about the events of the previous night.

Taking a deep breath then exhaling heavily, Heuberger headed toward Victor Reis's office, dreading whatever he was about to see.

Numerous townsfolk attempted to stop him and ask about what had occurred the previous night. All he could do was push forward, telling the concerned people of Burnmere, "We're working on it," and letting them know a town hall meeting would take place later that day in the church at three o'clock and to spread the word.

He was dreading the meeting, but in order to keep things from delving into chaos before help could arrive, some semblance of order would have to be restored.

He arrived at Victor Reiss's office and headed inside. The small office was scattered with autopsy and surgery equipment and tables for the recently deceased for Victor to work on. Today, all tables were occupied. Recently it had been the thirteen-year-old Aline Koltz.

Walking past the lifeless bodies of Hecht, Hartjenstein, Gustloff and Ada Shalner, he came to the last in the far end of the room. Everly Seiler. Reis looked at Heuberger and pulled back the blanket that covered the corpse. Instantly, Heuberger flinched at the sight in front of him on the table.

Everly had been stripped of her ragged clothes. Her naked body was peppered with a spray of tiny wounds where Heuberger's shotgun blast had hit. But that wasn't what caught both men's eyes.

Her breast area was covered in thin scratches, though none deep enough to bleed through to her clothing. Strands of thick, black fur clung to her body, primarily her pubic region. Clearly not human hair.

The doctor put his hand to his mouth, holding back the bile that had quickly formed inside. He was instantly nauseous and felt the need to turn away from the ghastly scene. "What in the *hell* did that?" he uttered in disgust, glaring at Reis.

Sighing, Victor Reis replied, "I simply cannot explain it. The fur, and it is indeed fur, appears to be from a wolf. That's not all. From what I gathered from an initial examination, she's recently had," he paused, looking at Heuberger before continuing, "intercourse." Pointing to dried blood close to her pubic region.

"Dear Lord, Everly, what did you do?" the doctor said, closing his eyes in disgust.

"I can't explain it. I'm not sure if whatever happened to her was the catalyst for her killing spree? Maybe it made her, I don't know—rabid? Possessed perhaps? If you believe that sort of thing." Reis said, mystified.

"Cover that up," Heuberger said grimly.

Victor Reis quickly obliged his request before adding, "Marco, her husband. While I certainly hope he survived whatever happened up there, I'm not sure how we can explain any of this to him."

"We'll figure something out. In a few hours we have the town hall meeting; let's deal with one thing at a time," Heuberger said morosely.

They both fell silent, looking over the four bodies in front of them.

"If this town ever needed a priest for spiritual guidance, it would be now. This is bad, Joachim," Reis said sadly, hanging his head and sighing heavily.

†

At three o'clock everyone in the small town of Burnmere gathered inside St. Joseph's parish. Even with barely one hundred residents still remaining in the town, the church couldn't hold everyone. The overflow were told to stand outside.

Doctor Heuberger couldn't believe the turn of events that had put him in charge of this meeting. He was little more than a doctor, a decent one, but that's where it ended. Walking up to the altar that would cease to be used for Mass until further notice, he wished to hell he was anywhere but in this house of God.

Glancing over at Reis, who nodded for him to get on with it, he cleared his throat to get the rambling crowd's attention. Much had been rumored throughout the day about the murderess Everly Seiler and her reasons for committing the crimes. One group of old men near the butcher shop conjectured that the woman had been possessed by an evil from the castle, and that its later destruction confirmed it. Heuberger wasn't sure how that confirmed anything, but he realized people needed their theories to rationalize what had happened.

Before Heuberger could utter a word, an elderly woman shouted out from somewhere in the crowd, "Just who is in charge here? How could you have let this happen! And after just burying Aline Koltz!"

"Ma'am, I assure you, none of us was in the jail when it happened. We aren't sure, and the girl's death was unrelated to this," Heuberger began, already becoming flustered.

A man cut him off, "I hear that Everly woman left the bürgermeister's house yesterday. What the hell was she doing there? She's married!"

Another face in the crowd, this one a younger man. "Why did Caspar, an upstanding enough citizen in our town, go up that mountain on some wild goose chase with two drunks and a strange woman that just rolled into town? Supposedly the sister of that young lady that disappeared. What's that all about?"

"I think an evil fell onto this town when she showed up! Then her sister arrived and last night happened!" a woman in the front row exclaimed.

Reis shook his head; this was going from bad to worse. He looked at Heuberger  who shrugged. This was going exactly how he had expected it to go.

An irrational woman in the middle of the crowd shouted, "I think this all stems from that Marco fella! Damn drunk that he is, chases his son out of town then vanishes up that mountain with a pretty little lady. Everly had had enough and took it out on us folks!"

"Don't blame him! That woman is a miserable old bitch, she killed a priest! She'll burn in hell for all eternity, mark my words!" a man in front of her retorted.

The woman shouted back louder than before, "Why don't you mind your business when I'm talking? I didn't ask for your opinion!"

"And no one asked for yours, Valerie!" the man retorted, this time standing to face her. She instantly stood up as well.

The chatter now grew louder and angrier.

"People! Please! We need to remain calm here! This is doing no one any good! We've called this meeting in order to set up a chain of command for the short term, so please, I need your help!" Heuberger pleaded. He wished his wife were here for moral support.

His words did little to calm the agitated crowd that was quicky descending into an angry mob. Kids began crying as mothers covered their ears at the growing use of strong language.

Everyone was low on sleep, scared, hungry and simply at their wit's end from the hard life in Burnmere. And now, uncertainly lingered across the entire town.

# Chapter 31:

†

# A New Leader Emerges

Marco and Juliette walked through the final stretch of trees into Burnmere, near the cottage where Lily-Rose had stayed. They made their way toward the center of town and along the way met Finn Sessler.

"Marco!" Finn exclaimed, pulling the reins back on his horse.

"Morning, Finn, where is everyone?" Marco said, glancing around at the empty street.

"Morning. And pleasure meeting you, ma'am, my name is Finn Sessler," he nodded and tilted his head slightly in her direction.

The exhausted and beleaguered-looking woman nodded back. "Juliette Burns."

There was a slight pause as Finn stared at the two haggard individuals. "Look, Marco, there's something you need to know. I hate to be the one to tell you this… But you need to prepare yourself. Especially if you're heading to the church," he said uneasily.

Sensing something was amiss, Marco pressed. "Finn, we're tired, banged up and honestly surprised to be alive. Out with it!"

Finn sighed heavily and climbed off his horse, standing in front of the large man. "Marco, something's happened here in town. It's," he paused then met Marco's eyes. "It's your wife. Something terrible has happened."

✝

The weather in Burnmere was beautiful but no celebrations were to be had. The fog had lifted, the castle was destroyed and, the townspeople would soon realize, the wolves in the forest had retreated deep into the mountain, away from any humans. Yet, tensions were at an all-time high in the tiny village.

Back inside St. Joseph's, the doctor was about to shout at the top of his lungs for everyone to just shut the hell up for one second so they could all talk rationally, but he didn't need to. A hush began to fall over the angered crowd. Starting outside then working its way up the pews until it reached Heuberger himself.

All eyes turned, watching the large man limping slightly and an unfamiliar woman favoring an injured arm walk up the middle aisle toward the altar and a wide-eyed Doctor Heuberger.

Marco and Juliette reached the front of the room then turned to the crowd. They were met with angry glares.

After a brief silence, Marco spoke. "The evil up on the mountain has been destroyed along with the castle it inhabited."

"Who is this woman? Do you know what your wife has done?" the angry woman who was getting ready to fight the man earlier said bitterly. "She murdered people! Our priest, the bürgermeister and Constable Hecht! Our schoolteacher! They're all dead!"

Marco was silent for a moment then replied, "I know, Finn Sessler informed me minutes ago."

"Well, what do you have to say for yourself?" the woman challenged.

Juliette, already agitated by this loud woman, took the stone out of her pocket and raised it high in the air. The brilliance of it emanated through the whole church. "Listen to what Marco here has to say!"

Silence once more fell across the crowd of people who stared in wonder and amazement at this small stone that cast various colors around the church.

Marco looked at Juliette and smiled in thanks. Turning to the crowd, and with the assistance of Juliette, he told the tale of her arrival, their trek up to the castle, battle with the vampires and werewolves then the ultimate evil, the Pricolici, and ending with the loss of Nick and Caspar and the collapse of the castle.

A long hush fell over the crowd as he spoke, and for many minutes after, as people's faces softened in awe and gratitude for what this man and woman had been through. Everyone sensed, from the appearance of the magical stone that shone so brightly, that they were in the presence of something clearly supernatural. It continued to display a light show against the walls of the church, freed of the confines of the black, alien parasitic presence that had encapsulated it for centuries.

Once the story was finished and most of the questions answered, one remained. Who would be the person to lead and guide Burnmere now, in its broken and beat-up shape? They all agreed someone should be elected, fair and square.

Heuberger was surprised and impressed with how well Marco handled the crowd, especially considering everything he had been through. He had kept his cool, and when it was all said and done, it appeared that the crowd, even Constable Hecht's widow, was satisfied with the crazy tale that had been told.

No one could deny the shaking ground, the birds leaving town, the numerous disappearances, the ominous fog, and, of course, the legend itself that seemed to collaborate what Marco Seiler had said. All of it had led to the devastating events of the previous night on the mountain as well as the town below.

"Last but not least, I would like to apologize to all of you," Marco said, hanging his head in shame, which immediately brought a new hush over the crowd. He continued, "I haven't been a good man. I know many of you blame Everly, but I take responsibility for not doing more. I've drunk to dull the pain of our lives together. I've fought some of you out of anger with my own personal demons. And this is what it has led to. Do with me what you will, but I lay myself before you, asking for your mercy. This town needs to come together, now more than ever, and if that requires me to be held accountable for what happened last night, I will answer for those crimes."

There was a pause, then Heuberger stood and cleared his throat, looking around him at the crowd of people inside the church as well as those standing in the back and directly outside. "I would like to make a recommendation. Many of you may not like it, but I see in front of me a man who deserves a second chance. Marco, I would like to nominate you as our interim constable. Provided we have a majority vote, of course."

Even in his exhausted state, Marco couldn't believe what he was hearing. His eyes widened and he quickly started shaking his head and raising his hand no in protest to this absurd notion.

"I second that motion," the woman who had been his strongest opponent throughout the discussion chimed in.

It seemed most of the townspeople agreed that Marco's unfortunate connection to the murderess Everly quickly became moot. She was a bad egg, always had been. And deep down, every person in the town of Burnmere knew it. The fault didn't lie with Marco; in fact, other than his heavy drinking, Marco had always tried to do the right thing. The drinking was simply the result of the awful excuse for a human he had unfortunately been linked to. Nor did the fault fall onto the bürgermeister or any of Everly's external circumstances. The fault fell on the woman's willingness to let evil in.

A hush fell over the church. Slowly, one by one, hands began to raise in unison. All in favor of making this one-time drunk, this man who had for so long been a laughingstock in the town of Burnmere, its new, if temporary, leader.

Juliette tried to suppress her emotions at what was happening. Finally, an underdog appearing to get his due. Her soft eyes shifted up to him. She barely knew this man but couldn't have been prouder.

Humbled by the town's unanimous support, Marco hung his head. Juliette, standing beside him, whispered, "I don't know you well, Marco, but damn if this doesn't feel good right now."

Not looking up, Marco smiled a genuine and deeply humbled smile of gratitude.

✝

The meeting was adjourned, and people filed out of the church. Though still a somber occasion, a new ray of hope had fallen across the people and town of Burnmere. All felt as though the end of the evil had truly come. The castle was destroyed, and the sunlit, beautiful sky promised a new and potentially prosperous time ahead.

Heuberger took Marco and Juliette to his office to get checked out. Marco would be fine with some rest but Juliette's arm likely needed to be put into a sling.

As she was being tended to, Victor Reis walked in, standing in front of Marco and crossing his arms. "Marco, I need you to see the bodies. I'm sorry, I know you probably need sleep but…"

Marco didn't hesitate. "I'll be over in a few minutes. I understand."

Nodding at the man's resilience and willingness to do this very unpleasant thing, Victor nodded at both him and Juliette then left them alone with the doctor.

"I'll be leaving tomorrow as long as my driver Daniel Kolb shows up," Juliette said quietly, suddenly feeling self-conscious.

"Of course. Juliette, I can't thank you enough for your help. We made a hell of a team. All of us," Marco replied, thinking of Caspar and Nick, two people that before the events of the past few days he had considered mortal enemies. He missed them both deeply and felt a sense of true loss. Not so with the woman he had been married to.

"I miss my sister. I will never forget the image of her in my mind, burning herself alive to kill that, that, thing," Juliette said grimly.

"I'm sorry, Juliette, truly, I am. The last few days are a blur of awful things piled upon awful things. That gemstone, many died for it through the years, you must protect it," Marco said watching her wince at the pain Heuberger was inflicting on her injured arm.

Doctor Heuberger said kindly, "Almost done, Miss Juliette."

"I have a pitstop to make at the coroner's then I'll walk you to Rozalia Sitek's cottage," Marco said as they made their way to the door, both thanking Heuberger for his help.

"Get some rest yourself there, Joachim, we have much to do. I'll get in touch with you in the morning," Marco said with a nod.

"One last thing, Marco, I'm sorry I did what I had to do last night. I'm no killer, but well, it was her or me," Heuberger said sadly.

"Thank you, doctor," Marco answered sorrowfully, "but it seems as if you did this town a service. I just wish you could have stopped this before it got this far. I should be the one apologizing; you never should have been placed in such a predicament. She was my wife and my responsibility. I will have to track down my son and give him the news, although I suspect he will have very little interest in his mother's death."

Heuberger nodded sadly as they left his office and headed to the coroner's office, a place neither of them wanted to visit in the least.

As they walked quietly to what was sure to be a house of horrors, Marco looked at Juliette. "You don't have to come in. This won't be pleasant."

"I'm coming in with you. Together to the end, or at least until tomorrow at noon," Juliette answered.

"I wish you'd be sticking around longer; we could really use someone like you to help us rebuild this town," Marco said kindly.

Smiling, she responded, "Thanks, Marco, but I think this stone needs to get as far away from here as possible."

He nodded in reply as they entered Reis's office, Reis greeting them solemnly. Both Marco and Juliette instantly became morose at the death that once again surrounded them.

Marco inspected the bodies of all three men, grimacing at their wounds. Upon seeing Fr. Gustloff's body, he made a sign of the cross then headed to Ada Shalner, sadly.

Reis said grimly, "Miss Juliette, I don't think you should see this," holding his hand on the cover of Everly's body, wating to pull it back.

"Whatever is under those covers, we've both seen worse up there in that unholy castle, trust me. She's certainly earned the right to be here if she so chooses," Marco answered, nodding for him to unveil the body.

"Suit yourself," Reis replied, sighing and pulling the blanket back.

Neither Marco nor Juliette flinched at Everly's naked body laying on the cold table. Surprisingly, it had very little damage done to it. The shotgun blast to her stomach was still there from the previous night, but the scratches were all gone.

"They're gone," Reis said shaking his head in puzzlement. "This woman had scratches all over her chest and stomach and they're gone. It's as if they healed themselves. I just don't understand it."

"What's that?" Juliette said, eyes widening at the black wolf's fur that remained on her body and around her pubic area.

"That I don't rightly have an explanation for," Reis replied.

"It said, 'Everly was so sweet,'" Marco said bleakly, thinking back to the words the wolf spoke into his mind when they had battled on the mountain the night before.

"The sooner she's buried, the better," he said shaking his head and turning away from the grizzly sight.

"The healing scratches, what do you make of them?" Reis asked.

Looking at the coroner, Marco shook his head. "I don't know. We've both seen more in the last few days than any human should see, so add this to the list. She's buried first thing tomorrow, got it?"

Nodding in resignation, Reis mumbled, "Got it."

Marco walked Juliette to the cottage where Rozalia Sitek happily accepted, free of charge, Juliette Burns into her home. "I'll get your belly fed, then get you all cleaned up and off to bed!" the old woman said happily.

Before entering the cottage, Juliette turned to face Marco. "Thank you for all you've done. It's certainly been an eventful couple of days; I feel like I haven't slept in weeks."

"You and me both," Marco responded, suddenly feeling awkward. She was incredibly beautiful, even tired and dirty.

Sensing the man's awkwardness, she leaned forward and gave him the slightest kiss on his dirty cheek, her soft lips barely brushing against him. An act of kindness he hadn't experienced since before he was married to the cold and uncaring Everly Seiler so many years earlier.

Blushing, he smiled at her then turned and headed to his house. The last place he wanted to be right now.

# Chapter 32:

†

# A Welcome Visitor

Marco cleaned himself up once inside his house, playing back the events of the past few days in his mind.

"I could go for a drink right about now," he said with a heavy sigh, before adding, "No you don't, Marco, those days are behind you. You may not feel worthy of the job, but it's fallen to you, don't let these people down."

He fell into his chair in the living room, his hip ached, and he remained hungry. He would deal with those issues and the many others lined up behind them later. He just needed to close his eyes for a few minutes. Sleep engulfed him in what felt like seconds.

Night fell across the mountain and town below. Not only were there no howls of wolves and the fog hadn't returned, but stars could be seen twinkling in the beautiful night sky. The people of Burnmere had all turned in early, as most had been up through the previous night after Everly's murder spree.

While the town slept, the moon glowed brightly in the night sky. Doctor Heuberger had seen to it that several men took shifts at the jail, standing by in case anything out of the ordinary happened. Marco needed at least one good night's sleep before taking on his new duties as interim constable. The man had much to do, but for now, he slept. All was calm in the night, except for an odd dream Marco had.

In it, he saw his dead wife Everly pull the blanket off of her naked body, previously lying dead in the coroner's office. She had changed. The shotgun blast was completely healed but the fur on her now much younger body remained. She barely looked like Everly at all. Her slim figure looked beautiful. Large, full breasts, milky-smooth skin that not a single wrinkle could be found on, and hair that hung down over her sensual body in flowing curls. Her eyes were full of new life and, if the moon hit them just right, they cast a yellowish glow.

She quietly slipped out of the coroner's office, into the full moonlight. Once outside, she began to change, her beautiful new body contorting and mutating into something horrific. Something very close to the black wolf.

She made her way quickly and quietly deep into the forest, where a single howl echoed through the trees.

Marco woke up with a jolt from his dream. Someone was pounding on his door, and he could see the sun through his dirty window. He had slept through the night. Shaking his head, he sat up, flinching at his hip as he walked to the door.

Victor Reis was waiting for him along with Doctor Heuberger. "She's gone!" Reis exclaimed as soon as the door opened.

Nodding because he knew, he chose not to share with them the dream he had awakened from. Marco stepped outside into the sunny dawn and the distinct lack of fog and gray cloud cover.

"I think you should have this," Reis said, handing over Samuel Hartjenstein's pistol and Constable Hecht's rifle.

Marco took them both, strapping on the pistol around his waist and slinging the rifle over his shoulder. The three of them made their way to Reis's office to confirm the missing body.

"What do we tell the townspeople? Heuberger asked as they walked quickly.

"We tell them the truth. They can choose to believe it or not. There will be no more coverups in the town of Burnmere," Marco said firmly.

"Anyone in this town looking for a deputy?" a man called out, walking toward the group slowly.

They all turned to see Caspar, bloody and dirty but very much alive.

Marco's eyes widened, and impulsively he ran over and threw his arms around the haggard man. "You're alive!"

Caspar grimaced at the hug and, with his unburnt hand, returned the embrace.

"Juliette, did she get out alive?" he asked as Heuberger began leading him to his office to treat the burns and a brief nod was exchanged between Reis and Caspar.

"Yes, she's alive and well. Let me go fetch her and we'll catch up with you. We have much to discuss, Caspar!" Turning to Reis, he said, "Change of plans. I'll come to your office as soon as I can—this is an unexpected surprise!"

Reis nodded in understanding and headed back to his office to await Marco's visit.

Marco headed to Rozalia Sitek's cottage, suddenly excited to see Juliette, quickly attempting to adjust his hair and clothes as he approached and then knocked on the door.

He was happy to see that she, not the old woman, answered the door, greeting him with a broad smile. She had obviously bathed, slept, and put on fresh clothes. She looked stunning.

They stared awkwardly at one another for several seconds before Marco spoke.

"Juliette, good morning. You, um," he stammered, "you look…beautiful."

Instantly, she felt her face grow flush and looked away then down at her dress. "Well, I don't have many clean clothes with me, but this works for my trip back home, I suppose. And you clean up pretty nice yourself, Mr. Constable!" she added with a slight smile.

He chuckled. "Well, thank you, Juliette." He ignored the sad fact that she was likely leaving in a few short hours, then said, "Do you have moment? I need you to see something down at the doctor's office."

Alerted by his sudden change in tone and facial expression, she quickly nodded. "I'll be right out." She gently shut the door and a minute later came back, letting Rozalia know she would be back soon to retrieve her luggage and thanking her profusely for her hospitality.

On the way to the doctor's office, Marco didn't tell her about his missing wife. He didn't want to worry her as she was preparing to leave soon.

"You have the gemstone?" Marco asked, glancing over at her as they walked side by side.

She wore a small leather satchel around her shoulder and pointed to it. "Yes, it's safe and sound." She patted it softly.

At Heuberger's office, after a few small knocks on the door, Marco pushed it open and they entered.

Juliette's eyes immediately grew large. "Caspar! You're alive!" she exclaimed and ran to where he sat on an examination table, the same one she had sat on earlier for her injured shoulder. She saw immediately that his hand was bandaged up and recalled the terrible burn he had received from the black tar-like substance.

Caspar wore a broad smile across his face. "So, the crew is back together again," he said, happy to see her.

Marco walked over and took a seat near him. "Are you up to talking? Or do you need some time?"

Nodding that he was good to chat, he looked at Heuberger who appeared to be leaving.

"Unless you have pressing matters, doctor, I would like you to stay. I want you to hear everything that happened up on that mountain," Marco said.

"Certainly," Heuberger responded, putting his hands behind his back and focusing on Caspar.

They all fell silent, waiting for Caspar to tell his tale.

# Chapter 33:

†

# Difficult Goodbyes

Caspar had indeed fallen with the Pricolici-Marcel mutation down through the rapidly crumbling interior of Castle Visimar. The creature's heart was punctured by Caspar, thanks to Marco's long knife, and since devoid of the life-giving gemstone it had previously clutched it its hand, it was vulnerable and mortal.

The castle was deep, but the fall lasted precious few seconds. The Pricolici landed with a hard thud onto the dirt of the dungeon floor. Caspar landed on top of it, the creature's massive size softening his landing.

Nearly having the wind knocked out of him, Caspar realized his good fortune at still being alive. The creature was still moving as well, its arms and large legs shaking from the impact. Black goo oozed out of numerous lacerations across its body, along with the large gash over its heart.

Caspar quickly scanned his surroundings, immediately seeing several coffins laying across the dirt. Rocks of all sizes were smashing down around him so he had to hurry. "There must be a way out of here!" he shouted.

He heard a roar and turned to see the Pricolici-Marcel mutation regaining its strength. He shook his head and crawled over in the dirt with Marco's knife still in his hand. Climbing up onto the beast, he didn't hesitate, slamming the knife once more into its heart. It bellowed out in anger and pain, swatting him and the knife away.

Landing several feet away, Caspar looked up at the creature as it got to its feet, a mess of black goo and broken body parts. Its neck was broken, and the head of the creature was at a nearly ninety-degree angle.

"You're not getting out of here alive, you sonofabitch!" Caspar bellowed in anger.

At this act of defiance, the creature tried to open its mouth but was stopped by a huge chunk of rock from above crashing down on top of it. The top half of the creature exploded, sending chunks of bone, partially developed muscle and a seemingly endless geyser of black tar-like goo spraying outward.

Caspar rolled out of the way as the large stone came to rest atop the leftover remains of the creature. "That'll do just fine," he said, getting to his feet while cradling his burnt hand. He still couldn't believe his good fortune at the creature's body cushioning his fall and thus, likely saving his life, but he wasn't out of danger yet, far from it.

"I've got to get the hell out of here," he uttered, once more scanning his surroundings. Rocks were landing all around him but he saw what could potentially be his escape out of the escalating destruction. A large entrance into the dungeon appeared to be halfway up the wall. Bars that once covered it had now been busted out from the shifting weight of the castle.

Picking his bruised body up, he scrambled up the wall toward the busted-out entrance, climbing on several large stones that had fallen earlier. The entire dungeon was shaking now. He glanced back once more, the ground beneath him littered with deadly pointed stones now embedded in the dirt.

Under the large rock that sealed its fate, all that was left of the Pricolici were legs and part of a torso, along with a large quantity of thick, black goo that was on fire again and appeared to be moving back to the lifeless body of the Pricolici.

"It's trying to regenerate itself!" Caspar exclaimed, watching on briefly as the gooey substance flowed back into the exposed torso of the creature. Another large chunk of stone fell in front of him, kicking up dust and more debris until he could no longer see what had happened to the Pricolici.

Not waiting another second for fear of being crushed by the caving in dungeon, Caspar leapt out of the opening, falling onto rocky soil. He picked himself up and began running away from the castle as fast as his weary feet could take him while rocks crashed around behind him. The ground shook as though an earthquake was occurring right across the soil he traversed. It was daylight, so he knew he had made it through the night in this hellish nightmare of a place.

Once he had run himself out of breath, he looked back. The castle was completely caving in on itself and crumbling to dust. Turning away from the destruction, his feet gave out along with his weary, bruised body and he collapsed into a small ditch off the path leading up to the castle. The last thoughts in Caspar's mind were of his traveling companions, Marco and Juliette. Did they survive or were they buried under the rubble of the castle? Did they escape only to find themselves facing an onslaught of wolves waiting to tear them to pieces outside? Then, blackness took over.

Caspar woke up, and it was nighttime once more. His body ached from head to toe, but he was alive. *Or am I dead and my purgatory is on this god-forsaken mountain?* He listened to the silence, there were no wolves howling. The smoldering remains of the castle were still there, so he knew it must have actually happened.

"Time to go home, if home still exists," Caspar mumbled. While he was still quite sore, he was rested. However, hunger and thirst wracked his body. "Food and water are down there," he said, looking toward Burnmere in the distance.

He began the trek back down the mountain after finding the path in the darkness. He walked through the night, defenseless other than a large stick he found along the weaving, winding path. He had no need for it, though, as he would find out later. The wolves had vanished from the land, as had the bats. The closer he got to Burnmere, the more thirst and hunger overtook him, but he pressed on, seeing the end of his long journey in front of him.

Only once in the middle of the night had he heard the distant howl of a wolf. This one sounded different from the other wolves he had heard over the years. More guttural and ferocious. He hurried along the path, thankful he only heard that menacing howl a single time before the night sky once more fell silent.

At long last, morning came, as did the sunlight. Caspar made it back to town, hungry, tired, thirsty and utterly exhausted, but alive and pleased to see the distinct lack of fog and gray cloud cover. *Maybe a miracle did happen and we destroyed the evil for good?* he thought, then remembered the one lone howl on his long walk.

†

"I don't think I've drunk so much water in all my life. And I have a full stomach as well. You never know just how good food is until you're without it for too long," Caspar said, exhaling after his long tale and grinning happily.

Marco looked warily at Caspar. "That howl you heard, I fear I may know what made it."

It was Marco's turn to share their own turn of events. The murders that occurred while they were up on the mountain and Everly's transgressions. Caspar listened in rapt attention to the story, culminating in Everly's corpse disappearing the previous night after her injuries had miraculously healed on the coroner's table.

This news came as a surprise to Juliette as well, who was as shocked at Marco's words as everyone else in the room, now silent, digesting all of the new and grisly information.

Marco's new position as town constable was then discussed, as was Juliette's imminent departure. She took the gemstone from her satchel, showing it to Caspar who stared at its sheer beauty, freed of what had been the frozen Pricolici itself, grasping onto it until the incantations could be uttered, freeing it to gain its new life.

"So, what now?" Caspar asked of the room as Juliette placed the gemstone back in the leather satchel.

"I must get to the town's entrance. My driver will be here soon. I need to get back to England; unfortunately, without my dear sister," Juliette said sadly, glancing at Marco.

Caspar noticed the glance. "You sure you don't want to stay a while? It seems as though we are in need of a schoolteacher. Our town is meager and small but maybe, just maybe, we've turned a corner after this nightmare. We could use all the help we can get, am I right...constable?"

Marco grinned at him. "Marco, just Marco, alright, deputy? Job's yours if you want it. Though you can still work out of the ironworks shop. With my help, of course. You owe me, remember?"

Smiling at Marco, Caspar thought for a bit. "Well, my hand is all messed up but it'll heal. So, if you think I can do the job, I'll take it. And I sure could use a spare hand in my ironworks. What are we going to do about a bürgermeister?"

"Let's keep that position open," Marco answered. "I think the will of the people should be good enough for now, we will hold regular town hall meetings and go from there."

"We should reopen the bar. I'm sure some in town could use a drink right about now. Caspar, think you could wrangle someone up?" Marco asked, looking at his new deputy.

Nodding and smiling, Caspar replied, "Yes sir, I'll handle it."

It was decided that, for the time being, Finn's wife Anna would do the schoolteacher duties until a permanent replacement could be found. Preferably one with a higher education. Juliette hadn't been of much help as she didn't know the townspeople, but she did know and understand what it would take to lead a class of students. She herself had great knowledge of such things from her years in college back in England.

When she brought up this fact, Caspar raised his eyebrows at Marco, as if to suggest her as a potential candidate for the job, but Marco shook his head. She had already made up her mind.

Leaving the doctor's office with the others, Caspar felt tired and his hand ached, but he was itching to begin his job as deputy. He was one of the most well-liked people in town and this would go over quite well.

Marco knew it as well, and it would help endear him to a town that had seen him as nothing but a drunk. He didn't want them to regret the decision and had decided quickly to surround himself with capable people to bring the town back to life. This was his new mission: to turn the town of Burnmere into a place of life, not death.

Juliette said her goodbyes to Caspar and the doctor.

"I'm truly sorry about your sister, Juliette, I wish there was a way to change how things went up there on that mountain," Caspar said as he gave her a quick hug. "That man could sure use a kind hand such as yourself around here, we all could. I hate to see you go, but God-speed to you. You and your sister shall never be forgotten, and you will always be met with open arms here in Burnmere."

"Thank you, Caspar. And I will keep the gemstone safe," she replied, not wanting to address what he had suggested about her remaining in town. They parted ways with a warm smile.

Marco walked Juliette back to the cottage to collect her things. From there they walked mostly in silence back to the entrance to the town. It was noon when they arrived and saw

Daniel Kolb, true to his word, riding up the dirt road atop his carriage with Baba in the lead.

As Daniel pulled up, Juliette turned to Marco and set her suitcase down. "Thank you for protecting us up there. Thank you for protecting me."

"It was you who pulled me up when I was about to give up, if you recall!" Marco exclaimed, thinking back to his tumble in the castle right as it was coming down on top of them.

She nodded and smiled. They both looked over at the schoolhouse where the desks and chairs and other items were being removed and taken back over to Samuel Hartjenstein's house, itself already being heavily renovated. His belongings were heading to the church until it was decided how to best disperse them and give back to the people of Burnmere whose money had funded the elaborate luxuries.

Marco cleared his throat awkwardly and looked into Juliette's beautiful brown eyes. "The schoolteacher job isn't set in stone just yet. It's not too late, you know. I know you want to get that gemstone as far away from here as possible, but maybe here is the safest place for it? All of us united, so to speak."

She smiled warmly and suddenly realized the finality of her departure. Her sister gave her life here, for them and this town. Her great-grandfather attempted to kill Antonin then one hundred years later, his great-granddaughter finished the task. It felt as though fate had played a hand in this all. Still, she had to return to England.

She didn't say anything for fear of bursting into tears. They had been through so much in such a short period and she suddenly felt as though she were abandoning all they had recently accomplished. So, she simply did the only thing she could think to do as she looked into this tall man's eyes. She leaned forward, rested her hands on his broad chest and gently kissed him again. This time on the lips.

Then, Juliette turned and handed Daniel her luggage. She climbed into his carriage as her driver nodded to Marco then turned and climbed aboard.

Marco walked over to Daniel. "See to it she gets back to the train station safe and sound. Here, this should cover the cost of your services." He handed Daniel all of the funds he had to his name.

Nodding appreciatively, Daniel tipped his hat and, with a flick of the wrist, old Baba began trotting away. Away from Burnmere and away from Marco. Juliette didn't look back. Not once. Instead, she cried softly to herself as they rode away. The weight of her decision pressed heavily on her heart, and the sooner she could reach the train station, the sooner she would be on her way back to Summerhost, England.

# Chapter 34:

†

# Evil Never Dies

Juliette rode in the back of the carriage in silence for a long period of time. Finally, Daniel, who sensed much had happened since dropping the woman off two days prior, looked back at her.

"Ma'am, I must say, I'm mighty glad to see you alive and well. But what of your sister?" Daniel hoped he wasn't overstepping his bounds.

Juliette wiped her still wet eyes and replied, "My sister is dead. So are a lot of other people, including the man that tried to give me a ride at the train station. I know we have a long ride to the station, but I don't think I have it in me to share the horrors I encountered."

"Miss, I'll have you know, I did pray hard for you and that village," Daniel said calmly. "Every town deserves a second chance. Every person deserves a second chance and I'm just glad to see you well. I haven't seen the sky above Burnmere, or this entire region for that matter, look this beautiful for as long as I've been alive. So, I figured something ultimately good must have happened."

Juliette opened up at this point and shared some of her tale. She produced the stone and showed it to him.

He smiled and said, "You keep that beauty safe, you hear me? That there stone is important, and something tells me more stories will be written about it." He stared at it as it shined brightly, casting colors his eyes had never seen.

"So, what now, Juliette?" Daniel asked after she finished summarizing her nightmarish experience for him.

"I told you much Daniel, do you actually believe it?" she asked.

"Why shouldn't I? I used to be a priest. I've seen and heard much and I've experienced much. Evil is real and evil never dies. Not until our good Lord makes His return someday, if you believe in all that, which I certainly do. Until then, it's up to us to make this world better, to help people, and to stop evil wherever and however we can."

"Daniel, do you like this job?" Juliette asked softly.

Surprised at this sudden change in conversation topics, he replied with a shrug, "Sure, I suppose so. I get to see the countryside. Meet new people, such as yourself."

"Have you ever considered stepping back into priesthood and becoming a man of the cloth once more?" Juliette pressed.

"Well, I suppose I always figured at some point the good Lord would show me the way back if that was indeed His will. So, I've just been waiting. Living life one day at a time."

"What would you say if I know of a parish that could use a man such as yourself to bring people together? People in dire need of not just worldly leadership in the law-and-order sense but actual spiritual guidance," Juliette continued.

He paused, contemplating what she was saying. He knew she spoke of St. Joseph's in Burnmere. She had told him about Father Gustloff's untimely death at the hands of the very evil he had spoken of minutes earlier.

"Interesting you should say that. I recall you telling me that town lost a schoolteacher, and they were in need of someone educated. What college did you say you went to again, missy?" Daniel said with a hint of playful smugness.

She liked Daniel. He was kind, funny, and compassionate. *But I must get back to Summerhost, mustn't I?*

She thought of burying her head in Marco's strong chest when her sister perished. She thought of forcing him to continue on to escape the falling debris of Castle Visimar. The hope they shared of surviving while so much death surrounded them. Marco's rise to leadership, not the least bit surprising to her. She saw it in him almost immediately and had admired him from the start.

"Well, I didn't right tell you what schooling I had, but yes, I am an educated woman. A woman whose home is Summerhost, England. Not Burnmere, Romania," she said, unconvincingly.

"And if that's the case, I suppose my home remains in Bucharest," Daniel countered, though no longer with a hint of playfulness.

Juliette thought back to her arrival in town. "When you left, I walked into that depressing town and one of the first things I saw was the tiny schoolhouse. The kids were outside, and all of them looked miserable. Even the schoolteacher looked sad and untrusting. And now, she lies dead on the coroner's table, soon to be buried." She paused, contemplating the state of Burnmere without a proper priest and without a proper….

"Those children, even if their number is small, need someone to lead them and teach them," Daniel said calmly, as if knowing exactly what was running through Juliette's mind at that very moment.

"The people need someone to lead them spiritually as well," Juliette shot back, a small smile growing across her face. Her mind went to her dear sister whose spirit surely looked down on Burnmere now. She thought of Marco. Tall, confident, and certainly the most unlikely hero she had ever met. Her smile turned wide as she clenched the gemstone in her satchel draped over her lap.

Baba felt her reins pulling back and came to a halt on the road, as did the carriage. Its master appeared to be making a course correction.

☨

Deep in the Carpathian Mountains, a newly reborn wolf creature ran through the trees. Its fur was silky and white, its eyes piercing and could change from green to yellow to red. It would be considered beautiful if it weren't for the fact that it was a cold-blooded killer.

Her mind relished her newfound powers as she ran through the forest on all fours. She had traveled far. Far from Burnmere where she felt vulnerable, where her old life had ended. Far from the mountain where her master's life had been snuffed out by meddling human beings. Out here, she was the alpha and would exert her power accordingly. The animals of the forest would come to fear her and, soon after, people throughout all the land would tell of a wolf blanketed in white. The stealer of infants and murderer of any that made the ill-fated choice to cross her path.

They would whisper her name in fear. The name *Everly* would be synonymous with terror. She would see to that. The last name Seiler was no more. That was her old life, her new life was just starting.

As she ran, she thought of her human self and changed at will, from wolf to woman. A beautiful woman, full of life and vitality and most importantly, *strength*. In her nakedness, she ran barefoot across fields and trees and streams. Animals of all kinds saw her and fled.

An inner voice whispered: *You will learn my ways and then you will find the stone once more and claim it as your own. In time, you will return to Burnmere, and it shall burn! But now, go find the son your human self gave birth to, and sacrifice him for me! Prove you are worthy of the gifts I have bestowed upon you!*

She continued running far away from Burnmere, knowing that in due time she would return.

# About the Author

Eugene Weaver was born on August 8, 1974 in Millersburg, Ohio. He and his wife Joani have been married for 21 years and have two boys. They currently live near North Canton, Ohio.

Eugene has been an avid lover of movies, music, and the arts nearly all his life. At 12 years old, he wrote his first novel, *Pivoron Mountain* in longhand cursive. At the persuasion of his boys thirty-six years later, he decided to take up writing once more. His first novel, *Thunder Stone Realm,* was published in 2023. It was followed by two sequels, *Survivors of the Realm* and *Return to Thunder Stone,* along with a fourth novel, another science fiction tale set in the same universe as his Thunder Stone trilogy, titled, *Battle for Quadrant 8304. The Amulet of Visimar* is his fifth novel.

www.ingramcontent.com/pod-product-compliance
Lightning Source LLC
Chambersburg PA
CBHW060608300726
48975CB00005B/1490